*St. Martin's Paperbacks Titles
by Jill Jones*

EMILY'S SECRET
MY LADY CAROLINE
THE SCOTTISH ROSE

THE SCOTTISH ROSE

JILL JONES

St. Martin's Paperbacks

This is a work of fiction. Only the characters of Mary, Queen of Scots and the historical entourage that surrounded her; Oliver Cromwell and his military officers; the Seventh Earl Marischal, his Countess, Elizabeth, and his brother, John Keith; George Ogilvy of Barras, his wife, Elizabeth Douglas, and her stepsister Ann Lindsay; the Reverend Mr. James Grainger, minister of Kinneff Kirk, and his wife, Christian Fletcher; and King Charles II are historical. Lynne Russell is a broadcast personality. All other characters are purely fictional, and any resemblance to any persons living or dead is entirely coincidental. Although the plot of this novel is based on the historical facts of the eras involved, all action other than that which is recorded in the annals of history is entirely fictional.

THE SCOTTISH ROSE

Copyright © 1997 by Jill Jones.
Excerpt from *Deep as the Rivers* copyright © 1997 by Shirl Henke.

ISBN: 0-312-96099-9

Printed in the United States of America

St. Martin's Paperbacks edition/February 1997

St. Martin's Paperbacks are published by St. Martin's Press, 175 Fifth Avenue, New York, NY 10010.

10 9 8 7 6 5 4 3 2 1

For my husband, Jerry,

with love always.

Thanks for being the wind beneath my wings.

ACKNOWLEDGMENTS

My deep gratitude to Mrs. Lesley Masson, BA ALA, Area Librarian, Stonehaven Library, Stonehaven, Scotland, for providing me with esoteric details on the history of both Stonehaven and Dunnottar Castle.

I also wish to thank Mr. David Taylor, proprietor of the Hook & Eye Lounge Bar in Stonehaven, for the excursion to the Kinneff Old Church, a journey not easily made by "outlanders," and for the wonderful Scottish hospitality.

Thanks to Mr. Alistair Scott of London, for facilitating many aspects of the journey to Scotland, and for his kind hospitality. Deep thanks to my friend Hubert Mornard, master jeweler of Belgium, for conceiving such a splendid chalice.

I am also indebted to the librarians at the Black Mountain Library, North Carolina, for their support in obtaining the research materials I needed for this complex story, and to Mr. MacGregor Grey, former scribe of the American Clan Gregor Society; Dr. S. Samuel Shermis, Professor Emeritus of Purdue University; and Mr. Hal Kaplan and Mrs. Norine Victor, for providing special insights and information to help me authenticate this tale. Many thanks to Dr. Olson Huff, Medical Director of the Ruth and Billy Graham Children's Health Center, Memorial Mission Hospital, Asheville, North Carolina, for information about the latest procedures being used to restore hearing to the deaf.

My thanks go, as always, to two special individuals whose creative and editorial talents are only surpassed by their encouraging support of my work, my husband, Jerry Jones, and my editor, Jennifer Enderlin.

And finally I wish again to thank my indefatigable traveling companion, Bonnie Sagan, aka "Anne Bonney."

"It is fortunate for tale-tellers that they are not tied down like theatrical writers to the unities of time and place, but may conduct their personages to Athens and Thebes at their pleasure, and bring them back at their convenience."

—Sir Walter Scott

PROLOGUE

◆

September 1561
Edinburgh Castle

They were liars to a man, and she knew it.

Their faces were respectful masks, but their eyes betrayed them. Hate lived there. And malice. Greed and jealousy.

Her uncle, Charles de Guise, had warned her it wouldn't be easy ruling these nobles, about which he'd declared there was little that could be described as noble. One, he surmised, perhaps two, might be trusted. Her half-brother, Lord James Stewart. Bothwell. But Charles had claimed that the rest of the Scottish lords gathered before her now to pledge their fealty were as snakes in the heather. He claimed that their recent fierce alliance with Protestantism was but a cover for their continuing intrigues that threatened the sovereignty of Scotland, and he had expressed doubt that she could reign successfully as a Catholic queen in a country so divided, especially over religion.

Even thusly forewarned, Mary, the young Queen of Scots, recently returned from her childhood in France, was determined to win them to her by showing tolerance, restraint, and respect for their ways.

Straightening to her full height, she held her head in a regal pose as the Earl of Arran placed the crown upon her auburn locks.

"As your most humble servant," said the Earl, "I welcome you home, Your Highness, and pledge my loyalty unto you."

Liar.

But Mary only nodded to him graciously, hoping the crown would not fall from her head in an accident that might be interpreted by these superstitious countrymen as portentous.

Next, the Earl of Lennox stepped forward and presented her with the golden sceptre. Kneeling, he bowed his head. "Your Highness."

At least he didn't speak his lie, the young queen credited him. "I thank you, Lennox, and pledge to serve you and yours truly and steadfastly."

Lord James came next, his smile warmer, more personal. He had pledged to protect her and stand by her as she took over the rule of this rough kingdom of Scotland, and Mary wanted to trust him. However, she was uneasy that he never let her forget that they shared the same father, King James V, and his pleasant manner did not successfully conceal his bitter resentment at his bastardy.

James laid the heavy Sword of State across her lap. "With these revered emblems of the kingdom of Scotland were you crowned Queen of Scots as an infant. In your long absence, my Queen, they were used in your place, representing the monarchy in Parliament." Mary did not miss his emphasis on the word "long" and suspected he wished it could have been longer still. She bit the corner of her mouth to repress the ironic smile that threatened the solemnity of the occasion.

One by one, the lords filed past her, bowing, kissing her hand, pledging their loyalty, extending their best wishes.

Lying.

When the farcical ceremony was complete, Mary surveyed her "nobility." How different were these men from the polished courtiers to which she was accustomed in France. These aristocrats looked more like outlaws. Dressed in the drab woolen attire common to the Scots and draped with what appeared to be rustic blankets, they presented none of the glitter, the sophistication, she'd enjoyed in the life she'd left behind.

Still, they were all she had, and she must make them her friends.

"My lords," she said, clearing her throat, "we are honored by your presence and your oaths of fealty, which we accept with humble gratitude. With your permission, we offer an oath of our own at this time." She could see from their expressions they were surprised at her deviation from the traditional formalities, but she wished to prove her mettle to them from the outset.

She would rule, not follow.

"Bring the Scottish Rose," she commanded a servant, who quickly bore forth a magnificent bejeweled cup on a silver platter. Made of hammered gold polished to a high sheen, the chalice was crafted to perfectly match the shape of a rose just beginning to open. Each petal was embellished with a large cabochon ruby set into a silver *cross fleur* bordered by tiny precious stones, the vibrant red of the rubies suggesting a rose of the same hue. Where the cup tapered to the stem, five sepals were enameled in green, with tiny but perfect pearls outlining them like dewdrops. The slender stem was sheathed in a second layer of gold formed to include thorns and leaves that authentically represented those of its botanical ideal.

She heard the intake of breath from the others, but it was not in admiration of the rose, as she had expected. Rather, it was a shocked reaction, followed here and there by a muttered "papist." She was shaken, but she ignored their rudeness and took the sacred vessel in her long fingers, holding it high for all to see.

"This was a gift to us from our Holy Father in Rome."

"I'll stand na more for this," said Lord Ruthven, heading for the door, his face almost purple with fury.

Mary regarded him steadily, although her heart was beating wildly. "Hear us out, Lord Ruthven, for 'tis not what you think." She had heard the rumors that the lords feared she would reinstate the old religion in the realm when in fact her intent was exactly the opposite.

Her quiet tone quelled his indignation, at least for the moment, and he turned to listen. "Upon the bestowal of this gift, His Holiness urged us to return Scotland to the Church, but we think this neither right nor reasonable. Therefore, we pledge instead with this cup that no man nor woman under my reign shall be persecuted because of their faith. All shall be free to follow the religion which best serves them." She paused, then added with emphasis, "Catholics as well as Protestants."

With that, Ruthven stormed out. At least he has made known his disposition openly, Mary thought, but she was discouraged at the hostile reception of what she had hoped to be an act of reconciliation. She went on, forcing a composure she didn't feel. "We hereby join this chalice to these regal Honours of Scotland, as a symbol of tolerance and religious freedom, of peace and unity in this kingdom."

At this, the room erupted in a mayhem, with shouts and oaths expressing the anger and outrage of her subjects who only moments before had sworn their loyalty. Appalled, she heard her name in context with whores and blasphemers, and she feared for a moment the chalice might be seized and destroyed.

"God's blood, Mary." James hurried to her, his face drained of all color. "What madness hath possessed you? Know you not the dangers of exhibiting such a papist symbol, much less of making it part of Scotland's royal regalia?"

Too late, Mary realized her mistake. Her uncle was right. These men did not want peace or unity. They had no tolerance, nor did they wish there to be religious freedom. A sharp pain slashed through the side of her abdomen.

Fighting tears, she bade the guard to rap on the floor with his pike, at which the lords lowered their voices to a muted growl. "Hear this, my lords," ordered the Queen. "We see our offer is not to your liking, therefore, we withdraw the chalice until such time as honest peace reigns in this land." She motioned to the servant to remove the cup. When it was out of sight, she continued.

"Even so, we shall tolerate your new religion, but we command you to respect our own. If any shall endeavor to bring harm to our person or members of our household or interrupt our worship in private Mass, the offense shall be punishable by death. Now begone." She waved them off as nausea threatened her in a most unqueenly manner.

Only James remained of the dozen who had just knelt at

her feet. "My Queen, you hath much to learn about the Scots."

"And they hath much to learn of me," she replied acidly.

"You mustn't press too hard too soon," he advised, then added smoothly, "Let me guide you in these matters. They will come around."

His tone was soothing, encouraging, but Mary knew that he, too, was lying.

ONE

❧

Aberdeen, Scotland
May 1996

Robert Gordon, Esquire, ran beefy hands through his graying hair and considered the dilemma he faced. Before him on the desk lay two letters and a small ancient book. One of the letters was written by his client, or rather former client, now that Lady Agatha Keith was deceased, directing him what to do with the other articles.

He fingered the other letter, taking care not to tear the paper that was fragile with age. The book he scarcely dared to touch at all lest it fall apart in his hands.

Robert Gordon had seen much in his days as a solicitor. He was old, and tired, and had no patience for this sort of hoax. If it was a hoax.

And what else could it be?

A final joke by an old lady he'd often considered to be mentally unbalanced?

He had visited Lady Agatha the day before she died. Well over a hundred years old, the dowager had sat hunched on a daybed by the fireplace in the family's ancestral mansion, her skin sagging, seemingly unattached to the brittle bones of her arms. But her eyes were bright and her conversation intelligent. There had been no sign of the senility that she had exhibited on his prior visits. She spoke as firmly as her ancient vocal chords would allow.

"I have made up my mind about something very important, Robbie," she'd quavered, handing him a large brown envelope with trembling fingers. "I want you to find this woman and give her what is in this envelope. I think she lives in America. She is my sister's great-granddaughter, and my only living kin, as far as I can tell."

Gordon had glanced at the envelope. It was addressed to "Taylor Kincaid. America."

He laughed softly. "Lady Agatha, surely you have a better address than this? I mean, America is a big country."

"Find her," the crone croaked. "It shouldna be that difficult. Her grandmother, my niece and namesake, ran away to New York in the late twenties. Near t' broke my sister's heart. But the girl wrote, giving an address, and she stayed in touch with her family in Scotland after she married."

Now she handed him a second envelope. "I have written it all down for you, all that I know. I have spent no small amount of money trying to locate her children, as my niece died just after the war. She had two children, a son and a daughter. The son, I have learned, was killed in Korea. The daughter married, and she had a daughter, this person named Taylor Kincaid." She paused for a moment. "Taylor," she repeated. "Odd name for a girl. She was born in Queens, according to the birth certificate, but that's as far as I got, and now I've run out of time. It's up to you, Robbie." She peered at him, her eyes as old as time. "I shouldna have waited so long."

The lawyer sat very still for a moment, astounded at the old woman's lucid recitation of the family's story. No one could convince him at the moment that Agatha Keith was not in full command of her wits. "What do you mean, you've run out of time, Lady Agatha?" he asked gently at last, although he supposed that for a woman of her age, every day was a miracle.

"I'll be dying shortly," she'd replied matter-of-factly. "It's long overdue, you know. I wish I had remembered this chore sooner. Could have done it years ago," she clucked. "Must've lost my mind there for a while. There's money in that envelope as well, Robbie," she added, pointing a bony finger at it. "Should be enough to cover your expenses and fees, even as high as they are."

Gordon started to protest, then thought it not worth the effort. "I'll do the best I can, madam," he replied patiently to the old woman whom he had served as lawyer for over forty years. Then another thought occurred to him. "Your will makes no mention of this Taylor Kincaid," he said. "Do your wishes remain the same as in the will we executed, what was it, five or so years ago?"

"Not another penny!" screeched the dame abruptly. "I'll not spend another penny on legal fees. Here!" She thrust a third envelope into his hands. "I have written a new will. Not much to it, you'll see. If you find my kinswoman, this Taylor Kincaid, what's left of my family's poor estate goes to her now. If you do not find her, or she doesna want it, then dispose of it as we decided before." She heaved a sigh. "Go now, Robbie. I'm tired."

The next day, Lady Agatha Keith was dead.

And although he was disinclined to do so, for to do nothing would be far easier and more lucrative, Robert Gordon, Esquire, had endeavored to honor the last wishes of his longtime client. He owed her that much, he supposed, although he faced lean times himself in his waning years, and she had made provisions for him in her previous will.

Still, she had enclosed a substantial sum to pay him to make a final attempt at finding her mystery relative, and he was a man with too much professional integrity not to make at least a minimal effort at doing so.

Using the details she had scribbled down for him, he had managed to locate the private investigator she had hired to find her descendant in the United States. The PI was able to supply the attorney with a history of his investigation, which ended when he located one Taylor Marie Kincaid, born in Queens, New York, in 1963. After that, he'd stopped looking, because Lady Agatha had told him she would not spend another penny on it, that she'd paid him too much already.

With a sympathetic smile from the far side of the ocean, Gordon had offered the man another thousand dollars to finish the job, with a bonus of five hundred more if he did it within the week.

The man had phoned today. Taylor Kincaid, he related, lived in Manhattan, and she was, he disclosed with unconcealed enthusiasm, something of a television star.

And in the five o'clock pickup, Robert Gordon had sent off two overnight packages to the United States: one to the investigator, carrying fifteen hundred dollars, the other to Taylor Kincaid, conveying a letter informing her of her inheritance.

After that, all he could do was wait.

And wonder.

What if the Taylor Kincaid located by the investigator was not Lady Agatha's great-great-niece? What would he do then with the two other incredible artifacts with which Lady Agatha had entrusted him?

For if they were authentic, they were also very valuable. Priceless even. And if there were no heirs, to whom would they belong?

The items had come as a complete surprise to Gordon. He'd never seen nor heard of them before. They were not mentioned in any of her earlier wills. That's why he believed they were a hoax, or, at the least, a fantasy created during one of the old lady's spells of delusion.

But if they were not a hoax. . . .

And if they belonged to no one. . . .

And if they were authentic. . . .

Robert Gordon leaned back in his chair and rested his hands on his vest. It could be that upon her death, Lady Agatha Keith had contributed substantially to his retirement fund.

Manhattan

Sweat trickled down the valley of her spine and pasted locks of straight blonde hair against her face. The odometer said she had skied three-point-two miles over the nonsnow, across the country of her living room. One-point-eight to go, she calculated, swinging her arms against the resistance of the machine and heaving for breath.

Why couldn't she have been born thin? she grouched silently. She always had to work so hard to keep in shape. Taylor Kincaid hated artifical exercise, although she didn't mind the real thing, like racing on long skis across a snow-covered countryside with a cold, bracing wind stinging her cheeks, or scuba diving in the temperate waters of some Caribbean bay.

But her busy schedule did not allow for the luxury of such vacations, and unfortunately, her diet consisted mostly of fast food eaten on the run. So at thirty-three, with a career that demanded both peak performance and a celebrity's good looks, Taylor had no choice except to do all she could to keep the pounds off, and twenty minutes a day en route to nowhere aboard the NordicTrak had proven to be the least offensive option. At least this way, she consoled herself, she was able to work out in privacy at home, where her leotard-clad body was unavailable to the lecherous stares of the musclebound mashers at the gym.

And while she exercised, she could catch up on the news of the day. A very efficient use of her time. She watched Lynne Russell's major red lips recount from CNN's newsroom the latest events of today's world . . . a train wreck in South America, a bombing in Asia, yet another snag in the Middle East peace process. . . .

How did that woman do it? Taylor wondered. How could she announce all those horrible things and still maintain a hint of a smile in her presentation? Taylor wiped a drip of perspiration from her eyebrow, glad that her own reporting style did not require such demanding theatrics.

Glad, too, that her stories were not on-the-scene reports of wars, murders, sensational trials, and such.

She'd stick to what she was good at . . . debunking the ridiculous myths and legends of the world, tales that perpetrated fear and ignorance, and proving that the so-called paranormal was just the normal dressed in superstition.

Combining a travelogue format with a touch of sensationalism and a dash of dry humor, she had developed an outrageous television series, *Legends, Lore, and Lunatics*. Her audience was eating it up, her ratings sky-high. The show was so popular, in fact, that the network was on her back to produce thirteen more episodes.

She grimaced. If only she had thirteen more good ideas.

The odometer clicked to four-point-zero, and Taylor checked her watch. Just a few more slides of the faux skis and she could head for the shower, after which, she would spend the evening in her dining room, which she had converted into a library-study-office, perusing the mountain of books she had brought from the library.

She *had* to come up with some story ideas. And soon. For while she reveled in her success, she was also beginning to feel tense and pressured. She'd been warned early on in her career, by veterans in the business, that it was difficult to sustain the interest of fickle viewers, who weekly had ever more program options in the *TV Guide* listings. She was learning that they were right when they'd told her, "You're only as good as your last show."

Despite this recent disillusionment at these overwhelming demands, she was determined she would adjust and keep on going, because she'd made a lifelong commitment to her career years ago when she'd learned that for her there was no option of ever having a family.

It was freak of nature, an odd birth defect, the gynecologist had told her. She couldn't bear children because she'd been born without a womb. He'd said she was perfectly normal in every other respect, and that this one deficiency should not prevent her from having a healthy sexuality as an adult.

But even as a maturing teenager, young to consider the ramifications of such problems, Taylor had been filled with grief and rage, for she was close to her family and had always wanted children of her own. So with her typical headstrong intensity, she'd vowed to follow another life path instead, one that meticulously avoided marriage, one that replaced the wife-and-mother role she had once longed for with that of super-achiever career woman. Nature may have taken control of this aspect of her body, but she'd sworn she would retain control of her life.

Maybe the glory of motherhood was just another highly

overrated myth, she told herself from time to time when the stress of her career left her wishing wistfully for a "normal" life, with a husband and family. Maybe it was just a myth, a legend, like the rest of the foolish notions she dealt with in her series. Maybe that's why she disdained them so intensely.

Her workout almost concluded, Taylor's breath came in sharp, painful gasps, and tiny pinpricks of light sparkled behind her eyes. She heard a buzzing in her ears and thought for a moment it was from the exercise, until she recognized the sound of the doorbell.

"Thank God," she uttered, happy to have an excuse to end the torturous ride a little early. Sliding to a stop, she stepped onto the polished hardwood floors, her knees only slightly more solid than Jell-O from the exercise. She clicked off the TV with the remote control and grabbed a towel.

"Just a minute," she called toward the front door. The buzzer sounded again, the noise grating irritably on her nerves. "Jeez." She wiped her arms and face and padded toward the intercom. "Who is it?"

"FedEx."

"Hold on." She peered through the tiny peephole in the door to ascertain that it was a legitimate delivery person. She wasn't expecting anything. But fan mail and hate mail had begun to arrive in equal measure daily at the network to compliment or complain about her controversial show. Had the lunatics found out her home address?

She unlocked the door to the restored brownstone and signed for the overnight letter. The young man making the delivery stared at her, smiling awkwardly, but his light blue eyes admired her unabashedly. "Are you . . . uh, *the* Taylor Kincaid?" he asked, his cheeks edged with crimson.

Taylor returned his smile. "Depends on who *the* Taylor Kincaid is that you mean," she replied lightly. She was still unused to her status as a television personality. Until *Legends, Lore, and Lunatics*, she had remained behind the scenes on her film projects.

"I've watched all your shows," he continued eagerly.

"You keep me on the edge of my seat. What are you going to do next?"

Taylor returned his pen and took the package. "The series still has a few weeks to run," she said, forcing a smile. "I'd spoil it for you if I gave away what I have coming up."

The young man grinned knowingly. "Right. Thanks, Ms. Kincaid. You can count me as one of your fans. Keep it up. There aren't many good shows left on television."

Taylor rewarded him with a sincere smile, then closed the door and leaned against it.

What, indeed, was she going to do next?

Stonehaven, Scotland

Cold weather seemed disinclined to go away this year. It was early May, but gales still blustered, peppering the air with frigid rain, turning the North Atlantic into a frenzy of angry gray swells whipped by vicious whitecaps.

Duncan Fraser shivered in the upstairs room of the small house that overlooked the twin harbors of Stonehaven and hastily threw on several layers of clothing. He was a big man, brawny and muscular, a marine petroleum engineer and sea captain who respected the fact that seasons did not always come and go according to dates on a calendar.

That they were, in fact, as unstable and unpredictable as life itself.

He reached for his wallet and keys on the bureau, then turned to go, hesitating just long enough to catch a glimpse in his mind's eye of this room in other, happier seasons, when he was first married and had awakened on that bed not as eager as now to head off to his harborside office and the dangers of his work.

Duncan shook his head and left the room, closing the door sharply behind him. Maybe he ought to move. This house was too empty. It harbored too many memories. He couldn't bring himself to even glance at the door that closed off the room across the hall. The one that had belonged to Peter and Jonathan. That door had been shut for four years.

With a glance at his watch, he hurried down the stairs, grabbed the yellow foul-weather jacket from the hall tree, and left the house, glad to be gone from it.

To all outward appearances, Duncan was a normally functioning human being. He went to work every day, came home every night, didn't bother his neighbors or make demands on his friends. Occasionally, he shot some billiards at the pub or played golf. But in reality his life functioned almost by rote. He performed with integrity if not enthusiasm his work as a consultant to the oil companies who operated the offshore rigs in the North Sea. He was the best troubleshooter in Scotland and was willing to be on call twenty-four hours. His office overlooked the harbor, where he also served as part-time Harbormaster. But the duty that gave his life meaning, if he could find any, was as head of the local Royal National Lifeboat Institution, Britain's team of volunteer rescuers on the sea. Although he shunned the accolades that often came his way from this work, he had been responsible for saving many local seamen from death in the icy ocean.

But when he laughed, the joy never quite reached his eyes. And he never cried, for he had no tears left. He'd spent them all.

For although Duncan Fraser was good at saving the lives of others, he'd failed miserably at saving those he'd loved the most.

TWO

✌

Aberdeen, Scotland

"Wait here," Taylor directed the two young men who lounged at the airport bar, "and don't overdo it on the local brewskis, okay? I should be back in an hour or so. Surely our bags will have shown up by then."

"Sure, boss." Barry Skidmore raised a half-empty pint glass to her.

"You got it," said the other, Rob Johnson, who at twenty-two knew quite a lot about everything.

Taylor turned and left the pair, appalled that these smirking, barely-post-adolescents were the top camera and sound graduates in the country. Still, they were good kids and fun to be around.

Flagging a taxi, she showed the driver the address she was seeking and settled into the rear seat of the vehicle with a weary sigh. It had been a long day.

Actually, it had been a long week, she decided, since the strange letter had shown up at her doorstep.

She hadn't known she had any relatives in Scotland, never heard of Lady Agatha Keith. Certain the law firm had the wrong Taylor Kincaid, she had placed a call to Robert Gordon, Esquire, but he had recited her family history accurately, at least as far back as she knew it, and together they'd decided that the old lady must indeed have been Taylor's great-great-aunt.

However, the lawyer had not seemed overly eager for Taylor to come to Scotland to claim her inheritance. If anything, he had downplayed the whole thing, explaining that Lady Agatha had been an eccentric, and that other than the mansion that was mortgaged to the hilt and would likely have to be sold, there was nothing left in the estate except some old papers.

The whole thing seemed at first so preposterous to Taylor that she had thanked the lawyer politely, saying she'd get back to him, and laid the letter aside. The incident served, however, as a catalyst to spur her research in a new direction.

Scotland.

She'd never done a show about Scotland, but surely such an old and trampled upon country would have a wealth of myth and folklore just waiting for her to set straight.

She spent the next several days poring over books on Scottish history and traditions, still ignoring the letter that beckoned every so often from under the stack of paperwork on her dining table. She skimmed biographies of major Scots personalities, from William Wallace and Robert the Bruce to Rob Roy, from Mary Queen of Scots and Bonnie Prince Charlie to Robert Burns and Sir Walter Scott. But other than the continuing mystery of Queen Mary's complicity in the death of her husband, and the ongoing debate as to the existence of the Loch Ness monster, she found little material that suited her format. Tales of Scottish witchcraft remained possibilities, as did the origins of the ancient Pictish standing stones that dotted the barren northern landscape.

But, she wondered, were these folk tales controversial enough to sustain a thirty-minute show?

Several times she came close to giving up on the Scottish idea entirely, but the letter continued to demand her attention. At last, Taylor decided she would make a trip to Scotland. She was intrigued, she admitted, by the idea of being descended of Scottish nobility, even if her inheritance was worthless, as the lawyer had assured her it was. And even though she did not have a solid story angle, she felt like she might come across something once she arrived.

She'd better, she thought as she gazed out the window of the taxi en route to the lawyer's office. It was expensive to hire a crew and fly them to Scotland without a predetermined story line. But maybe they'd get lucky and come up with something quickly.

If only she believed in luck.

Everything about the offices of Robert Gordon, Esquire, was old. The building in the oldest district of Aberdeen had likely been there since Rob Roy was a lad, Taylor decided when the taxi pulled up to the front door. The reception area of the law firm was illuminated only by the light of a single lamp and the rather morose day that filtered its grayness through the windowpanes. It was furnished with equally morose shabby chairs and rundown tables. These were not, she decided, the digs of a high-powered law firm, the type she would have expected someone like Lady Agatha Keith to retain.

The lawyer himself was an aging gentleman who appeared suddenly from a darkened doorway. He wore a nondescript brown suit and yellow tie. Huge brushy brows overhung thick, black-rimmed glasses that magnified his dark eyes into grotesque, bulging orbs. "You must be Taylor Kincaid," he said politely enough, but Taylor discerned beneath his heavy Scottish accent a distinct note of disappointment that she had arrived.

"Mr. Gordon?" Taylor extended her hand, which he shook briefly.

"I apologize for the lack of a secretary," he said, knocking tobacco from a pipe into a metal ashtray, "but I only work part-time these days. I keep trying to retire," he added with a hint of dry amusement, "but some things, like this business of Lady Agatha's, seem to keep me tied to this place."

Taylor was unsure whether or not to be sorry for the elderly fellow. He seemed somewhat pathetic, and yet, she sensed he could be putting on an act for her benefit. At any rate, she smiled.

"Thank you for letting me know about my great-great-aunt," she began. "I must say, I am still quite surprised. And curious, too."

Gordon motioned for her to precede him into the next room, which was equally disheveled, but which took on a warmer, cozier glow from a series of a lamps scattered around the chamber. "Please, sit down. Would you care for coffee? I know you've just got off the overnight flight from the States, and you must be tired."

That was a major understatement, Taylor thought. "I would love some coffee. Black, please."

The brew was bitter and lukewarm, as if he had made it hours ago. Or yesterday, and rewarmed it in the coffeemaker, a possibility for a man who had no secretary to tend to his needs. Taylor didn't much care. All she wanted was caffeine in her veins.

Polite formalities completed, Robert Gordon settled into the large chair behind the paper-strewn desk, and Taylor sensed a hesitation. She leaned forward expectantly, but did not speak. At last, the brow-incrusted Scotsman picked up one of the papers from his desk and handed it to her.

"I suppose this is as good a place to begin as any, Miss Kincaid. It is a letter Lady Agatha gave to me the day before she died."

Taylor took the letter and began to make her way through the unsteady handwriting. It was written to Robert Gordon and was comprised mainly of a recitation of Lady Agatha's attempt to locate her distant relative, a surprisingly savvy effort for an eccentric centenarian thought by many to be mentally unsound, Taylor decided. It was the conclusion of the letter that was most astounding, however:

I began this search after I came across some items in an old file I had completely forgotten about. They were passed along to me late in my own life by my mother, who received them from her father's mother. I believe them to be both authentic and valuable, although they could be forgeries and worthless, a joke played by a prankster upon a long-ago ancestor. Of these things I know not and care little. But I promised to pass them to my descendants should I decide to take no action upon them, which of course I never did, not knowing what action was to be taken.

Now that I have discovered that I indeed have an heir, I wish for you to locate her and give these things into her keeping, with the same directions as I was given. I have also revised my will, for I now wish to leave what little there might be left in my estate to this descendant, Taylor Kincaid. As you will see, Robbie, I have made provisions for you as well, although I am enough of a traditionalist to believe the heir of my bloodline is the appropriate benefactor of my worldly goods.

It was signed in an almost illegible scrawl—
"Lady Agatha Keith."
Taylor gazed at the letter for a long moment. She understood now the reason for the lawyer's near antipathy toward her—she had taken his place as beneficiary of Lady Agatha's "worldly goods." But other than the mysterious articles that had provided the old woman the impetus for finding her long lost heir, Taylor wondered what other "worldly goods" she might have inherited that the lawyer had thought would be his own. A debt-laden mansion didn't sound like much of a prize for an old man like Robert Gordon. Rather, it sounded like he'd be stuck with liquidating the estate and be lucky if there was anything left over.

In interviewing people for her stories, Taylor's style was to ask one or two pertinent questions and then keep her mouth shut. She learned a lot this way, and exposed herself little. She placed the letter back on the desk. "What items is she referring to?" she asked, looking across at Gordon expectantly.

After a long pause, he handed her a brittle piece of paper and a small, loosely bound book. "Be careful," he warned. "Whether these are what Lady Agatha believed them to be or not, they are very, very old. I have scarcely touched them since she gave them to me, thinking that one more opening might break them apart."

Taylor scrutinized the letter. The penmanship was antiquated in style, and the language stiff, like a very old form of English, but the content was remarkable. "Who was Elizabeth Douglas Ogilvy?" Taylor asked, looking at the scrawled signature at the bottom. "And what is this all about?"

Gordon explained that in the year in which the letter was dated, 1652, Governor George Ogilvy and his wife Elizabeth Douglas, along with some other brave Scots, saved the "Honours" of Scotland—the royal crown, sword, and scepter—from the hands of Oliver Cromwell's army. "It all took place just south of here, at Dunnottar Castle, just outside of Stonehaven."

"She mentions here 'another relic, a secret member of the Scottish regalia.' " Taylor ran her finger on down the difficult script of the letter. "The Scottish Rose, this rose-shaped golden chalice that she claimed once belonged to Mary Queen of Scots." She looked up at Gordon. "Have you heard of it?"

"Never." The lawyer steepled his fingers. "She also mentions a letter written by the queen, expressing her wish that this so-called Scottish Rose become part of the Honours. There was no such letter in the envelope your aunt gave to me, and to my knowledge, no such chalice has ever been associated with the Honours. That's why," he said, with a significant pause, "I am inclined to doubt the authenticity of these items."

Taylor gingerly picked up the little book, and understood Gordon's concern for its condition. The hidebound cover was very fragile, and it cracked even as she opened it with utmost care. The handwriting on the pages was elongated and elegant, the words written in French.

Taylor glanced at Robert Gordon. "But this could be the diary she mentions?"

"It could be, madam. I have not yet translated it nor had it examined by experts." He raised his shaggy brows and his shoulders simultaneously. "I told you that Lady Agatha was quite an eccentric. As a Keith, she could have inherited these two items exactly as she said, and they could be authentic." His lips twisted in a mirthless smile. "But then again, she could have been playing a joke on me."

Robert Gordon helped the young American woman into the taxi and waved her off before deciding where to proceed from here with this most unusual business. Returning to the gloom of his offices, he sat heavily on the arm of a chair and picked up the slender volume he'd convinced Taylor to leave in his custody until she was through with her exploring in Scotland.

He should have translated it before now, but he hadn't expected her to show up so soon, if at all. Now, he hadn't much time, and there was much he had to consider before making certain decisions.

He took the book to his desk and flicked on a high-intensity lamp. Then he laid a legal pad next to it and found a pen that worked. He must first discover if the letter, but more importantly, the diary were authentic. If the dated entries met the parameters of history, his next step would be to call on John Doggett, a shrewd antiquarian he knew who could validate it forensically.

And then . . . well, time would tell.

Carefully opening the diary, he turned to the first page and squinted at the letters inscribed on paper as thin as a wafer:

24 August 1561
Holyrood Palace

My native land continues to disappoint me. I have been upon this soil less than a single week, and already I have felt the sting of prejudice that the new religion has put upon those of us who still practice the old. I have vowed upon the Scottish Rose to defend the right of all to worship as they please, that neither Catholic nor Protestant should come to harm for the practice of their religion, but this very day, as my priest said a private Mass in the Chapel Royal, we were attacked and would have been injured, perhaps murdered, had not my brother James interefered. I will write a proclamation tomorrow and have it posted at the Mercat Cross that any future attacks will be punishable by death. My life and those of my servants will not be endangered by these foul haters.

Even though I gave my word to the Holy Father upon accepting the rose chalice that I would work toward returning Catholicism to Scotland, His Holiness could never understand from the distance of Rome the brutal facts of my reign. I arrived to find my realm in shambles. My nobles fight for power among themselves like snarling dogs after miserable scraps, and Knox's Reformers spout hatred from the pulpits. How I ache to help this poor country, my native land, but I understand more clearly as each day passes the concern of my uncle toward my lords, and I wonder how I can ever reign successfully in a land so bitterly divided. . . .

There it was. Mention of the Scottish Rose in the very first entry. Robert Gordon reached for his handkerchief and blotted the beads of perspiration on his brow. This diary couldn't be authentic, he thought, frowning. If Queen Mary had had such a chalice, it would have been recorded somewhere in history, and not just on the pages of her most private journal.

He pushed his chair away from the desk. On the other hand, he argued, maybe he was just ignorant of its existence. Gordon looked at his watch. There was still time. Quickly, he closed down his office and headed toward the university library to which Queen Mary had once bequeathed a collection of Greek and Latin volumes. If there were mention anywhere of the Scottish Rose, it would be here.

THREE

Stonehaven, Scotland

The dart hit the mark with a thud, and the crowd in the smoky pub cheered the venturesome American woman who claimed she'd never thrown darts before. Taylor Kincaid allowed herself a small, gratified smile and chalked up her score.

It was about time something went right for her today.

She had left the lawyer's office more than a little troubled, feeling as if she might have made a mistake in allowing him to keep the intriguing letter and diary. Not that she didn't trust him, but because the artifacts might provide her with just the story she had come to Scotland to find. Not so much Elizabeth Ogilvy's letter, for Gordon had said it was history, not legend. But she was intrigued by the mention of the "Scottish Rose." Gordon claimed he had never heard of such a chalice, supposedly once owned by Mary Queen of Scots. If the letter proved to be authentic, perhaps the vessel would provide a legend she could investigate.

She was anxious to know if the diary supposedly written by the queen contained references to the rose chalice, but since she couldn't read French, and Robert Gordon claimed to be fluent in it, it seemed like a good idea to let him translate it and have it evaluated for authenticity while Taylor explored other story options. Maybe she'd get two segments out of this trip.

She'd made a photocopy of the letter and obtained a written receipt acknowledging her ownership of the artifacts, but as she'd prepared to leave, Gordon made a statement that had curiously unsettled her. It wasn't anything sinister. He'd merely emphasized how he had loyally attended to Lady Agatha's every wish and whim, which had not always been easy. But Taylor knew instantly that he considered the letter and the diary to be his, and that he resented her intrusion on his claim. She also got it that for all his assurances that these were likely a hoax, he didn't believe that.

She started to change her mind and take the items, but it occurred to her that her search for other Scottish legends would likely take her into the wild countryside with only back-packs and camera gear. No place to stow relics that were literally crumbling away from age.

Scolding herself for being foolish and paranoid, Taylor left them in the lawyer's care after all. She zipped the photocopied letter along with the rest of her valuables inside the pouch strapped around her waist and headed back to the airport.

From there, her day had gone completely downhill.

Their baggage and equipment did not show up for several more hours, during which time, her young film crew proceeded to sample the many varieties of Scottish ale, which rendered them witless in short order, leaving her to handle everything alone. The car rental agency had screwed up their reservation. There was no minivan available, so the three of them had jammed into the only car left on the lot, a tiny Ford Escort, and headed south, the bulky gray metal cases that contained cameras, film, and other gear crammed beneath their feet and piled on their laps.

Taylor had hoped to have time to take a look at one of the nearby Pictish standing stones, but with all the delays, it was late afternoon before they arrived at their destination, the small town of Stonehaven. They had barely made it inside the quaint old inn they had booked in the heart of town when the clouds that had threatened all afternoon let loose with a violent storm. Taylor craved the warmth of a cozy room and a peaceful nap, but her room was freezing cold. When she'd complained to the innkeeper, he'd looked at her as if she'd lost her mind. "But 'tis spring," he'd said as if that would explain away her discomfort. "There'll be no need for heat again 'til November."

A hot bath at last warmed her bones, but when she tried to nap, she was too tired to sleep. And too hungry. She'd had nothing to eat since the plastic breakfast on the airplane. Feeling responsible for her crew, she knocked at the door to their room and invited Barry and Rob to come along, knowing they'd be worth more tomorrow if they fed their hangovers tonight. The inn, however, had no restaurant.

Maybe there *was* such a thing a luck. Bad luck.

The innkeeper directed them to the nearest eating establishment, the Hook and Eye lounge bar around the corner. Undaunted by the lightning that streaked across the darkened sky and the rain that poured down in sheets, the trio made a run for it.

Now, with a satisfying supper and a couple of lagers in her stomach, Taylor felt better about the world. She was especially pleased about winning the dart game.

Maybe her "luck" had changed.

She'd bested the local champion, a large fellow with blond hair and ruddy skin who grinned at her with a good-natured but somewhat perplexed expression. "Your next pint's on me then," he said in a thick Scottish accent. "Not bad, for a woman."

She brushed off the sexist remark with a patient smile, tucking a strand of long, blunt-cut blonde hair behind her ear. "Thanks," she replied. "A half pint'll do." She'd learned long ago not to take offense at such comments, which were often dropped inadvertently by men who found her abilities surprising "for a woman." She'd also learned the value of making friends with the locals, for they'd saved her backside more than once in unpleasant situations in countries where the language and customs were foreign to her.

The bartender brought her a half pint of a golden brew, and the chilled beer felt good against her throat. She smiled at her defeated opponent and raised the glass in thanks, but a sudden blare of loud music made further conversation difficult. With a silent toast to the jukebox gods for rescuing her, Taylor excused herself. Experience had also taught her what to expect any time she let a man buy her a drink.

Some things were universal.

And any involvement with a man, other than on a casual basis, was not in her game plan.

"Nice going, boss," Rob said, edging a chair away from the table for her with his booted foot as she joined her crew in the next room. "You sure you never did that before?"

Taylor sat down, giving him a sardonic smile. "I'll never tell." She glanced out the window at the downpour. "I wonder when this is going to let up?"

"Looks like we might be stuck here for days," Rob observed, eyeing his beer glass with an affectionate grin.

"And would that be such a terrible fate, lads?"

Taylor looked up to find the dart player hovering above them.

"The ale is plentiful and the food's good," he said. "Many's a storm I've weathered in the Hook and Eye. Care if I join you?"

Taylor wasn't certain how to gracefully say no to the man, but she never had the chance. She watched, aghast, as both Rob and Barry leapt to their feet like two trained dogs, eager to give him a seat. But it wasn't the boys his eyes were on as he took a chair. "Name's Fergus," he said, extending a hand. "Fergus McGehee."

"How do you do, Mr. . . . McGehee," she said, accepting his handshake, then withdrawing her hand again quickly. "I'm Taylor Kincaid."

"And I'm Barry Skidmore, and this is Rob Johnson," piped up the young man with a beaked nose and sandy hair so curly it was almost kinky.

"Americans, I take it?" The man's gaze left Taylor's face just long enough to acknowledge Barry's introductions. "What brings you to these parts?"

Before she could stifle them with a warning look or a swift kick under the table, the two young film makers, fresh from school and just a little full of themselves at being on this assignment with the almost-famous Taylor Kincaid, eagerly filled in Fergus McGehee about their job, their boss, and *Legends, Lore, and Lunatics*.

Taylor sent a die-now look at Barry and Rob, but it was too late. The burly Scotsman turned to her, new interest in his eyes. "Ah, so 'tis legends you're after then?" he replied, his words so heavily accented he was almost hard to understand. "So what's brought y' t' Stonehaven? Th' story of th' rescue of the Honours of Scotland at Dunnottar Castle?"

Taylor looked up at him sharply. "I thought that was history, not legend."

"Oh, 'tis history for sure. Every child in school around here has t' memorize that story," he said with a laugh.

Taylor paused. "Have you ever heard of something called the Scottish Rose?"

"Scottish Rose?" He laughed. "Sounds like a loose woman, or a brand of whiskey. No, I don't know of it. What is it?"

"Just a legend I heard about today," she replied, amused at the Scotsman's bawdy humor, "but not from around these parts, I guess."

"Guess not. No, most tourists come t' th' castle because of th' Honours story, but if it's legends you're after, *real* legends, then it'd be th' Ladysgate that y' want."

Taylor couldn't recall having read about anything called the Ladysgate. "Is that the same thing as the Pictish Maidenstone?" she asked. "We're going there tomorrow, if the weather lets up."

Fergus brushed the air with his large paw of a hand. "Nay, there's nothin' special about th' Maidenstone, except 'tis said to be very ancient. Have y' not heard o' th' Ladysgate?"

Taylor was suddenly aware that a few others had trailed into the lounge behind Fergus McGehee and were listening to the conversation. Her cheeks grew warm.

"No. I can't say as I have," she answered, feeling suddenly tired again and not wishing to be in the spotlight. She finished the last of her lager. "What's the Ladysgate?" she asked politely, hoping he'd make it short so she could escape as soon as possible.

Another man pulled up a chair and sat backwards across it.

"Some say 'tis a haunted place," the newcomer replied earnestly, but Taylor suspected he was jesting with her. "Others, they say 'tis a gate to th' land of th' fairies." Laughter tittered through the small crowd, but it had a nervous edge to it, and Taylor's antennae went up.

"The land of the fairies?"

Fergus McGehee leaned toward her, his big arms resting on the table between them. "Haunts, fairies, who knows?" he said, his mysterious smile the perfect segue into his story.

"Once upon a time there was a wealthy laird in this land, with a bonnie wife named Melinda. But he was a greedy sort, not content with th' land he owned, although 'twas already vast. So he set upon a plan t' enlarge his kingdom. Now, th' border between his land and that of his neighbor was a stream. So th' laird ordered his vassals t' divert th' flow of th' stream by diggin' a channel through his neighbor's property, enlargin' his own by th' size of a rich meadow."

"Augh, th' villain!" one of the listeners said in mock horror, causing the group to erupt in merriment. Even Taylor was caught up in the laughter, not knowing if she was being fed a true legend or a line of baloney. One and the same, as far as she was concerned.

Fergus let the laughter die down, then regained center stage. "But unbeknownst t' th' laird, his serfs had disturbed th' bones of eleven ancient souls buried for centuries beneath th' earth of his neighbor's property. Druids they might have been. Or Vikings. And th' souls, raised up from their slumber in th' Land of th' Dead, exacted their revenge upon th' laird. They built th' Ladysgate, a giant granite arch that now stands yon upon th' shore, and through it, they called in enchanted voices t' th' lovely Lady Melinda. Bewitched, she followed th' voices, and when she stepped through th' portal, she simply disappeared, never to be seen again."

Fergus McGehee was a skilled storyteller, and even Taylor found herself spellbound. "Where is this place? Does it really exist?"

"Oh, aye. It does indeed. But you wouldna want t' go near it, even today."

Here comes the punch line, Taylor thought, bracing herself to be the gullible brunt of a local joke. "Why not?"

"Because," piped up a young woman from behind her. "Melinda is not th' only one t' have disappeared through th' Ladysgate. There've been others. . . ."

"Others?" Taylor glanced across at Barry and Rob. Were they thinking the same thing as she, that maybe they'd hit upon their story? She gave them a discreet wink. "What others?"

"Well, we dinna have all th' names," Fergus said in mock apology. "But down through th' years, there's been many a disappearance reported. Although some were men, most of th' unfortunates have been women. That's why it's called th' Ladysgate."

Taylor leaned toward Fergus. "Can you take me there?"

He gave an uneasy laugh. "Now? 'Twould hardly be a good idea in this storm."

"Of course not now. I'm a film producer, not a fool. But your story is interesting. I'd like to see this granite arch, by the light of a sunny day."

"If th' rain lets up, I'll take you there tomorrow," Fergus offered. "Y' can see it from land, but y' canna get to it because th' level of th' ocean has raised up over th' past centuries and th' shoreline has eroded. Th' best view's from th' sea."

"The sea? You mean we have to go there by boat?" The adventure suddenly lost its luster. She wasn't afraid of boats, but neither was she fond of them.

"Aye." Fergus smiled at her hesitation. "But there is nothing t' worry about. I am a seasoned captain."

Taylor heard a stir from a booth in the far corner of the room and realized suddenly someone had been sitting in the shadows watching them, listening. The man now stood up, his tanned, rugged face set in hard lines, his eyes hard, almost angry. The height and breadth of his body seemed to fill the room as he approached them. Taylor's eyes grew wide, and she felt her heart lurch.

"Stay away from those rocks, Fergus," he growled, his ice-blue eyes fierce beneath heavy brows that were drawn tightly together.

Fergus McGehee looked up at the man, and Taylor saw the color drain from his face. "Ye'll not be tellin' me what t' do, Fraser," he replied hotly, standing to meet his opponent.

The man called Fraser walked slowly over to the table where Taylor sat with her equally wide-eyed young companions, wondering if these two grizzly sized men were about to exchange blows. Fraser glared first at Fergus, then allowed his gaze to travel over the rest of the locals who had drawn around the storyteller. "You people know better than this," he said, as if he were a grandfather admonishing wayward children. "Don't stir up trouble."

Then he turned his attention to Taylor. The electric blue eyes seemed to burn straight through her.

"It is no ancient curse that causes people to disappear through the Ladysgate, Miss Kincaid," he explained with a somewhat patronizing attitude. "It is the giant boulders that lie beneath the surf . . . and the foolish sailors who dare to bring their craft into those treacherous waters." He looked again at Fergus. "You've been cited before. Stay out of there, or I'll personally see to it your license is revoked . . . permanently."

With that, he strode toward the front door, reached for a yellow vinyl jacket that hung on a coat rack there, and shrugged into it as he stepped out into the storm.

Behind him, the group murmured among themselves and broke up, moving back into the room where Taylor had played darts. She looked across at Fergus. "Who was that?" she asked, frowning. She was confused and disturbed by the instant and electric attraction she had felt toward the man who had just left. "What was that all about?"

"He's Duncan Fraser," Fergus replied coldly, the good nature gone completely from his voice. "He takes care of problems out on th' rigs. But he's also a Master Mariner and the Harbormaster, and head of the Royal National Lifeboat Institution here.

"And sometimes"—he added sourly—"he thinks he's God."

Dodging the sheets of water that poured from roofs and gutters, Duncan pulled his collar closer about him, wishing for all his life he'd never laid eyes on the blonde. But there was no way he could have ignored her. From the moment she walked in the front door, her presence seemed to permeate and enliven the whole place. And watching her throw darts in the next room, her body trim and athletic, her stance bold, her eyes shining at the challenge, his attraction to her had been immediate and visceral. It wasn't just her fresh-faced, feminine appeal that had kept his eyes riveted on her, but rather a way she had about her, a confidence, a radiance, a daring. . . .

How on earth had she ended up in his accustomed lounge bar? Few Americans, especially sexy blonde American women with the brass to accept a challenge for a dart game, happened into the Hook and Eye. A part of him resented her, as if she had invaded his private space. For certain she had shattered his peace of mind.

Duncan had been about to leave, recognizing the threat she posed to his well-ordered, emotionally guarded existence, when she'd come back from her victory at darts, beer glass in hand, hair swinging, the flush of triumph on her face, and he'd found himself abruptly anchored to his chair, unable to run. Only when that idiot Fergus McGehee started spinning his nonsense had Duncan been able to gather his wits enough to mobilize.

He hoped the American woman wouldn't listen to McGehee. Nobody had any business going near the Ladysgate. It was the most perilous stretch of water along the coast. But he'd seen the look in her eye. She was a daredevil, that one. Likely, she would persuade McGehee to take her to those damnable rocks where more than one fool had lost his life. Would the threat of losing his captain's license be enough to keep Fergus away?

From the way the man had looked at Taylor Kincaid, he doubted it very much.

Duncan sloshed down the narrow streets of the ancient village that had been his home for all of his thirty-nine years, heading like a homing pigeon for the harbor, annoyed at how the American woman had so easily thrown him off balance. Yet, strangely, he felt as if he'd just been given a jumpstart or something. He suddenly noticed the cool prick of the rain against his skin, the vivid yellow of his jacket, the smell of the ocean in the air. Not that these were anything unusual. It was just unusual that he noticed them.

Rubbish. Of course he'd noticed things like that before.

He was on RNLI duty today, and even though he hadn't received any summons on his pager, he decided to check in at the Life-Boat station, just in case. In a storm such as this, one never knew when a call would come.

Besides, he had nothing else to do.

The Royal National Lifeboat Institution maintained a post in a cramped, weathered building near Duncan's own office at the edge of the harbor. The boats of fishermen were moored there, along with other larger vessels, his own included, most of which ferried men and materials to the many offshore rigs that sucked oil from beneath the ocean floor. As the volunteer harbormaster, Duncan Fraser was vigilant always in his stewardship of these ships that were in his keeping.

Letting himself into the protection of the one-room shack, he knelt and lit a fire in the small stove, then shook out of his jacket and hung it on a nail hammered into the wall. Glancing at the answering machine, he noted that the red light burned steady. No calls from landside. He tuned in the calling channel on the VHF and listened for a few moments, but there was almost no radio traffic.

Quiet day. Surprising in this weather. But sometimes storms kept prudent sailors in port. It was the calm, flat days that often proved more deadly, when fog crept in on the unsuspecting seaman, stealing away all visibility, turning the world into a white-shrouded nightmare. Duncan dreaded fog rescues the most.

After checking with his regular contacts on the rigs, Duncan contented himself that all was well for the moment. He picked up a magazine and settled into his wooden swivel chair, propping his feet on the desk. He opened the glossy pages and stared at them, but his thoughts raced immediately to the forbidden, and the image of Taylor Kincaid filled his consciousness.

It had been four years, no . . . much longer than that if he were honest about it, since Duncan had felt that kind of spontaneous, gut-level attraction. In fact, he wondered if he'd ever been drawn this powerfully to a woman. With Meghan, it had been different. He'd fallen in love with her as a schoolboy. They'd grown up together, and the allure was somehow . . . different. Less intense. Less . . . sexual.

Oh, Christ, he had to stop thinking like this.

Slamming down the magazine, Duncan went to the sink and filled a ceramic mug with water. He plugged in an immersible water heater and moments later sifted a packet of instant coffee into the cup. The bitter drink warmed him, but he could not sit still. He stalked the office like a caged animal. What was wrong with him? In foul weather, he was usually content to read, work a word puzzle, wait in patience knowing that at any moment he might have to respond to trouble, whether on the rigs or on the sea.

But not this evening. Unable to settle into his normal routine, he finished the coffee, donned his jacket again, and stepped out into the storm. He began the long climb up a nearby footpath that led to the top of the hill, pretending he was going there to scan the shoreline in case a mariner had gone aground. But he knew that was a lie. When he reached the crest where the roadway curved sharply in a tight U away from the ocean and continued its climb up onto the lonesome moors, he stopped.

Instead of looking out to sea, he looked straight down. As he always did. The railing had been repaired long ago, and the scrubby gorse had grown over the ugly scars in the underbrush left by the plummeting vehicle, but Duncan could see it all, just as it had been that night. Oblivious to the weather, he stood and stared down the steep slope where Meghan's car had lurched over the cliff in the darkness, taking with it everything in his life that he had loved and cherished.

FOUR

ꝫ

Robert Gordon returned from the library thoroughly perplexed. None of the librarians or historians to whom he had spoken had ever heard of the Scottish Rose. They had suggested he contact some of the history professors, but he didn't have the luxury of that kind of investigation. It wasn't a mysterious rose chalice that concerned him at the moment, or served his interests. It was the diary.

His facility with the French language was rusty to say the least, and it had taken him a good hour to translate the first diary entry. It was late, and he was tired, and yet, at one entry per hour, it would take him a couple of days to finish. Did he have a couple of days?

No. But he could work at home, where he could have a bite to eat and a pot of fresh coffee to keep him awake.

He wrapped the fragile diary carefully in a sheet of newspaper and placed it in his briefcase. He donned his weatherproof coat again, turned out the light in the office, and walked in the rain the few blocks to his apartment. He was oblivious to the weather, however, because his mind wasn't on his surroundings. Rather, it was on a time long, long ago, and the book in his briefcase. Most remarkable, he thought, that it had come into his hands. He could hardly wait to see what secrets it might reveal. A short time later, by the light of the swag lamp over his kitchen table, he resumed his translation where he had left it off:

30 October 1562
Aberdeen

The dreadful Huntly affair has at last come to an end. What started as a visit to our Highland dominions has ended in the downfall of one of our most dangerous enemies, ironically also our sole Catholic ally, John Gordon Lord Huntly. He was Catholic only when it suited him, however, and hungry for power—one of the most contentious lords in our land. We have reason to believe that because of our mutual religion he sought to murder Lord James, and Maitland and Morton had we stopped at Strathbogie. We believe he sought to establish a Catholic coup and marry us off to his loathsome son, Sir John Gordon.

He was present in Edinburgh Castle when we vowed upon the Scottish Rose to bring peace and religious tolerance to our country, but he scorned our good will. He has paid dearly for that mistake. We bestowed upon our brother Lord James the northern Earldom of Moray coveted by Huntly. We were forced to hang Alexander Gordon, Huntly's son who refused us entrance to our own castle at Inverness. James accompanied us on this northern invasion, and through his valor, we were victorious on the Hill of Fare. Huntly escaped in the end, but only into the arms of death, as the disgrace of defeat caused him to burst and swell, and he fell from his horse in front of his captors. His corpse has been disembowelled and embalmed in a keg of vinegar, and will stand trial in Edinburgh for his treasonous acts. It is as well he will not be witness to the execution of Sir John, which will eliminate one more traitor, even though Catholic. It will be difficult for us to explain these actions to our Holy Father.

Robert Gordon let out a low whistle. He knew well the grisly story of Huntly's pickled corpse being tried by the Queen. As for the rest of the details in this entry, they could be easily checked in the history book he had brought with him from the library.

It was late, but adrenalin and the constraint of time urged Robert Gordon to turn to the next page.

The following morning, the rain had ceased, but the sky remained a leaden gray, and the sea roiled beneath the keel of the small fishing boat. Taylor swallowed over her growing nausea, wishing she hadn't been so headstrong in her demand to go to the granite arch known as the Ladysgate. Still, this trip was not a vacation, and since the locals had assured her this was by far the most intriguing legend in all of Scotland, she was anxious to find out if it was indeed a valid myth around which to build a show.

"Don't you think we should turn back?" she shouted into the wind toward the man who stood at the helm with his back to her. But Fergus McGehee did not reply, and Taylor realized he couldn't hear a word she said. He looked strong, at ease in spite of the rough seas and fretful weather, and Taylor attempted to take comfort from his assured manner. She glanced at Barry and Rob and grinned slightly. For once the two were speechless, both hanging onto the sides of the boat for dear life. They'd assured Taylor they were totally dauntless when they'd been hired for the production team, but their bravado, she noticed, was something of an overstatement.

She peered across the choppy water, hoping they were getting closer to their destination, and hoping as well they could put ashore nearby so she could regain her composure.

" 'Tis there, on th' horizon," Fergus called, turning his head to her, his voice carrying easily downwind. He pointed straight ahead.

Taylor squinted, focusing as hard as she could in the direction he indicated, but all she saw was the dark flat line of the horizon where it met a dull gray sky. Moments later, however, she discerned that the horizon was not flat at all, but rather a ridge of cliffs that dropped in a cascade of dark rock into the sea. As they came closer, she noted that to the right of the cliffs, green hills also rolled toward the sea, their slopes gentler, more approachable than the high craggy rocks.

And then she made out the Ladysgate. A huge stone archway, it stood stark and naked and alone some ways out from shore. A shiver, but not from the cold, crawled down her spine. She had seen haunting sights before, but this one was remarkably eerie.

Taking a small camera from her waterproof bum-bag, as the waistline pouches were called here, she snapped off several shots for later reference, then secured it behind the zipper once again.

"Rob, why don't you get some footage from here, then work into some closeups when we get nearer?" she instructed the camera man. "And Barry, think we can get anything in this wind? I've got the lavaliere around my neck."

"We can try, boss," the young man said, reaching for the silver metal case that protected the sound equipment. "I hope this stuff doesn't get wet."

"Leave the equipment inside the case," she instructed patiently. "Just crack the top open enough to get the cable out, then turn the case so the lid creates a windbreak. Here, hand me the cord, and I'll plug in."

She laughed to herself when she saw the mixture of skepticism and admiration on Barry's face as he handed her the end of the sound cable. It was his first time in the barrel, but not hers. She'd gone on camera in worse places. He'd have to get used to it if he remained on her crew. Keeping her weight low, she eased forward, edging past the bulk of Fergus McGehee, who started in surprise.

"What're you doing?" he asked in alarm.

"Going forward. I want to get some footage as we approach."

Fergus shook his head. " 'Tis not a good idea. You'll get soaked. Besides, we can't get too close. There's a strong tide and huge rocks just beneath the surface."

"I'm not afraid of getting wet. You just drive the boat and get us as close as you can. The telephoto will do the rest."

But he suddenly slowed the engine, throwing the vessel forward abruptly in a surge of inertia before it achieved a stable course again. "Ahh-hh-hh!" Taylor cried out, grabbing for the back of a bench seat for support. "Watch it, would you?" She appreciated that Fergus had reverted to a slower, more comfortable speed, but she'd been damned near rocked overboard by the sudden unexpected motion, and her faith in the seamanship of the man she'd hired to take her on this trip slipped a notch.

Finally ensconced in the curve of the minimal metal bowsprit at the very front of the boat, Taylor managed to plug the cord into the mike and closed her expensive rain jacket over it securely. "Can you hear me? Testing. Testing. . . ."

Barry nodded and gave her a thumbs-up. She saw his lips move, but the wind stole away his words.

"Can't hear you, so you'll have to signal what you need," she spoke loudly. "Am I audible?"

Another thumbs-up and an okay sign.

"Is Rob ready? Let me know when to start." Taylor was used to improvising in front of a camera, because she always knew her material well beforehand. She'd queried Fergus for a long time the night before, after the man called Duncan Fraser had made his rude exit. Taylor had taken copious notes about the Ladysgate and the legend that surrounded it. Today might be her only chance to get the film she needed from this vantage point. She had no desire to make another trip by boat to this spot if she could avoid it.

She saw Rob hold up his hand and begin to count down by his fingers. Five. Four. Three. Two. One. He pointed at her.

"On the rugged coast of northeastern Scotland, a grim ridge of rocky cliffs and stony hillsides fall into a boulder-laced sea," she began. "Nearby stands a granite archway, chiseled by wind and water over aeons, and now subsided into the ocean. This arch is called 'the Ladysgate' and through it, according to the legend told by those native to this bleak and barren land, many people, mostly women, have disappeared from time to time, never to be seen again. We are approaching the formation now by sea. . . ."

Taylor turned to look behind her in the direction the boat was traveling and drew in a sharp breath. "What the hell?"

Behind her, the scene she had just described was vanishing before her eyes. A heavy mist, suddenly rolling in from nowhere, clutched its vaporous tentacles around the Ladysgate, and it disappeared in a thick fog. Just like that. She'd never seen anything like it. For the first time in a very long time, fear dropped into the pit of her stomach. Not bothering to disengage from the audio cable, Taylor scrambled back to midships, where Fergus McGehee gripped the wheel with white knuckles, his face pale and distraught.

"What's happening?" she demanded.

"Looks like we've got a bit of a spring fog droppin' in on us," he replied easily enough, but Taylor sensed his deeper concern. "It's best we be gettin' on back now." He steered the boat to the left, and she saw his lips move in a curse just before a large wave hit the the ship broadside, almost swamping it. The young men in the stern yelled and grabbed for the gunwales, and Taylor heard the thud of their equipment cases striking the side of the boat even as she lost her footing and landed butt-first on the craft's hard sole. Fergus held tightly to the wheel and rode the wave through, at last turning the boat toward the open sea. He gunned the engines, but the vessel seemed to make no headway. Indeed, it appeared to Taylor, who had pulled herself up onto the bench seat, that the craft was moving steadily backward instead, as if of its own volition. It was swirling slightly from side to side, like a leaf bobbing in a rapid stream, caught in the current of the strong incoming tide.

And then Taylor realized to her horror that no one on board wore life vests. In their eagerness to get to the site of the Ladysgate, no one, not even the captain, had given a thought to safety.

"The life jackets!" she called. "Where are they?"

Fergus pointed to the bench in front of him where she sat. "In there. Quick. Get them!"

Seeing that both young men were frozen in terror, Taylor jumped up and lifted the seat. Inside, several orange life vests were lined in a neat, dry row. How could she have been so stupid?

Quickly, she pulled the clumsy vests one by one from the box and handed them to Fergus who passed them back to

Barry and Rob. The Scotsman held the wheel and revved the engine for all it was worth, but the force of nature was stronger than the motor's power, and the boat tossed and bounced helplessly through the fog, heading ever closer toward shore. Cursing her carelessness, Taylor grabbed a life jacket for herself, then dropped the cover of the bench and sat on it again, fighting to keep from being slung from one side of the pitching vessel to the other.

"Can't you do something?" she yelled, unable to believe that she had allowed herself to end up in such a precarious situation and angry with the doltish captain who had assured her they would be fine. She wished she'd paid more attention to that Master Mariner, Duncan What's-his-name, last night. She had no time to reflect on her poor judgment, however, and her anger turned to terror as she felt a sickening scrape, and Fergus McGehee's fishing boat sliced its hull on a submerged boulder. "Oh, God," she uttered.

But a large wave picked up the boat, now completely at the mercy of the sea, and thrust it forward, lifting it off the first rock and crashing it onto another. Please, Taylor prayed, oh, please get this damned boat close enough that we can make it to shore if it breaks apart.

The sky turned suddenly darker, the way it does when a cloud passes in front of the sun, and Taylor looked up to find herself in the jaws of a monster, a voracious sea creature with a mouth that gaped from the surface of the water to someplace high above, its upper teeth hidden in the dense fog. She never knew if she screamed as the great sea demon flung her from the boat into the icy waters of the North Sea and prepared to devour her alive.

Duncan Fraser had a gut feeling that something was wrong. He'd been in rescue work for two decades, and he had learned to trust his instincts. In times past when he'd had this sensation, the radio had crackled shortly with a call for help.

He pulled up the blinds that covered one of the windows of the RNLI shack and studied the boats moored in the harbor or tied to the docks. A shroud of fog hung barely above the weatherbeaten hulls, threatening to drop at any moment. He scrutinized each boat, mentally ticking off the name of its captain, taking roll of the vessels that belonged in Stonehaven harbor. He stopped and went over them again.

Someone was missing.

McGehee.

Surely the fool wasn't crazy enough to ignore the fog warnings that had been broadcast for the area today. Often after a spring storm such as yesterday's, a fog would follow, a thick, soupy fog no sensible mariner would dare sail into by choice.

Irritably, he dropped the blinds again and picked up the phone. It took only a few calls to find out what Fergus was up to, and when he did, Duncan sat down heavily in his chair, rubbing his eyes and shaking his head. That idiot! That fool!

But he wasn't sure to whom he was referring, whether to Fergus McGehee or to the woman who'd hired him.

They were in trouble. He sensed it, and yet, there was nothing he could do at the moment. No call for help had come over the radio. If they'd left sometime after daybreak, they had not been gone long enough to consider them overdue. His stomach knotted, and his frown deepened.

There was nothing he could do.

Nothing except wait, and hope his gut feeling was wrong.

FIVE

༃

A cold wind shrieked down the barren hillside and struck Taylor squarely in the face, jolting her into consciousness. She opened her eyes to a sky filled with gray clouds scudding anxiously in the wind. She blinked, then tried to move, but every muscle seemed riveted painfully to the earth.

Memory trickled back, filling her with shock and horror. She recalled being thrown from the boat into the icy waters at the base of the Ladysgate. She remembered hearing the screams of the others on board. And then nothing. Closing her eyes again, Taylor let out a small, anguished moan.

She was alive, but what about the others?

With great effort, she raised herself to a sitting position and looked around, but she saw no one.

That's odd, she thought instantly. How did I get here? Instead of being on the shoreline, she was sitting on the lower slope of the hillside. Not far away, the monstrous granite archway loomed, appearing even larger and more threatening than it had from Fergus McGehee's boat. With sudden alarm, Taylor realized that the Ladysgate was no longer surrounded by water, but now stood squarely on dry land.

A dream, she thought immediately in an attempt to quell her panic. She was awake in a nightmare. Maybe she was in a hospital somewhere, rescued rather than drowned, doped up on drugs and hallucinating heavily.

"Barry!" she called, her weak voice lost in the wind. "Rob!" She stood on shaky knees and became aware that her clothing was soaked. Clammy jeans clung to her legs, and layers of shirts and sweaters hung in heavy, wet folds about her torso. But her discomfort was not her first concern.

Where were the others?

She cried out their names again and staggered down the hillside, stopping short of the formidable arch. "Oh, God, what have I done?" she croaked, scanning the desolate shoreline, searching for some sign of her film crew and the captain she had coerced into taking her on this dreadful misadventure.

She glanced at her watch, but there was only an ugly scrape where the Rolex had earlier encircled her wrist. She uttered a silent curse. Looking to the sky, she saw that the sun hung low in the west. She guessed the ship had been wrecked around noon. Maybe the others had survived, but because she'd somehow ended up inexplicably so far from the water's edge, they had been unable to find her and had gone for help. "Can anybody hear me?" She summoned strength to her voice and called in every direction. But the only reply was the cry of the gulls that dipped and swooped into the ocean as they fed.

Taylor tried to get her bearings. She knew that the ocean lay to the east, and Stonehaven was a few miles to the north. She scanned the countryside, hoping to find some less strenuous terrain for the hike back to town. She clambered up the hill again, which was strewn with bare rocks and looked curiously as if it had been wasted in the not too distant past, perhaps by fire. There were no trees, only a few scraggly shrubs and a covering of low grass. In the distance, she heard the bleat of a sheep, and her gaze followed the sound, coming to rest on a low, wattled dwelling farther up the next hill.

Maybe there would be a telephone there.

Taylor reached what she decided must be a farmer's cottage and knocked at the rough wooden door. Although she saw a trail of blue smoke rising from the chimney, no one answered her summons. She knocked again. "Anybody home?"

After a few moments, she tested the latch. The door was unlocked. She pushed it open a few inches. "Hello? Anyone here?"

She felt like Goldilocks entering the home of the three

bears, but any reluctance she felt toward being an intruder was quickly overcome by the welcome warmth of the fire crackling in the hearth. Taylor couldn't resist the temptation and crept inside. Holding her hands to the flames, she rubbed her fingers briskly, restoring circulation to numb, cold flesh. Then she turned and gave her backside a chance to thaw while her gaze traveled the single room of the dwelling, searching for the telephone.

Through the gloom of the pale light that filtered in through two small, high windows, she beheld surroundings of extreme austerity. The shanty was crude, primitive almost, built of clay and whitewashed inside and out. A small cot covered with a sheepskin was placed along the wall immediately to her left, close to the fire. Opposite her was a rustic cabinet and a chair with animal hide stretched across the seat and back. Several wooden pegs were set into the walls, and from one, a woolen garment draped almost to the floor. It was a drab olive green or brown, with a faint pattern of plaid woven into the fabric. Along the wall to her right, a wooden plank mounted on legs that looked like tree trunks served as a table. On it were a tankard, a bowl, and a knife, along with a blackened cooking pot.

But no telephone.

And no other amenities, such as a bathroom.

Stretching her aching muscles, Taylor marveled that people still lived like this at the end of the twentieth century. Were the owners of this hut just painfully poor, she wondered, or was it their choice to live in the ways of their ancestors? She had visited other lands where country folk had made it clear they wanted no part of the complexities of modern civilization, and sometimes, just a little, Taylor had wondered if their more simple lifestyle wasn't preferable to her own frenetic existence.

She brought her mind back to her immediate dilemma. She must get back to Stonehaven as quickly as possible. If the others had not been rescued, she had to get help to search for them. Oh, God, she prayed again, please let them be okay.

Her clothing, although warmer now, was still soggy, and

she knew the moment she stepped outside into the wind, she would be chilled again almost immediately. Perhaps it would be better to wait in the protection of the cottage for the farmer to return. Maybe he would have a vehicle, and she could pay him to drive her into the village. She felt for the pouch at her waist and unzipped it, glad she'd bought a heavy duty, waterproof one. The camera and film cartridges inside were actually dry, as was her small coin purse and the photocopies of the letter she'd made at the lawyer's office. That seemed like ages ago, although she knew it had been only a little over twenty-four hours. She retrieved a small hairbrush that she had also tucked into the bag, along with a compact and lipstick and a roll of breath mints. Never knowing when she might have to step in front of the camera, Taylor never traveled without at least minimal cosmetic supplies close at hand. She stroked her long hair vigorously, deriving warmth from the stimulation of the bristles against her scalp.

Deciding to wait for the owner of the cottage to return, she slipped out of her jacket and heavy outer sweater. She was tempted to remove the cumbersome jeans as well, but decided it would be inappropriate for her to completely disrobe in the home of a total stranger. Instead, she moved the solitary chair in front of the fireplace and hung the wet clothing over it to dry.

Outside, the wind gusted suddenly, whistling eerily around the windows. Taylor shivered. Her undergarments were still wet, she was starving, and her whole body ached with bruises and fatigue. She eyed the woolen blanket on the peg. She looked at the cot.

So she'd be Goldilocks. Quickly, she stripped bare and wrapped herself in the coverlet, then draped her underwear over the chair to dry with the rest of her sodden clothes.

If only she knew where they kept the porridge. . . .

Duncan had spent the day trying to ignore his gut feeling, but by late afternoon, he was seriously concerned that the one boat gone from the harbor had not yet returned. Where in the name of God was that idiot McGehee? He knew Taylor Kincaid had hired him to take her to the Ladysgate, but they'd had plenty of time to take a scenic tour and be back by now. Even though there was no real emergency, Duncan had radioed every offshore rig and vessel passing within fifty miles of Stonehaven, but no one reported having seen or heard from the fishing boat. He hesitated to call the neighboring RNLI stations, not wanting to create problems where there probably were none. He stared out the window vacantly, trying to decide what he should do. There was no emergency, no call for help.

And yet. . . .

His gut feeling shouted at him again.

Damn it! He slammed his palm against the wall, shaking the windowpane. He couldn't stand by any longer, waiting. He had nothing more to go on than a hunch, but things just didn't feel right.

He looked at his watch. It was six o'clock, but as it was late spring, the sky would stay light for several hours yet. Since there was no emergency, he would take his own boat, rather than one of the RNLI rescue craft, but with its powerful engines, he could easily make the trip down the coast to the area around the Ladysgate and be back before dark. Provided, of course, he found nothing and wasn't delayed. The fog had lifted, although clouds still hung in a low ceiling overhead. There was a chance, always, that it would descend again.

Duncan rested his hand on the receiver of the telephone and drummed his fingers. One of his rules of sea rescue was never to go alone. Another was not to needlessly risk another's life. Should he call in a backup?

Since there was no official emergency, he decided against it. He often took his boat out alone. The weather had calmed considerably, and checking the tide tables, he determined that he would get to the rock formation at slack tide, although he knew the current could still be strong. He did take the precaution of donning his heavy rescue gear, if for no other reason than it would keep him warm and dry. Exiting the Life-Boat station, Duncan headed toward his boat that was secured to the dock in the harbor. He hoped this was all in vain, and that before he got very far he would spot the other vessel returning to the harbor and could himself turn back.

Whatever the outcome, Duncan planned to make good on his threat to revoke McGehee's license. Or at least suspend it for thirty days. The damned fool.

The late afternoon sun settled under the layers of clouds as Duncan stepped aboard the heavy crew boat tied to the dock. He started the two huge inboard diesels, and they thundered reassuringly in the engine well. He untied the lines, and with the ease that comes from long experience, he backed away from the pilings. He turned the boat toward the neck of the harbor and gathered speed as he reached the end of the jetties and headed into open water.

Taking action helped relieve Duncan's anxiety, and the crisp ocean air cleared his thoughts. The weather had remained relatively calm all day, he reflected, looking for reasons not to worry. If McGehee had run into fog or a squall, perhaps he'd had had the good sense to take refuge in another harbor farther south.

Yes. That's likely what he'd done, Duncan tried to convince himself. But he set his course for the Ladysgate anyhow and gave the engines full power, quickly bringing the heavy craft to maximum speed.

Thirty minutes later, he could see the dark outline of the arched stone looming ahead of him, silhouetted in the late evening sun. If it didn't pose such a hazard to navigation, the area would be a popular destination for pleasure boaters, he knew, for it was a breathtaking view. But most sensible seafarers stayed safely away.

Unfortunately, Duncan had never considered Fergus McGehee either sensible or safe, and certainly not much of a seaman.

Duncan drove the boat hard, wondering just why he was so determined to save McGehee's ass, especially if he wasn't sure it even needed saving. But he knew it wasn't McGehee's backside he was concerned about. The particular, rather appealing, backside he was worried about belonged to one of McGehee's passengers.

One blonde female passenger.

One blonde female passenger he had no business being interested in, but one, for the life of him, he couldn't seem to get off his mind.

Duncan Fraser had been a bachelor for four years. Or more exactly, a widower. He was determined to stay that way, even though he was a man to whom family at one time had meant everything, because he never, ever wanted to go through the pain again. The pain of losing those you love.

After the deaths of his wife and sons, he'd grown reclusive, dealing not very well with the guilt he felt for their accident. Guilt that pointed a finger squarely in his face for letting his wife drive that night, for allowing his sons to get in the car with her when she came to the Life-Boat station to pick them up the night of the accident. He knew she'd stayed too long at the pub after work and had had far too much to drink. He knew her tendency toward reckless driving. Why had he not taken them home himself and then returned to his vigil at the station?

A simple act. A responsible one.

And one he hadn't given a thought to at the time. Not until he'd heard the ambulance, and his friend from the police had knocked on his door, his face grave and ashen. Duncan would never forget that look.

Three crosses now stood in the churchyard near the edge of town. He visited them from time to time, less frequently as the years went by. He had loved Meghan, in spite of her reckless ways and the fact he knew she had not always been faithful to him. But the boys, oh, Christ, how he'd loved them. He would have stayed with their mother no matter what for the sake of Peter and Jonathan.

But now they were dead.

Salt spray lashed his face, tasting like tears. He forced the powerful boat onward, lunging across the waves, speeding over the coastal waters as if the air rushing past his face would blow away his torment.

Reaching a point far away enough from the Ladysgate to avoid the submerged rocks but close enough to check out the area, Duncan shifted into idle, slowing the boat and letting it bob among the waves. He took out his binoculars and surveyed the shoreline, but he saw no sign of life nor any debris that would indicate a shipwreck. He tried to focus on the water near the arched formation, but he was too far away to see anything in the deepening shadow it cast across the waves. Cautiously, he moved the boat forward again. The rocks that lurked beneath the surface posed little threat at the moment, for they were sufficiently covered by the high tide. But a high tide did not mean the absence of a strong current. Duncan inched his way over the ocean's floor lest he be caught in the treacherous current that had earned its reputation as a killer.

And then he thought he saw something. A tiny dot of orange stood out against the dark water, spotlighted by a ray of lingering sunlight. Duncan's heart began to beat harder. It looked like a life jacket.

An empty life jacket.

Acting on impulse, he revved the engines and sped toward the floating object which drifted just the other side of the Ladysgate. As he neared the maw of the giant monument, he realized his mistake. With a sudden sickening horror, he saw that the force of the current was overpowering his ability to steer clear. Frantic, he turned the wheel, trying to make his way back toward the open sea, but he succeeded only in turning the boat dangerously broadside to the rocks. The sound of water being sucked through the narrow pass grew louder. He reached for his radio.

"Mayday! Mayday!" he called, furious that he'd let himself get caught in such a situation. "This is the motor vessel *Intrepid*. I'm located at the Ladysgate, south of Stonehaven. I'm caught in the current and have lost steerage. Mayday! Mayday!" He released the broadcast button, his voice clutching in his throat. "Oh, my God," he uttered and watched helplessly as the force of nature dragged the craft between the legs of the archway.

Praying that he would somehow ride through the danger, he looked up to see what faced him on the other side. But instead of the clear view he'd had when he spotted the life jacket, he saw nothing but a wall of dense, swirling fog which swiftly enveloped him in its deadly embrace.

Robert Gordon made a fresh pot of coffee. The clock read two A.M. But the story unfolding before him was like history come alive, and with each entry he translated, he became ever more convinced it was authentic. He was especially intrigued with the entries that related to northeastern Scotland, his own home.

4 November 1562
Dunnottar Castle
   We are at last en route to Edinburgh once again, and we welcome a respite from these sad affairs. We were forced to witness the execution of Sir John Gordon to give the lie to the stories he had spread that we had encouraged him in his wild matrimonial schemes. We deplore bloodshed, but the executioner was clumsy with his axe, making the ordeal even more dreadful. We are grateful for the hospitality of the Earl Marischal and his Countess, Lady Keith, here at the fortress of Dunnottar where we shall linger a few days until we regain our strength to continue the journey.
   Riding south from Aberdeen along the coast, we came across a most remarkable rock formation. Our host the Earl called it the Ladysgate, for it is rumored to steal away fair maidens who pass through its portal into the land of the faeries, never to be seen again. We are disinclined to believe such nonsense. However, we found ourself wishing suddenly we could disappear through such a portal. Perhaps on the other side, in the land of the faeries, we would discover the peace and harmony so absent from our affairs in this land.

SIX

Duncan expected his boat to be torn to shreds at any moment as the force of the current threatened to drive it onto the rocks he knew littered the subsurface along this coastline. The closer to shore it impelled him, the greater the danger. He pressed the broadcast button on his radio and once again called for help, but the air waves were strangely silent, and after a few moments, he gave up. If anyone was near, they would have heard him and would bring help. And if not, well, he wouldn't be the first mariner to meet his fate in this place.

The fog seemed to thicken even more, for now he could see nothing farther than the hand in front of his face. Knowing it was safer to do nothing at all at the moment rather than try to fight the current and fog to avoid rocks he couldn't see, Duncan switched his engines to idle, allowing the boat to make its own way on the current. It rocked and bobbed almost gently, the soft, gray shroud muffling the sound of the engines. Duncan's skin crawled at the eerie calm. He sensed its false security.

Hastily, he felt his way around the boat, gathering a few emergency items and zipping them into the pockets of his waterproof suit. A flashlight, a hand-held radio, a compass, a small first aid kit, a tin of sardines, a flask of whiskey. And then he sat at the helm and waited.

It was imperceptible at first, the sensation of changing directions, but Duncan felt the boat begin to turn about. His heartbeat, already racing with apprehension, slammed against his chest. Was the tide turning? Could he make it safely back to open water?

His hope turned to icy terror, however, as he realized the vessel wasn't just turning about, but rather was beginning to spin. Whirlpools were common in these waters. Had he become caught in the vortex of one of the powerful surges created by the clash of currents?

Oh, God.

To his further alarm, he heard the engines shut down. What in hell had caused that? He had plenty of fuel.

The craft swirled and churned in the clutches of the current for what seemed an eternity. Duncan, fingers white on the useless steering wheel, felt the boat scrape and knock against hard rock as it was swept even closer to shore. He closed his eyes and met images of his sons. If he died now, would he meet them on the other side? He wasn't a religious person, but the thought gave him comfort.

And then, oddly, it was over. The boat steadied itself and continued afloat, apparently unscathed. Duncan let out a long breath and tried to see through the fog, which seemed to be dissipating. He heard a sound like tires scrunching over a gravel driveway and was thrown forward slightly. The vessel continued to rock, but Duncan knew it was no longer totally afloat. Cautiously, he left the helm and made his way toward the bow. The waves continued to buffet the boat from astern, pushing it farther each time onto the sandy shore.

He released a hoarse expletive into the mist, but being aground was better, he decided, than being sunk. Securing a heavy line to a forward cleat, he scrambled down the ladder and tied the rope around an enormous rock, wedging it beneath its weight, leaving some slack for tidal changes. Nothing short of a hurricane would free it.

Duncan heaved a sigh of relief, grateful to be alive. He had no idea how he would ever get the boat out of this pickle, but for the moment, it and he were safe. He should have listened to his own advice and stayed away from the Ladysgate. And then he thought about his reason for coming here in the first place.

The nonemergency rescue of Taylor Kincaid and the two young men who had accompanied her. And Fergus McGehee. Disgusted at his overreaction, Duncan emitted a guttural sound and started climbing the hill toward the road at its crest that led to Stonehaven.

Upon reaching the summit, however, he saw no sign of the road. He frowned and scratched his head. Damned strange. How could he have missed it? He took out his compass and knew he hadn't lost his way. The road should be here. Right where he stood. Maybe it was a few paces farther on. The fog continued to cloak the area, obscuring visibility. Maybe he hadn't walked far enough.

But half a mile farther on, Duncan sensed something was wrong. He knew these parts. He'd grown up here. The village where he'd spent many summers with his grandmother was nearby, and he'd roamed these high moors like a wild goat when he was a lad.

It was impossible that he was lost.

Ahead, he made out the faint outline of a cottage. He picked up his pace and headed toward it. Maybe he could get a lift back to Stonehaven from the farmer. But as he approached, the hair on the back of his neck stood on end. This was no ordinary cottage or farm shelter. If he didn't know better, he would swear it was a . . . a crofter's lodge. He'd seen such places in the Highlands, but modern construction had long ago replaced such primitive hovels in this part of Scotland.

"What the hell?" Duncan asked aloud. He went to the front door, which was low and made of rough planking, and knocked. No answer. He raised the wooden latch and cautiously opened the door.

"Hello? Is anyone here?" Receiving no reply, he stepped inside, where it was warm and dark and smelled of wood smoke. His eyes took a moment to adjust to the gloom of the dusky cottage. When his gaze fell upon the chair by the fireplace, he raised his brows and drew in his breath sharply. Feminine lingerie lay scattered atop heavier garments—several sweaters and a jacket. He glanced around and spied a lump on a small cot against the wall. Perceiving that someone was sleeping under a brown blanket, Duncan started to return to the door and knock louder, when the lump stirred and tossed long blonde hair as it turned to face him in its slumber.

Taylor Kincaid.

"Well, I'll be damned," Duncan said, awash with relief that she was safe. But what in the hell was she doing here?

Asleep.

Naked.

His noise did not awaken her. She appeared to be in a deep sleep, so Duncan allowed his gaze to linger upon her. She lay with her head propped on one arm, the other long slender limb curled gently atop the coverlet. Her shoulders were bare, and her skin glowed in creamy silkiness in the firelight. He stared at her openly, hungrily, and felt long-forgotten desire tighten his gut. Her face was a study in delicate beauty, relaxed now as it was, unetched by care and determination. Her cheekbones were high, her nose straight and narrow, and pale blonde eyebrows arched gently against a broad forehead. She could be a model, Duncan thought, and then remembered that she was instead a TV star.

And then he saw the bruise.

It was just beneath her left eye. At first he thought it was a play of the light, but stepping closer, he saw an ugly purple mark on her fine skin. His desire changed to alarm. What had happened to her? Had someone struck her, knocked her unconscious and. . . .

He glanced at the pile of clothes. He didn't want to think about it, that she might have been attacked, raped, and left for dead. The nausea of dread sickened him. Don't let it be, he prayed as he stepped toward her and gently touched her shoulder. Her skin was warm beneath his fingers.

"Miss Kincaid?" He shook her slightly. "Are you all right?"

Taylor's eyelids flew open and she let out a small, startled scream. "Who . . . what? What are you doing here?" she demanded, scrambling to a sitting position, her arms poised to strike. Duncan felt his own relief that he had been mistaken in concluding that she was the victim of foul play. She seemed quite capable of defending herself.

"I . . . came looking for you," he said gruffly, trying to ignore the fact that the blanket had slipped, exposing the top of her breasts. "When McGehee's boat didn't return, I got worried. What happened to you?"

Only then did a bleak, frightened look cross her face, replacing the earlier confidence. She drew the blanket closer about her and ran a hand through her hair, brushing it away from her face. She gingerly touched the bruise and winced. "I . . . I'm not sure. Where are the others? Have you seen Barry and Rob and . . . what was the captain's name? Fergus? Is everyone okay? What about the boat . . . ?"

"How about one question at a time?" Duncan replied with a quiet patience that belied his anxiety to learn what had happened to her. He knelt and took the flagon of whisky from his pocket. "Have a sip of this. It'll warm you."

Her gaze locked on his for a long moment before taking the whisky, and he saw there half frightened animal, half curious television reporter.

He also thought he might drown in those blue depths.

She took a swallow of the single-malt whisky and made a face as the amber liquid slid down her throat. "Where are the others?" she said, her voice raspy.

"I don't know," he answered, wishing he had better news for her. "What happened? Did the boat go down?"

Taylor returned the flask and shivered. "I don't know exactly what happened. It seemed like we were being drawn, sucked almost, toward that dreadful rock. Fergus tried—I know he did—to get away, but the last I remember, I was flung overboard. I . . . I don't know what happened to the boat, or to. . . ." She covered her mouth with the back of her hand, stifling a sob. "Oh, God, I wish I'd never gone near that place. . . ."

Duncan, a veteran of regret, reached for her hand. Her fingers felt small and cold beneath his, like a child's. He wanted to embrace her and comfort her, but he refrained, afraid of the danger of the physical attraction he felt toward her. He cleared his throat. "Don't worry. I'm sure we'll find them." He looked around. "I don't see a telephone in this place, and I have no idea who lives here. Maybe we should start back for town."

He half expected her to pull away from him, but instead, she squeezed his hand and gave him a weary smile. "Thank you. I think I'm okay. Maybe a little bruised here and there. I must have been knocked unconscious. I'm lucky I was washed ashore. I don't think I ever even got my life jacket on. . . ." Then her bottom lip began to quiver in spite of her effort to keep a brave face. "I . . . I hope the rest. . . ."

Duncan returned the squeeze, then released her hand and stood up. "I'm sure they're fine," he said, sounding more confident than the felt. "If that damned McGehee had any sense, you'd not be in this predicament."

"It was not his fault," Taylor flared. "I'm the one who insisted. . . ."

"And he's the one who took you, the greedy bastard."

"Get out of here! What right have you to come barging in on me like this anyhow?"

He heard fear and near-hysteria in her voice, but suddenly, his earlier concern and sympathy were overwhelmed by anger and disgust at the recklessness displayed by the pair of them. What if those two young men had been lost? Whose fault would it be? They worked for this woman. They followed her orders. If she had insisted on making the trip, had they had any choice in whether or not to go along?

He really didn't want to know. "Get dressed," he ordered, his jaw tightening. "I'll check on my boat and wait for you outside."

"Don't bother," Taylor called to the burly figure that ducked out of the low doorway. Fergus was right. The damned man thought he was God.

And yet she was utterly grateful that he'd come looking for her.

Throwing back the rough woolen coverlet, Taylor hurried on tiptoe to the chair where her clothing was now crisp and dry by the fire. She slipped into her panties and bra, appalled that she'd stripped bare and gone to sleep, leaving herself so vulnerable to anyone who happened along. What if the owner of the cottage had stumbled in and had not been the same sort of gentleman that Duncan Fraser, God complex and all, had proven to be? It wasn't like her to be so foolish.

She noticed a few more bruises as she hurried into the rest of her clothing, but other than that, she seemed unscathed by her ordeal. She dreaded another boat ride, but she would be glad to get back to Stonehaven and the warmth of a hot bath— if the innkeeper had left the water heater on. She hoped fervently she'd find the others there, safe and sound.

Outside, she was dismayed to find the daylight almost gone. "What time is it?" she asked the man who was clad head-to-toe in bright yellow vinyl and who, she decided suddenly, looked more like a Martian or some kind of cartoon character than God. Irrationally, Taylor began to laugh.

"What's so funny?"

She laughed harder. She laughed until her sides ached. Until her mouth hurt. Until she became aware that she was no longer laughing but rather sobbing hysterically in the arms of the yellow Martian.

"Shhhh," he said, holding her against him, enfolding her in his strong arms. He rocked her gently until she caught her breath and calmed down. Taylor closed her eyes, grateful that this man did not laugh at her weakness. In fact, he seemed to understand her terror. She leaned into his broad chest and did not move for a long while, letting his quiet strength steady her trembling body, calm her jangled nerves. For the first time in many years, she allowed someone to be stronger than herself. Recalling Fergus' accusation that Duncan sometimes thought he was God, she smiled. Right now, that was okay with her.

She didn't mind being held in the arms of God.

The thought threatened to set off another round of hysterical laughter, which she squelched with a determined swallow.

"I'm okay now," she murmured, gathering her own strength at last and pulling away from him. "Let's go. Where's your boat?"

"We're not going by boat."

"Why not?"

A dark look clouded Duncan's ruggedly handsome face. "She's aground." He pointed down the hill, and her eyes widened when she saw the large vessel sitting high and dry on the pebbly sand. "How in the world did that happen?"

Duncan shook his head. "I don't know." Then he turned on his heel and headed toward Stonehaven. "Come on. It's getting late."

The dried sea salt in her socks rubbed against her skin, blistering her toes and ankles as she tried to keep up with him, but Taylor was determined not to complain as she followed Duncan over the rough terrain. She could tell he was upset about his boat, but she also knew he was a native and a rescuer and would soon present her at the doorstep to her hotel. However, after stumbling for the umpteenth time, she called out at last. "Isn't there a road around here?" she asked, thinking it unnecessary to take such a difficult short cut. "And do we have to walk so fast?"

The tall Scotsman didn't answer. Maybe he hadn't heard her. "I said, is there a road nearby we could take back to town?" she repeated in a louder voice.

He stopped and turned to her, a strange look in his eyes. "Yes, there is a road."

"Then why don't we . . . uh . . . take it?"

Taylor wasn't sure she caught his reply as Duncan resumed their brisk pace, but it sounded something like, "We would if I knew where it was."

Surely not. This man was from here. Part of the local rescue team. But he was used to rescues at sea. Maybe he didn't know the land quite so well. Taylor stopped to catch her breath.

"Are we lost, Mr. Fraser?" she called after him. She saw him slow his pace and straighten perceptibly before turning to face her again.

"No, Miss Kincaid, we're not lost." He sounded annoyed. "We're following the coastline. Stonehaven is just beyond that next hill. Now," he added gruffly, "shall we stand here chatting all night or get on with it?"

Taylor didn't reply, afraid her temper would explode at his

patronizing manner. However, he seemed determined to get back to the village, road or no road, and she wasn't about to be left alone at night on this lonely Scottish shore. The sky had finally grown dark sometime past ten o'clock, and save for the golden aura to the east that presaged a full moon later, there was nothing to light their way except the small flashlight he kept trained to the ground a few feet ahead of them. At least, she thought, trying to find comfort in something, the fog had broken up.

They crested the hill, and Duncan halted, scratching his head. "That's odd," he muttered.

"What?"

"Where are the lights? That's Stonehaven, I'm certain of it. Do you suppose there's been a power outage?"

Taylor didn't reply. But she did peer into the darkness, straining her eyes to see the tiny village barely discernible at the foot of the high hill where they stood. She looked up at Duncan and was alarmed by the queer expression on his face.

"What's wrong?" she whispered.

His voice was hollow in reply. "I don't know," he said one more time.

SEVEN

Holyrood Palace
3 March 1563

The weather outside our window is as bleak as our life, and as cold. How we long for a brisk hunt in sunny France, as in the days of our youth! Alas, those days have passed, we fear never to return. Our beloved uncles art dead—the Duke of Guise murdered by Huguenots, and Francis struck down by the will of God.

In Scotland we fare little better. The poet Châtelard, whom we loved, but only for his beautiful song and verse, took into his head a madness, and betook himself into our bedchambers, not once, but twice, vowing his love for the Queen in a way most inappropriate! The first intrusion was discovered by our grooms of the chamber, but the second assault was upon our own person. Whether he was mad or the agent of one who wished me dead, we knowest not. He was brought to trial, found guilty and executed in the market square at St. James. He was a favored poet, for he wrote in our beloved French style, and we shall miss him. It saddens us to know that one so young and beautiful and close in loyalty, or so we believed, would return to our court from France in the employ of traitors with murderous intent. Is there no one we can trust?

Our health and our spirit art worn by these things and the tiresome habits of our nobles. They bicker and fight amongst themselves until we think we might lose our wits. None trusts the other, and we trust none of them, save Moray, our brother. Elizabeth, although she writes with great sympathy, will not be our friend and we are still unreconciled with no hint of the establishment of the promised meeting. We have suffered from the cold of Scotland and the illnesses to which we have succumbed these past few months.

It hast been two years since the death of our beloved husband Francis, and we have not until of late truly wished for another husband. Now we long for a strong, loyal consort to support and defend us and to carry part of the burden that we find increasingly unbearable. But who wouldst that husband be? Maitland and Moray ask us daily. The Archduke Charles of Austria, or our cousin Henry of Guise? Never Charles, poor Francis' brother, for we find him vile and vicious, even at only twelve years! Don Carlos of Spain? Or the king of Denmark or Sweden? Or shouldst we marry a Protestant and bind together the religious wounds of our realm? A Catholic queen and a Protestant king? It is not the fate desired by His Holiness, and yet, it might be the wise resolution to our unending dilemma. Then might our subjects and their unhappy queen dwell together in a peaceful Scotland.

Peace in this land is our most fervent wish, and yet, we seest now that the world is not that we do make of it, nor yet are they most happy that continue longest in it. . . .

The lawyer went to the window. The sun was just beginning to bleach the night sky with the pale light of dawn. He felt odd, ill at ease almost, at this intrusion into the intimate thoughts of this long-dead queen. He'd never thought much one way or another about Mary Queen of Scots. Never wondered, never cared whether she was guilty of the crimes for which she was executed. But here, on these pages, he began to understand and sympathize with the young queen's woes. According to these pages, she had wanted nothing more than peace among her nobles and the freedom of her people to worship as they pleased. To these ends, she had pledged the Scottish Rose.

The Scottish Rose. There it was again. . . .

Something was wrong. Very, very wrong. Duncan Fraser knew every inch of this land. He knew there should be a road under his feet. He knew this was the promontory of his nightmares, where his wife's car had plummeted down the cliff on an equally dark night four years before. And below, the village of Stonehaven should be twinkling with lights as his friends and neighbors went about the business of life—eating supper, drinking in the pubs, putting babes to bed, watching television—those ordinary activities of nighttime that required electric lights. Instead, if his eyes didn't deceive him, he saw a few lights, but of a very different kind. They looked like torches.

"Come on." He grasped Taylor's hand and led her down the steep slope. Maybe he was having a bad dream, he thought wildly as they scrambled over stone and thick patches of gorse. The events of the past few hours had a certain dream quality about them . . . his powerful and heavy boat becoming stranded on totally dry land, discovering a beautiful woman naked in bed, being unable to find a familiar roadway. And as they made their way down the hill, Duncan saw there was no paved footpath, no park bench, no trash barrel. It must be a dream.

At the foot of the hill, he stopped for a reality check. He took in a deep breath and saw the mist on the air as he exhaled. He felt Taylor's hand in his, her skin warm and soft. Just clearing the horizon, a brilliant full moon dispelled the darkness. These things were real. This was no dream.

What wasn't real was the village of Stonehaven. He led Taylor slowly down the darkened unpaved street, his frown deepening with each step. Some buildings he recognized, the very old ones, but the newer ones simply didn't exist. Panic gnawed at the edge of his consciousness, and Duncan fought to control the apprehension that knotted his stomach. He heard a strange noise, a clattering sound, like horses' hooves striking hard ground, and he pulled Taylor into the safety of the shadows of the doorway of an old stone building.

It sounded like horses because it *was* horses. Three riders raced through the main street of town, shouting at the top of their lungs. "Halloo! Awaken, countrymen! Beware!" The riders began pounding on doors along the street, bringing angry responses from inside.

"Why ye be callin' so late?"

"Th' divil take ye. Sound asleep I was."

"Awake! Arise! The bloody English have taken the Earl Marischal prisoner! They're marching now for Dunnottar Castle!"

Duncan felt Taylor tug at his sleeve. "Is this some kind of movie they're filming?" she asked, her voice hopeful.

A movie. Could be. Mel Gibson had filmed scenes from Hamlet a few years back at nearby Dunnottar Castle. Advertising firms sometimes used the area as a backdrop for commercials. The riders were certainly in strange costumes and spoke with a heavy antiquated accent not heard in real life. It would explain why the lighting had been replaced by the torches he'd seen from the hilltop. But it didn't explain where the houses of his neighbors had gone, or the roadway, or the park bench. A movie company, even one committed to utter authenticity, didn't tear down dwellings and highways.

The dream shifted and became a nightmare.

"Could be," he answered, "but I don't think so."

"I don't see a camera crew," Taylor agreed, and Duncan felt her fingers tighten around his arm. "Duncan, what is going on?"

"I'm sure there's a logical explanation." But he'd be damned if he knew what it was. There was no apparent logic to what they were witnessing, and there was danger here, too. He could feel it, but he didn't want to alarm Taylor. "Follow me to the Life-Boat station," he said under his breath. "I'll phone my friends at the police and find out what this is all about." He put his finger to his lips. "Come on."

Keeping to the shadows, he led Taylor toward the harbor. Hopefully, McGehee and the others would be there, and there would be a rational explanation for everything that seemed at the moment altogether incomprehensible. But as he turned the corner of the narrow street that should have ended at the doorway of the RNLI shack, he saw clearly that it ended instead at the water's edge. The building that housed his engineering office was gone as well.

"What the bloody hell?"

"What's the matter?" Taylor asked tremulously from behind him.

Couldn't she see what was the matter? he thought irritably. Or was it just *he* who was hallucinating? He wheeled around and put his hands on her arms. "Does anything seem . . . extraordinary to you?"

"Extraordinary? Oh, only that half the houses in town seem to have disappeared, and a bunch of hairy, filthy men have just ridden in to announce that the 'bloody English' are about to invade. Other than that, I'd say everything was pretty ordinary."

Her tone was light, but he felt her begin to shake, and he feared she would relapse into her earlier shock-induced hysteria. "Stop that," he said gently.

"Stop what?"

"Shaking."

"Was I shaking? Oh, do forgive me," she replied sarcastically, and Duncan knew her mockery was an attempt to hide her fear. "Listen, could you just call me a cab? I think I want to go back to New York."

Duncan didn't blame Taylor for being scared, but he couldn't appreciate her levity. His nerves were frayed, too, not just from the day's events, but even more by the chimerical nature of what seemed to be happening around him. Nothing made sense. Normally, he was the world's most rational human being. He was dependable, cautious, the rock to which others clung. Normally, he found logic behind the seemingly illogical and laughed in the face of fear.

But nothing about this moment was normal.

Nothing.

Suddenly, impulsively, he pulled Taylor against him and pressed his lips to hers. He felt her stiffen in surprise and alarm, but then she yielded and melted against him like warm butter. Oh, God, what was he doing? He barely knew the woman. And yet, the feel of her body grounded him. Gave him an anchor in the storm of the surrealistic events that seemed to be engulfing them.

This, if not normal, was at least real.

"What are you doing?" Taylor regained her momentarily lapsed senses and pushed against the huge wall of Duncan's chest, gasping to catch her breath. "What . . . what was that all about?" she sputtered, not wishing to acknowledge how his fierce kiss had stirred her.

Duncan's only reply was to stare at her for a long moment, and watching his face, Taylor saw an astounding progression of emotions lash fitfully across his rugged countenance. There was confusion, uncertainty. Distress. Then an inexplicable anguish, followed by a dark look that could only be described as rage.

But not one sign of apology for his brash behavior. Instead, he took her arm and almost dragged her down a dark side street. Only when they were safely hidden in shadow did he speak.

"I don't know what I'm doing," he said roughly, "and I don't have a clue what the hell is going on. But we'd better stay inconspicuous until we find out."

Taylor wished he'd given her a more reassuring answer. He was, after all, supposed to be the rescuing hero. He was probably right about remaining inconspicuous, but looking at him still dressed in his yellow weatherproof gear, she thought it unlikely. "Then you'd better get out of that outfit you're wearing," she advised with a small grin. "You're like a beacon."

Duncan scowled at her but did not reply. He did, however, remove the bright yellow jacket and pants which he rolled up and stashed behind a bush. Beneath the foul-weather gear, he wore a heavy navy blue oiled wool sweater and dark pants that blended with the night around him.

"Let's go," Duncan said, taking her hand once again and heading in the direction of the town center. Taylor did not protest, although she was perfectly capable of making her way through the darkness. But she had been through so much in the last forty-eight hours, she didn't want to think. She just wanted this man to do his job and get her back to the warmth and safety of the inn and find that Barry and Rob were alive and well.

Then . . . maybe . . . she would think about Duncan Fraser and the unsettling kiss he had just ventured upon her lips.

The sound of more riders entering the village jolted her back into the alternate reality they seemed to be caught up in, and Duncan pulled her against the side of a building. With caution, they peered around the corner to see a growing crowd of townspeople gathering by torchlight to learn what further news the riders brought about the events that had taken place in the south.

"General Lewis has left Stirling Castle," one called out breathlessly, "marching for England!"

A cheer went up, along with murmurs of it being about time for Cromwell to get a taste of Scottish vengeance. The speaker continued. "Nay, hold, countrymen! 'Tis not all good tidings we bear. Perth has fallen to Cromwell! The city surrendered without a fight, but many of our fellow countrymen and women have taken flight." With this, a communal moan ensued from the crowd.

"Are the bloody English coming north?" someone shouted anxiously.

The rider's horse reared, as if the animal shared the common fear that rustled through the crowd. "Not Cromwell himself," the rider answered, "but he has dispatched General Overton with orders to take Dunnottar Castle!"

A cry of terror and despair rose from those huddled together in the night. An old man shouted indignantly, " 'Tis too much! We've only just recovered from Montrose's wicked plunder of our village!"

"I canna bear it! I lost my bairns in th' fires when they burned the village," cried a woman.

"But what want they with Dunnottar Castle?" another woman's voice questioned. " 'Tis only a lonely outpost."

At that, the voices stilled momentarily in brief consideration of the question. But no one seemed to have a ready answer. The English were a confusing lot.

The horseman continued. " 'Tis forecast that Overton and his army will arrive before two weeks hath passed. Flee now, or seek safe harbor in th' castle, if ye dare! Ogilvy will need all th' help he can muster now that th' Earl is imprisoned!'' The riders spurred their horses, which reared in protest, then sped off into the darkness, headed north to warn the citizens of Aberdeen.

Taylor felt Duncan's hand leave hers, and he drew her back, pressing her shoulders against his chest, enfolding her securely in his strong arms. "I'm almost certain it's not a film set,'' he said grimly, his lips next to her ear.

She felt her stomach turn over, and she twisted in his embrace to look up at him. "But . . . but what else could it be?''

"I think it could be . . . another time. . . .''

"Another time? What do you mean, another time? I don't understand.''

"Neither do I,'' he replied. He frowned at her thoughtfully. "When you were thrown overboard, did you . . . uh . . . were you washed through the Ladysgate?''

Taylor stared at him, then scowled sardonically. "Oh, for heaven's sake. You're not going to try to tell me we've somehow been taken back in time.. . . .'' But she shut up when she saw that was exactly what he meant. "Surely you can't believe that nonsense.''

"Then you come up with a better explanation for this, lady,'' he snarled. "Where did the Life-Boat station disappear to? Where did the road go? Where are all the houses in Stovehaven? The ones that have been built for two hundred years but somehow don't seem to be here?''

"Don't get testy,'' she snapped back, feeling the bile of panic rising in her throat. "I don't have the answers. But I know it's just not possible that we've been thrown into another time. It . . . it just isn't possible,'' she repeated, but her voice trailed off in misgiving. She turned to watch the chaotic scene in front of her. People were pouring into the street, crying and consoling one another all at once. She kept hearing the name Cromwell repeated in words of fear and hatred. Of course, Taylor had heard of Oliver Cromwell, but she had no idea of the role he had played in Scotland's history. "If . . . and I'm not saying this is the case," she began, "but if we somehow are having . . . let's call it 'matching dreams' about being in the time of Cromwell, what time . . . uh . . . would that be?"

Duncan did not reply immediately, and she thought at first he hadn't heard her. Then he answered. "Around 1650, I think."

"Around 1650! No way! This is absurd." The weight of the idea snapped her reason like a twig. With the strength of a sudden adrenalin rush, she tore free of his grasp and darted into the crowd. "What's happening?" she cried. Fear and exhaustion pushed her into hysteria. "What is going on? Somebody, please! Explain yourselves."

EIGHT

She was gone before Duncan could restrain her. He watched with sickening apprehension the expressions on the faces of the townspeople who grew quiet at this sudden intrusion. Surprise. Fear. Distrust. Even in his own time, Duncan's small town was wary of newcomers, unless they were tourists and quite temporary. He doubted seriously if the Stonehaven he was beginning to believe he had stumbled upon, the Stonehaven of some long-ago day, knew what a tourist was. In this Stonehaven, strangers would be severely suspect, especially in dangerous times such as these appeared to be.

He didn't wait to see what would happen next, but chased Taylor into the street, shoving his way through the crowd that was now encircling her. He grabbed her roughly by the arm. "Be still, woman," he commanded in as strong a Scots accent as he could summon. He felt foolish and theatrical and was not at all certain she would react like a meek seventeenth-century wife. His gaze took in the astonished faces of those who for the moment had forgotten their fear of Oliver Cromwell and had focused their attention instead on the mad woman in their midst. "Pray, forgive my wife, for she is distraught by all that has befallen us since Cromwell's troops marched on Perth."

Taylor stiffened at his reference to her as his wife, but he shot her a warning glance. Did she realize what danger she was in? Fortunately, she had the sense to remain silent, but her eyes were wide and wild, and Duncan was unsure for how long she would remain docile.

"Ye come from Perth?" asked one of the men in the crowd. "What did th' bastards do?" His eyes glittered, hungry for lurid details.

Of which Duncan had none. " 'Twas a terrible day," he improvised with a sad shake of his head. "Most all I knew fled when word reached us that the English were at the edge of town." His mind was racing for his next tactic, because an historian he wasn't, and it was but a matter of time until he made a mistake and his prefabricated story would fall apart.

If nothing else was familiar to him, he did recognize the old part of the village. This *was* Stonehaven. His family had lived here for generations. He straightened and looked through the crowd, catching the eyes of several men. "I am Duncan Fraser," he said, drawing himself to his full six-foot-three. He towered over the other men. "Have I a kinsman in this town?"

The crowd murmured and several looked around as if searching for someone. After a long moment, a tall man stepped forward. "I am Kenneth Fraser," he said. "Are ye my kinsman indeed? I know no Frasers in Perth."

"I come originally from Aberdeen," Duncan replied truthfully, since he had indeed been born in the hospital there, although that had been in the 1950s. In true Scottish tradition, his father had made sure he and his sisters knew of their ancestral lineage as they grew up, and it occurred to Duncan that possibly he was addressing one of his own forebears.

Now it was he who had gone mad!

Stay calm, he told himself, feeling his heart pounding in his chest. Next to him, his "wife" trembled, and he knew any wrong move could spell disaster for them both. "My father was Angus Fraser, and his father William Fraser." Duncan silently thanked his grandmother and great-grandmother for choosing such common names for their sons and hoped like hell Kenneth Fraser might have heard of some kinsmen coincidentally of the same names.

The lanky Scotsman lifted his torch to look Duncan straight in the face. "I know of these Frasers," he said at last. "Welcome, kinsman. Ye look weary from thy journey. Come t' my house. Take food and rest. Then we can ken what step next t' take.''

Duncan let out a deep breath, then turned to Taylor. ''Are you all right?''

She raised her face to his. ''Yes,'' she said in a small voice. And then those luminous blue eyes filled with moisture. ''No.'' Duncan wanted to pull her against him again, to assure her he wasn't going to let any harm befall her, but he felt the stares of the people around them.

''Let's go with my kinsman, wife,'' he said quietly, smiling at her and brushing her hair from her face. She did not return the smile, but nodded and allowed him to place his hand at her waist. For all her strength and independence, Taylor Kincaid was still in shock, and Duncan hoped he merited the trust he knew she was placing in him. He would not let her see his own fear and confusion. He would instead do everything he could to protect her.

Kenneth Fraser's house was a small, weathered abode that perched near the harbor, on the far side from where Duncan's house stood in 1996. Being a wooden structure, it was not one of those houses that had stood the test of time and remained in the Stonehaven Duncan knew. But in the bright moonlight, the two-basined harbor it overlooked was infinitely familiar. Except that it appeared full of debris. ''Was a ship wrecked nearby?'' Duncan asked before going into the house.

''Tha' 'twas part of Montrose's evil,'' Kenneth replied, his voice filled with resentment. ''Not content t' burn th' town down, he sunk all th' ships in th' harbor as well. We've had th' veery divil of a time araisin' 'em again. Ye'd have thought he was an Englishman, instead of a fellow Scot.''

''Perhaps I could help,'' Duncan offered, watching as his host doused his torch in a bucket of water and placed it to dry into a holder fastened to the outside of the house. ''My skill is as a seaman.''

Taylor, who had remained miraculously silent as they walked down the narrow streets to their host's home, gave him a snide glance at his claim of seamanship. He supposed she didn't think much of his seafaring skills, since he'd managed to land high and dry in the middle of this strange adventure. But he didn't care what she thought. He was glad to see a return of her quick wit, even if it was aimed against him. It would serve to stabilize her emotions.

Duncan tried to tell himself that his protective feelings for her were simply those of a professional rescuer. But even as this flashed through his mind, he knew there was nothing simple about his feelings, or the woman toward whom they were directed. Taylor Kincaid had not yet stolen his heart, he decided, but she had most definitely laid seige to it. In spite of their strange circumstances, for the first time in years, Duncan felt alive, felt a purpose to his existence, more purpose than just to rescue Taylor, although he wished to God he knew what was going on and how to get them back to present-day Stonehaven. There, he could explore his feelings for her further, see if they were real, or if they sprang only from their mutual distress of the moment.

But this was neither the time nor place for him to be thinking about his personal life.

Right now, he had to concentrate on a more important job.

Keeping them alive.

They entered the tiny house, stepping into a single room partitioned by a woolen blanket the color of mud and lit solely by a fire that burned in a small grate in one corner. A blackened cooking pot hung from an iron frame next to the fire. A rough-hewn wooden table with benches along both sides took up most of the room, and next to the table, a short, stocky woman stood anxiously wringing her hands, her dark eyes filled with questions, her weathered face lined with fear.

"My wife, Greta." Kenneth nodded toward her. "Greta, 'tis here we have a kinsman come directly from Perth. He is Duncan Fraser, and his wife . . ." He looked expectantly at Duncan, who realized he was to introduce his own "wife." But "Taylor," he suspected, was not a name that would set well with these folk. Even in his own time, most Scots gave their children more traditional names. So he improvised once again.

"This is . . . uh, Janet," he said, and wasn't surprised when Taylor's head jerked toward him. Her mouth moved, but no words came out, and Duncan hurriedly continued. "She's . . . she is in a strange state of mind, I ken, with all that has happened." He brushed the bruise beneath her eye gently. "With some food and rest she will be as good as new. She's a strong lass," he added, giving Taylor a warning press with his hand on her shoulder. He felt her flinch, but she remained silent.

"Have ye some food left in th' kettle, wife?" Kenneth went to peer into the pot.

"Aye," Greta replied, prying her suspicious eyes away from the strangers and going for two crudely carved wooden bowls that stood on the table. She filled them from the pot and without a hospitable look of any kind handed them both to Duncan. From the slimy texture and rich odor, Duncan guessed this was a poor man's version of haggis. He knew Taylor would likely gag on it.

He afforded the woman a nod of thanks, then turned to her husband. "Kinsman, we thank ye for thy kindness in taking us in," he said to Kenneth, hoping his language sounded appropriate. "I fear that my wife is too weary to eat. Is there a corner where we might rest for the night?"

With a glare, Greta took the bowls back and slopped the unwanted food into the pot again. "Ye shall have th' best we have to offer, although 'tis nothin' royal," she sniffed, not hiding her resentment that he had refused her food. She pulled back the curtain which separated the sleeping quarters from the main room. Rushes were strewn over the dirt floor, and along one wall lay a gray-brown pallet covered by a sheep's hide.

"We'll not take thy bed," Duncan protested, but Greta shushed at him.

"Aye, ye will, and make no more talk about it." She scowled. "We have another we can make down for ourselves before th' fire," she added as if proud of such wealth. "But my husband has much he must tell me first, before we sleep."

Looking into Taylor's tired face, Duncan made no further protest. His own fatigue washed over him in a huge, gray wave. "We thank ye then, kinswoman," he replied.

Greta closed the curtain between them, and Duncan turned

to face Taylor. Suddenly there was fire in those blue eyes, and a burnish on her cheeks. He could tell she was about to explode. But he put his finger to her lips and shook his head, warning her not to speak. He took her hand and drew her down onto the pallet beside him.

"Get some sleep," he whispered, leaning back against the wall. Perhaps if she slept, she would awaken with a more rational mind, and a better attitude. He fought going to sleep until she was under control, but his own body screamed for rest. "We'll sort this out in the morning."

Exhausted, confused, and frightened, Taylor was both astonished and appalled at the way Duncan seemed to be taking all this in stride. "Sort things out in the morning! You have got to be kidding." She gritted her teeth, trying to keep her voice low. "How can you even think about sleeping? We have to get out of here!"

"And go where?" he growled.

Taylor backed off, since no answer came readily to her mind. "Well, you can at least quit playing your little games," she said, nursing her anger, for it gave her a much-needed vent for all the rest of the chaotic emotions that threatened to overwhelm her. "Where do you get off giving me another name? And where in the hell did you come up with Janet? And about me being your 'wife,' excuse me, but. . . ."

Duncan leaned forward, and Taylor shut up when she felt the big man's powerful grip around her wrists. "Get hold of yourself," he whispered urgently. "We're strangers in a place and time that neither of us understands, and until we figure a way out, we had better behave like we belong here. *Both* of us."

Taylor glared at him, ready to spit back an angry retort, but she saw the raw anxiety in his eyes and realized that he was taking their predicament seriously, even if he didn't let it show. Somehow that reassured her, and she relaxed a little. She felt his grip loosen, although he did not let go of her, and a lopsided grin crossed his lips.

"Besides, Janet's not such a bad name. It was my mother's."

She failed to see the point. "Well, it's not mine, and I'd thank you to use the perfectly good one I was given."

"It may be a perfectly good name for the twentieth century," Duncan replied patiently, "but if we are indeed in some long-ago time in Scotland, a name like Taylor could get you into a lot of trouble."

Taylor stared at him stubbornly. "Why?"

"It's not . . . well, a . . . *traditional* name like they used to use in Scotland. It would likely sound alien to these people." He let go of her altogether and leaned back, a scowl replacing his attempt at good humor. "Sorry if you don't like it. But it was the first thing that popped into my head. The part about your being my wife, too. I doubt if single men and women traveling together would be welcomed in this time."

"Welcomed? That woman didn't seem very welcoming, for all of her offers of hospitality, even if she believes I'm your wife. And what the hell *time* is this, anyhow?" Taylor was denying with all her will that they had somehow transcended time and that even as they bickered here in this strange place, Cromwell's army was advancing toward them.

There was no way this could be happening. Time travel didn't exist except in science fiction novels. It was right up there with UFO sightings and Bigfoot on her list of ridiculous phenomena that some people claimed for truth. And yet, what other explanation could there be for what was going on around them?

She saw Duncan's eyes close, and she was incensed that he was ignoring her. And then she heard a low gurgling sound. He was snoring! The damned man was asleep!

Taylor crouched at the edge of the pallet and pulled her knees up, hugging them to her chin. She felt a hard knot at the back of her throat. Her muscles ached from the battering they'd taken in the ocean and from the long hike into town, and her eyes burned from forcing back tears. She was unnerved, emotionally drained, uncharacteristically afraid, and generally unhinged. And the only person available as a sounding board against which to express her frustrations had managed to slip easily into a sound asleep. Jerk!

But angry as she was, her own body was betraying its need for nourishment and rest. Why Duncan had refused the food offered by the woman named Greta was beyond her. Surely he was as hungry as she.

Taylor stood up and loosened her jacket, trying to get comfortable. She needed to go to the bathroom but suspected there wasn't one, and she wasn't about to interrupt the man and woman who spoke together in low tones just the other side of the curtain. She was so exasperated at Duncan she didn't want to lie down next to him, but at the moment, she had no other options. She knelt on the sheepskin and as best she could in the semidarkness, studied the sleeping form of the man who thought he was God.

But Duncan Fraser was only a man. A big, rugged man with an athletic body that would be more at home out-of-doors than in heaven, she decided. Clad as he was in dark clothing, his form melted into the shadows of the room, leaving only his face discernible in the low light. It was large as well, with handsome features—a wide brow, finely shaped nose, and tanned cheeks just beginning to show the stubble of beard. His hair was the color of burnished copper. He was, she admitted, one altogether good-looking Scotsman. And she remembered how safe she had felt in the shelter of his arms. Under other circumstances, Taylor reflected, she might be tempted to bend her rules concerning men just a little. . . .

She drew in a tired, ragged breath and fell forward on her hands, then collapsed altogether, scarcely feeling the rough fleece graze the skin of her cheek before she slipped into a deep sleep.

It was past ten o'clock in the morning when Robert Gordon resumed his task. At dawn, he had run out of energy and gone to bed. He arose refreshed and eager to continue. He decided to remain at home where he would be uninterrupted by any business calls that might come into his office. Then he laughed at the notion. He had no business. His last real client had been

Lady Agatha Keith. As a lawyer, he was washed up. A has-been. At this point in his life, and his career, the only important business he must attend to was that which lay in front of him now. But though he was intrigued by each page, he felt an urgency to make his way through the diary by the end of the day, so he skipped several entries and continued his translation:

April 1565
Stirling Castle

Last month, the first of our lovely and loyal Maries was wed—Mary Livingston writes of her deep happiness as the bride of Lord Semphill's son. Maitland is courting the belle Mary Fleming, and the others each have their own favorites. Their enthusiasm on the subject is beginning to turn our own thoughts to romance. Four years have passed since we were widowed, and we admit to these pages we are sorely inclined to find a husband soon.

Our good cousin, Elizabeth, has sent a handsome choice northward to our dominion, Lord Darnley, the son of the Earl of Lennox. He has been in our presence here at Stirling since the winter, and although there are those in our court who dislike him, we have attended him personally during his protracted illnesses, and we find him not only handsome, but gay and charming, and in need of our succor. We tire of the daily diatribes of those who would make the choice of husband for us, for we know their choices are not in our best interest, but rather their own. We are, in fact, tempted to go against all their choices and marry to spite them. The thought lifts our spirits. Darnley would do nicely in this respect, although our own uncle has written that he disapproves of my attentions to the *gentil huteaudeau,* the agreeable nincompoop, as he calls him.

We tire of our uncle as well as our court. We tire of constantly being counselled, as if we had not a brain in our head. We tire of living this lonely existence without the comfort of a consort. Darnley even has his Catholicism to recommend him to us.

Yes, even as we write these words, we are convinced that we shall marry Darnley. Surely since it was Elizabeth who sent him, she must mean for it to be. Our union would be perfect, for, like us, he is a descendant of Henry VII of England. Our issue would be directly in line for the throne of both England and Scotland, after Elizabeth of course. Perhaps Darnley is the key to peace between England and Scotland, although our marriage would in the beginning, we fear, cause a great uproar amongst our nobles. But we shall give him the title of King Henry and the power to quell their dissent.

Oh, yes, we shall marry Darnley, to suit ourself and spite our lords. We shall send an emissary to Elizabeth this very day.

To spite her lords? Robert Gordon was astounded. The Queen had married Lord Darnley out of spite? How different this account than that of recorded history, which stated that the Queen had fallen hopelessly in love with the hated son of Lennox. But if she hadn't loved him, it might explain her later complicity in his murder. Suddenly the pages he was painstakingly translating became an intriguing murder mystery as well as a record of perhaps Scotland's most infamous royal.

NINE

༄

When her eyes opened again, Taylor awoke to violet-blue predawn light filtering through a crudely glazed window above where she lay. Blinking away the fuzzy remnants of sleep, she tried to remember where she was. She lay comfortably against something large and warm that held her in a protective embrace into which she instinctively cuddled . . . until she realized it was Duncan's body.

Taylor bolted out of his arms, remembering everything. She had hoped it was all just a nightmare, that she would awaken in 1996 in the old inn in Stovehaven, where Cromwell and his troops were forever tucked away in history books. Instead, she remained in the sleeping quarters of the shanty belonging to Kenneth and Greta Fraser, curled up against a man she scarcely knew.

"We've got to get out of here." Taylor shook Duncan roughly, not wanting to think about how she momentarily had relished the security and comfort of his embrace. Those kinds of feelings were dangerous and misplaced at the moment, born of the circumstances, not of rational thought.

Duncan was awake instantly, and together they emerged from behind the curtain into the main room of the house. Kenneth and Greta were seated by the fire, their faces drawn and weary. Taylor felt guilty that she and Duncan had taken their sleeping space. They looked as if they had stayed up all night.

"Good morning," Taylor managed, wishing she could affect a Scottish accent.

Greta looked at her with a forced half-smile, but it was her husband who spoke. "Are ye feelin' better after some rest?"

Taylor nodded. The initial shock of yesterday's events had worn off, and she had begun to assimilate the dreadful possibilities their situation presented. With a return to more rational thinking came also a return to her normal instinct for self-preservation. Something about their "kinsmen's" tense attitude, especially Greta's, raised goosebumps on her skin.

Kenneth stood and dipped something white and runny from the same pot the mystery meal had been served from the night before. "Take some gruel," he said, handing a bowl to each of them this time. "It'll warm ye. We dinna know what th' day will bring, and we must all be ready."

Taylor's stomach growled. She tried to remember the last meal she ate and couldn't. Gruel sounded like "cruel," but something was better than nothing, she decided, accepting the bowl with a murmur of thanks. The gruel was palatable enough, tasting a little like oatmeal, and she quickly downed the entire bowl.

"Ah, I knew ye'd be hungry." Greta said, her scarcely concealed contempt mollified somewhat that this time her food had been accepted.

When the two had eaten their fill, Kenneth said to Duncan, "Hath ye a horse, or came ye on foot?"

Taylor saw Duncan hesitate a tiny fraction of a second, obviously not having made up the part of his story that would explain exactly how they had arrived here. But he recovered almost immediately and continued to weave his tale.

"We have no horse," he said, attempting to mimic their host's accent. " 'Twas taken from us by Cromwell's men. Lucky we was t' encounter a tinker who let us ride as far as Arbroath on the back of his wagon."

Kenneth looked thoughtful. " 'Tis said th' governor of th' castle is in dire need of strong men," he said at last. "I went out again last night and met with my friends in the village. We will ride for th' castle early this morning t' learn if this be true. We've decided 'tis safer in the castle than in yon wild hills. Will ye ride with us, kinsman, if I can find ye a horse?"

"Aye," Duncan replied without hesitation, and Taylor lost

all hope that they might instead make their way to the Ladysgate and into their own time once again. She was feverish to return. It was, she'd decided fervently, far better to debunk a myth than to experience it.

Kenneth turned unexpectedly and surveyed Taylor from head to foot. "Kinsman, pray tell, why doth thy wife dress as a man?"

Taylor looked down at her jeans and started to protest, but Duncan replied quickly, his face suddenly fierce, as if he'd been affronted by the question. "Why, ye know as well as I, kinsman, what th' English would do if they captured a woman. Would ye not protect thy wife by disguising her in like manner?"

Kenneth nodded, but added, "Hath she no woman's clothing? She will be ill-received among th' rest dressed like this."

Duncan shook his head. "We escaped with our lives and naught else," he said soberly. "All we have is what we are wearing."

Taylor's hysteria threatened to resurface at the absurdity of this little scene, but she wasn't sure whether to laugh or scream at Duncan's theatrics. But his statement was true. All they owned was upon their backs.

Their host looked at his wife. "Hath ye such as would fit her?"

Greta was several inches shorter and many pounds heavier than Taylor, but she nodded, although hesitantly. "Aye, husband. There is . . . your elder sister's dress. I put it away in the chest when she died. She was tall, like this lass."

Taylor raised her brows. A dead woman's dress? This was too much. "I . . . I'm fine, really, I mean, you don't need to make such a fuss. . . ."

Kenneth approached her, a queer look on his face. "Thy speech is strange, kinswoman," he said quietly. "Ye stand taller than th' other women in th' village, and thy hair is more golden than most and oddly styled. I fear ye'll attract attention as an outlander. It could be dangerous for ye, and for us as well. Ye must," he warned, "hold thy tongue."

Taylor felt like retorting that she would do no such thing,

but his tone of voice restrained her. She glared at him, but nodded reluctantly.

That understood between them, Kenneth turned to his wife. "We must hurry," he said urgently. "Give Janet th' clothing, then bundle together all that we can carry. Kinsman, cover thyself with this mantle, for thy clothing is not of our shire either."

Shouts met their ears, and Kenneth opened the door. "We're coming." He motioned to Duncan to follow him.

As he passed Taylor, Duncan bent his head and pretended to kiss her, as a caring husband would his wife. Instead, he whispered into her ear. "Do anything you have to," he warned, "but speak as little as possible, and under no circumstances give away our secret. It could get us killed."

Duncan rode hard through the early morning mists alongside Kenneth Fraser and several other townsmen, quickly covering the short distance to Dunnottar Castle. He knew it was important for him to join in, to be a part of the activities until he could figure out a way to escape, but he was worried sick about leaving Taylor with Greta. Something about that woman made him uneasy.

Duncan was familiar with Dunnottar, for as a castle ruin in the late twentieth century, it was a popular tourist destination that attracted visitors from around the globe. In the mid-seventeenth century, however, it was still very much an active fortification, one of the most dependable strongholds on the coast, Kenneth had told him. As a child in school, Duncan had been taught the story of Dunnottar's most glorious moment in history . . . when it served as the hiding place of the Honours of Scotland, revered symbols of the independence of the Scottish people, and kept them from the destruction intended by Cromwell's invaders.

Although nothing had been mentioned yet of the presence of the Honours at the castle, the timing was right, and, incredibly, it appeared that he might be about to take part in that very history. The notion was staggering.

The riders raced along a path much farther inland than the

road Duncan knew. He had expected they would ride along the coast which would have afforded him a glimpse of the *Intrepid*, hopefully by now floating free on the incoming tide. Somehow, he tried to assure himself, the boat would provide a means of rescue from this crazy time warp. If it had brought him through the Ladysgate into this time, it stood to reason it could make the passage in reverse, returning he and Taylor into their own time.

But at the moment, nothing stood to reason.

And until he could figure how to effect their escape, he had to keep his wits about him in this strange and primitive era. He'd vowed he would protect Taylor, and he intended to keep that pledge, no matter what.

Duncan learned from the clipped conversation between his fellow riders that they were on their way to meet with George Ogilvy, a man he had heard of only in history books. Ogilvy, he recalled, had been the governor who defended Dunnottar in the absence of the seventh Earl Marischal, who had spent the latter years of the civil war locked in the Tower of London. Duncan searched his mind for the details of the story, which was Stonehaven's favorite legend, next to the Ladysgate, of course, but all he could remember was that somehow, with few men and low provisions, Ogilvy had staunchly defended the castle, his king, and the Honours of Scotland. But the particulars escaped him.

Guards at the castle gate scrambled to attention upon the arrival of their small party. "Halt!" cried a sentry who crossed his pike over the first entrance to the castle, almost at the foot of the castle rock. "Who goes there?"

"We hail from Stonehaven," replied Kenneth, undaunted, "t' learn if 'tis true that th' Earl Marischal has been arrested and taken away t' London."

The guard did not soften his stance. "What business is't of yours?"

Kenneth dismounted. "We come as friends of George Ogilvy of Barras," he said, stepping to within inches of the guard's face. "We've heard 'tis good strong men he needs t' defend Dunnottar. Pray, admit us t' see him." He turned and indicated his band of men with a glance. "Ye can see he might need the likes of us when th' bloody Roundheads come t' fetch th' Honours."

"How know ye of th' Honours?" the guard challenged immediately.

Kenneth laughed. "As Sheriff of Kincardinshire, 'tis not much I do not know."

"Sheriff?" The guard instantly dropped his challenge. "I beg pardon, sir. Yes, of course, Governor Ogilvy will be most anxious t' see you."

Duncan raised an eyebrow, surprised to find his rustic "kinsman" was an officer of the law. Dismounting with the rest of the men, he held tightly to the reins of his borrowed horse, as he'd been directed to by the others, guarding the animal carefully as they were led to the summit. One of the men had remarked earlier to Duncan that horses were almost more valuable than gold, as they were in demand by both the English and Scottish armies to replace those that were killed in the fighting, and by common folk as a means of escaping the fray. Duncan considered himself lucky to have been loaned one for this excursion.

George Ogilvy of Barras was of medium height, rather stocky, but his stance was proud and professional as he greeted his visitors. " 'Tis not many good Scots we have seen come prepared t' defend this castle rock," he said, shaking his head as if he could not comprehend why every loyal Scotsman in the neighborhood had not immediately rushed to the cause upon hearing of the events that were unfolding. "These are confusing times, however, with Royalists fighting Roundheads, Catholics fighting Covenanters, and Presbyterians fighting everyone."

"And what are ye fightin' for?" Kenneth asked him.

Ogilvy straightened and looked him directly in the eye. "Why, for king and castle, sir," he said, almost indignantly.

"And for what lies within the castle?" Kenneth pressed.

Ogilvy scrutinized the local sheriff, assessing how much he knew. "Yes," he said at last, "for what lies within th' castle that was brought hither not long before th' Earl Marischal was abducted by th' scurrilous English.''

"So 'tis true that th' Earl has been captured then?'' Kenneth continued.

"Aye,'' Ogilvy replied morosely. "Just before they forced him t' go t' London, he managed t' smuggle this t' me,'' he said, reaching into his deep coat pocket and producing a large, heavy key. "And with it, orders that I am t' keep Dunnottar and all within safe until the English are defeated and King Charles II is restored t' his rightful throne. That, good sir, is what I fight for.'' Duncan saw the pride in his eyes, and he respected the honor and loyalty the man exhibited to his absent superior.

"We stand ready to defend th' castle and th' Honours,'' Kenneth came to the point at last, "with th' condition that our families may join us behind th' castle walls.''

Ogilvy looked worried. "There is a problem with provisions,'' he said. "And ammunition. I dinna ken th' slowness of the General Commissary. Six hundred bolls of meal was t' have been delivered here already, but I've received less than half that. I suspect,'' he scowled, "th' rest can be bought on th' streets of Aberdeen.''

Kenneth turned to his men. "Ye ken th' conditions here. Wish ye still t' bring thy women and bairns into th' castle for what will likely be a long siege with low provisions over th' winter, and there bein' no guarantees any of us will come out alive?''

It didn't sound like much of an offer to Duncan, but he had decided if he and Taylor couldn't make an escape through the Ladysgate, then they would go with whatever decision his "kinsman'' Kenneth made. But Olgivy's option must have sounded more hopeful to the rest, who agreed to the man to bring their families to the castle.

" 'Tis likely th' English will raid our homes and kill our cattle and sheep,'' said one. "Here at Dunnottar, more provisions may or may not be forthcoming, but we ken well what will happen t' our families if left without shelter t' forage on the moors for th' winter.''

"Aye," the rest of them agreed.

Ogilvy nodded grimly. "Bring ye thy wives and bairns then," he said, "but also thy chickens and livestock and all thy food, as we will need every sustenance available to us." Then abruptly he bowed his head in prayer. "God grant us His grace and mercy. God protect and defend us. God smite our enemies and return unto us our anointed King. Amen."

"Amen."

Needing a visual tool to help him through the historical details of the translation, Robert Gordon laid out a time line on a legal pad. He made note of the diary dates, then compared them to the accounts of the same events recorded in the history book.

They matched in every instance.

If this diary wasn't authentic, the forger had had a detailed knowledge of the Queen's life. His pulse quickened. He should call in John Doggett right away, for he knew him to be the most knowledgeable, if not always the most scrupulous, antiquarian in the area. If Doggett determined this was the real diary of Mary Queen of Scots, it would be one of the most monumental documents ever to have emerged from the shrouds of history. More important even than the famous Casket Letters.

And more valuable.

Perhaps he should call Doggett immediately.

But no. Gordon could not resist finishing the translation first.

Holyrood Palace
5 September 1565

Elizabeth has withdrawn her blessing of our marriage to Darnley. Our nobles hate our choice of husband. But we are hurt most by the treacherous betrayal of our brother. James is perhaps the greediest of all, we can see clearly now. Not content with the wealth and power we bestowed upon him in awarding him the Earldom of Moray, he has rebelled against us now, taking to his side

Châtelherault and Argyll, once our powerful allies, now our dangerous enemies. Moray claims that our marriage to Henry Darnley poses a threat to the Protestant religion in Scotland, but his motives are far less noble, we are certain. For until our marriage, he enjoyed the greatest power in the land next to ourself, and now he cannot abide that his power has been usurped by our husband. It would be easy to hate our brother.

We have taken steps to crush his rebellion. We have put him to the horn for treason, as he has refused to appear before us and explain his churlish behavior, in despight of our assurance of safe conduct for him and eighty of his legion. We have outlawed Châtelherault and Argyll as well, and seized the properties of Moray, Rothes and Kirkcaldy. We stand ready to march against the rebels if necessary, but have not enough resources to carry forth this campaign with any great expectation of victory. We have pledged certain of our jewels, among them two of the rubies from the Scottish Rose, to raise the funds that we need, and we have sent an urgent plea of our Holy Father to aid us in this cause. We regret having to profane the chalice, but our brother's actions leave us no choice.

Our heart is heavy, and we vacillate between anger and despair. We sought only peace and the companionship of a loving husband, but we have instead stirred the hornets in their nest, and truth be told, in our own nest we are finding little of the harmony and marital bliss that prompted us to marry Darnley in the first place. Still, we stand resolute to our decision. We are the annointed Queen of Scotland, and we shall bend our subjects to our will, if they will not see it on their own.

TEN

Taylor had thought Duncan was being overly dramatic when he'd warned her that their lives might be in danger. But after the men were gone, she almost jumped out of her skin when Greta came toward her carrying a huge long-handled knife.

The gnomelike woman held it up as if in threat, the steel glinting in the firelight, then turned it and handed it to Taylor. "Take this," she said gruffly. "Ye might be aneedin' it soon. They say th' English'll not arrive for some days, but y' niver know. If we're lucky, Kenneth'll get us out of here and safely into th' castle before the butchers get here." She shook her head. "If we dinna flee soon," she sighed, " 'tis likely we're done for."

"Done for?" Taylor wished like hell this was a script for a screenplay.

Greta Fraser looked at Taylor as if she were addle-brained. "Y'know . . . deed." She came closer and squinted up at the taller woman. "I'd rather be deed than tortured by that lot of bloody infidels." Her tone was confidential. "I heerd th' tales of what they done t' th' poor unfortunates who din't escape when Montrose burnt us out in '45."

Taylor's skin crawled. This woman was no actor. Her words were undeniably urgent, her fear real. Taylor accepted the knife with a solemn nod. Then Greta dug through a large oaken trunk and handed Taylor a wrinkled, well-worn garment. "Put this on," she said, shaking dust from the rough brown fabric. "Ye'll not seem such th' stranger then." She gave her a pair of shoes as well that resembled ankle-high moccasins.

Taylor offered no argument. She went behind the curtain to change clothes, not from modesty, but rather to prevent Greta from seeing her other modern attire. She kept on the lingerie and Wintersilks that comprised the first layers of her garments, not wishing to give up more protection from the cold than she had to. Slipping the dress over her head, she wrinkled her nose at the odor that permeated it. Still, Greta was right, she told herself, now she didn't look so much like a stranger. But she didn't have to look like a barbarian, either. She brushed the tangles from her hair and started to apply lipstick, then thought better of it, not knowing if there was some means of reddening the lips in this place. Zipping the brush and lipstick back inside the bum-bag, she fastened it securely around her waist, where it was effectively hidden beneath the large, loose skirt. Inside, the small camera seemed undamaged, and she hoped she would have the chance to discreetly snap a few shots of this incredible journey.

After this ordeal, she thought wryly, she was certain she'd have to change the focus of the show. Maybe name it something like *A Lunatic Rethinks Legend and Lore*.

She folded her jeans and sweaters into a neat pile, tying them along with her sneakers into a bundle within her jacket. Then she ventured again into the main room, holding the knife in one hand. "How do I look?"

Greta eyed her critically, then nodded. "As ye should." She took the knife from Taylor and showed her where to place it in her belt, hidden in the folds of the rough fabric.

"There. It'll serve ye well, but pray God ye'll not need it. Now, I must make haste t' be ready when Kenneth returns."

Greta bustled around the little house, which was no larger than the living room in Taylor's New York apartment. She threw clothing and rough bedding and the newly washed cooking pot and some rustic-looking utensils and cups and plates into a pile on the floor. She picked up several other small items of her household and added them to the collection. "There," she said at last, dusting her hands together, "that ought to do it."

Taylor had watched all of this with the animation of a statue, fascinated that Greta was so matter-of-fact about tearing down her household, no matter that it was meager, and leaving everything behind. She couldn't imagine her friends at home doing such a thing. Of course, her friends at home didn't have Cromwell's troops bearing down on them.

She forced back a wave of hysteria invoked by the thought. "How . . . how can I help?"

Finished with her immediate chore, Greta turned her attention fully upon Taylor. "Y' can help by remainin' as hushed and hidden as possible," she said, her voice suddenly terse and cold, no longer attempting to feign goodwill. "And for certain stay away from my Kenneth." She took a step closer and regarded her guest with jealous eyes. "Ye didna come from Perth, did ye?"

Taylor froze. Duncan had warned her not to give away their secret, but unlike him, she had no ready reply. "What makes you say that?"

"Ye come through th' Ladysgate, din't ye?" the woman went on, nodding her head in answer to her own question.

"I . . . I'm afraid I don't understand," Taylor said, adrenaline shooting through her. "What are you talking about, the Ladysgate, I mean?"

"Dinna play stupid with me, lass," Greta warned. "Ye know verra well what I speak of. Everyone knows th' place is bewitched." She walked in a slow circle around Taylor, her eyes gleaming. "There've been others come here, like you, whose talk and dress and manner is not of our time."

Taylor's eyes widened. "What others?" Curiosity quelled her fear, and her reporter's intuition began to take charge. "When? How . . . ?"

"They's come through th' big arch, from time t' time. Most of them women, although some men've strayed through. Strange they's been, all of 'em. Some of them ravin' mad." Greta shook her head. "Some say 'tis th' work of th' divil," she whispered malevolently. "And if they find out ye'r one of them, ye'll not be spared th' stake."

"The stake?" Taylor squeaked.

Again Greta looked at her as if she'd taken leave of her senses. "Aye, th' stake. Th' others was burned at th' stake, they was, because th' townspeople thought they was witches and th' messengers of th' divil."

Taylor went cold all over. She'd read a lot about Scottish witches in her research. And about the ignorant, superstitious people who had murdered thousands of innocent women accused of witchcraft. "Do . . . you think I come from the devil?"

Greta gave a nervous laugh. "I dinna know what t' ken. Ye seem harmless enough. Yet I'm afeered that some mischief shall befall us for takin' ye in. Already, I seen th' eyes starin' and th' tongues waggin.' "

"Then we musn't stay here," Taylor replied immediately. Not only did she not wish to place Kenneth and his wife in jeopardy by their presence, but she hoped that Greta, thinking she was about to get rid of them, would quit this creepy conversation. "As soon as the men return, my . . . uh . . . husband and I shall be on our way."

She couldn't wait. Surely they could make it back through the Ladysgate before all hell broke loose here in this time. Why had Duncan gone with the villagers this morning? she wondered, her earlier irritation returning. And when would they get back?

"I'm afeered it'll not be that easy, Janet," the woman continued, and Taylor suspected Greta of deriving some twisted satisfaction in scaring the bejeebers out of her. "Some of th' others tried it, goin' back through th' Ladysgate, if that's what ye be athinkin'."

It was as if Greta had read her mind, and Taylor wondered just which of them was the witch. "What happened to them?"

Greta shrugged. "Th' last one I heard tell of came through in my mother's time. She was one of them what talked too much, and it dinna take long for th' witch hunters t' arrest her. She pleaded with them t' let her go back through th'

Ladysgate, and they did. But instead of disappearin' soon as she stepped through, she appeared again on th' other side. That's when they nabbed her and tied her t' the stake.''

She emphasized the word *stake* in a most unpleasant manner, and Taylor shuddered. ''You mean, nobody who comes through the Ladysgate is able to return through it?'' She found it difficult to believe that she was discussing this as if it made sense. But with each passing moment, the reality was more and more difficult to deny.

''Oh, some's got through it.'' Greta's nonchalant reply was encouraging. ''At least accordin' t' th' tales that's been handed down.'' She paused. ''But who knows? Th' tale tellers have been deed a long time.''

''Deed'' or alive, until this misadventure, Taylor would never have believed a word of anyone's tales of the Ladysgate. It was her job *not* to believe such folklore. It was how she made her living. But at the moment, she would be a fool not to suspend her disbelief in time travel and the legend of the Ladysgate and at least take warning from Greta Fraser.

It could, she feared, mean the difference between life and death.

Left with that choice, the concept of time travel became infinitely more believable.

After Greta's grim tales, Taylor, aka ''Janet,'' had no illusions about the fate that might await them if they remained in this time. These people believed in legends and lore, like the Ladysgate and witchcraft, and although she wouldn't classify them as lunatics, they *were* ignorant and superstitious, and therefore dangerous. She had no doubt that her life, and Duncan's, were in jeopardy. She felt a pang of regret, knowing that it was her headstrong insistence on visiting the Ladysgate that had drawn Duncan into this predicament. But then she reminded herself that she hadn't asked for his help. He'd come to her rescue totally of his own volition.

Why? She hadn't had time to wonder until now. Why had Duncan Fraser come looking for them? Had Fergus radioed for help? She didn't recall that he had. It had all happened so fast there hadn't been time. The thought of Fergus and Barry and Rob brought a hard knot to her throat. Where were they? Had they gone through the Ladysgate, too? Were they nearby, aware that they were no longer in the twentieth century, that they were about to be attacked by English soldiers? Or had they managed to avoid those terrible jaws of granite and survive the turbulent seas that had caused her to fall overboard?

Please, please, let them be safe.

Greta's frightening indoctrination had convinced Taylor that if she wished to survive to see the twentieth century again herself, she had better learn fast how to become part of the seventeenth. There must be a way out, in spite of Greta's stories to the contrary. But until she found it, she was going to have to remain sequestered and inconspicuous behind an old-fashioned dress and a shy demeanor.

From this vantage point, however, she would be able to observe the villagers, making mental notes of every detail that might later come in handy in writing a script, or maybe even a book, about this adventure. She had come to Scotland to get a story. It seemed as if she'd found a dandy.

If she survived to tell about it.

Feeling ill at ease around Greta, Taylor stepped into the street for a breath of air. It was a beautiful late summer morning, with a brisk breeze blowing off the North Sea. Looking about, she recognized the uniquely shaped harbor, but otherwise, this Stonehaven looked little like the one they had left behind. Of course, she hadn't seen much of it in the twentieth century, but this village was eerily primitive. For comparison, she tried to envision seventeenth-century Manhattan for a moment and came up with an even more primitive image—white men trading beads to Indians in exchange for an island.

Something rustled in an alleyway across the street, and Taylor jumped. She turned her head, expecting to see a giant rat or a stray cat and was surprised to see instead a small, filthy boy crouched by the side of a building, gnawing hungrily on a scrap of someone's garbage. His face was so dirty it matched the mud-smeared rags he wore. Her heart lurched in compassion. Hesitantly, she took a step toward him. He looked up at her with wide, frightened eyes, then leapt from his hiding place and dashed away down the street, leaving Taylor regretting that she had interrupted his pathetic breakfast.

"Leave him be," Greta called from her front door. "Th' boy's touched, he is." She tapped her own forehead. "He'll not survive another winter, and it's good of't."

Taylor was shocked. "What do you mean?"

Greta motioned to her to return to the house, peering around anxiously lest someone might have seen the strange woman make an overture to the boy. Inside the dim house, she shut the door firmly behind Taylor. "The bairn's mother was a witch. And if ye be seen 'round him, ye'll have even more chance of bein' accused of th' same," she hissed. Taylor saw the threat in her eyes.

"There are no such thing as witches, Greta," she replied, trying to restrain her aggravation. "That's just foolish superstition."

Greta's fat fists landed on her plump hips. "Naw that's na way t' talk." She frowned. "Of course, there's witches. Everyone knows about 'em." She wrinkled her face into a puddle of distain. "Th' most famous was named Janet, in fact," she added as if unsure that her visitor wasn't the witch just named. "Janet Beaton. Lover t' Lord Bothwell, she was. Some say 'twas her bewitched him and gave him th' potions that he later used t' seduce Queen Mary."

Taylor stared at this intense little woman, who obviously believed every word she uttered. "Queen Mary?"

"Mary Queen of Scots, of course," she scoffed at Taylor's ignorance. "She must've been enchanted t' kill her own husband for th' likes of Bothwell." She shook her head, considering this almost century-old gossip as if she'd read it in the morning paper. "Although 'tis common said that her husband, Lord Darnley, was no good man either."

Taylor was fascinated at this recital of history by an obviously ignorant peasant woman. Where had she learned all the details about the love life of a queen who had been dead almost a century? From legends, she guessed, and stories handed down by word of mouth from one generation to the next.

Taylor was steadily gaining a new respect for that which she had once disdained.

She wondered briefly if the woman had ever heard about the Scottish Rose, but Greta seemed as if she had spun all the tale she had to tell. So Taylor pressed her on another matter. "Who is the boy? What is his name? And where is his mother?"

"Ye'd better learn 'bairn,' " the other woman uttered. "Na ane calls a child a boy or girl." She sat on the rough wooden bench at the table. "His name is Pauley, and his mother is deed. Fell from th' cliffs, she did, just near th' Ladysgate. 'Tis whispered she was killed by th' faeries for bein' th' wife of th' divil." She smiled maliciously, revealing several missing teeth. "But then, that's just a tale."

"Was she . . . one who came through the Ladysgate?" Taylor asked tentatively.

"Nay, she was th' daughter of a crofter who lived nearby. His lodge is just up th' hill from th' Ladysgate. Ye might of seen it. Nobody lives there anymore. They's all deed."

Taylor recalled the small hut where she'd taken shelter and fallen asleep by the fire. Although barren, that hovel appeared inhabited. Greta must be talking about another place, she decided.

Their further conversation was interrupted by the sound of the arrival of the men returning from the castle. Greta jumped to her feet and ran to the door, but Taylor pulled her heavy skirts around her and moved to stand by the still-glowing coals in the grate. She knew her hostess meant well in lending her the clothing, but the dress smelled funky and looked worse, and she was in no hurry for Duncan Fraser to see her in it.

And then she wondered why she cared.

The men tromped in. There were six of them, including Kenneth and Duncan, all dressed in rough, rustic garments made of similar fabric as the dress. Duncan gave her a quick glance in which she saw first surprise, then a flash of amusement, and then approval, that she had changed into the costume of the day. She returned his greeting with a small smile, anxious to hear his news, hoping it included word that they would soon be leaving this town and this time and this insanity.

Instead, she learned that he'd enlisted them in service at Dunnottar Castle, where they and the other villagers would join forces with the Royalist governor to defend the castle and the Honours of Scotland, just as she'd heard had taken place in history. She shook her head, stunned, but kept her mouth shut. If they were locked inside the castle, how would they ever get back through the Ladysgate? Maybe when she got him aside, she could explain their precarious situation and he would go with her to make an attempt at a return to their own time.

Because *she* would make that attempt, with or without Duncan Fraser. She had no desire to play cowboys and Indians with this group of primitives.

"Word from th' south has it that Cromwell's general will reach here in little more than a week," Kenneth reported to his wife. "Governor Ogilvy needs forces now to prepare for a long siege. Are ye ready, wife?"

Greta appeared pale and shaken, but she broached no argument to her husband's decision. "Aye," she murmured. Then she looked from Taylor to Duncan and back again at Kenneth. "What about them?" she asked, her voice betraying the fear and distrust Taylor knew she harbored against the two strangers.

"They go with us. We'll need all the strong men we can muster."

Greta stared openly at Taylor. She shook her head. " 'Tis a bad business," she uttered.

ELEVEN

Duncan could see from Taylor's face that she was struggling not to strike back at Greta's rude declaration. That she was trying to control her quick tongue seemed a miracle, and he wondered what had come over her. Quickly, he went to her and took her hand, pressing it in reassurance. "Ignore her," he murmured. "The woman's just afraid."

Gazing into Taylor's pale, grim face, he saw a demand for an answer. *Why are we going to Dunnottar instead of the boat?* Maybe they wouldn't go to the castle but instead drop out of the group of refugees on the way. But only if the *Intrepid* was floating free and ready for them to make a dash for it. Otherwise, they'd be safer with the villagers. They must continue their play-acting, at least for a while.

"Are ye ready as well, wife?" he asked, the old-fashioned words sounding awkward even as his eyes pleaded with her to go along with the ruse.

She glared at him. "Aye, *husband.*"

A short while later, Duncan and Taylor, Kenneth, Greta, and their cow and two chickens joined the others from the town who had chosen to take refuge in the castle. The raggedy band gathered at the foot of the hill, milling about with mounting anxiety as they awaited others they expected to join them. Duncan was aware that he and Taylor were the focus of many curious stares, but it appeared that Kenneth's sponsorship prevented any overt challenges to their presence. After what Duncan had learned about events in the not too distant past that had nearly destroyed their village and their lives, he couldn't blame them for distrusting strangers. Spies, he had been told, were commonplace in this time.

At last, the motley crowd seemed to have swelled to include all that were expected, and Kenneth, as sheriff, gave orders. "Stay together," he warned. "We will be allowed as a group to enter the castle, but once we are admitted, th' gates will be locked behind us. See t' your bairns and womenfolk."

Duncan leaned over and spoke in Taylor's ear. "Are you okay?"

She narrowed her eyes. "Okay? What's *okay*? They don't say 'okay' in this time, do they?"

The stress of the last two days and his own frustrations at not having a plan of escape left Duncan with little patience for Taylor's petulant behavior. He took her roughly by the arm and led her away from the crowd and into semi-privacy behind a large bush. "What is wrong with you?" he demanded, furious.

"What's wrong?" she shot back. "What's wrong is that instead of trying to get us back to the boat and our own time, you seem to be taking some perverse pleasure in joining in this jolly little war that's about to happen. I can't believe you've got us going off to spend the winter behind the walls of that creepy old castle with a bunch of ignorant, superstitious peasants who would just as soon burn me for a witch as look at me."

"Burn you for a witch . . . ?" Duncan decided Taylor clearly had snapped. But before he could press her to explain herself, footsteps sounded nearby, and they turned to see a small, wraithlike figure vanish into the shadow of a nearby building.

"Wait here," Duncan ordered and ran after whoever had been watching them. But turning the corner, he saw no one. He paused, listening, and thought he heard a faint sound, like someone's rapid breathing. Silently, he moved in the direction of the sound and jumped in alarm when a small brown creature darted from behind a heap of foul-smelling rubbish and dashed down another street. It looked to be a child!

Wanting to catch the youngster and reunite it with its

mother before it was left behind, Duncan pursued the child, quickly overtaking it and grabbing it in his strong arms. Thin arms and legs kicked and flailed at him, and the creature grunted unintelligibly as it struggled.

"Pauley!"

Duncan heard Taylor call out from behind him and turned to face her. The child, a filthy, stinking boy of about seven, stopped his struggle momentarily when he saw her.

"You know him?" Duncan asked, startled.

"Oh, my God," Taylor replied, rushing toward them. "They're going to leave him behind." She reached over and touched the boy's face. "His name's Pauley. He's an orphan," she explained quickly, then glanced around to see if they were observed. "They say his mother was a w-i-t-c-h," she spelled, not wanting the boy to understand the ugly, ignorant slur Greta had made against his mother.

"Surely you are joking," Duncan said, incredulous. "Who told you that?"

"The same good woman who warned me that I might be accused of being a witch, our kind-hearted hostess Greta," Taylor said grimly, taking a small piece of hard bread from her pocket. The morsel was eagerly snatched by hands that hadn't been washed in days . . . or months. Maybe never. The child ate like a ravenous beast. "That dreadful woman said he was 'touched' and that the villagers believe he is the child of the devil." Her voice was strained, husky, but she continued. "She told me he . . . wouldn't survive the winter, and that . . . it was a good thing."

"Good Lord," Duncan replied, shocked at such cruelty. And yet, remembering when and where they were, a chilling reality struck him. Witchcraft was a common belief in these times. Persecuting so-called witches was a way of getting rid of those who did not fit in with the local society. Like this boy.

Like Taylor.

He wished now he'd never left her alone with Greta, who had obviously entertained her with tales of Scottish witch hunts. But a dilemma now loomed large before them. "What are we going to do with him?"

"Well, we can't leave him *here*," Taylor pronounced. She stood and faced Duncan, defying him to argue with her, and he was surprised at the determination in her eyes. She hadn't seemed the motherly type, until now.

"But Taylor, if these people have left him to starve on the streets, which it appears they have, what makes you think they will allow him to go to the castle? Food there is going to be even more scarce, and . . ."

"Screw the castle," she flared. "If we go to that castle, we'll never get out of here."

Duncan understood her point, but she did not understand their options. "We may not get out of here anyway," he returned harshly. "We may not be able to float the *Intrepid.* And if we do, it may not take us back to our time. Do you want to be huddled here in Stonehaven when Cromwell's troops arrive to burn the place down and . . . and who knows what else?"

"I can always put my jeans back on so I'll look like a man," she snapped. And then she sighed. "I suppose you're right," she said, in a calmer voice. "But what about Pauley?"

Duncan could see it was no use arguing with her, and he himself had no wish to leave the child to die of hunger. But from what Taylor had just told him, he doubted that the superstitious people of Stonehaven, his own kinsmen included, would agree to take the boy.

He hoisted the wiggling, grunting bit of humanity to his shoulder and together, the three of them headed back to the others. As they approached, he heard a murmur begin to sweep through the crowd, and he knew things could turn ugly. His heart went out to the urchin, who through no fault of his own was feared and hated by the villagers. He thought fleetingly how unfair life was, in this time and his own. This child had lost his mother; Duncan had lost his children and their mother. The world, he decided, could be a cruel place, no matter what time you lived in.

"Hist! See who comes yon, husband," Greta cried out

loudly enough for all to hear. "I said t'would be a bad business t' let th' pair of them come."

The undertones grew louder, and Duncan heard for himself the hateful charges against the waif named Pauley.

"Son of a whoring witch, he is!"

"Should've been drowned when he was born."

"The divil's in him."

"Tha's wha's wrong with him, tha's why he canna speak."

Duncan stopped in his tracks and automatically reached one hand behind him to shield Taylor. He glared at the gaggle of snarling citizenry. "What say ye against this lad?" he demanded, summoning all his theatrics and his fiercest expression. "What hath he done t' deserve thy scorn?"

Kenneth stepped to the front of the crowd, his face dark as a thundercloud. "Kinsman, ye hath been welcomed in thy time of need, but ye intrude in business that is not of thy knowing.

" 'Tis but a lad," Duncan scowled back. "Whatever his mother's crime, 'tis not of his own doing."

" 'Tis th' divil's offspring," Greta snarled. "He brings bad luck. He canna go with us t' th' castle."

"But he'll starve if he stays here," Taylor blurted out, stepping from behind Duncan.

"I warned ye about him," Greta frowned at her, "and about yer words," she added, reminding Taylor-Janet to speak in the tongue of the others. "The bairn should niver abeen born, and th' sooner he dies, th' better."

Duncan now shared Taylor's undisguised shock and contempt, and in spite of his better judgment, he made a decision. "My wife and I'll not be joinin' you in th' castle, then, kinsman. We shall make do as best we can on our own. We canna in good Christian conscience leave this lad t' die."

Kenneth's expression hardened. "Ye hath made a grievous error, kinsman. Th' evil bairn's life may cost ye your own and that of thy woman."

Duncan felt Taylor squeeze his hand, and that sealed it. He nodded grimly to the other man. "I thank ye for thy good counsel, kinsman, and for thy lodging and food. Hath ye any further instruction to give us for th' days to come?"

"Aye," the other man replied shortly. "Hie ye from this land quickly, and let no one know th' history of th' evil thou carryest with thee."

Taylor was not sorry to see the villagers go, nor was she afraid at being left behind. These people were dirty, ignorant, and cruel, she had decided, and she wanted no further part of them. All she wanted was for the three of them who remained behind to go to the Ladysgate and attempt to make an escape into the future. Pauley, who had accepted reluctant refuge in Duncan's arms throughout the ugly scene, had nothing to look forward to in this time. If they took him back into their own, he would at least be cared for. They could find a foster home for him, make sure he was well nourished and given proper medical care. It beat the hell out of starving to death all alone in a deserted village.

"Give them time to get far ahead of us," she voiced her thoughts, "then let's go back to the Ladysgate." She turned to Duncan. "Maybe the tide has come in by now, and we can take your boat back through the arch."

Duncan nodded. "It's worth a try." Then he set the small boy on his feet, and the child bolted away as quick as lightning. "Damn!" Duncan swore, and once again pursued the pitiful urchin. Taylor watched, her heart aching for the frightened youngster who had suffered so much abuse in his young life.

Knowing that she was unable to bear children, Taylor had consciously avoided being around them, because they reminded her of her loss. She avoided Christmases with her sisters' families, although of course she sent presents to her nieces and nephews. She sent money to Big Brothers/Big Sisters, mainly because one of her friends was in charge of that charitable organization in her area, but she made no contribution of personal time. She'd never been interested in the idea of adoption, or the possibility of being a foster parent. And she scrupulously avoided long-term relationships with men that would force her to confront the issue of having a family. Even if a man swore he did not want kids, she didn't trust that later he might not change his mind.

But something maternal had sprung to life when she'd first seen Pauley, and she knew she could not leave him to the fate Greta had assigned him. Pauley seemed to have other ideas, however, and it took Duncan almost half an hour to round him up again. "I don't think he wants to go with us," he said, hauling the boy back to where Taylor waited. "In fact, I don't think he likes us much."

"Can you blame him?" Taylor said softly, her heart melting. "After the way he's been treated by those awful people?"

How could they gain his confidence? She remembered something she'd put in the waistline pouch—a day or two ago, or over three hundred years in the future, depending on how you looked at it. She set the bundle of clothing on the ground and raised her skirt, turning her back to Duncan modestly. Reaching beneath it, she unzipped the bag and brought out a roll of Breathsavers. She peeled away the foil wrapper, noting that the boy had suddenly stopped squirming and was watching her with curiosity. She flicked off one white circle and held it up to him.

"Do you like candy?"

Pauley just stared at her.

"Want a mint?" she asked again. She put the circlet on her own tongue and smiled. "Mmmm," she said in an exaggerated manner. "Good." Then she held out another to the boy. He looked at her with intense distrust. "Go on. Take it," she encouraged, but she didn't force it into his hand, sensing intuitively that he needed to make his own move to accept the gift.

Slowly, his thin arm reached for the candy, which he slipped into his mouth. He made a face at the tart flavor of wintergreen and quickly spit the mint into his grimy hand. But he did not throw it away. Instead, he seemed fascinated by it, and turned it over and over until the wet white surface looked more like chocolate. Taylor grimaced but didn't interfere, waiting to see what he would do next.

He put it into his mouth again and bit it in two with a loud crack. And then, to her delight, he let out an impish laugh. It was not normal laughter, however, but rather more of a gurgle and a grunt, and she recalled suddenly a remark one of the townspeople had made, something about Pauley not speaking.

"Pauley?" She said his name when his head was turned away, and he did not respond. She stepped closer to Duncan, who was watching her closely, and snapped her fingers next to the boy's ear. Again, there was no response. "The boy's not touched," she said, suddenly understanding. "But I think he might be deaf."

Duncan adjusted the child's weight on his hip. "I suspected he might be," he replied. "He didn't pay any attention when I was talking to him after I caught up with him. I thought at first he was just frightened, but I think you've hit on the real problem."

Taylor touched the boy's hair, and the child jumped nervously. "Poor kid," she murmured. "Think of the treatment he must have been through, just because he's deaf. Those people actually think he *is* the son of the devil, don't they?"

"I'm afraid so. But what are we going to do with him?"

"What do you mean? He goes with us, doesn't he?" Taylor was amazed that Duncan would consider anything else. But the brawny Scotsman shook his head.

"That's not our decision to make."

"What?" Amazement turned into incredulity.

Duncan held Pauley slightly away from him and looked into his grimy, frightened, defiant face. "This little lad has to *want* to go with us. If we force him, I'm just going to be chasing after him again and again."

Taylor knew immediately that Duncan was right. Pauley had been accustomed to avoiding the villagers, and she and Duncan were no different as far as he was concerned.

Then suddenly, he pointed a thin finger at the package of mints Taylor still held in her hand. "You want another?" she asked, then felt foolish, knowing he couldn't hear her. She held up the package and pointed to it, then touched Pauley's mouth lightly. The boy's eyes lit up, and it was all the answer Taylor needed. But she made the motion of nodding her head, then gently tipped his head up and down with her fingers. Pauley was deaf, but he was also obviously bright, for he caught on in an instant. Taylor pointed to the candy again, then to his mouth, and his little head bobbed eagerly.

She gave him a mint and a warm smile. "He's certainly not retarded," she said to Duncan. "Maybe there is some way we can get him to understand that we will take care of him if he goes with us."

"Put yourself in his place," Duncan warned. "Trusting us to give him a candy mint is one thing. Going along with us into a modern power boat that to him probably looks like some sort of dragon is quite something else."

"He needs time to get used to us," Taylor replied, seeing Duncan's point.

"But we may not have much time. Ogilvy said they are expecting the leading edge of Overton's troops any day now."

Taylor shook her head in disbelief. "I'm still having a hard time with this whole thing." She paused reflectively, then added, "Don't you think it would be better for the child in the long run to force him to go with us? After all, if he stays here, he'll starve or be killed by the invaders."

Duncan raised his brows and shrugged. "Let's start from where we are at the moment," he said at last, and he put the boy down again. "Let's see if he runs."

But although Pauley backed away and looked up at the two of them with large, questioning eyes, he did not take off as he had before. Duncan squatted down to Pauley's eye level. He smiled broadly and held out his hand. The boy looked at the bear-sized appendage, then back into Duncan's eyes. He chewed his bottom lip. Taylor watched, her heart flooding with love and compassion for the frightened child, and with admiration for the gentle giant who was trying to coax him to come back into his arms. He had no reason to trust the strange man, except that he had been shown kindness in those arms, and protection. Would that be enough?

Tentatively, Pauley's thin arm unfolded from across his chest, and with a small smile, he placed his tiny hand in Duncan's. The man nodded, and the boy mirrored his gesture.

Yes.

Then Duncan did a remarkable thing. He spoke to the boy with his hands.

Gordon skipped a few entries, those he could tell from a brief scan recorded Mary's personal grief at the ill-treatment she was receiving from her new husband. Apparently his foppish arrogance continued to win him only enemies, and even in his role as a newlywed, he was not always prompt to the Queen's bedchamber. Robert Gordon raised an eyebrow, thinking how much like an afternoon television drama some of this Queen's diary resembled.

Holyrood Palace
January 29, 1566

Surely the Lord is on our side, not theirs. The Lord, and happily our subjects as well. Not our nobles, but our people, those true Scots who came to our aide and delivered us a sound victory over Moray and the rest in the Chaseabout Raid. We will seal the defeat of these treasonous lords by attainting their properties at the forthcoming session of Parliament in March. Perhaps if they have nothing to return to, they will remain in England to annoy Elizabeth and leave us in peace.

Our spirits are high after this victory, and these recent betrayals have taught us that we need not depend upon our nobility, nay, we should never depend upon these worthless, greedy troublemakers. Instead, we are gathering around us those whose loyalty we can count upon, such as our secretary, the Italian Davie Riccio. We care not that those highborn scoundrels spread rumors against us, saying that poor little Davie and we are lovers. Absurd, as anyone in our court is daily witness to our actions. Riccio is, at best, an excellent opponent at cards.

We have heard yet another rumor, that our own husband Darnley is jealous of Riccio. Another absurdity! He has scarcely taken time away from his hunting and hawking with his craven cronies to bless us with his presence at court. We care not, other than it presents our private discord to the world, for we already have what we want from him, as we carry in our belly now the heir to the throne of England.

TWELVE

༄

It was ridiculous, of course, but Duncan could think of no other way to start communicating with Pauley. Using the sign language that he had learned when training to become part of the RNLI rescue force, he motioned to Pauley that they wanted him to go with them. But the boy responded only with a queer look that revealed his suspicions of these strange hand movements.

"You know sign language?" Taylor's voice reflected her own surprise.

Duncan nodded, but did not take his eyes off the boy. "I'm not proficient," he replied, "but I can usually make myself understood. That is, however, with deaf people who already know the signs. Which obviously isn't the case here."

"He's watching you, though. I think he might be very clever. Keep trying."

Duncan pointed first to himself, then to Taylor, moving his hands to indicate they were together. Then he let his fingers walk in the air. Then he pointed to Pauley, and back to himself and then to Taylor, and then used the walking motion again. But Pauley only stared at him. "Humm," Duncan murmured, standing up. "I don't think he got it."

"Let's see what happens if we start walking and invite him to come," Taylor suggested. "I just hope the little fellow doesn't think we're leaving him." She gave her bundle to Duncan, then turned and smiled and held out both her hands toward Pauley. "Come with us," she said as she motioned to him with her fingers.

Taylor and Duncan both held their breath for a long moment. Pauley looked up at the grown-ups, wrinkled his brow thoughtfully, and then a grin of comprehension slowly crossed his face. With only slight hesitation, he put his hand in Taylor's and together, the three refugees began to climb the hill, leaving the deserted village of Stonehaven behind them.

Neither adult said a word for a long while. Duncan wondered what Taylor was thinking. He knew so little about her. Was she married? Or had she been? Did she have children? She seemed so natural with the waif at her side, he guessed she probably did. But what kind of mother left her children behind to go adventuring around the world like this woman obviously did? Duncan recognized the anger behind this thought and knew it was not directed at Taylor, but rather at the memory of his own wife's disinterest in motherhood. It had been a source of conflict between them on numerous occasions.

And what about the boy? Was it fair to him to take him from this primitive place in time and thrust him into the madcap world of the 1990s? Duncan did not want to become emotionally involved with the child, and yet, Pauley would need someone strong to stand by him and help him make the astounding adjustments that he would face. What if Duncan accepted this responsibility, only to have the boy removed at a later time and placed in a foster home? He wanted no part of that picture. He could not stand the loss of another child, even this little orphan who didn't belong to him.

But Duncan managed to get a grip on his thoughts. He was projecting events that likely would never happen. He didn't even know if they would make it back to the twentieth century, or if they invited him, whether Pauley would choose to go with them. Duncan was against forcing him, but if the opportunity arose for he and Taylor to make an escape through the Ladysgate, how would they communicate to Pauley what he was about to get into? There were just too many questions for which he had no answers. A part of him wished perversely he had never known of Pauley's existence. His presence was making an already difficult situation even tougher.

Reaching the crest of the hill, the threesome paused for breath and looked out over the slate blue sea. A fresh wind blew up short whitecaps close to shore, but beyond, the ocean rolled with peaceful, undulating splendor.

Duncan heard Taylor emit a heavy sigh, and he turned to see a pale and pensive look on her face. "You okay?"

"Yes," she replied, but he could tell she was troubled.

"What are you thinking?"

"About the others who were in the boat when I went overboard. Do you suppose they are around here somewhere, too?"

Duncan considered that a moment. He hadn't seen Fergus's boat or signs of any wreckage either on the twentieth-century side or this side of the Ladysgate. Since the *Intrepid* had been swiftly grounded, he thought it unlikely that Fergus's boat had come through the arch, since it was nowhere in sight. He doubted that her young crew members and Fergus McGehee had met the same fate as he and Taylor, but he had no solid answer to give her. "I didn't see the flotsam of a shipwreck when I was looking for you," he replied. "I imagine they got pretty wet, but remained afloat, even though you fell out. Chances are, they made it back to Stonehaven and are looking for us at this very moment."

"It's a strange thought, isn't it," Taylor remarked, "that they are possibly walking on this same hillside or in Stonehaven, but we can't see them. Sort of like parallel lives. Do you think such a thing is possible?"

Her face expressed her deep concern for the others who had been with her in the boat. Duncan wanted to reach out and smooth away the furrow between her brow, to give her a kiss of reassurance on her cheek. To hold her in his arms and protect her, and feel the magic that her presence engendered in him. "I can't say what I think," he replied instead, more perplexed than he'd ever been. About more things. "Let's go."

After another quarter of a mile or so, Pauley suddenly pulled his hand away from Taylor's and ran on ahead of them. Where other children might have let loose a squeal or a shout of delight, for his face revealed that he was excited about something, Pauley's voice remained silent. But he turned as he ran and motioned eagerly with his arms for them to hurry.

"Wonder what he's up to?" Taylor asked, gathering the full skirt high around her ankles and quickening her pace.

Far in the distance, they saw the crofter's lodge that had given them shelter . . . had it been only yesterday? Oddly, it appeared that the hut was the source of Pauley's strange burst of enthusiasm.

But Duncan hurried, eager to cover the distance to the croft as well, because at the foot of the hill far below it, he hoped he would find the *Intrepid* safely moored to the boulder but afloat once again, ready to facilitate their escape.

But as they approached their destination and he strained to see down the steep incline, he perceived that the boat remained exactly as he'd left it, stranded on the sandy shore.

Later that night, Taylor sat cross-legged on a cushion next to the hearth in the crofter's lodge. She stared into the firelight that flickered in the low grate, trying to get over her disappointment that they had not escaped. When they had reached the top of the hill overlooking the mysterious granite arch, she had expected they would make a beeline for the Ladysgate and 1996. But Duncan had refused to go through the portal without his boat, and Pauley would not go near the place at all.

Disgusted with them both, she had impulsively determined to make the attempt alone, but at the foot of the arch, she'd turned and looked back. Duncan stood tall and handsome, his coppery hair glinting in the sun, his eyes silently urging her not to go. In his arms, Pauley appeared to wipe away a tear. For an instant, they were the family she had once longed for but could never have. She knew it was ridiculous, that it was only the strain of their mishap playing with her emotions. And yet, the sight of the two of them had been enough to keep her in the seventeenth century.

So here they were, waiting on a tide that might never come in, either high enough or in time for them to escape the encroaching army. At least for the moment, she consoled herself, she was warm and dry, and they'd had something to eat. She even had a decent bed to sleep on later, this large cushion borrowed from the *Intrepid*. But from all she'd heard in the village, she believed that time was short. They *had* to get out of here soon. Maybe tomorrow she could convince the stubborn Scot that their lives were more important than any damned boat.

She could thank Pauley for the minimal creature comforts she was enjoying at the moment. After she'd decided to stay, he had led the two of them back up the hill to the deserted crofter's lodge where Taylor had taken her first refuge. The child had proven an amazing resource by showing them a nearby cistern, where they had all drunk thirstily for several minutes. Then he'd gathered straw and sticks and produced a crude flint that lit the fire that now crackled and kept them warm. Pauley could not speak, but from his actions and his familiarity with the hut, they surmised the boy came here frequently. Taylor wondered if Pauley had seen her wash ashore, and if it was he who had lit the fire that had warmed her and dried her clothing that day.

Unable to bear the stench of the dress Greta had furnished her, Taylor had changed back into her jeans and laundered the soiled garment as best she could, hanging it out to dry on a low bush nearby, just in case, God forbid, she would have need of it again.

Duncan had retrieved the cushion she now sat upon, as well as canned goods, dried meat, instant coffee, a tin of crackers, and a couple of cooking utensils from the boat's small galley, and Taylor had created a simple meal which they devoured with relish.

Behind her, Duncan whittled at a piece of wood with the long knife Greta had given Taylor, while Pauley watched in fascination as the stick became a small wooden boat. The boy seemed comfortable now with the two strangers who had mysteriously shown up in his life, and Taylor thought sadly that likely they were the first adults to show him care and kindness in a while, perhaps ever. He had eaten as heartily as Duncan, and Taylor had watched in satisfaction and amusement, paying no attention to his lack of manners. She knew little of the growth patterns of children, but she guessed he was older than she'd first thought. He behaved like he was maybe ten or twelve, although his body was small and underdeveloped.

"I think his mother lived here," she speculated aloud, breaking the silence. "Greta told me that she was the daughter of a crofter who lived out here somewhere."

"What happened to her?" Duncan asked, glancing at Pauley.

"She died in an accident," Taylor replied, glad that the youngster could not hear what she was saying. "Fell off a cliff somewhere near here."

The knife slipped in Duncan's hand, and he swore suddenly under his breath. He dropped his carving, which fell to the floor with a clatter. At the man's sudden motion, Pauley ducked in instinctual self-defense and ran into the protective shadows of a darkened corner, his eyes wide.

"What happened?" Taylor jumped off the cushion and faced Duncan, shocked at the look on his face. It was as if someone had struck him. Blood seeped from a slice in his finger. "You're hurt," she said.

"It's nothing," he growled, putting his finger in his mouth and bending to pick up the unfinished wooden boat. "Just a nick." Duncan motioned to Pauley to come back, and when the boy summoned the courage to return to him, the big man put his arm around him and tousled his grimy hair. "Sorry, lad," he said.

Watching Duncan with the boy, Taylor's curiosity about the Scotsman increased. Until this moment, she'd sized him up as a well-meaning and dutiful man, but also a rather autocratic, dominating male chauvinist with a God complex, just as Fergus had said. And yet before her eyes he was patiently teaching the abused child how to love and trust others. He put the knife in Pauley's hand and showed him how to safely shave the wood, carving with strokes aimed away from his body. He spoke to the boy in low tones, although he knew Pauley could not hear him. The way he treated the boy seemed out of character, at least as she had defined it.

Then a sudden thought jolted her. His behavior with Pauley was unmistakably fatherly. Did Duncan have children of his own?

She had, for some reason, probably because of the way he had kissed her, assumed he was single. And he had not once mentioned wanting to get back to his family. Wouldn't he have been as anxious as she to go back through the Ladysgate this afternoon if he'd had a wife and children worried about him back in twentieth-century Stonehaven?

Ambivalent emotions enveloped Taylor. She'd set rigid rules for herself, limiting her involvement with men. She'd never allowed a serious relationship to be an option, certainly not with a married man. But she could not deny that more than once in the last twenty-four hours, she'd found herself reliving the feel of this man's kiss and the sense of security and protection she'd felt in his arms. And she could not deny his appeal at the moment. His broad shoulders were like the Rock of Gibraltar. His face by the firelight was rugged and handsome. But it was the tender look in his eyes that was her undoing. If he were to make the slightest overture to her at the moment, she was afraid her heart would undermine her resolve to keep her distance.

She attributed this fleeting vulnerability to their enforced intimacy and unusual circumstances and would be glad when morning came and with it, hopefully, their return to the twentieth century where she would also return to her normal, rational self.

Pauley yawned, and Duncan took the knife and toy boat from him. "Time for bed, little fellow," he said aloud, then signed his words with his hands. Pauley emitted a short gurgle, then made the same signs with his own grubby fingers. "Good lad," Duncan said.

"Shouldn't he wash up or something?" Taylor asked, not knowing what to do with any child, much less a dirty ragamuffin such as this.

Duncan turned to her, his expression amused. "Have you

ever been around a small boy before? They're not always that easy to clean up.''

"You sound like you speak from experience. Do you have children?'' The question was out before Taylor knew it, but the moment she spoke, she regretted it, for the amusement vanished from his face instantly. His shoulders drooped, and he stood up. He went to the table, and Taylor jumped when he unexpectedly drove the knife heavily into the rough wood. When he turned to her again, his look was distant and sad.

"I *had* children, once,'' he said, running his hands through his hair and looking away again. "They were killed, a long time ago.''

Working throughout the day, Robert Gordon made steady progress, his French improving quickly with the practice, speeding his progress. By four o'clock in the afternoon, he placed his call to John Doggett. A machine took his message and promised that the antiquarian would return his call as soon as possible. Gordon was becoming more and more convinced the diary must be authentic and could have stopped the eye-straining exercise, except that he was held spellbound by the story as told by the Queen herself.

Holyrood Palace
March 19, 1566

We shudder to recall the terror we have endured the last few days, and we are revolted at the utter treachery of our husband. Had it not been for his greed, and the jewels embedded in the Scottish Rose, we and the heir to the throne of England and Scotland would be dead.

We wish to record this foul deed lest we later be murdered by our husband to protect his complicity in the scheme. We were in our supper room with Erskine and Standen and Davie Riccio when a band of our jealous lords, led by our own traitorous husband, burst in upon us and brutally murdered Riccio right before our eyes. Our own life was imperiled when Ker of Fawdonside pointed a gun at our belly and threatened to kill the heir.

We were held captive in our apartments for over two days under the harshest and most terrifying conditions. Our only ally was the weak will and cowardice of our husband, for it was easy for us to convince him that his fellow conspirators planned to kill us, and that once we were dead, his life would be forfeit too. We believe that to have been the case, for the brutes care only for power, for control of Scotland, and they would never abide Henry Darnley as their king, despight their promises. We bribed Darnley to help us escape, offering him one of the rubies from the Scottish Rose, but the blackguard demanded two. We had no choice but to pry loose two more of the lovely jewels from the chalice, but we were grateful that we had it to rely upon.

Darnley sickens us with his pathetic vacillation. We managed to make our way out of the palace, but had to cross the cemetery and the newly dug grave of our murdered secretary, over which Darnley had the audacity to lament his loss of a good and faithful servant.

It was the courage of our loyal Stewart of Traquair, the captain of the royal guard, and Erskine, and our page Standen that we effected our escape successfully. Once we were clear of Edinburgh en route to the safety of Dunbar Castle, our beloved husband, in his panic, flogged our horse mercilessly, taking no heed as to our advanced condition of impending motherhood. We raced at a frantic pace over several miles, until at last we slowed our horse and cried out for him to have a care for the life of the bairn that we carry. But the vile recreant merely reined in and paced restlessly beside us, stating that he cared only his life, which he rightfully said should not be worth a pisspot when they discovered his treachery. If the bairn died, he said, we could have another. Never have we hated anyone as we do Darnley now. We promised him then, and we swear it now, if the bairn dies, we will personally turn a dagger into his own perfidious heart.

We have defeated the traitorous assassins, largely with

the aid of our loyal Bothwell, who was marked for death by Riccio's murderers, but who managed to escape their butchery by jumping out of the rear windows of the palace, past the lion pit. We met up with him at Dunbar, where he joined forces with Lords Atholl, Fleming and Seton and other men loyal to us. Their ranks swelled from just a trickle to the river of strength that flowed behind us when we returned this day triumphant to Edinburgh. We will hunt to the death those who committed this heinous crime, but unfortunately, we must abide Darnley some time longer, as he must acknowledge the legitimacy of our heir, which will not be born until June. After that time, it will be difficult for us to call him husband.

Robert Gordon was a civil attorney, had never tried a criminal case. But his eyes glowed with the intrigue of this revelation. She would turn a knife into his perfidious heart? It would be difficult for her to call him husband? Even if Mary did not participate in the murder of Darnley at Kirk O' Field, it was clear from these pages that Mary Queen of Scots hated her husband.

He raised his shaggy brows and turned the page.

THIRTEEN

❧

Pain sliced Duncan's heart as surely as the the knife had cut his finger only moments before. He knew when he looked at her again, he would see pity in Taylor's eyes, like the pity that still reflected occasionally in the eyes of his friends and neighbors in Stonehaven, even after all this time. Duncan Fraser hated pity. It was a useless emotion. No amount of pity could restore his sons to him, and its very presence was an odious reminder of his guilt in their deaths.

"I'm sorry," he heard Taylor whisper, but he did not reply. He was glad Pauley had not heard the sound of the knife striking the table, for it would have frightened him. He put his hands on the boy's shoulders to gain his attention, then pointed to the cot and nodded. The boy did not argue, but took the woolen blanket from its peg and lay down beneath it with a smile and a look of deep contentment on his wretchedly filthy face. In a moment, he was asleep.

Duncan closed his own eyes, wanting to erase all the tender feelings that were flooding through him at the moment. It was hard enough fighting his attraction to Taylor Kincaid. He could not allow himself to become attached to this urchin as well. The whole situation where the child was concerned was impossible to begin with. Even if he and Taylor managed to return to their own century, it would not be right to drag Pauley along with them. He belonged in this time, in this place. He tried his best to convince himself of this, but his heart, instead of listening, was arguing back.

This boy had nothing to live for in this time, it said. He was neglected, abused, in poor health, starving. . . . Why should he be left to this fate?

Duncan didn't have the answers to any of these questions when he returned his attention to Taylor. "What did you say Greta told you about him?" he asked heavily, taking a seat on the cushion in front of the fire, leaving the only chair in the place vacant for Taylor.

She cleared her throat. "She told me that he was 'daft' because he was the child of the 'divil.' She accused his mother of being a witch and said that folks here think that she was thrown over the cliff by the faeries because she was the wife of the devil." She sank onto the chair behind Duncan, her legs almost touching his back, and let out a long sigh. "Can you believe such horrible ignorance?"

"There is horrible ignorance in our own time," Duncan pointed out. "It just takes on different forms."

The fire began to burn low, and Duncan reached for a stubby, gnarled piece of driftwood to fuel it again. "He's a remarkable survivor," he said at last, searching for a way to repair the awkwardness that had dropped between them at his vehement response to her questions about his children.

"Who do you suppose his father was?" Taylor asked quietly.

Duncan had an unpleasant suspicion about that . . . incest was not uncommon in the lonely wilds even in the modern age, and it had been more prevalent in ages past. But he didn't share this with Taylor. "Who knows? Obviously no one who gave a damn about him. . . ." He heard the bitterness in his voice.

He felt a soft touch on his shoulder. "This must be very painful for you," Taylor said. "I'm a good listener, in case you need one."

He touched her hand. Her skin felt like silk, cool and soft and smooth. She curled a slender finger around one of his massive ones. He grasped all of her fingers and ran his thumb along the feminine fingertips. He was tempted to tell her about Peter and Jonathan. And Meghan. He'd never talked to anyone about them, or his guilt, or his anger, or the desolation that comprised his life in 1996. He hadn't eased his burden, because he found it difficult to share his private torment, even with close friends. Odd that he would consider doing so now. Taylor was a virtual stranger. Besides, he argued, deciding against taking her up on her offer, she didn't need any more problems. She was having a hard enough time coping as it was.

With her other hand, she combed her fingers through his hair. Her caress was tender, comforting, pleasurable. It had been a long time since he'd felt a woman's touch, and suddenly his entire being was starved for more. Starved, indeed, for a meaningful human relationship. Perhaps that was why he had allowed himself to become so taken with the raggedy child that now slept soundly on the cot.

It was a dangerous, vulnerable place to be.

"My guess is that high tide will be around dawn." He changed the subject, attempting to steer clear of the dangerous emotions that Taylor threatened to unleash. "If there is any way that boat will float, we'll try to get out of here tomorrow." He felt Taylor withdraw her fingers, and he missed their warmth.

"Can't we just push it into the water?" she asked.

"The thing weighs thirty tons."

"Oh."

Duncan could feel the heat of her body where her legs skimmed his back. He turned and looked up into her face. Her skin was radiant in the glow of the firelight. Her golden hair, freshly brushed, hung sleek and straight, curling just slightly beneath her chin. Her lips were pink with twentieth-century lipstick.

Unable to resist, he took both of her hands in his, entwining their fingers. His eyes searched her face for any sign that his overture was unwelcome, but her steadfast gaze held his, her eyes inviting him to swim in their wide, blue depths. He drew her from the chair and moved to make room for her beside him on the cushion. Fleetingly, he wondered if there was a man in her life, or a family, but as she did not resist him, he decided that must not be the case.

He cupped his large hands around her fire-toasted cheeks, feeling beneath his fingers the fine bone structure, the soft skin. He saw her eyes close and her lips raise to meet his. His heart thundered as he bent to taste their sweetness. At first, he kissed her as a boy relishes the first taste of an ice cream cone, gently, savoring the delight to come. But the very softness that met his lips, the smell of her and the taste of her replaced his gentleness in an instant with a surge of desire. He let his kiss shift into one of greater passion, and he embraced her with a desperation born of years of empty days and long, lonely nights. With a hunger for warmth and understanding. With a need for a woman that suddenly welled within him, blinding him to all forethought and consequences.

He felt her return his kiss with equal passion, her response seemingly as hungry and desperate as his own. They fell back against the cushion. He cradled Taylor's head in the crook of his arm and with his lips never leaving hers, ran his hand along her slender arm and over the curve at her waist. She pressed into him, and he heard a small moan escape from her throat.

The sound reached his rational mind somewhere through the fog of his passion and rapped on the door of his sensibility. What on earth was he doing? His body ached for this woman, and yet, to simply satisfy that animal desire in the heat of the moment was to violate the integrity with which he strove to live his life.

He released Taylor with regret but determination. "I . . . I'm sorry," he said, breathing heavily. "I don't know what. . . ."

Taylor gave him an enigmatic look, an odd mixture of frustration and relief which was immediately replaced by a small smile. She touched her finger to his lips, and he felt her trembling. "Shhh," she whispered. "It's okay."

Later, Taylor lay alone on the cushion by the fire, sorry that Duncan had felt obliged to leave her for the night and sleep on the *Intrepid*. She blamed herself for what had transpired between them. She'd sensed his despair and had felt the need to reach out and console him. But she'd responded to him for another reason as well, she admitted. She needed consolation of her own. She'd read somewhere that people caught up in unusual events, like being trapped in earthquake debris or held hostage, often did extraordinary, out-of-character things they could not later explain.

And their situation definitely fell into the category of "unusual events."

Two days ago, she'd never heard of Duncan Fraser. She thought the Ladysgate was just another primitive legend perpetuated by ignorant people and that time travel was the invention of fools and dreamers.

Then, suddenly, all that had changed in a dreadful, inexplicable chain of events that shook the very foundations of her existence. Her fast-held beliefs, or rather disbeliefs, in such supernatural hogwash as time travel had been blown apart.

As had, it would seem, her determination to remain at a safe emotional distance from this man.

She was sorry he'd left, but grateful at the same time, for she didn't trust herself at the moment, even though consciously she knew her feelings for Duncan sprang from their bizarre circumstances and nothing more. She was also glad to have some peace and some time alone. It gave her a chance to try to sort out what had happened to her and to consider what might happen next.

If she allowed herself to accept as reality that she had actually traveled through time, regardless of the horrific situation she seemed to have landed in, she should be making more of the experience than she was, professionally speaking. Instead of panicking and wanting only to find a means of escape, she should be taking better advantage of the opportunity to record this incredible adventure. When she somehow made her way back into her own time, and she would not allow herself to think otherwise, this would make a great movie.

Now that she had clear proof that some myths, such as the legend of the Ladysgate, had their basis in truth, she would have to give up *Legends, Lore, and Lunatics* and put together another show. Or write a screenplay or a book. At the moment, she wasn't certain what path her career would take after this. With a small stab of guilt, she considered the shows she had produced in the past and wondered if any of the legends she had taken so lightly, even poked fun at, had their basis of truth behind them as well?

She sighed. Too late to do anything about it now. Oddly, worrying about the future of her once all-consuming career seemed pointless to Taylor at the moment. First, she had to get back to that future.

Pauley stirred in his sleep, and she glanced at the boy. Now there was something important to think about. And the real dilemma she faced. If this unutterably pathetic child fled with them into the future, what responsibility would she have for his life? Unlike Duncan, she felt they had every right, even an obligation, to take him away from this awful place. He needed medical help. He would receive an education. In their time, he would be treated as a member of the human race instead of some unwanted animal.

Duncan's reluctance to take him along made Taylor believe he wanted no part of helping the boy. Maybe it had to do with the deaths of his own children. It would be understandable if he did not want to get emotionally involved with another child. She wondered what had happened to his kids. And his wife. After his terse explanation that the children had been killed, he'd offered no further information about the circumstances, and she didn't press him, sensing that his emotional wounds were still very raw.

But if Pauley went with them into the twentieth century, and if Duncan declined to be involved with the child, then his welfare would be up to Taylor. Was she ready for that responsibility?

The entire concept of motherhood was foreign to her.

And single motherhood, she'd observed from the lives of some of her friends, could be a nightmare.

But Taylor was not inclined to run out and find a daddy for the boy. Her entire adult life had been carefully planned and executed to ensure her personal freedom. Her reaction to being unable to have a child had made her selfish in that way. She didn't want to be tied down to a family.

Or at least she didn't think so.

She weighed the idea for a moment and decided that the best option would be for her to find a loving family to adopt him. But looking upon the sleeping boy, her heart opened into a larger space than it had ever encompassed, and she knew that she'd passed the point of no return where he was concerned. Whether Duncan agreed with it or not, she would somehow convince Pauley to take her hand when they went through the gateway. She would deal with the consequences on the other side.

But would they make their escape that easily? She recalled with a shudder Greta's tale about the woman who'd tried unsuccessfully to return through the Ladysgate and had been burned as a witch instead.

Or what if the tide rose sufficiently to float the boat, enabling them to go back through the structure, but on the other side it was still the seventeenth century? She wondered what sailors of that time would think of the modern power boat, and decided that it would scare them witless. They might be attacked with cannons, like in the days of old.

But then, she thought, unable to suppress an ironic grin, these *were* the days of old.

Another even more startling idea occurred to her. What if they went through and ended up in yet another time period?

She groaned. The very thought gave her a headache.

The most likely scenario, she decided, would be that they would not make good their escape before the threatened invasion by Cromwellian troops. What then?

They would have no choice but to take refuge in Dunnottar Castle. She grimaced at the thought of having to associate with the likes of Greta Fraser, and she was uncertain just how safe they would be. What if Greta decided to spread the rumor that Taylor was a witch? It was possible, especially if they showed up with Pauley.

Taylor tried to remember what Kenneth had reported about conditions at the castle. The governor, what was his name, Ogilvy, had said that food would be scarce . . . wait a minute!

Ogilvy.

Quickly, she reached for the zippered pouch which was

slung over the back of the chair. Ogilvy. Wasn't that the . . . ?
In the confusion of the events of the last two days, Taylor had
completely forgotten about her meeting with Robert Gordon,
and the photocopied letter in her bag.

By the light of the fire, she dumped the contents onto the
cushion . . . the camera and film canisters, lipstick, hairbrush,
the remaining candy mints, a small notepad, a ballpoint pen,
and yes . . . there it was, the photocopy of the letter.

Her hands trembled slightly in excitement as she unfolded
the paper. She made her way again through the cramped handwriting and strange spelling:

In this the Yeare of Our Lord Sixteen Fifty-two—
To my Lady Keith, Countess Marischal,
    'Tis with great trepidation that I attempt to smuggle
this message to you, for I am at extreme risk of revealing
a secret not ken even to my husband, the Governor of
Dunnottar and servant to your husband, the valiant Earl
Marischal.
    But the winter has been long and harsh, and food
scarce, and our small regiment filled with complainte.
With the coming of springe, we have been warned by
our spies that the heavy English guns will be moved
from Dundee to our very doorstep, and when we must
endure the battering of these cannon alongside our hunger and discontent, God only knows how long we can
sustain. My husband has been loyal in his pledge to the
Earl Marischal to hold the castle and the royal regalia
for the King, but events are moving swiftly, and he must
needs arrange for the removal the croun, suord and sceptre to a safer repository, for they will surely fall to the
English if Cromwell's troops penetrate the castle walls.
    But 'tis with another relic, a secret member of the
Scottish regalia, that I treat with thee in this communication. When Mrs. Drummond, that brave dame, brought
forth in safety and secrecy the Honours of Scotland from
Stirling to Dunnottar, she also carried upon her person
a fourth relic, the ''Scottish Rose'' she called it, and a

diary and a letter written by Mary Queen of Scots, expressing her most fervent wish that the Scottish Rose become part of the royal regalia when strife ended and the warring factions in Scotland were united in peace. Alas, will that day ever come?

The Scottish Rose is a golden chalice shaped like a single rose and once studded round with rubies, although only one now remains. The unfortunate Queen placed the cup in the safekeeping of her loyal serving women just before she was imprisoned in Lochleven Castle. Descendants of these ladies have passed it down through the years, keeping it ever secret but within close proximity to its brother Honours.

Because of Queen Mary's wish that it remain secret until peace and unity are achieved in our poor kingdome, I am not inclined to move the chalice to the new hiding place of the other Honours. Instead, I have taken measures to hide it deep within the belly of the castle rock.

I fear that all in the castle may die for protecting the Honours, but it is our duty to defend these sacred emblems of Scotland. I write you this in the event we are murdered by Cromwell's men, so that a woman of virtue such as yourself will know of the existence of the Scottish Rose, and when the blessings of peace and unity come at last to our land, you, or your own representative, will find it and eventually install it in its rightful place alongside the croun, suord and sceptre.''

Your humble and loyal servant,
Elizabeth Douglas Ogilvy

"In the year of our Lord 1652," Taylor repeated softly. Next year. Could it be? Could this letter supposedly written to her own ancestor not even be penned yet? She went to the window and gazed out into the night, thinking about the story Robert Gordon had told her about Dunnottar Castle and the Honours of Scotland. And the letter's referral to the Scottish Rose. Was that what lay ahead of her if they didn't escape tomorrow?

Her fingers lingered momentarily on the camera. If indeed this was 1651, and Cromwell's army was headed this way, then the Honours of Scotland were likely in the castle. Along with Queen Mary's Scottish Rose, if Mrs. Ogilvy's letter was for real. Taylor could hardly suppress the sudden excitement that thrilled through her. She wished Duncan were there to expand on the story, but decided she must be careful not to ask him about the Scottish Rose, since Mrs. Ogilvy had indicated that its existence was secret.

Dunnottar Castle, although not her choice of lodgings for the upcoming winter, now held at least some redeeming hope for Taylor . . . hope that she would discover the secret member of the regalia . . . Mary's Scottish Rose.

FOURTEEN

⁂

The tide rose to its crest by dawn, never approaching the level needed to launch the *Intrepid*, and since it was just past the time of the full moon, Duncan believed it would be another month before they could expect the tide to reach its maximum again. Nothing short of a hurricane swell would set the heavy craft back in the water.

He leaned against the boat and scratched his head, wondering again how in the devil it had ended up so stranded. But then, how in the devil had all the rest happened either? He pushed away from the hull, which on dry land revealed a crust of barnacles beneath the waterline. Slowly he walked several hundred feet in the direction of the granite rock formation known as the Ladysgate. It, too, was standing on dry land.

He'd read in nautical books that the level of the oceans had risen over the past few centuries. He stared through the gap. It looked innocuous enough. What would happen, he wondered, if he walked through it? Right now. Without thinking about it. Would he just come out the other side? Or would he be met with the wild waves of the ocean that pounded this arch in his own time? If they successfully recrossed time, unless they made the attempt by boat, he decided, they would risk being drowned.

Duncan drew in a deep breath and started the climb up the hill to the crofter's lodge and the sorry duty of informing Taylor that there would be no boat ride today. He just hoped she didn't insist on striking through the portal anyway.

But when he stepped inside the door to the hovel, he sensed

something different in her attitude. Something had changed since yesterday's petulant display of bravery, which he'd recognized as fear in disguise, when she'd mocked him for not wanting to go through the Ladysgate with her on foot. Thank goodness Pauley had made it clear he wanted no part of such a venture.

Today, Taylor stood before him clothed in the tattered dress he knew she hated, and she had made ready to go to the castle. Her back was straight, her eyes bright, eager even. He frowned slightly, curious to know what was going on inside that beautiful head.

"The castle is our only choice," she told him resolutely. "I could see from here the water wasn't going to make it to the boat," she explained her readiness. "But we'd better hurry. Remember, Kenneth warned us we have only a short time before the soldiers arrive." He noticed she was speaking rapidly, and her voice was a little too chipper. What was up with her?

"Are you sure you want to go there? We'll likely be thrown in with Kenneth and Greta again," he warned, testing her resolve, not totally trusting her new attitude toward remaining in this time. Duncan glanced at the boy who played on the cot with his new toy boat. He noted that Taylor had somehow managed to clean his face and hands, although his clothes were still stiff with soil. "It could be dangerous for the boy, you know."

"No, I don't *want* to go there," she snapped. "But like I said, it seems like our only option right now. I'll just have to keep a close watch on Pauley." She hesitated a moment, then added, "Duncan, why is Cromwell so interested in Dunnottar Castle? Isn't this sort of an out-of-the-way place? What is it those soldiers are after?"

He returned his gaze to Taylor, curious about the inexplicable gleam of excitement in her eyes. He wasn't certain he liked it. "Sit down, and I'll tell you what I know of this time and this place," he said at last. "Then you can decide if you want to take part in its history or not.

"When Cromwell gave the Royalists a good thrashing at

Dunbar, on the southern coast," he began, "the Scots fled to Stirling Castle, where he would have a hard time routing them. But instead of trying to take the castle, which was more or less invincible, Cromwell went north and took Perth, cutting off the Scots' supply lines. The King's general decided to take advantage of Cromwell's move to the north and stupidly left the safety of Stirling, marching south again to invade England, where eventually he was defeated.

"When Cromwell at last took Stirling, he was furious to learn that the prize he thought he'd find there had been smuggled out of the castle and taken north, to Dunnottar, as rumor had it, this considered the most secure castle in all of Scotland."

"What prize?"

"The Honours of Scotland," he said, doubting that an American would know what that was. "The crown, sword, and scepter that for centuries had been emblems of the independence of the Scottish people and of their loyalty to the King. Cromwell hated any vestiges of royalty, and he swore he would find and destroy these symbols, just as he did the English crown jewels."

Taylor drew in a sharp breath. "He destroyed the crown jewels of England?"

Duncan laughed. "Don't worry. The Queen's got more. You can see them in the Tower of London. But to finish your history lesson, if we are in the time we think we are, the Honours are hidden in Dunnottar Castle even as we speak."

"And Cromwell's men are on the way to get them." She nodded thoughtfully.

"Aye."

"Do they succeed?"

"Nay."

She was silent a moment, then turned and looked at him with a single but serious question in those enormous blue eyes. "Duncan, you know the history. If we go to the castle, will we survive?

"Maybe."

Edinburgh Castle
1 June 1566

We are heavy with child, and burdened with care lest we die in giving birth. The night is stormy, and we have sent away all except the midwife, who sleeps in the next room. As we lie alone upon this bed which is already draped in blue taffeta and velvet in honor of the birth of a royal child, we wonder what the future holds for him, or her. For any of us.

We have forgiven Darnley for his part in the Riccio affair, but we will never forget it, and we watch our back carefully. That is why we are in the safety of Edinburgh Castle to await the arrival of the bairn instead of our chambers at Holyrood, and why today we have drafted a will ordering that all of our worldly goods should be transferred to the heir, without distinction, and that Darnley shall not inherit anything. We cannot prevent him from inheriting if the child does not survive, but we have charged our two most loyal nobles, Bothwell and Erskine, with protecting the child from Darnley's evil, for we doubt not he is capable of killing his own son to satisfy his greed for power and fortune.

In the same document, we annexed our most precious jewels, including the Great Harry, to the Scottish crown, but we did not include the Scottish Rose, for we doubt that even our most faithful nobles would honor our wishes, such remains the rancor between the religious factions in the land. Instead, we have entrusted the chalice to Mary Seton until the danger has passed. If God grants our survival of the birth of this bairn, the chalice shall once again be returned to its use at our private Mass. If we do not survive, we have given Mary S. a separate letter indicating my wishes for the future of the chalice.

The Queen did survive, Gordon knew, at least that time. But that separate letter . . . did it exist?

Duncan, Taylor, and Pauley, looking for all the world like a typical seventeenth-century family, appeared at the castle gate and asked for admittance. "I am kinsman of Kenneth Fraser," Duncan said, "come with my wife and bairn t' serve his Majesty King Charles in th' defense of this castle."

Taylor bit her lip to keep from laughing out loud. He sounded more like he was trying out for a play than to gain admittance into a castle. But he must have been convincing, for after some debate among the gatekeepers, they were allowed to enter.

Taylor's levity soon changed to an uneasy foreboding, however, as they climbed the stone steps and ventured ever deeper into the mighty fortress. Their choice of refuge meant they would not leave this place until the siege was lost, which according to Duncan would be some time next spring. He had reassured her, however, that their chances of survival here were good, better than if they opted to flee into the wilderness. She wondered again briefly about the fate of her camera crew and the captain. Were they somewhere out there in the wilderness? Would she meet up with them inside the castle if they, like she and Duncan, were taking refuge there? Or had they been drowned in the twentieth century? Guilt riddled her once again. She should never have made that boat trip.

But there was nothing she could do about it now.

She had to think of the future, not the past. Duncan's history lesson had fleshed out Robert Gordon's earlier account of the daring rescue of the Honours of Scotland. She believed now she was about to witness that event in history. Witness it, and record it, hopefully on film, certainly in her notes. If nothing else good came of this mishap, she might come away with the start of the next phase of her career.

What she wouldn't give for a video camera right now, she thought as she progressed up the steep climb. No production studio in Hollywood could create so authentic a setting for the drama that was about to unfold in this ancient stronghold.

Her heart began to beat heavily, however, as they approached the summit. She felt Pauley's little hand tighten around her own and gave it a reassuring squeeze, even though she needed reassuring herself. He looked up at her, his eyes revealing both trust and fear. Would she protect him? She read his silent message clearly. She answered with a nod and a smile, trying to squelch her own misgivings about his safety.

Duncan strode confidently a few feet ahead of them, as they had decided would be appropriate for a man of this day to do, even though the thought of such behavior gagged Taylor's feminist nature. There was much about 1651 she could live without.

They progressed through a succession of heavily defended bulwarks before reaching the flat, grass-covered area upon which the Earl Marischal and his predecessors had created an impressive group of structures that were not visible from below. A two-story building spanned the entire length of the rampart on their right where men milled about, watching them curiously. Directly in front of them was a church, and to their left was another, grander edifice that Taylor decided must be the palace. A man approached them, a guarded look on his face.

"That's Ogilvy," Duncan whispered to Taylor. She smoothed her dress. They had decided before leaving the crofter's lodge that their best protection for Pauley would be to attempt to secure a position for Taylor as a personal servant to the governor's wife, and for himself to volunteer to sail aboard the vessel Duncan knew from history the castle had available to it. Otherwise, they would likely be thrown together with the ragtag, "divil"-fearing crowd that had left them behind in Stonehaven.

"Are ye not th' kinsman of yon Kenneth Fraser?" Ogilvy recognized Duncan, and his greeting, though cautious, was not unfriendly.

"Aye, my honorable Governor," Duncan replied, duly respectful.

"Why did ye not arrive with th' rest from th' village?"

Duncan hesitated. He and Taylor had decided telling the truth was the best strategy for achieving their aims. "Th' others from th' village refused t' bring with them this orphan lad," he said, filling his voice with compassion. "He is a simple lad, who has been rejected by the others because he is deaf. My good wife . . . Janet''—he laid his hand upon her shoulder—''couldna bear t' leave him t' such a fate.''

''What say ye, 'deaf'?''

Duncan touched his ear. ''He canna hear, sir.''

''Oh, *deef* i' tis ye say. Thy tongue, my good man, is foreign t' mine ear. From whence d'ye hail, and what brings ye t' Dunnottar?''

Duncan recited his story about escaping from Perth just ahead of the invasion of Cromwell's army, and Taylor watched with satisfaction as the governor believed every word. Duncan's performance was getting better and better. Then he offered what she hoped the governor could not refuse.

''I am a sailor, sir,'' he said. '' 'Tis my skill upon th' sea that'll serve ye best.''

''How so?''

''Ye told my kinsman that y're expecting a long siege, and that food was scarce. Hath ye not a vessel moored behind th' castle fortifications that could be used t' sail for victuals if provisions become dire?''

Keep it up, Taylor thought, pressing her lips together nervously. You might land the part yet.

Ogilvy studied Duncan openly. '' 'Tis a possibility t' be considered, as there's a small ship anchored in th' cove just behind th' castle. But there's not a qualified captain amongst us. Are ye a sailor of enough skill and experience t' stand as captain of it?''

''Aye, sir. I have stood behind the helm for many years upon th' sea. 'Twould be th' best service I can offer.''

Ogilvy extended his hand. ''Then welcome. What be thy name?''

''Fraser. Duncan Fraser.''

Then Ogilvy turned to Taylor. ''Hath ye skills at serving a lady, madam? My wife's companion, Ann Lindsay, is . . . t' be leaving us soon on a gallant errand, and I fear that Mrs. Ogilvy will sorely miss th' presence of another woman. Ye appear t' have a good demeanor.''

Taylor dropped an awkward curtsey. '' 'Twould be my

honor to serve thy wife,'' she replied humbly, hoping she could adequately disguise her American accent.

"Now, about th' bairn.'' Ogilvy turned his attention to Pauley, but not for long. "He shall have a good scrubbing and other clothing before he enters my household. See t' it . . . uh . . . what be thy name?''

It was an effort, but Taylor managed it. "Janet,'' she said. "My name is Janet Fraser.''

FIFTEEN

✕

Their acceptance into the castle household had been far easier than Duncan had expected, but he suspected that Taylor's beauty had something to do with Ogilvy's decision to assign her to wait upon his wife. It was an excellent outcome to their dilemma, however, and he was gratified, although it meant he would be separated from her most of the time.

And that, illogically, threw a shadow upon the rest of their good fortune.

Duncan had spent an almost sleepless night tossing and turning in one of the small bunks aboard the *Intrepid*, for his mind would not let go of the idea of Taylor Kincaid. She was everywhere in his senses. The unquenched passion they had shared on the pallet by the fire had ignited flames within him that had been dormant so long he'd thought they had died out.

Walking behind her now, she side by side with Ogilvy who was talking to her in an animated manner, as if they were well acquainted, Duncan felt a surprising rush of jealousy, a possessiveness that didn't make sense, but there it was. He watched the long skirt sway at the curve of her hips, admired the way the bodice fitted her slender torso. On Taylor, the homely rag looked almost sexy.

But his attention was jolted from thoughts of Taylor by a rude shout. "So, kinsman, I see ye decided t' follow us after all. But 'tis no good ye've done us bringin' in that cursed child."

Duncan turned to Kenneth Fraser, whose formerly friendly face was distorted and threatening. Glancing over his shoulder,

Duncan was relieved to see that Ogilvy had led Taylor and Pauley into one of the structures of the quadrangle and out of sight of this confrontation. He returned his attention to his "kinsman."

"What do ye care if I take responsibility for th' lad?"

" 'Tis not a lad, but a bairn of th' divil," Kenneth replied, as if Duncan might be part of that same fiendish family. "Know ye not th' dangers of bringin' th' evil among us? 'Tis like t' curse us all when Cromwell's army marches upon us."

Duncan shook his head. "He is no child of th' devil, kinsman. He is a starving, misused lad who brings no curse among us. Why doth ye fear him so?"

But Kenneth's fury was beyond reason. "Ye'll see," he growled. " 'Tis a bad business, just as Greta foretold."

Duncan raised a brow, thinking quickly. "Thy wife has th' power of foreknowledge?"

Kenneth blinked, then glowered. "Of course not. Only witches can foretell the future."

"Then how can thy good dame know whether th' lad is a bad business or not? Unless . . . she can see into th' future. . . ."

His implication was clear enough and quieted the other man abruptly as he became suddenly aware of the stares of his fellow villagers. Kenneth turned on his heel and quit the scene. Duncan knew he'd won this round, but the incident did not bode well for the peace and security of those who would spend the long winter cooped up with one another inside the castle.

Ogilvy returned alone. "What was that commotion about, Fraser?" he asked with a frown.

" 'Tis th' villagers who fear th' lad," he replied.

"Ye must keep him away from th' others," Ogilvy replied. "We can ill afford dissention within our poor ranks." But then he brightened. "With any good luck, King Charles will send troops and supplies soon, and we will be rid of th' damnable English from Dunnottar Castle, even from all of Scotland. 'Twill be a glorious day, that, and one I pray for with my every breath."

Good luck, Duncan thought glumly. "Are my wife and th'

bairn safely housed?'' he asked, feeling a little more comfortable with the archaic language that fell from his lips. He was surprised at how easily it came to him, and he hoped it sounded natural to Ogilvy and the others.

''Aye. My Elizabeth is much satisfied t' have such a ladysmaid as Janet. And as for th' bairn, he was doomed for th' basin even before I took my leave.'' Ogilvy laughed. ''Now, I will show my new captain his quarters.''

The quarters were comprised of a small apartment, one of seven lined in a row that had originally been built to house guests of the Earl Marischal and his Countess. Each had its own fireplace and separate entrance. ''I trust this shall be sufficient for ye and thy wife?'' Ogilvy said, proud of the accommodations, knowing they had been meant for men of far higher rank than Duncan Fraser.

Duncan was familiar with the structure of the quadrangle, although in his time it had been nothing but a ruin. In the twentieth century, these tiny rooms were but bare stone walls with both the second floor and the roof missing, exposing what was left, little more than a pile of rocks, to the further erosion of the elements. But in Ogilvy's time, the space was cozy if not luxurious, certainly preferable to the miserable crofter's hut or Kenneth Fraser's hovel.

''We thank ye, Governor,'' he said, meaning it sincerely. ''This shall serve us well.''

Duncan hadn't expected to be lodged in so fine a manner, and certainly not with Taylor, but then, the governor believed her to be his wife. No matter what age they were in, husbands and wives were expected to share a room.

And a bed. . . .

He just wondered what ''Janet'' would think about the arrangement.

Three months later

Outside, the wind whipped fiercely around the buildings of the quadrangle, and a heavy rain battered against the door.

Inside the small quarters, Taylor and Pauley huddled in front of the fire, and Duncan paced behind them like a tiger in a zoo.

"I'd rather be us than them," Taylor commented, speaking of the battalion of Cromwellian soldiers who were likely getting drenched in their encampment which surrounded Dunnottar Castle on three sides. "At least we're warm and dry," she added with forced optimism.

"And facing winter with no food," Duncan replied with equal pessimism. He was in an ugly mood, and Taylor was afraid to ask why. She put her arm around Pauley, who shivered beneath the blanket that was wrapped around him. She drew him closer. Although the boy had gained a few pounds through the efforts of Taylor and Elizabeth Ogilvy, he was still thin and frail, his body seemingly unable to avoid sickness. He was a walking winter cold, and Taylor was frustrated that there was nothing much she could do to relieve his symptoms. No aspirin, no nose drops. No Kleenex even. The best she could do was keep a supply of clean rags available to him and try to keep him nourished. At the moment, she suspected he was running a slight fever, and she was seriously worried that Greta's prophesy that he would not last the winter would come true.

Duncan's own gloomy forecast did nothing to lift her spirits. They had known from the outset that food might be scarce but had held out hope that the promised supplies would arrive before Cromwell's soldiers. But all their hope hadn't changed history. The provisions never came. The castle gardens had produced some fall vegetables, which stretched their supplies somewhat, but the small contingent inside the walls of Dunnottar Castle faced a winter diet of little more than thin gruel and bread. Taylor remembered November in New York, with the promise of the holidays putting an extra bounce in the step of shoppers, who thought nothing of the abundance that surrounded them. She would never take that for granted, she promised, providing of course, she survived and managed to see New York again.

She was disappointed, too, that after three months in this

virtual prison, she had laid eyes on neither the Honours of
Scotland nor the Scottish Rose. Elizabeth, in fact, had never
once mentioned the treasures, and Taylor was beginning to
believe the letter and the diary were indeed a hoax. Taylor had
been tempted to ask her employer about the rose chalice, but
reminded herself that she was not supposed to know of its
existence.

She had not told Duncan of her intent to document this
journey into the past for future use either, for she sensed he
would deem it too big a risk. He had purposely left any connection to the twentieth century aboard the *Intrepid*, including,
much to Taylor's chagrin, the first aid kit that contained medicines that could have eased Pauley's discomforts this winter.
"It's better that we don't bring things with us that would support their superstitions," he'd told her. Good thing he didn't
know about the camera and film in the zippered pouch, or the
flashlight that she'd filched from the boat when his back was
turned. He also didn't know about the Scottish Rose, nor the
photocopied letter. Maybe she'd tell him about them in time,
when and if she found out the chalice did indeed exist.

"Would you stop pacing?" she demanded of Duncan at
last. His restlessness was getting on her nerves. "What's
wrong with you tonight?"

Duncan went to the door and leaned against it with both
arms, as if to keep the world barricaded safely away. "Sorry,"
he gritted, his jaw tight. "I'm just fed up with the dissension
around here. Governor Ogilvy is the only one with any back-
bone. He's standing firm, as he's been ordered to, refusing to
surrender the castle. But you should have seen our esteemed
Colonel Leighton when the summons to capitulate came today
from General Overton. He was ready to dance to any tune the
English wanted to play. And as second in command, Leighton
carries a lot of weight with the garrison. He's stirred up trouble
already."

"Duncan, these people are frightened and they're hungry.
You can't really blame them. . . ."

"They chose to come here," he barked at her. "They knew

the circumstances in advance. And, by God, they should stick by the commitment they made to Ogilvy.''

''You're forgetting one thing,'' Taylor replied quietly, summoning patience.

''What?''

''You know the outcome of this siege. They don't.''

This gave Duncan pause, and Taylor saw him relax a little, but she could tell he was still cross. ''Is Pauley asleep?'' he asked after a long silence.

Taylor shifted her weight to peer beneath the blanket into the small face. ''Out cold.''

Duncan lifted the slight form and moved him to the double bed the child had shared with Taylor since their makeshift ''family'' had moved in together for the duration of the siege. The big man tucked the blanket carefully around the boy. ''And that's another thing,'' he growled as if looking for additional fuel for his anger. He pulled a second chair to the fire, opposite Taylor, and sat down, leaning toward the warmth, his arms resting on his muscular legs. ''I'm tired of having to hide little Pauley away from those idiots from the village who continue to carry on against him with their bogeyman stories.''

Greta and her gaggle of cronies had launched a verbal campaign against both Pauley and Taylor the day they arrived. Taylor was tired of it, too, but she had ignored it as much as she could and carefully stayed out of their way. ''I know,'' she murmured, heartsick for the little boy. ''But what else can we do? Until we have a chance to go home again. . . .''

Duncan shot her a quick glance, then looked away, and Taylor knew what he was thinking. She continued to be haunted by the same doubt. . . .

What if they couldn't go home again?

A long silence fell between them, filled only by the sound of the storm's unabated fury. At last Duncan spoke. ''Taylor,'' he said, ''there's something else.'' He let out an audible breath. ''Ogilvy has called on me as his ship's captain to take John Keith to France with a letter asking for help from the King.''

Taylor sat very still, stunned by the unexpected news. Her

blood ran cold at the thought of Duncan setting out on an extended journey in that leaky tub Ogilvy called a sailing ship, and she had no desire to be left alone on this godforsaken rock. She knew she could get along without his help, but she'd become accustomed to it, and to the companionship of a fellow traveler from the twentieth century. "Is this part of the script, Duncan?" she almost shrilled at him. "You never said anything about sailing off to France. . . ."

"It's . . . a part of the story I didn't know," Duncan answered.

Taylor wanted to choke him. "Will it accomplish anything?" she asked, doubting it very much. John Keith was the Earl's younger brother who had stayed in the castle as part of its tiny garrison of defense, but from what Taylor had seen of him, he had none of the courage of Governor Ogilvy. She wasn't sure that he wouldn't just run away as soon as his feet hit dry land and the safety of the Continent.

Duncan's knowledge of what had taken place here, read from history books some three hundred and fifty years in the future, until now had assuaged her fear that they would die in this siege. He'd told her that for the most part, things had resolved themselves without a lot of bloodshed. But history, she had learned, did not record the daily incidents that filled her with apprehension. Like the threats against Pauley. And the danger that Duncan now faced. "Did . . . or does . . . the King send help?"

Duncan sat back in the chair and rubbed his eyes. "I don't remember for sure," he said wearily. "I don't think so."

"Then don't go," she implored. Taylor was surprised by the acute sense of loss she felt at the prospect of Duncan's departure. She knew she could cope on her own. But she was well aware that Duncan's presence had kept Kenneth and Greta effectively at bay. With him gone, would she and Pauley be safe? And what of his safety? She sensed the mission he'd been given was fraught with far more danger than any twentieth-century power boat rescue. If he sailed for France, Taylor believed it likely he would never return.

The thought devastated her, more than she could have imagined.

During the three months they had been together, she and Duncan had cohabited like brother and sister while presenting themselves as husband and wife to the outside world. To Pauley, they became like adoptive parents.

But never had they been lovers.

Not once had Duncan approached her again the way he had the night they'd spent in the crofter's lodge. Not once had he attempted to cross that boundary between platonic and passionate. And Taylor had purposefully kept her distance. She could not deny that she was sexually attracted to the robust Scotsman, and she'd caught him with a certain look from time to time that revealed his own desire plainly enough. But they seemed to have an unspoken agreement on the matter.

He had at last told her about the tragic accident that took away his family, and Taylor knew that although she cared deeply about Duncan, he was clearly emotionally unavailable to her, and she had warned herself not to let her feelings go any further. At the moment, however, she wasn't sure she had heeded that warning.

Duncan, who had remained silent for a long while, spoke again at last, his voice interrupting her disturbing thoughts, bringing her back to the issue at hand, his trip to France.

"It's not that simple, Taylor," he said. "If I don't follow Ogilvy's orders, then I'm no better than Leighton. We don't sail until late December. Maybe the governor will change his mind by then, or," he added irritably, "maybe we'll wake up and find out this was all just a bloody nightmare."

Jedburgh, Scotland
October 16, 1566

We are feeling unwell this evening, having returned from a hard ride to Hermitage Castle where we visited Lord Bothwell, our Lieutenant of the Borders. We learned earlier in the week that he had been injured in an ambush, and since we were in this nearby village holding a justice eyre, we thought to make a quick visit to ascertain his condition for ourself. We were assured it was but a half day's ride, and it being dangerously close to the English border, we had no wish to stay overnight there. We left at dawn, stayed but a short while, and returned, arriving back at the bastel-house after sunset. It was a torturous ride over the treacherous, boggy Liddesdale moors, and we are paying for it now. The ache in our side is burning, and we feel feverish all over. Perhaps we should have listened to James, who tried to dissuade us from making the trip. However, even though we have reconciled him into our court again after the Riccio affair, we have little ear for his counsel.

The trip is behind us now, at any rate, and we are gratified that even though Bothwell appeared to have sustained serious wounds, he did not seem as if he were approaching death. He has been a good and loyal servant, both to our mother and ourself, and we pray for his speedy recovery.

It was all unfolding just as history had recorded it. Riccio's murder. The Chaseabout Raid. The birth of King James V. And now enters Bothwell. Robert Gordon picked up his pen again in excited anticipation of what was to come. He could hardly wait to hear what Mary had to say about the events at Kirk O' Field.

SIXTEEN

❧

A bloody nightmare, Duncan thought. That's exactly what this was. In fact, it seemed for the last several years his life had been just one bloody nightmare. Marital problems. The accident. His guilt and loneliness. Then this bizarre journey through time into the harshest conditions he had ever experienced. And added to all that, his struggle to keep a distance between himself and Taylor Kincaid.

The latter was becoming the hardest part of this particular nightmare. Being thrown into her intimate presence every night, he was finding it next to impossible to conquer his growing attraction to her. Taylor was brave and beautiful and compassionate and resourceful, and when he was around her, Duncan was tempted to relent of his determination to avoid another serious relationship. Except for one thing. Taylor had told him she'd never been married and had no children. She was several years younger than he, and he suspected she was a woman whose biological clock was ticking. As attracted to her as he was, Duncan had no interest in starting another family.

Especially in 1651.

So, with the exception of his one slipup the night in the crofter's lodge, he had carefully kept their relationship strictly as that of two survivors thrown together by a monumental accident. He would not allow his sexual desire to cause another accident, a biological one. There was no machine on the wall in the men's room to provide protection, and if he lost control and followed where his instincts wanted to lead him, she could become pregnant.

Aside from his personal preferences concerning another family, Duncan would do nothing that might put Taylor's life in jeopardy, and he believed a pregnancy in this era would be life-threatening. So he slept on a pallet by the fire every night, trying not to think about the beautiful woman who lay in the bed so close to him.

The enforced intimacy between them, necessitated by their masqueraded identities, was wearing on his nerves, however. Maybe it would be just as well for him to take off for France. But the thought of leaving Taylor and Pauley behind to fend for themselves amidst the growing animosity of the villagers went against every grain of his protective instincts.

They were not only endangered by the threat of the peasants, but if something should happen to him, he believed they stood little chance of returning through the Ladysgate, considering the conditions he believed awaited on the other side.

Altogether, his situation was aggravating enough to make him want to chew nails.

As if she were reading his thoughts, Taylor stood and moved behind his chair, and with cool, slender fingers began massaging the back of his neck. He was surprised, for she rarely made a move to touch him.

"I'm sorry," she murmured. "We mustn't get at each other's throats." She moved her fingers to his temples. "We have to stick together. We're all we've got."

Her words struck a chord deep in his heart. *We're all we've got.* She'd said it as if they had very little in this brutally primitive time, but it occurred to him suddenly that he had far more here than in the twentieth-century life he'd left behind. All of a sudden, the emptiness of that life slammed into him.

Here, he had Taylor. And Pauley. A family . . . of sorts.

But he didn't want a family, did he?

Duncan closed his eyes. He didn't know what he wanted. Except he didn't want to think any more. He breathed deeply and allowed Taylor's fingers to ease the painful tension that seemed to pull his scalp down over his ears. She worked at the tightness at the back of his neck, the knotted muscles of his shoulders, along the tops of his arms. He felt his body begin to relax, and a warm glow crept through him. "Where'd you learn to do that?"

"My massage therapist. He's the best in New York."

He.

Duncan stiffened again, hating the idea of a man, even a professional therapist, massaging Taylor's exquisite body.

"Relax." She laughed, seeming to guess his thoughts again. "Ralph's not interested in women. But he sure knows how to get the kinks out."

He tried to laugh with her and ease up once again, but her steady touch against his skin was beginning to speak to a need deeper than muscle relaxation. The warm glow was turning into a fever that spread from where her fingertips met his skin into the depths of his being. He emitted a low groan, trying—sort of—to fight the sensations that she was arousing in him. But the truth of the matter was that he wanted her. Painfully. Her touch, coupled with the pent-up desire he had stored away all the nights he'd observed her as she prepared for bed, added up to a craving he could not, nor any longer wished to, control.

Without thinking, he took Taylor's hands and drew her into his lap. He encircled her with one arm and ran his free hand through her long, luxurious hair, bringing her lips close to his. "Tell me to stop," he said raggedly. He closed his eyes and held her, waiting for her to save him.

But she didn't. Instead, she brought her mouth to his, warm, open, ready.

When their lips met, passion shot through him like lightning, with voltage enough to ignite those fires of physical desire that had begun to smolder again since he'd been with Taylor. Fires that sparked the need for intimacy he had denied for so long.

He buried his fingers in locks of silken gold and crushed her against him in desperation, fearing she might pull away from his embrace. She smelled of the essence of lavender, tasted of the thin red wine that was one of their few remaining luxuries. Consumed by the driving demand for her that rushed through him, and with the permission of her own ardent response, Duncan began to satisfy his deep-seated longing for Taylor. His mouth trailed kisses from her lips, down the white skin of her throat, while his fingers worked awkwardly at releasing the tiny pearls that served as buttons along the front of her dress.

Pauley stirred on the bed, and they both froze, but the boy did not wake up. "Maybe we shouldn't . . . ," Taylor began, but her protest was quickly claimed by Duncan's kiss. Maybe they shouldn't, but they were going to. . . .

He carried Taylor to the bed and laid her down gently, then with equal tenderness, picked up the boy and moved him to the pallet by the fire. "He'll be warmer there anyway," he said, turning back to Taylor, who had finished the job with the pearls. She leaned back against the primitive bedclothes, her breasts freed from the confines of the handsome blue gown, an elegant present from Mrs. Ogilvy that replaced the coarse and begrudging gift of Greta Fraser.

Duncan drew in his breath. She was exquisite, her smile evocative. He wondered if she knew her power of seduction. He suspected she did when next she slipped the dress away from her altogether, and unashamed at her nakedness, invited him with her eyes from where she reclined against the pillow. He tore free of his own clothing and joined her in bed. The firelight flickered over her pale skin, turning it to bronze. With his tongue, he traced the shadows of the flames across her belly and upward to her breasts, where with kisses gentle— then not so gentle—he reheated their passion that had been temporarily interrupted to attend to Pauley.

He wanted to prolong this delicious pleasure, but oh, God, it had been so long. His body was now in control, and he had no rational mind. He felt himself become one with her, and they were together for the first time as the husband and wife they had pretended to be for these many long weeks. She moved against him with the rhythm of a wife who knows the measure of her husband's needs, and her own. His body cried out for release as she tormented him, drawing him ever nearer, ever deeper into her essence.

And then he felt her shudder and give out a low moan of pleasure, a sound that triggered his desperately needed release.

Sometime in the night, the storm abated, but Duncan was aware only of Taylor's body curled next to his and his sense that somehow, with her, his nightmares could come to an end.

Taylor awoke before dawn, but Duncan was already gone. She saw that before leaving, he had added wood to the fire and moved Pauley back into the bed next to her. She closed her eyes and wrapped her arms tightly around her nakedness, re-calling the exquisite pleasure she had found in Duncan's arms. She lay very still, relishing the new feelings that tingled throughout her. Her body was aglow, but not just from sexual fulfillment, she realized. There was something deeper about her feelings for Duncan.

They were the feelings she had tried all her life to avoid having toward a man. Feelings of caring. And commitment. Of wanting a future with him. She knew better, fought the idea, but she couldn't ignore that Duncan's caresses last night had presented her with a summons to life, a mandate unlike anything she had ever experienced, a wake-up call to discover a more profound meaning of human existence.

Sliding out of bed, she donned her sleeping gown to ward off the chill morning air, then snuggled back under the covers. She was sorry Duncan hadn't awakened her before leaving to start his day, but in a way, she was glad, too. She treasured the intimacy they had shared in the night, but she needed some time to sort out her feelings.

Disturbed by her earlier self-talk that included words like "caring" and "commitment," she warned herself against reading more into their interlude than was there. It could have been but a moment of passion, a much-needed release for them both, and ironically, she was glad she didn't have to worry about getting pregnant.

Taylor was unsure whether she wanted something more be-tween them than an occasional moment of passion, even if he returned safely from his pointless errand to France. It went against her carefully controlled life plan. She'd always been strong, committed to her career, certain that a loving relationship could only lead to eventual disappointment, since the family she would want from such intimacy could never be. The tender emotions that surrounded her at the moment left her feeling vulnerable, afraid even.

And yet, a new awareness sang in her blood this morning. She felt more alive, more vital than at any time she could remember, and in her heart she knew that Duncan Fraser was a man who could make her reevaluate her priorities.

And because of that, he was a very dangerous man.

She wished she knew more about him. That he was a passionate lover there was no doubt. And Taylor knew from the way he treated Pauley, and the deep pain on his face when he'd told her about his own children's deaths, that Duncan was a caring father. But how was he at being a partner?

A life mate?

A . . . husband?

The ''h'' word scared her, and Taylor abruptly forced herself to rise and face the day, shaking off these and other troublesome thoughts. Her hair, she noted as she brushed it vigorously, had grown long and uneven. Fit for little other than a braid, Taylor managed with some difficulty to twist it into control, tying the end with a bit of ribbon given her by Mrs. Ogilvy. Her hairdresser on Forty-third Street would be appalled. She wondered what Duncan thought of the way she looked, so crudely groomed in this harsh and rustic environment.

She slipped into the blue wool gown, the cut of which revealed the white of her throat, the promise of her bosom. It was far from lovely, but elegant in comparison to the rank brown rag given her by Greta. The low neckline was edged with Belgian lace, which also graced the hem of the full skirt. Beneath it, she wore underwear that was fashionable for ladies of the day, but Taylor doubted that it would sell very well at Victoria's Secret.

She wished she could wash her clothing more often, but American-style hygiene was not the order of the day at Dunnottar Castle in 1651. In this time, she found reason to be grateful for the one advantage of her birth defect, that she didn't have to suffer the monthly "flux," as Mrs. Ogilvy called it. But this thought disturbingly led right back to her feelings toward Duncan.

He had lost two sons. If he remarried, wouldn't he want more children? She thought it likely.

Despair and anger raged through her as she sank into one of the two small chairs in the room. Damn it, she had dealt with this disappointment twenty years ago. She'd thought she'd put it behind her once and for all. And now here it was again, reminding her why she'd vowed not to get involved with men. Taylor sighed. It likely didn't matter anyway. Theirs was a fairy-tale relationship at best, and when, if, they returned to their own time, nothing would be the same.

Still, she reminded herself to dig the trenches a little deeper around her heart.

The morning was freshly washed from the midnight storm when she and Pauley emerged from their quarters. Cool, brisk air stung her cheeks as they hurried across the flat green yard of the quadrangle toward the suite of rooms formerly used by the Earl and Countess but presently occupied by the Ogilvies. Unfortunately, unless she wanted to enter the Countess' chambers through the secret passageway from the old church, Taylor had to pass the well and the stairs that led below to where Greta and many of the village women from Stonehaven were assigned as cooks and other menial servants. An encounter was usually unavoidable. She pulled Pauley beneath the protection of her arm and straightened her back when she saw Greta approach. She was certain the woman waited for her purposely every morning just to taunt her with her evil superstitions.

"I prayed in th' storm last night that th' divil would take his child back," the woman said, her words filled with both righteousness and rancor.

"We thank ye for thy kindness, madam," Janet Fraser replied with sarcasm that was lost on this rude, hate-filled woman. Taylor quickened her step, and together the woman and child hastened up the stone stairway. Behind her, she heard Greta hiss.

Get us out of here, Taylor prayed silently to whatever gods happened to be in charge of this isolated mountaintop of superstition and grief. Oddly, however, she found a small place in her heart to forgive, even pity, the woman whose harsh life and times transfigured her from a human being to something almost animal.

"Oh, there ye be, m'dear." Mrs. Ogilvy's voice was uncommonly bright this morning.

"Janet" dipped a curtsey to her and ushered Pauley ahead of her into the room. "Aye, madam," she replied in the manner she'd learned was proper of her station, "Sorry that I'm a bit late. The . . . uh . . . storm kept me up last night, and I overslept."

"I thought ye were goin' t' tell me 'twas thy handsome husband kept ye up," the other woman laughed, and Taylor's face turned bright pink. "He's a manly one, that," Elizabeth continued. "He should be able t' give ye many healthy bairns."

Her unexpected comment knocked Taylor completely off center. The blush drained from her cheeks, taking her normal color along with it. Bairns. He might be able to give them, but she would never be able to have them, she thought caustically, irritated to be facing the subject again so soon. Maybe it was just as well he was leaving for France. Their pretend marriage was resurrecting some painful old sorrows that were best left buried.

Mrs. Ogilvy gave her a worried look. "Are ye all right, my dear? Ye look sorely pale of a sudden."

Taylor shrugged and nodded with a forced smile. "Yes. I am fine, madam."

Mrs. Ogilvy came to her and touched her face, raising her chin and forcing Taylor to look into her eyes. "Ye wouldn't be with child now, would ye?"

Get off it! she wanted to scream at this woman suddenly. But her momentary temper turned immediately to shame. Mrs. Ogilvy had no way of knowing that Taylor could never bear children, and Taylor shouldn't get angry at the woman's genuine concern. "No, madam," she answered as calmly as possible. "That good fortune has not yet been visited upon me."

Mrs. Ogilvy sighed and turned to look out the east window at the early morning sun sparkling on the waters. "Perhaps 'tis just as well, Janet, for who knows what fate shall befall us here?"

A knock sounded at the door, and Taylor was glad for the interruption. Governor Ogilvy poked his head in. "Are ye available, ladies, t' accept th' company of Mr. Grainger, th' minister from yon Kinneff Kirk, who hath come t' call?"

Elizabeth and Janet exchanged startled glances. "How did he get in?" Mrs. Ogilvy voiced Taylor's question. "I thought we were under siege."

Her husband laughed. "Oh, but we are, my good wife. It is certain that Mr. Grainger brings more than th' holy word with him. If Colonel Dutton has let him pass, 'tis likely with still another demand for capitulation. However," he added cheerfully, "Mr. Grainger is well known t' be a loyal Scotsman through and through. Come. Join us in the receiving room. Let us hear what news he brings."

Taylor signed to Pauley to remain in the room, and she left him sitting on a blanket on the floor, playing at a game much like marbles. She followed Mrs. Ogilvy through the Earl Marischal's richly appointed chamber with its unique and surprisingly accurate timepiece built into the stone mantle. It was not yet eight o'clock. The minister must rise early to tend to his scattered flock, Taylor thought wryly.

But the minister was not alone in the sitting room, she discovered to her consternation. Behind him, Duncan Fraser rested an arm on the stone window sill and stared out to sea. If the strength of his profile defined the strength of his character, Taylor thought in the fraction of a second in which she beheld him, he was a noble man indeed. His face was set, as if chiseled from stone, his broad brows thoughtful, his jaw firm. He stared intently, as if looking at the infinite, and she wondered what he was thinking. When he turned to the others, his brilliant blue eyes were fierce just before he cloaked his thoughts behind a collected demeanor and brought his attention to the moment.

"Madam Ogilvy," he said with a bow. Then his gaze met Taylor's, and she felt her color rising again. He offered her an equally polite bow, but his greeting was distant, a formality and nothing more. Taylor's earlier unsettling thoughts concerning a possible future with Duncan, based on last night's intimacy, fled beneath the cool address, and suddenly she flushed again, but this time with anger. What had she done to deserve this?

The minister stood and greeted the women and the governor effusively. "It is good t' see ye well, madam," he gushed, kissing Mrs. Ogilvy's hand as if she were the Queen. "We have been so worried t' know thy state here at Dunnottar."

Governor Ogilvy motioned for everyone to be seated, and all found a chair except Duncan, who chose to remain behind the chair of the minister. Taylor wondered if he were serving as a guard at the moment. "Our state is a sorry one indeed," the governor said. "I have little refreshment t' offer ye, other than some bitter wine and th' clear water of our well."

"Th' only refreshment I need," said Mr. Grainger, "is t' know that ye and thy lady, and those in th' castle, are well and sound."

Taylor's mind flitted to the boy left playing on the floor of the Countess's chamber. He was neither well nor sound. Nor safe from the others should he wander away from her protection.

"Hath ye a word for us from our besiegers, kind Reverend?" Ogilvy got right to the point, to the slight embarrassment of the preacher.

"They would not let me pass otherwise," he replied with an apologetic smile. "Aye, here 'tis." He took a folded scrap of parchment from his coat pocket and handed it to Ogilvy, who read it, an amused look creeping over his countenance as he finished. "Th' bloody English will never understand th' mind of a Scotsman," he said with forced good humor. "Do they not know that th' Honours are t' us symbols of Scotland itself? That t' relinquish them t' be destroyed by the ilk of

Oliver Cromwell would be t' send a message t' every true Scot that th' end is come?''

Taylor's head jerked up. The Honours?

"So 'tis true then," the minister replied. "Th' Honours are here. We had heard rumors."

"Would ye like t' view them, Mr. Grainger? Then perhaps ye, and all in this room, in fact, will have more cheer for th' challenge we have accepted."

Taylor's gaze locked with Duncan's and she forgot her earlier pique. His face was impassive, but she was unable to suppress a grin of excitement. They were to see the Honours at last! She had begun to believe that the royal regalia of Scotland was only another myth, and on her bad days, she'd silently accused Ogilvy of being a deranged megalomaniac in defending what appeared more and more to be a losing cause. But then she'd remembered the history lesson.

And now they were about to see the Honours. She hoped they were worth the wait, and the struggle, and the starvation and everything else the people in Dunnottar Castle had suffered on their behalf. . . .

SEVENTEEN

❧

The small party followed Governor Ogilvy's stout but muscular form down the stairs, past the well and across the quadrangle where the refugees from Stonehaven and other neighboring villages milled about and watched them with open curiosity. Duncan reached for Taylor's hand in a show, she supposed, of husbandly protection, performed for the benefit of his "kinsman." Even though she was still confused by his earlier cold greeting, she dared not withdraw her hand in front of these people.

They approached the ancient tower, and Ogilvy ordered the guard to stand aside and let them pass. They filed through a narrow, mildew-blackened passageway and up a circular stair, coming to a halt in a small exterior room with gunports overlooking the south side. From his pocket the governor withdrew a large key with which he unlocked the door to a dark little room that looked to be no more than a closet. He stepped inside for a moment, then returned, carrying in one hand a slim golden scepter with an elaborate crystal and gold finial. In the other, he held a magnificent sword of impressive proportions, sheathed in an intricately embellished scabbard. Taylor was not the only one to draw in an audible breath.

"Th' scepter," Ogilvy said solemnly, holding the emblem high, "has represented Scottish royalty for more than a hundred and fifty years." He handed it to Mr. Grainger, whose eyes widened in veneration.

Then Ogilvy drew the long blade of the sword away from its protective holder. "Th' sword of state and its scabbard were gifts t' King James by the 'warrior pope,' Julius II.'' He ran his fingertips along the wide steel blade, obviously in awe of the responsibility that had been given him for its safekeeping. He handed the sword to Duncan, and Taylor read his excitement in spite of his stoic expression.

Finally, Ogilvy went back into the cubicle and returned with the *piéce de rèsistance*, the royal crown of Scotland.

"Oh, dear," murmured his wife. "It's so . . . splendid!"

Splendid was an enormous understatement. The crown of Scotland gleamed even in the dim light, as if giving off an aura of its own. The circlet was bejeweled with rubies and pearls and other precious stones, set among golden *fleurs de lis* and *crosses fleury* and enameled circles that ringed the headpiece. Four arches of gold rose from the circlet to the apex, each richly ornamented with gold and red enamelled oak leaves. At the top, an orb of blue enamel studded with golden stars supported a cross that was decorated with eight huge pearls and bore an exquisite purple stone, probably an amethyst, Taylor guessed. The bonnet of the crown was of purple velvet, slightly faded but incredibly regal nonetheless.

" 'Tis is not th' original crown of Robert the Bruce," Ogilvy continued, almost apologetically that the original circlet of gold had been lost over the ages. " 'Tis an adaptation of James V, who thought his father's crown unsuitable for his royal head."

The Honours of Scotland did not disappoint Taylor. In fact, they far exceeded her hopes and expectations, both in their glory and in the reverence in which the people of Scotland obviously held them. She glanced at the tableau before her eyes, the small group gazing spellbound upon the regalia, and wished like hell she could capture this Kodak moment on film.

Later, in the privacy of her quarters, Taylor removed the photocopied letter from its secret sanctuary in her zippered pouch and read it again. She'd seen the Honours. She knew that part of the letter was real. And now she was convinced that somewhere, very nearby, lay another, even more astonishing treasure.

The Scottish Rose.

Craigmillar
November 1566

We are still quite weak from our near-fatal illness in Jedburgh, and our troubles with Darnley continue to plague us, so much so that often we simply wish to be dead. We have acquiesed to the wishes of Moray, Argyll, Bothwell, and Maitland and retreated with them to the privacy of this gloomy pile of rocks where tonight we have discussed our mutual dislike, or rather hatred, of the king, and what, if any, resolution can be had. Maitland approached us saying that some means could be found for us to divorce Darnley, but as always, his offer came with a steep price . . . that we pardon Morton and Ruthven and the other vile conspirators who killed Riccio. So desperate are we to be rid of Darnley, we agreed to his demands. What difference will it make? We have already allowed our own disloyal brother to return. We want with all our heart to be forever free of Darnley, a man we once thought we loved but whom now we hate with a passion. But we must be certain that such a divorce will not prejudice our son's claim to the throne. Maitland suggested there might be other means to get rid of Darnley, but he has assured us that whatever ensues, nothing will cause dishonour upon us, as all will first be approved by Parliament. Tonight we may sleep soundly for the first time since we met Darnley, thinking that happily he will soon be out of our life forever.

Oh, my naïve Queen, Robert Gordon thought. It was a fault she never overcame, trusting in those around her. Quickly, he thumbed through the history book to the reference to the secret meeting between the Queen and her nobles at Craigmillar. Yes, he thought it was so—Bothwell had been there as well. But she made no mention of him in her diary. Odd, thought Gordon, since her reputation was about to be destroyed by accusations that Bothwell was her lover and together they had plotted the death of Darnley. Of course, those charges could have been false.

Or the diary could be a fake.

Sleeting rain slanted against the door to their quarters, and Duncan saw Taylor shiver where she stood by the fireplace. Her hair, recently brushed, fell softly across her shoulders, its pale blonde burnished by the firelight and gleaming with an almost angelic halo from the backlighting. She wore a white nightgown, perfectly modest, and yet the silhouette of her body beneath the puritanical gown aroused him more than if she'd been wearing sexy lingerie.

He looked away, feeling again the apprehension that had gnawed at him since he had made love to her just over a month ago.

What if Taylor was pregnant?

In the heat of his passion, he had given protection only a passing consideration, but in cool afterthought, he had agonized over losing his control. He had been short with Taylor the morning after, a response she neither understood nor deserved, stemming from his own conflicted emotions. But if he'd made her pregnant, it would mean she must endure that condition alongside the cold and hunger he knew lay ahead for those inside Dunnottar Castle, an environment that could threaten her life and that of the baby. And he wouldn't be here to help.

It had been one hell of an irresponsible act on his part.

In less than two days, he was due to set sail for France with John Keith and an emergency plea for help that he'd remembered would not be answered until too late. If he thought the journey would be successful, Duncan would have been anxious to get under way, but his foreknowledge that it was an exercise in futility made it difficult for him to muster any enthusiasm for the trip. Especially if Taylor's condition was what he suspected it might be.

Duncan had been married for fifteen years, and he knew a woman's cycle. Although since he and Taylor had made love he had tried to distance himself as much as possible from her by volunteering for the night watch, it was unavoidable that they should spend some time together in the intimate chamber that they shared. And he'd seen no sign that his suspicions were unfounded.

He must know, he decided, tormented, and he must know tonight. If she was indeed pregnant, maybe he should reconsider going on the perilous ocean voyage. He was torn between duty to the governor and duty to Taylor. In his heart, he knew he belonged here, by her side, to protect her from the villagers and do what he could to provide food for her and the rest who were cooped up here under desperate and hopeless conditions. But his honor called him to serve as he'd promised Oglivy.

But wouldn't that duty be better served by finding more food for the beseiged Scots? he silently argued the point. He'd already made several forays by boat into the towns and villages beyond the circle of Cromwell's encampment and had managed to bring in enough rations to sustain the raggedy troupe and their families, but only minimally. They needed not just food, but medicine and blankets and clothing, all those things so readily available in the twentieth century, so missing from this one, he thought sadly. With him away, there was no boat, no captain, to scavenge for the meager supplies that *were* available.

Taylor took a seat and invited Pauley into her lap with a smile. They had learned some rudimentary sign language, and the pair seemed to have no difficulty understanding one another. She had been trying to teach him that speech existed, as his own voice continued to emit only spontaneous grunts when something surprised him. Duncan watched her place his little hand on her throat, and then she spoke aloud. "I love Pauley," she said, then signed the words.

Could the child understand the concept of love? Duncan wondered, knowing the boy had likely never been loved by anyone before. But his doubts were answered by the child's response to Taylor. Pauley made a valiant effort to speak, although it resulted in not much more than a gurgle. But he signed "I love you" to her, then planted a wet kiss on her cheek.

Duncan felt a hard knot at the back of his throat. Here before his eyes was all that he had ever asked of life. A woman who cared, a child he could love.

But if the three of them returned to 1996, would it be the same? Or would Taylor take off on her television adventures, leaving him to find a proper home for Pauley? Or . . . would she take Pauley with her?

The thought of either of them leaving his life again filled Duncan with the same desolation as when his family had been wrenched from him by the accident, and he realized with a start that somewhere along the way of this misadventure, he had done the forbidden.

He had allowed himself to fall in love with Taylor.

And to love the frail youngster who had been deposited into his life by this strange twist of fate.

And, now, was there to be another child in the picture?

Duncan wasn't sure he wanted any part of it—loving a woman, having a family once again. He'd been there before, and the pain of that loss was carved on his heart forever. He stood at a crossroads. He did not have to take on any of this. He could get on the ship, head for France, and never look back. If he didn't ask, he would never need to know if Taylor carried his child. He could simply disappear over the horizon, into the mists of time.

Even as he entertained these thoughts, however, he conceded their folly, for to run away was against everything Duncan Fraser stood for.

And the family in front of him, as make-believe as it was, represented everything he'd ever wanted. Watching Taylor rock Pauley gently, he knew that if she were pregnant, the child would be a joyous addition to his life, despite the difficulties it would present. He had to know! He tried to figure how best to approach the subject.

"Care for some wine?" he asked at last, breaking the protracted silence.

"The stuff tastes like vinegar," she replied, making a face, "but it's better than nothing, I suppose. Sure."

He filled a metal goblet and handed it to her, but she made

a face and set it aside after only one sip. "I'd call that 'self-rationing' wine," she laughed. Then she looked up at him, a question in her eyes, as if she knew he wanted something of her. "What is it, Duncan?" The woman seemed to have an uncanny ability to read his thoughts. "Come, talk to me." She motioned to the other chair.

"You know I'm supposed to sail tomorrow at midnight," he began, sitting next to her. She remained silent, a listener. He continued. "Before I go . . . there's . . . something I need to know."

Taylor tilted her head slightly. "What's that?"

Duncan slugged awkwardly through his embarrassment. "It's rather, uh, personal," he said, finding this more difficult than he had thought. She raised a brow but nodded for him to go on. He hesistated a moment, then continued. "You know, last month, when we . . . made love?"

Taylor's wide, blue eyes seemed to melt, their expression changing from curious to tender. "How could I forget?" she replied softly, and in those eyes he read a clear invitation for him to come into her arms again. Since she had not spoken to him of her feelings about that incident, nor had she touched him again, not even for a neck massage, her unmistakable welcome came as a complete and disconcerting surprise. And it made things damnably more difficult.

He took both of her hands in his and felt the smoothness of her skin against his own calloused fingers. Caught between the two adults, Pauley grinned with delight at the perceived attention he was getting. But Duncan's concentration was totally upon Taylor. He cleared his throat. "What I need to know is . . . well, is there any chance that you might be . . . that you are . . . uh, pregnant?"

Her smile vanished, and she stared at him. "Pregnant? Why . . . why do you want to know if I'm pregnant?"

"Because, if you are, I don't think I should leave."

High color stained her cheeks. "What the hell difference would that make?" She dropped his hands and stood up abruptly, setting Pauley on his feet.

"I . . . well, it would be extra difficult on you if. . . ."

"It's difficult on me now, and I'm surviving," she pointed out. "If you're thinking of changing your mind, do it because it's more important for you to be here than off on this wild goose chase. Not because you've got a guilty conscience about possibly having fathered a child."

"Guilty conscience!" Duncan was bewildered by her inexplicable indignation. He, too, stood up, almost knocking his chair over. A curt reply sprang to his lips, but the truth cut it short.

He *did* have a guilty conscience.

Guilty for loving her. Guilty for leaving her. Guilty of not wanting to go. Guilty of looking to her for an excuse. And yes, guilty of possibly having fathered a child. If Taylor was pregnant, he didn't blame her for being furious with him.

He turned away and ran his hands through his hair, his emotions a confused mess. He didn't know what to say next. At last, he faced her again.

"Look, Taylor, I only want to do my duty by you . . . ," he started, even though the words sounded lame in his ears, but she saved him the effort of continuing.

"Your duty! I thought your *duty* was to take John Keith to France to get the King to rescue us from this godawful situation." The way she emphasized the word "duty" left no doubt of her scorn of the ill-fated trip.

"You are more important than John Keith, or King Charles, or any of the rest of it," he almost shouted. "Don't you know that by now? If you're going to have a baby, I should be here to provide food and safety for you."

"And if I'm not, you're off to France, and I can fend for myself?" Her voice was icy.

He saw her point immediately and understood why she was so upset. Why was he only willing to change his plans if she was carrying his child? She needed his support regardless of her condition. Damnation, he hadn't meant to imply that she was more important to him if she was pregnant than if she wasn't! He wished he'd never started this conversation. He wished he'd never agreed to make the voyage.

But he'd signed on as Ogilvy's captain, and suddenly he

was chagrined that he had let emotion get in the way of that duty. He had never in his life evaded his responsibilities. "Yes," he said with a heavy sigh. "I am going to France."

"Well, I suppose a man's gotta do what a man's gotta do," she snapped with a toss of her blonde tresses.

"Look, you know this wasn't my idea," he snarled, losing patience. "Don't make it any harder than it already is."

"You're the one who is making it harder on all of us, going off on a totally impossible mission. . . ."

Their quarrel suddenly was interrupted by the sound of crying. Duncan saw Pauley crouched in the corner by the door and realized to his horror that even though he could not hear their words, had been watching them, and the child clearly understood a fight. Before either of them could stop him, he lifted the latch and dashed out the door into the icy, wet night.

EIGHTEEN

❦

"How is he?" At midmorning, Elizabeth Ogilvy stepped through the doorway and entered the room where Taylor kept a silent, and solo, watch over the small, unconscious figure on the bed.

The boy had managed to evade their search for over an hour, long enough to suffer from severe exposure to the icy wind and rain. When Duncan had at last found Pauley and brought his almost lifeless body back to their quarters, they had worked together feverishly to dry him and warm his skin, although the child remained unconscious. Neither of them had spoken a word.

When they'd done all they could, Duncan had left abruptly, and Taylor had taken it as his way of laying unspoken blame on her for the child's condition. She had, after all, started the fight by senselessly overreacting to his question.

Before taking his leave, Duncan had removed her belongings from the old chest that held their meager possessions, and Taylor guessed he was taking the trunk for his sea voyage. Since she had not seen him again, she assumed he was gone for good. Grief knifed through her heart.

She wished to God she could rewind that horrible scene and play it again differently. His question about her being pregnant had caught her totally off guard, for she had thought he was asking to make love to her again before he left. It was an offer she was not going to turn down.

Instead, he had raised the issue that she had begun to dwell upon more and more as her feelings for him grew—his possible desire for more children and her inability to bear them. If he felt strongly enough about her being pregnant to forgo his sworn duty to Governor Ogilvy, didn't that say volumes about his desire for more children?

Damn.

Taylor knew he meant well in offering to stay behind if she was pregnant, but her heretofore carefully concealed, even denied, fury at him for going at all and leaving them alone in this godforsaken place had erupted, taking over her senses. She'd nursed her anger throughout the night, holding on to it to keep her alert in case Pauley should need her.

But as night rounded into morning and she'd begun to think more rationally, she realized she was angry with herself, not Duncan. She was angry at her own weaknesses. At being afraid to stay behind alone. At allowing herself to love Duncan, as she knew now that she did. At wishing, after all these years, that she *could* get pregnant.

She hoped that Duncan hadn't boarded his ship yet and would return so she could explain why she'd lost her temper. He needed to know. If he wanted children, he'd have to find another mother for them. She could give him a lot of things . . . love, companionship, an interesting life partner, money even.

But not children.

It hurt, and it might well mean the end of their budding relationship, but then, she thought bitterly, better to nip it now with the frost of truth than let it go on under false pretenses.

Marriage, and motherhood, both still carried a lot of ambivalence for Taylor. For all its reputed blessings, she reflected, looking down at Pauley on the bed, being a mother was a lot harder than she'd thought. Caring for a child meant more than making peanut butter sandwiches and reading bedtime stories. Especially caring for this particular child.

"He's not doing very well, I'm afraid, madam," Taylor answered Mrs. Ogilvy, her heart like a rock of ice.

Elizabeth handed her a covered dish, and Taylor accepted its welcome warmth between her freezing fingers. " 'Tis a thin broth,'' the governor's wife said, "made of th' heart of th' last sheep in th' castle. Perhaps when he awakes, he can partake of it, and it will give him strength.''

"Ye are most kind, madam.'' Taylor made herself smile, even though her throat was constricted painfully and her eyes stung with tears she could not shed. "I'm sure it will do him much good.''

Elizabeth started toward the door, then paused and turned to Taylor. "Janet, when thy husband embarks for France, ye shall be alone. Would ye consider moving with th' bairn into th' room adjoining my quarters? 'Tis warm there, and we can see t' th' lad together.'' She hesitated. "It would give me great comfort,'' she added, "for without thy husband t' protect ye, I trust not those who wish ill upon both ye and th' bairn.''

Taylor nodded. "I accept with deep gratitude, madam,'' she said. She meant it sincerely, for she, too, suspected that Greta and Company would take Duncan's departure as a sign for increased harassment. "I share thy fears.''

"Then have Captain Fraser bear th' bairn t' my chamber before nightfall. He will be safe there, and I will look after him myself, in case ye would like t' . . . take leave of one another in private.''

Elizabeth Ogilvy kissed Taylor lightly on the cheek and was out the door before Taylor could admit that no such leavetaking was in store. Alone in the room, Taylor placed her hands on the knot in her stomach and started to allow her tears their much-needed release when almost immediately, Duncan banged through the unsecured portal, opening it before him with the old chest.

"Close the door behind me and throw the latch,'' he said urgently. Taylor's joy that he had returned spilled out in a spontaneous cry. She asked no questions, just hurried to lock the door, then turned to see him place the large wooden box on the floor in front of the fireplace. "We haven't much time,'' he said. "There are some things here I'll need to teach you to use.''

Taylor blinked in surprise when he opened the lid and

brought out an orange plastic container that looked very much like a fishing tackle box.

"What in the world?"

"Shhh," he said, looking around as if worried that someone might see them, although only the two of them, and the boy, remained in the tiny quarters. He opened the box, and Taylor was dumbfounded to see that it was a well-equipped medical kit.

"Where did you get that?"

"Last night, after I brought Pauley back, I went to the *Intrepid*, and. . . ."

"You did what? How . . . ?"

"Would you shut up?" Duncan looked at her in exasperation. "I went by sea," he said, as if it made all the sense in the world for him to go out in a boat with the wind whipping wildly and rain pouring in sheets of sleet and ice. "I took the tender and rowed there in the cover of darkness."

"But . . . that's a long way. What if Cromwell's patrol . . . ?"

Duncan gave her a quick grin. "Do you really think those fellows, who have no more wish to be here than we, would actually put to sea in a storm like that?"

"No," she replied with a quavering smile, half angry with him for taking such a chance, half delighted at this explanation for his mysterious disappearance. "Only a crazy Scotsman would do something like that."

She watched him sort through the contents of the kit. There were vials and bandages and splints and little bottles with labels on them. At last he found what he sought . . . a syringe. Expertly, he removed a sterilized needle from its protective paper and attached it to the syringe. "Burn the packaging," he instructed her. "And you must hide this case and mention it to no one. If these people find it, you'll be branded a witch for sure."

He filled the syringe with a liquid from one of the bottles, then gently rolled Pauley over, wiped a spot on his little buttocks with alcohol, and administered the shot. "Antibiotics," he said. "If he has an infection, this should get him on the road to recovery. I suspect he's been carrying a low-grade condition for a while. I wanted to go for this sooner, but didn't have the opportunity . . . or the emergency.''

The man continued to amaze Taylor. ''Are you a doctor, too?''

Duncan gave a short laugh and disassembled the syringe. ''Hardly. But they train you pretty well for the Institute. Sort of like paramedics. Now, let me show you what's in this bag of tricks. . . .''

Holyrood Palace
21 January 1567

We are recently returned from a harsh but necessary trip to Glasgow to bring our husband back to Edinburgh. He has suffered another bout with the pox, the *roniole*, not the small pox, and is in need of an extended and undisturbed period of recovery. We did not recall him out of love nor any wish to be near his person, which we find vile and contemptible, especially in its present state. Rather, we made this move upon the advice of Maitland, who wisely pointed out that it was safer for us to have Darnley where he is more easily controlled than loose in Lennox country where he might plot against us. The fool is easy to persuade, as we discovered after Riccio's murder. A soft word, a kind invitation, an intimation that he is to be returned to favor at court, and he was eager to leave his self-imposed exile.

By his own choice, he is now lodged in the old provost's house at Kirk O' Field, where he will abide until he is recovered enough to return to Holyrood. We shall maintain visitation quarters in a chamber directly beneath his, although we are anxious to learn of any progress that may have been made in our absence concerning a divorce.

The history book dated Darnley's murder at Kirk O' Field in mid-February, and Robert Gordon eagerly turned to a page dated the eleventh.

Holyrood Palace
11 February 1567

We are both horrified and shocked at the conspiracy that was worked before our very nose to kill Darnley. We never dreamed when Maitland said he would find other means than a divorce to be rid of him, that he was referring to murder. We are doubly shocked because we believe that the lords who spoke of divorce to us at Craigmillar sought to murder us as well. We have learned the old provost's house was filled with gunpowder the very night we last visited Darnley, and had we not left to attend the masque in honor of Bastion's wedding, we would have died in the explosion along with our husband.

We have heard rumor that many of our grand lords, including Moray and Bothwell, were not only involved, but designed the very plot among them. With such as these we fear for our life, the life of our child, indeed, the life of Scotland. As we sit at table to write these words, we see by our candle's glow the battered but still lovely Scottish Rose, and we despair of it ever joining with the Honours of Scotland. What hope is there for peace and unity, when rogues such as these murderers dare to kill a king and nearly so an annointed queen? What reason is there to hope, what reason any longer to care?

Later in the day, Duncan carried the boy to the new quarters he and Taylor would share in the Ogilvys' household. She'd wanted to come along, but he'd asked her to wait for him in their own room. Pauley was better already, and he seemed soothed to find his adoptive "parents" back on terms, even if they were strained.

Although Duncan still wished he could convince the governor this voyage was unnecessary, during his long night in the rowboat, he had decided unequivocally he would go if Ogilvy insisted. He'd been wrong to entertain the idea of staying at Dunnottar, even if Taylor was pregnant. He'd volunteered in the beginning to be the ship's captain, and it was what had secured his place, and Taylor's, in the upper order of the castle where they had lived in relative safety and comfort. He owed it to the governor to obey his command.

And pregnant or not, Taylor had proven she was most capable of taking care of herself and Pauley. He still hated to leave her, but he felt a little better knowing she now had some twentieth-century ammunition against Pauley's ill health. He was concerned most, however, about the ongoing threat from Kenneth and the villagers. He'd heard their open taunts, and even though he'd warned his "kinsman" to back off, he knew the minute he set foot on board the ship, Taylor was at a greater risk than before.

He had spoken at length about his fears to Governor Ogilvy, who had assured him he would take personal responsibility for their safety in Duncan's absence, and he was greatly relieved to learn that Taylor and Pauley were being brought into the main residence. They were safer there than they ever had been in the guest quarters, and under the watchful eye of the Governor, Duncan was certain they were as protected as they could possibly be under the circumstances.

With Pauley comfortably tucked in and Elizabeth Ogilvy hovering over him like a benevolent mother hen, Duncan turned to the last of his affairs that needed settling before he set sail for France.

Taylor.

He couldn't leave without making up with her. Even though he didn't understand why she had reacted so vehemently to his concern about her being pregnant, he knew that for all her bravado, she was likely filled with fear. He didn't blame her for being afraid. Hell, he was afraid. Who wouldn't be afraid in this insane set of circumstances?

He wished he could rescue them both from their fears, but since that was an impossibility, he would have to settle, hopefully, for reconciliation. He still didn't know if she was pregnant, but he wasn't about to ask again. He reached the door to the quarters they had shared for the last four months, and as he'd made a practice of for all that time, he knocked before entering.

Taylor's heart leapt at the familiar rap at the door. After Duncan had left with Pauley, she'd quickly washed up, brushed her hair, and changed into a fresher frock. He had asked her to wait here for him, and there was a command in his voice she did not question. Either he wanted to apologize or ream her out, she wasn't sure which, not that she cared, for she felt she deserved both. But she needed a chance to set things straight between them.

"Come in."

He filled the doorway with pure male power, and his eyes were fierce when they met hers. Good God, now that Pauley was out of the way, was he going to pick up their fight where they had left off? Taylor's stomach cramped. He slammed the door behind him, the vibrations sending the latch sliding down into place and a shiver down her spine. Without speaking he strode across the small room, dropping his heavy, snow-covered mantle to the floor behind him. Before she could utter a word, he flung his arms about her, drawing her into a forceful embrace, and his lips seared hers in a kiss that melted away her doubts and fears. His face was bearded now, the scratch of it rough against her chin, and yet she pressed against him, threading her fingers through his hair, bringing him closer, and still wanting more. He smelled of winter air and woodsmoke. Of man.

His embrace communicated all that she needed from him. His strength surrounded her with courage, his tenderness enveloped her in forgiveness.

"Forgive me," she heard him whisper into her hair.

"Forgive me," she replied.

His lips returned to hers in a renewed assault that bespoke of his pain and fear, his passion and torment. Taylor knew he did not want to leave her. She knew, too, the kind of man he was, dedicated to principle and utterly loyal. Her earlier anger at him for leaving shifted to admiration, and she allowed her heart to fill with the love she'd given no other man.

"Make love to me, Duncan," she murmured, running the palms of her hands over his broad chest, feeling the strength of his muscles, the heavy beat of his heart.

Cupping her face in his hands, he looked into her eyes. "I want you," he said raggedly. "God knows how I want you, Taylor."

He was torn, she could see, and she didn't understand why. They had forgiven each other. The door behind them was locked. Nothing stood between them but their clothing. Which she began to remove with deft fingers. She started with his belt buckle, and then the buttons to the rough breeches that had replaced his modern clothes through the kindness of the governor.

"Oh, my God, Taylor, what you're doing to me . . . ," was all he said before he picked her up in his powerful arms and carried her to their bed. Tonight, she thought briefly as they frantically raced to remove the remainder of their clothing, she would love him as if they *were* the husband and wife they pretended to be.

But secretly, in her heart.

They would not talk about marriage, or children. Not tonight. He didn't need to know about all that. Not now. He might never return, and it wouldn't matter anyway. She did not want to waste the few precious hours they had before he was to leave.

For if he never came back, at least she would have the memory of tonight. A treasured memory of how, once upon a time, she had cherished a man as a woman cherishes a beloved husband. She had not thought herself capable or desirous of these feelings that now filled her with greater happiness and serenity than she'd ever known. If nothing more ever came of their time together, she would have this to remember.

NINETEEN

༝

The small chapel seemed to shiver beneath the winter winds that blasted through the cracks between the rough windowsills and the ancient rock walls. Taylor had once considered prayer just another superstitious practice, but when Mrs. Ogilvy had suggested that they pray together for the safety of Duncan's ship and crew, and the success of their endeavor, she eagerly joined her employer on her knees on the stone floor of the chapel. When they were done, the two women embraced tearfully.

"I know this is hard on ye," Mrs. Ogilvy said, her voice soothing and filled with understanding. "But ye must be proud of thy husband. He is a brave and honorable man. With God's grace, we'll see him again 'ere th' spring comes."

Spring. It seemed so far away to Taylor on this dreary December day. It was the winter solstice, the darkest night of the year, and Taylor's mood reflected the earth's barren sorrow. "I beg a favor, madam," she asked, wanting some time alone to gather her energies to face this bleak time without Duncan. "I . . . I would like to set our chamber straight. Perhaps you would wish to offer it to some other family during Mr. Fraser's absence. Its fire is quite welcome on these nights."

Mrs. Ogilvy took her hand and gave it a reassuring squeeze. "I understand. Go. I will care for Pauley and take up the matter of the chamber with my husband."

Taylor curtsied and hurried out of the front of the chapel. She darted a furtive glance toward the kitchen house but saw no sign of Greta. The weather was still foul, although the rain and snow had let up.

Inside the small quarters, she closed the door and leaned against it, at last letting her tears flow. She had held them bravely in check for many long hours, through her quarrel with Duncan, Pauley's crisis, even her last farewell to the man who had loved her so tenderly and passionately there upon that bed. Oh, God, why had she ever gotten them into this mess?

She threw her kerchief across the room. Damn, damn, damn!

She jerked the bedclothes away from the rude mattress, thinking to launder them straightaway, but instead of throwing them aside in a pile, she held them against her and smelled the scent of man and woman, together in love. Her control slipped further, and she sank to the floor.

She should never have allowed those thoughts to enter her mind late last night when Duncan had come to her. Those thoughts of marriage beds and husbands. For it made the cold reality of this morning even more cruel. She had no husband. No marriage bed. And the only man she had ever loved, maybe ever *would* love, was gone, and she despaired of his return.

Taylor sat motionless for a long time, her mind and heart weary from the effort of fighting tears, of being brave. But she was brave, and she knew she must continue to be brave, if not for her own sake, then at least for Pauley's. And maybe prayers got answered. Maybe Duncan would somehow miraculously return in that rat-infested, dry-rot mottled sailing ship. She sniffed, then straightened and went to put some more wood on the fire.

She was consoled by only one thing. Whether Duncan came back or not, he had given her a gift before he left, even though he didn't know it. It was nothing tangible. No diamond ring. No golden band. No promise of all his tomorrows. But something even more precious . . . a moment in time, when she had become not Taylor Kincaid, television star, or Taylor Kincaid, dauntless career woman, or even Taylor Kincaid, freak of nature. Just Taylor Kincaid.

Woman.

Three days into the voyage, the weather finally relented enough that John Keith managed to come out of his cabin and join Captain Fraser on deck. Duncan eyed him, feeling both sorry for his acute attack of *mal de mer* and a little amused at the way nature had reduced him from a swaggering would-be hero to a cowering lump of flesh.

It wasn't that Duncan didn't like John Keith. He just hadn't cared for the man's braggadocio just before they'd left. Keith was convinced that he was going to France to save the day, and his older brother, the Earl Marischal, would be forever in his debt because of it. With some concentration, Duncan had finally recalled from history that John Keith suceeded in doing nothing of the sort. Instead, he fumbled and faltered at every turn along his way, losing all his money to bandits and ending up in Paris very late, coming before King Charles poverty-stricken and embarrassed.

Duncan did not, however, tell him that at the moment.

Nor did he tell him yet that they had been blown severely off course, and that landfall would likely be somewhere in the Low Countries, not France.

Which, after he'd taken his last bearings using a crude sextant that he'd found on board, he'd remembered as happening in history as well.

Everything was going just as he recalled from the history books. And for some reason, he and Taylor seemed to have been swept into this distant past, not merely as accidental tourists, but rather as active players in the scenario. He groped to make some sense of it all.

How could they enter the picture from the future and take part in events in the past? And if either of them did anything that was contrary to recorded history, how would it affect everything else that followed? Was it possible, desirable, or dangerous to change history?

These and similar disquieting thoughts had taken hold of Duncan in the dark of night, during his lonely watches when the wind and waves threatened to wash him and his fellow sailors into the treacherous sea. Yet as baffling as they were, they served to take his mind off other equally disquieting thoughts.

Like his desire for a woman that kept leading him to make mistakes, such as making love to her again the night before he left. Wild horses could not have kept them apart, and she'd wanted him as well, but before his passion had completely obliterated all reason, he would have given the Honours of Scotland for a condom.

He must return to Dunnottar Castle and take Taylor and Pauley away safely and without delay. Back in twentieth-century Stonehaven, maybe he and Taylor could sort out their feelings for each other and make decisions about their future, or non-future, based upon rational thinking and the relative safety of their modern civilization. If she wanted children, he would consider it, but only in a place and time where competent medical professionals were immediately available.

After this voyage, he would have fulfilled his obligation to Governor Ogilvy, and to history, he supposed, since *somebody* had to be the captain on this trip. He wondered idly, if he hadn't taken responsibility for this journey, who would have? There was no one else in the castle who was qualified to sail the derelict vessel. Was that the reason he had been thrown back in time, to perform this specific duty for his native Scotland? Was it himself he'd always read about in those history books?

Ridiculous.

But it was even more ridiculous to try to answer such preposterous, insane questions, so he focused instead on the most important issues facing him right now.

Staying alive and returning to Taylor.

Almost two months had passed since Duncan's ship had sailed, and there had been no word of him, or John Keith, or rescue from the King. At last, in desperation, Governor Ogilvy managed to locate and dispatch another captain to complete Duncan's mission, which all in the castle but Taylor believed to have ended in tragedy.

Taylor lingered at the window overlooking the North Sea,

as she did so many of her long, idle days, waiting, watching for, believing in Duncan's return.

The Castle of Dunnottar appeared clean and fresh under a light blanket of snow, the whiteness of which hid the dark suffering of those who weathered the winter siege within. Starvation had taken the lives of some, and others hovered on the brink between life and death, their bodies too weak to throw off the ravages of winter illnesses.

Taylor rarely left the protection of the Countess's suite, but she heard the stories of the terrible conditions suffered by the refugees and the soldiers in the garrison. She thought guiltily of the precious medicines she kept hidden in the wooden trunk, the tiny vials of antibiotics and ointments from the twentieth century that had saved Pauley's life and could likely save others. More than once she was tempted to bring the medicine forth, but Duncan's warning rang in her ears.

The villagers were desperate to blame their plight on someone, and Taylor had learned she was "it." She and Pauley. Elizabeth Ogilvy had warned her of the rumor that was being spread among the peasants that it was her fault, and Pauley's, that food was scarce, that the winter had been extraordinarily harsh, that Cromwell's troops had come in the first place. The good woman feared for their lives if they ventured out of the protection of the Earl's private living quarters.

Taylor tried to resent these accusations but instead found she was deeply sorry for these superstitious people who firmly believed, thanks to Greta, that she was a witch. If they needed a scapegoat, she didn't mind being it . . . but from a distance. Using modern medicine, however, would definitely be considered magic, and though the bearer of magic might work miracles, she might also be condemned to death.

It was this kind of folk tradition that she had so deplored in the twentieth century, more so than the tales of flying saucers and monsters from the deep. This kind of superstition preyed on the fears of primitive peoples even in 1996 and kept them enslaved to their ignorance. But unlike in that age, which seemed like many lifetimes ago to Taylor, there was no forum like *Legends, Lore, and Lunatics* from which to uproot these beliefs.

The ever-present hunger in her belly and threats on her life, however, were nothing compared to the terrible anxiety for Duncan that grew more intense as each day passed without word from him. He had been gone for over six weeks, and she was discouraged and filled with despair although she refused to believe the worst.

Everywhere, gloom permeated the castle. Tempers were short, and even Governor Ogilvy began to lose hope. If she didn't have Pauley to care for, Taylor thought she would completely lose her mind.

A sharp rap on the door interrupted her morose thoughts, and Taylor turned her gaze away from the empty ocean. "Come in."

Mrs. Ogilvy, followed by a woman Taylor had met several times, Christian Grainger, the minister's wife, hurried into the room and shut the door securely behind them. "Janet, my husband has decided we must remove th' Honours from th' castle. There are rumors that Colonel Leighton is stirring up th' garrison t' pressure Mr. Ogilvy to surrender."

"Surrender!" *But it's not time yet*, Taylor wanted to say, but she bit her tongue. Unless Duncan's memory of history was in error, she knew it would be spring before the Governor finally capitulated.

"Aye. Th' coward ought t' be horsewhipped." She turned to Mrs. Grainger. "But there are those among us"—she smiled at the woman warmly—"with courage enough for all. Christian has a plan to save th' Honours, but it will take great daring. Tell her, my dear. You can trust Janet completely."

The woman blushed beneath Mrs. Ogilvy's effusive praise. "As you know, I have been visiting Mrs. Ogilvy regularly these past few weeks. The English Colonel Dutton allows me t' enter the castle, for he is a Christian gentleman, even though an Englishman, and I have told him I come t' bring th' Lord's word t' the Governor and his lady. The Colonel has become used t' my presence, and I believe it would be possible for me t' smuggle th' Honours out on my person."

''But my husband thinks this is too risky,'' Mrs. Ogilvy broke in. ''He does not wish t' endanger th' life of this good woman, who would surely be put t' death should she be caught.''

''Does he have another plan?'' Taylor asked innocently, although she knew full well what was about to unfold. Her heart began to beat harder in spite of her efforts to control her excitement. It was happening! She was about to witness the rescue of the Honours of Scotland! Where was her film crew when she needed them? But she sobered quickly at the thought of Barry and Rob. She was certain by now they had not gone through the Ladysgate, and she prayed they were safe and sound in 1996.

''Aye. Mr. Ogilvy believes that since th' English have become lax in their vigilance with Mrs. Grainger, they might also become unmindful of a peasant woman who wanders th' shore at th' foot of th' castle gathering dulse in her creel.''

Taylor nodded, encouraging the woman to continue the story that she had already been told by Duncan.

''After a time, when they no longer pay attention t' th' gatherer of dulse, we can lower th' regalia over th' castle wall t' her, where she will hide th' crown, sword and scepter in her creel and take them away safely to Kinneff Kirk. Mrs. Grainger and her husband have sworn t' hide th' Honours in th' church and t' protect them with their lives.''

''It sounds like a good design,'' Taylor remarked, masking her excitement beneath an outward calm. ''When do ye plan t' begin th' scheme?''

She saw the other women exchange a glance. Then Mrs. Ogilvy took Taylor gently by the arm. ''Sit down, my dear. We have an idea t' discuss with ye.''

An hour later, Mrs. Grainger stood and bade farewell to Janet. ''Good-bye for now, my new 'kinswoman,' '' she said with a conspiratorial smile. ''My husband and I shall make ready for thy arrival in a few days.''

When she left the room, Mrs. Ogilvy looked at Taylor, who was astounded at what had just taken place. She had hoped to observe the rescue of the Honours, like a reporter covering a late-breaking story. But now this!

"Are ye certain ye wish t' carry out this plan?" Mrs. Ogilvy asked, her eyes searching Taylor's, seeking the slightest sign of hesitation. " 'Tis a dangerous assignment should it go afoul."

Taylor stood and went to the window, hoping but not expecting to see a tiny dot on the horizon that might be Duncan's ship returning home. Finally, she voiced her thoughts to her friend and employer. "For two months, madam, I have watched in vain through this window for my . . . husband's return. For two months, I have paced this floor, unable t' relieve my anxiety even by a walk in th' quadrangle for fear of being attacked by those whose superstitions have slain my reputation. For this time and longer I have worried for th' life of this bairn. And now ye offer me not only escape from those who would harm me and th' bairn, but give me a means to repay thy kindness and hospitality." Taylor turned and took the hands of the governor's wife. "Oh, Mrs. Ogilvy, I vow t' ye I wish fervently t' carry out this plan for ye and Mrs. Grainger. Two kinder, braver women I have never known."

She was still dumbfounded at this latest turn of events, but she meant every word of her vow. Duncan had sailed for France out of a sense of duty; she would participate in this scheme for much the same reason. But also, she hoped, it would distract her from the constant and growing fear that Duncan Fraser had perished.

"Good," Mrs. Ogilvy replied, obviously satisfied that her serving woman was honestly eager to participate in the perilous plan she and Mrs. Grainger had laid out. "I will inform my husband, and the necessary preparations will be made. But first. . . ."

She went to the privy closet that was separated from the main part of the room by a velvet curtain. "There is something more I would ask of thee. . . ."

Taylor watched with growing curiosity as the matron dug around among various items of household goods and clothing stashed in the tiny room, at last retrieving a tattered pouch of some sort. She turned to Taylor, a strange smile on her face.

"All the world knows of the crown, sword, and scepter," she said, "but only a few loyal women in Scottish history have known about this, a sister in the royal regalia."

Taylor held her breath, hoping but not daring to believe what Mrs. Ogilvy might have in the pouch.

Elizabeth carried the small parcel to the bed, where she sat down and untied the drawstrings with great care. "What you are about t' see," she continued dramatically, "is a legacy from Mary Queen of Scots. She called it her 'Scottish Rose.'"

And with that, she produced an exquisite if somewhat battered golden chalice uniquely shaped in the form of a rose. Only one large ruby remained of the five that had apparently at one time adorned the petals, and the enamel had chipped from the sepals and leaves. Still, it was a remarkable object.

Taylor's throat tightened, and blood sang in her ears. So it was true! Those artifacts she'd inherited were authentic! "My God," she whispered. "What . . . ? Where . . . ?"

"Would ye like t' hold it?" Mrs. Ogilvy said, presenting it to Taylor. "For ye are truly a brave woman of Scotland, and I am about t' ask thy help in preserving this secret regalia from th' English as well."

Taylor felt herself shift into overwhelm. Her hands trembled as she accepted the lovely cup from Mrs. Ogilvy. "What is the story behind this?" she managed, wanting more information than what she'd learned in the photocopied letter.

"Let me read it from the hand of Queen Mary herself," Elizabeth Ogilvy replied. She went to a writing table and turned the key to the inlaid wooden box that rested there. Inside lay a small, loosely bound book. Taylor thought she might faint. For although it was newer, in far better condition than it had been in Robert Gordon's office, it was the same diary she had inherited. The diary that in her own time was hopefully locked away securely in the lawyer's vault, unless he was working on the transcription.

"This letter accompanied the diary of the Queen when Mrs. Drummond gave it and the rose chalice into my safekeeping,"

Mrs. Ogilvy said, taking a separate page from between those that were bound.

Taylor wondered if Robert Gordon had this letter as well. He hadn't mentioned it. But before she had time to ponder the question, Mrs. Ogilvy's voice commanded her attention:

Edinburgh, Scotland
By command of Her Royal Highness Mary, Queen of Scots, inscribed on this the first day of June in the yeare of our Lorde 1566.
The bearer of this letter is hereby charged with the duty of protecting and defending the Queen's Scottish Rose, the golden chalice which has served and sustained her Grace during her reign in these times of peril and provocation. It is the most sincere wish of Her Majesty that the warring factions in this land will unite and peace will at last reign throughout the kingdome. In the event that Her Majesty will be unable to witness these goode thingis in her own time, she hereby charges the Keeper of this chalice to protect and preserve it as a symbol of Her Majesty's Royal Spirit, that Spirit being of peace, good will, and tolerance toward all religions. When these thingis are accomplished, the Keeper of the Rose is to join it into the company of the known Honours of Scotland, that is the croun, suord and sceptre, so that the Scottish Rose will reign alongside its brother regalia in a place of honour for all time.
Until this time of peace be achieved, the Keeper is charged with secrecy lest the enemies of peace find and destroy this symbol.

Mrs. Ogilvy looked up at Taylor, obviously relishing her role as Keeper of the Rose. "It is signed, 'Marie R.' and sealed with the device of Mary, Queen of Scots."

Taylor stared dumbfounded at the paper in Elizabeth Ogilvy's hands, knowing that somehow she had become involved in perhaps the most intriguing and important Scottish legend of all. At last, she said in a quiet voice, "What is it ye wish of me, madam?"

TWENTY

୬

Amsterdam

Duncan surveyed the sailing ship that was supported by huge wooden beams leaning against each side of it in the shipyard, wondering how any clear-thinking sailor would ever venture forth across the ocean in such a tub. And yet he'd done exactly that over two months ago, when the boat had been in even worse condition. And he was about to do it again, as soon as he and his mates could launch her again.

The trip south from Dunnottar had been dangerous and would have been deadly under the command of a less experienced captain. They had left in a storm which followed them out to sea, where it buffeted the ship mercilessly until most aboard were sick and wet and miserable. They were blown off course, and with holes in the rotten wood of the ship, it was a miracle they had managed to stay afloat long enough to wallow into a port in Holland. John Keith had taken off for France by land in search of King Charles, and Duncan had set about the task of repairing the ship. With little money and few allies, it had not been easy, but his knowledge of boat-building, so far advanced from the shipwrights of the day in Amsterdam, had secured him work that sustained his personal needs and provided scrap materials with which to repair his own ship.

Every day away from Taylor had been lived in agony for her safety. He'd heard bits of gossip from time to time, sometimes relating that the castle had fallen, at others that the governor had defeated Cromwell's army. Duncan tried to believe neither but to remember instead what he had read in his history books, that the siege lasted until the spring. He must return before then and somehow get Taylor and Pauley out of harm's way.

During this time away from her, Duncan had come to realize not just that he loved Taylor, but *how much* he loved her. And how certain he was that, if she felt the same, he wanted never to be away from her again. Ever. In their short and difficult time together, she had somehow not only cauterized his old wounds but also rekindled the fire of his spirit. She had taught him to live again, to feel, to love.

A difficult voyage lay ahead of him, but not an impossible one. He would return to Taylor, even if he had to swim to get there.

Taylor's mind reeled, not only at the proof she continued to be presented with that her inheritance was authentic, but also that she was actually on the scene when Mrs. Ogilvy's letter had been written! Shortly after receiving her instructions concerning the Scottish Rose from the governor's wife, Taylor attended her as she penned a desperate letter to the Countess, the one she would read again in Gordon's office some three hundred and fifty years hence. . . .

But only now, in this time, did she understand the full impact of her words. . . .

> *"I fear that all in the castle may die for hiding the Honours, but it is our duty to protect these sacred emblems of Scotland. . . ."*

With this letter, Mrs. Ogilvy passed to the Countess, Lady Keith, Taylor's ancestor, the duty of preserving the knowledge of the existence of the Scottish Rose, but it was to Taylor she passed the responsibility for the physical safety of the chalice itself.

"I know a place, a secret cave in th' belly of this castle rock," Elizabeth told Janet, "where th' rose will be safe until we can come back for it. Only ye and I will know of it, and

I would die before I would give it away t' the English. Will you swear th' same?''

''Aye, madam,'' Taylor answered without a blink of an eye. ''But pray, Mrs. Ogilvy, why hath ye chosen t' entrust this secret t' thy serving woman?''

''The secret has been handed down through trusted servants since th' time of Queen Mary,'' she replied, taking Taylor's hand. ''But ye hath become more t' me than my serving woman, Janet,'' the woman added. ''Ye are also my trusted friend. And I feel almost like a grandmother to thy 'bairn.' But,'' she said, laughing, ''there is another more practical reason why ye must be th' one t' secure th' Scottish Rose in the cave. I am rather, uh, too stout t' go into th' tunnel, whereas thy slender body will easily make th' passage behind th' rock that guards th' entrance t' th' cave.''

Taylor had to suppress a giggle. But she found no reason for laughter in Mrs. Ogilvy's next words. ''Ye might also find it difficult, however, once ye reach the goal. The portal to the cave itself is tiny. I knew it as a child when it was easy for me t' enter. I think it will take a child''—she looked directly at Pauley—''t' enter it still. It is much I ask of ye, Janet Fraser, but t' ensure th' successful outcome of our task, I believe ye must make Pauley a part of th' plan.''

Taylor was aghast at the idea in the beginning, but Mrs. Ogilvy gave her little chance to object. Pauley's health had returned, she pointed out, and although he was still frail, he was stronger than he had been since Taylor brought him into their present quarters. Taylor knew that, in her own gentle way, Mrs. Ogilvy was calling in a chip for the kindness she had bestowed upon her and Pauley. She knew, too, that this errand must be extremely important to her or she wouldn't have asked. Having lived and worked closely with Elizabeth Ogilvy since late August, Taylor knew the depth of the woman's loyalty and dedication to that which she had pledged herself. ''He will be safe,'' Elizabeth assured her. ''Ye'll go under cover of darkness, by th' light of a waxing moon, when th' rest of th' villagers are asleep. I shall send ye with an unlit torch and a lighting stone t' show ye th' way once inside th' passage.''

Taylor dressed carefully for the mission before Mrs. Ogilvy came to fetch her. Beneath the blue woolen dress, she wore her twentieth-century jeans and long underwear. She wished she could don her sneakers for more sure footing, but decided against it as being too dangerous in case she was caught. Beneath her apron, she carefully attached the zippered bag in which she carried Duncan's flashlight, her camera, and the remaining candy mints, in case Pauley needed a little bribe along the way. Over all, she wore a dark, hooded mantle.

She believed the boy understood what was going on. She had signed to him as best she could what Mrs. Ogilvy was asking them to do. Together they had watched her draw a map of how to get to the secret cave, and Pauley actually pointed and nodded his head, as if he knew exactly what she was talking about. It was possible, Taylor supposed, that Pauley had been to that cave before, exploring his environs just as Mrs. Ogilvy said she had as a child. He was quick and sure-footed, and, she thought with a bite of irony, she didn't have to worry about him making noise.

Wind whipped at her cloak, and Taylor attempted to tighten it around her body, although with the unwieldy rushes she carried tucked beneath her arm to provide her a torch later, such an effort was difficult. She and Pauley made their way noiselessly along the parapet toward the southeasternmost corner of the castle wall. Only inches from them, the sheer cliffs dropped off into blackness. Taylor's heart thundered, and she tightened her grasp around the Scottish Rose. She had hoped to put it in her pouch, to free both hands for the difficult descent to come, but it was too large, and she had no pockets other than in her jeans.

Pauley hurried ahead of her, and being unable to call out to stop him, she walked faster than she would have liked over the uncertain terrain in order to keep up. At least he seemed sure of the way. She didn't know what she would do if he took a wrong turn. But he stayed exactly on the path Mrs.

Ogilvy had indicated, and shortly they arrived at the break in the wall she'd said led to the path. At last the boy paused, and Taylor caught him by the arm. "Slow down," she mouthed, giving him a smile and a gesture that asked for his sympathy in letting her catch her breath.

The night was dark, but the pale crescent moon shed enough light for her to make out the path. Until they reached a place where Taylor believed no one would see them, she was afraid to turn on the flashlight. She had wanted to show it to Pauley beforehand, but had not had the chance. She knew he was likely to be afraid of the twentieth-century "candle," but she was counting on his trust of her to keep him from freaking out.

She signed to him, "go slowly." He nodded, and they began the perilous climb down the narrow, overgrown path to where Mrs. Ogilvy had said they would find a boulder protecting the entrance to the passageway that led to the cave where she wanted Taylor to place the rose chalice. Taylor went ahead of Pauley this time, to break his fall if he should lose his footing, and also because she wasn't sure he knew where the entrance was and might lead them past it.

Down into the darkness they half-walked, half-slid. Taylor was almost glad for the dark of the night around them, because she suspected if she could see the vertical angle of their path clearly, she might lose her nerve. How far was this place? she began to wonder when they had traveled along the way for several minutes. Had she missed it?

The path took an unexpected turn, which Taylor would have missed had not Pauley grabbed at the hem of her cloak and pointed out the twist. Likely he just saved me from stepping off this cliff, she thought, swallowing her fear and continuing on. Another few minutes brought them to a large boulder that seemed to block the path, although she eventually discerned the outline of the trail to the right of the rock. This must be the place, she said, her lungs heaving from the exertion and her heart racing with excitement. Pauley took her hand and drew her to the left side of the boulder, opposite where the path led. There, inconspicuous unless a person knew where to look, was a slender opening between the rock and the mountain that spawned it.

Pauley passed easily through the opening, but Taylor wasn't sure she would be able to follow him. Mrs. Ogilvy was right. There was no way her stout body could have squeezed through here, if she'd been able to make it down the hill at all. But Taylor was thinner than she'd ever been as an adult as a result of the scarcity of food in the castle, and she edged herself through the portal sideways with no problem. Inside, it was blacker than black, making the nighttime outside seem as day. Taylor took the torch from under her arm, glad to be relieved of that scratchy and useless burden. Instead of seeking out the "lighting stone" and piece of metal given her by Mrs. Ogilvy, she reached beneath her apron and unzipped the pouch. She smiled when her hands touched the cold, smooth metal of the flashlight. She just hoped the batteries would hold out until they had finished their assignment.

She clicked it on, and she saw Pauley, who was several feet away from her, freeze in alarm. His eyes grew wide with fright, but Taylor knelt down on the cold rock floor of the passageway and motioned to him to come to her. Reluctantly, he did as she bade, and she gave him the flashlight to hold. He turned it over in his hands, then looked at her questioningly. She put her hands around his on the light, then showed him where the switch was. Together, they turned it off, then on again. In the gray-blue illumination emitted by the instrument, Taylor nodded and smiled. Then Pauley did likewise, but he quickly handed the thing back to Taylor as if unsure that it wasn't dangerous.

With the light shining before her, and Pauley trailing behind, Taylor edged through the narrow passageway that wound into the very heart of the castle rock. High above, Mrs. Ogilvy kept a vigil for their return while, hopefully, the rest of those confined to the fortress slept unawares of their sojourn. Silently counting her paces, as she'd been directed to do by her employer, Taylor tried to think brave thoughts to keep from choking on her fear. She felt her body start to shake, as it had done the night when the first awful suspicion had started to sink in that they had traveled through time. The night Duncan had held her and comforted her and protected her. . . .

Stop it, she scolded herself silently. Don't think about Duncan. Not now. Think only about the work at hand. One step at a time. One step at a time.

After the appropriate number of steps, she beamed the light across the cold, wet slash of wall. It fell upon a small indentation at the base that cast a black shadow against the shimmer of the wet obsidian.

"Bingo."

The hole in the wall was low to the ground and less than two feet wide, but she crouched down and flashed the light through the opening. On the other side, she saw a rounded room big enough for Pauley to stand up in.

"Well," she said aloud, as if the sound of her own voice would calm her jangled nerves, "here we are." This had to be the place. She turned to the boy, who still showed some fear of the flashlight, but who also seemed unafraid of this cave. Taylor signed, asking him if he would crawl through the narrow space, and with an enthusiastic grin, he nodded. Placing the pouch containing their treasure on the floor, she helped him through the small space, keeping the light on so he wouldn't be suddenly entombed in darkness.

She started to hand him the Scottish Rose, then remembered why she'd brought along the camera. Here in the depths of the mountain there was no one but a small deaf mute boy to witness her use of such "witchcraft," and she was not about to forgo the opportunity to photograph this relic before leaving it in its hiding place. She did not know what she planned to do with the evidence once she returned to reality, as she considered her own time to be, but while she existed in this alternate reality, bad dream, or whatever-it-was, she wanted to document as much as she could without jeopardizing her safety and that of the little boy she now considered to be her own.

Quickly, she laid the flashlight down on the flat stone floor of the entrance between her and Pauley. She unzipped the bag again and took out the small camera. She saw Pauley peering out at her curiously. What would he do when the camera flashed? Taylor wondered, but if he decided to run, there was no place for him to go. Still, she did not want to frighten the child, so she motioned for him to come back out of the cave for a moment. She showed him the camera and put it into his hands, as she had done with the flashlight. She let him hold it as she slipped the golden rose-shaped cup from its protective pouch and set it next to the flashlight. Then she encircled Pauley in her arms and held the camera to his eye. He peered through the viewfinder for a second, then nervously handed the camera back to Taylor. Not releasing him for fear he would run away when she took the picture, she adjusted the camera and pressed the button.

The chamber exploded with light, and she knew if Pauley could have screamed, he would have. He struggled to get away from her, but she held him firmly and closely against her and began to rock him gently. She hummed a tune and placed her throat on the top of his head so he could feel the familiar vibrations, for she'd often rocked him to sleep like this when he was so sick. Slowly, he calmed down. Maybe this was a good experience for him, Taylor thought hopefully, a way to begin preparing him in this time for all the magic that he would encounter when she returned with him to 1996.

She wanted to take another shot, but she didn't want to risk terrifying the boy completely, so she decided one would have to do. In a few moments, Pauley recovered his composure, and, to her surprise, he indicated he wanted to look at the camera. She let him hold it again, then she took it and secured it in the waistline holder. She noted that he watched her carefully and knew that he would remember what was in the "magic bag," as she'd begun to call it. Her fingers touched the roll of candy mints, now almost half gone, and she flicked one loose and handed it to Pauley. "To reward you for your bravery," she said, wishing he could hear and understand.

The boy took it eagerly, then Taylor asked him to go back into the cave. She wasted no time now. With one long last look at the Scottish Rose, she put it back into the pouch, tied the drawstrings, and handed it through the entrance to Pauley, who placed it on a rock ledge that jutted like a natural shelf on the far wall. Taylor signaled "okay" and nodded with a smile, then motioned for Pauley to come out of the cave.

The pair made their way back to the rock that covered the entrance to the passageway and squeezed out into the icy night air. Taylor considered dousing the light from this point onward, but it made the return trip up the mountain safer and faster, and she wanted nothing more at the moment than to return quickly to her quarters and the warmth of her bed.

They reached the break in the wall safely, and Taylor turned off the flashlight and zipped it back into the pouch. She helped Pauley through the niche, then stepped through herself. But when she reached the other side, he was gone. Damn, she thought. The kid was like a mountain goat. He'd probably already made it halfway back to their chambers by now.

But a rough hand covered her mouth as a strong arm imprisoned her in a vise grip. "Keep thy tongue, ye wicked woman," a guttural voice hissed. "We shall soon rejoice t' be rid of ye and thy evil bairn."

TWENTY-ONE

༄

The ring of the telephone startled Robert Gordon, bringing him immediately out of the almost trancelike state into which he had drifted while reading the ancient diary. "Yes?" he said into the receiver.

"John Doggett here, Gordon. I got your message. What's on your mind?"

At first Gordon was hesitant to share the incredible treasure he'd received from Lady Agatha Keith even with a known expert in antiquities, but he quickly remembered an idea that had crossed his mind earlier in the day. So he gave Doggett a brief rundown on his acquisition of the diary and the Ogilvy letter, as well as his opinion of how well what he had recently translated fit into the historical timeline. He could tell by the man's reply, he had his immediate interest.

"Would you like me to come right away?"

"Would tonight be agreeable? Say eight o'clock?"

Doggett agreed, took down the address of Gordon's office, and rang off. Gordon ran his hands through his hair, his heart pounding so heavily it almost hurt. He looked at his watch. It was three o'clock in the afternoon. Could he make his way through the rest of the entries before eight? He'd certainly give it his best shot, because he wanted to know the truth of what had happened to Queen Mary, and because he wanted even more to know where to look for the Scottish Rose. . . .

Holyrood Palace
16 April 1567

They have acquitted Bothwell of Darnley's murder even though we and the rest of the world knows of his authorship in the deed. Lennox, who brought the private process against Bothwell, feared to come to Edinburgh, since Bothwell's four thousand men roam the streets, and having no one to make the charge, the jury had no choice but to acquit. We have mixed feelings about his acquittal, for we abhor and detest rank bloodshed, especially of a royal. At the same time, we shall not miss Darnley. Marrying him was the most monumental mistake we have ever made in our mistake-ridden life. Even so, we are left bereft of any husband at all, and we are still in want of a strong, dependable consort. We are despondent, and our health continues to deteriorate. The pain in our side recurrs so often it is almost constant. Our only happiness is in knowing that soon we will visit our son Stirling, and that his father is no longer a threat to his well-being.

Today we attended Parliament, to which Bothwell carried the scepter, and we had a strange premonition that he would also have liked to have worn the crown upon his own head. Bothwell has long been our friend, a stalwart lord when others turned traitor. But we begin to discern in him a certain greed for power that we have found refreshingly lacking in him heretofore. Even so, he is a strong lord and has served us well since our arrival in Scotland. Could we entertain the idea of Bothwell as husband?

Taylor struggled against her captor, who lifted her as easily as if she were a child and carried her for some distance before setting her on her feet again. He did not release her, however, nor uncover her mouth. She could see Pauley flailing against the strength of a large man she recognized as one of Kenneth's friends from the village. The man let out a low growl.

"He's a wild 'un, this," he snarled. "At least he canna

make a noise, th' little beast.''

She recognized the voice that replied and knew that it was Duncan's own "kinsman" Kenneth who held her prisoner. "Light th' fire,'' he ordered, and Taylor's eyes grew wide in terror. *The stake.* She'd seen the gleam of malice in Greta's eyes when she'd told Taylor about the witches in times past that had been burned at the stake, and Taylor had no reason to believe that Greta wouldn't delight in torching her very own witch.

Oh, my God.

Taylor froze as the flames grew from a single spark into a roaring bonfire that sent sparks high into the night sky. Her heart seemed to stop, and the sheer horror of what was about to happen paralyzed her. When Kenneth felt her cease to struggle, he removed his hand tentatively from her mouth. "There's a lass who respects her fate,'' he muttered. "Where's Greta?''

"You people are mad,'' Taylor said, finding her voice at last.

Greta pushed her way through the mob. "Ye art th' one tha's mad, woman o' th' divil. Ye thought ye'd get away with thy evil doin's, goin' about charmin' th' Governor and his lady like ye have. But we've been watchin' and waitin', knowin' ye'd make a mistake. And a sure fine one ye made tonight, trespassin' out alone like this, likely on th' divil's own errand.''

"Let the lad go,'' Taylor said, trying to ignore the hateful vengeance in the woman's voice. "He's done nothing. . . .''

But her plea was interrupted by a furious curse from Kenneth. "No, by damnation, th' lad must die!'' he roared. " 'Tis th' evil bairn who's caused our woes. I knew his mother, and never a more accursed witchy woman spirited this earth. She deserved t' die, and so must her offspring.''

Taylor's blood ran cold. Kenneth knew Pauley's mother? Then a terrible suspicion hit her.

"How know ye of th' bairn's mother?'' she demanded quickly, and in a strong voice. "She was not of thy village. Could it be . . . ye art th' father of this bairn?'' The accusation spilled from her lips before she had time to consider the ramifications of what she was saying. But she had effectively caught him off-guard and seized the opportunity to jerk free from his grasp. Another man ran to snatch her again, but she turned all of her pent-up wrath on him and the others, facing them with such boldness that they backed away.

"Beware of crossing me," she warned, "ye who call me a witch." She could see her words begin to play with their superstitions. "So might it be. But whatever I am does not remove the stain of sin from this man's hands. Ask him, if ye dare." With a sudden inspiration, she hastily reached beneath her cloak and apron, unzipped the waistline pouch and grabbed the flashlight. Switching it on, she directed the beam into Kenneth's face. The mob emitted a communal cry at this sorcery and edged away even further.

Taylor took advantage of their surprise and fear and pressed forward with her charges. "Did not th' woman ye accuse of being a witch enchant you? And did ye not sire this poor bairn within her? Is that not th' reason ye pour thy venom upon him, and wish t' see him . . . deed, t' protect your secret sin?" She could tell from the man's expression that her suspicion was dead on.

"Nay, 'tis not true," he denied her charge vehemently. " 'Tis th' lies of this blasphemer," he continued, looking around to find support among his fellow witch-hunters. But his voice and his manner betrayed him. Taylor watched, astonished, as Greta moved toward her husband, her eyes now filled with suspicion.

"Swear it, husband," she demanded. "Swear it on th' book o' th' Lord, for if ye so swear and then tell a lie, ye shall be doomed t' th' fires o' hell."

But Kenneth Fraser would not swear. Instead, he fought back. "This woman is th' devil in th' flesh," he said, pointing to Taylor, "whose false words are meant t' poison th' minds o' God-fearin' folk. Believe her not!"

Some of those in the crowd gave a shout of approval and began to close in on her again, but Taylor shouted, "Halt! Stay ye away from me, and let the bairn go free." She swept the beam of light over the faces of the villagers, seeing even as she did so the fear her actions instilled in them. But how long could she sustain this charade? Out of the corner of her eye, she saw Pauley squirm loose and take off into the darkness of the night.

Run, Pauley! Run! Taylor mentally willed the child into the safety of the governor's dwelling, knowing that when he returned without her, Mrs. Ogilvy would rouse the rest of the household who would come to her rescue.

Rescue.

Her mind flashed to the man who had sought to rescue her once before, in another time. Likely, he ended up dying for it in this one. *Oh, God, Duncan!* she screamed in her mind. Duncan!

But Duncan wasn't here to come to her rescue, and she hurriedly tried to collect her thoughts again and decide what might save her skin.

Time.

She needed to give Pauley time to rally the Governor's men. But this crowd was turning uglier by the minute, angered that the boy had escaped.

The mob crept forward, their voices mingling in threats and epithets, and Taylor retreated a few steps. But to her horror, her back ran into the stone wall of the ramparts. There was no place for her to run. Sweat poured from her forehead, and her heart was pounding so hard she thought she might faint. She heard something fly past her ear and hit the wall with a thump. Another missile struck her skirt, and then she felt a sharp pain as a rock struck her forehead. "Death to th' divil-woman," Kenneth cried, gaining courage once again. My God, she thought panic-stricken, they're throwing rocks at me. They intend to stone me to death!

"Oh, no you don't, you heathen bunch of nincompoops!" she screamed at them, reaching again into the hidden pouch. She brought out the camera, brandishing it in one hand and the flashlight in the other, like Princess Leah with a light sword. Where the hell was Hans Solo?

"Get away from me or I'll capture your soul with this machine, and you'll all go straight to hell!" she called out, waving the black box at them threateningly.

Again, their primitive simplicity worked in her favor, and

they ceased pelting her with stones. Determined not to show her fear again, she advanced toward them. "Bubble, bubble, toil and trouble, fire burn and cauldron bubble," she cackled with every ounce of theatrics she could summon. They wanted witch? They were going to get witch. . . .

She dug into her Wizard of Oz repertoire.

"Ep-pe, pep-pe, kak-ke!" she said, hopping ridiculously onto her left foot. "Hil-lo, hol-lo, hel-lo!" she screeched, hopping onto her right. "Ziz-zy, zuz-zy, zik!" She landed on both feet again. The Winged Monkeys should be here any second.

Then she held the camera to her eye and aimed it directly at Kenneth and Greta. Snap. The flash worked its magic, lighting up the bewildered, frightened, angry faces of Duncan's kinsman and his "bediviled" wife. Snap. Another flash was all it took to disperse the crowd, sending the vulgar wretches scattering into the night.

Taylor's knees were weak, and she thought she might throw up, but she forced herself to stand firm, and with halting, painful steps, made her way toward the safety of Governor Ogilvy's quarters. She had gone barely a few feet, however, when she heard shouts, and the Governor and two of his personal guards followed Pauley to where she stood quaking in the aftermath of the violence. The boy ran to her and clung to her skirts, sobbing fiercely.

"Madam, is thy person unharmed?" Ogilvy said, his face blanched with horror. "What happened?"

"We must leave this place at once," Taylor breathed when she could find words to express her outrage. "They . . . they think I'm a witch. They were . . . going to kill us both."

"Duncan!"

The call came from far away and yet he heard it distinctly. "Duncan!" It sounded again, louder, more urgent. Terrified.

Duncan jolted out of the narrow bunk, his feet thudding against the planks of his cabin. He was shaking and cold and dripping the sweat of fear. Nightmare. It was only a nightmare, he told himself, but the premonition that engulfed him was so strong it sickened him.

Taylor had called his name.

Taylor was in terrible danger.

He rubbed his hands across his face, trying to remember what he'd seen in his dream. There had been fire, and shouts, and the sound of rocks hitting against other rocks.

Duncan threw on his heavy cloak, donned his boots and climbed up the companionway to the deck into the black pre-dawn of the ship's second day at sea. His first mate was at the helm, giving Duncan his first respite in over twenty-four hours. Maybe he was so tired he was hallucinating.

Duncan!

The cry echoed again in his ears, a memory from the dream. But it was too strong, too clear, to be an hallucination. Taylor was calling for him. He felt it to the marrow of his bones.

"Can't you make this thing move any faster?" he groused at the mate.

"Sails is trimmed t' th' best, sir," the man answered, and when Duncan looked up, he knew his mate spoke the truth. The sails were full and as well-trimmed as they were capable of being. The wind was brisk, with no hint of a storm. The sea was as flat as the North Sea ever got. They should be flying, but he guessed that the heavy, old-fashioned ship was making less than five knots headway.

At this rate, it might take more than a week to traverse the distance that in the twentieth century would be a matter of hours in a modern vessel.

Duncan slammed his fist against the stern rail, every fiber of his body raging in frustration. Taylor's life was in danger. He was certain of it. And there wasn't a damned thing he could do about it.

Never in his life had he felt so helpless.

Before dawn broke, Taylor and Pauley bade a tearful farewell to Elizabeth Ogilvy. "Oh, my dears, I shall miss you terribly," the woman sobbed. "You have been such a blessing. How I hate those horrid people out there. . . ."

"Do not hate them, madam," Taylor said softly. "They know not what they do. They are driven by their fear. We shall see one another again, I am certain. In the meantime, Mrs. Grainger will bring our news one t' th' other.''

''Yes, yes, of course,'' the Governor's wife tried to sound as if she was consoled, but Taylor knew otherwise. The Governor's personal guards lifted the wooden chest between them, and the four crept out of the castle, retracing the path to the cave Taylor and Pauley had taken only a few hours before. When they came to the big rock, she and the boy glanced at each other, but they continued on, circumnavigating the boulder to the right-hand side and clambering on down to the sea.

The first rays of morning found them half way to Kinneff Kirk.

TWENTY-TWO

꒰

Duncan Fraser never thought he would become a pirate, nor that he would be gratified to be one. He had orders to scavenge for food and supplies before returning to Dunnottar, although after his unsettling dream, he was determined to sail straight for the castle instead. He regretted his return home would only provide the additional food he had stocked the vessel with in Amsterdam, but it would have to suffice. He could always make another scavenger run if he needed to, unless . . . he wasn't there.

Duncan had determined his course to run parallel to the Scottish coast, and when he'd spotted the merchant ship just off Scurdie Ness, he knew the fates were with him. He had come alongside her by night, issued one shot across her bow, and ordered the captain to surrender. Since the ship had little firepower with which to retaliate, his command was obeyed.

Duncan wondered if pirates in this time always had it so easy. . . .

The vessel was laden with a rich supply of victuals, precious cargo indeed for one semistarved, ocean-weary sea captain anxious to move on to the besieged Dunnottar Castle.

Duncan left his own vessel in the hands of his first mate and took over the helm of the merchant ship with a lightness of heart he had not felt since the beginning of this whole misadventure. "Dinna worry, Mr. Young," he said to the skipper, who was to be for a short time his prisoner. "Ye can have your ship back as soon as we make this delivery. Ye be a good Scotsman now, is it not true?"

The youthful captain of the vessel glowered at Duncan. "Aye, but that'll not save my skin when I return without th' goods I came for," he growled. "Th' lords in Edinburgh sent me with ample coin t' purchase these goods from far t' th' north of th' English threat."

"Th' lords in Edinburgh cannot have as desperately empty bellies as th' courageous patriots who defend their king and yours at yon Castle Dunnottar."

Under sail again, with fair winds and steady seas, the two vessels made good time, but still it seemed like an eternity until the call came from the crow's nest, announcing that Dunnottar Castle was in sight. Duncan climbed to the first spar and peered through the spyglass. A useless piece of equipment, he decided, unable to hold the fortress in his vision for the bobbing of the boat upon the waves. As they grew nearer, however, he saw with great relief that the royal standard still flew from the battlements. Governor Ogilvy had held firm!

And so far, so had the history books.

It was early March, and he knew that Cromwell's troops had likely moved their heavy artillery from Dundee by now, so he changed course to put farther out to sea until darkness would cover their return to the small cove protected by the cliffs and the castle. After this horrendous voyage at sea, he was almost home. Almost back to Taylor, in whose embrace he planned to drown himself. He wasn't about to take any action that might drown him in the sea instead.

Taylor, with hair of golden silk and skin as soft as a cloud, a lover who had captured his heart and his mind and his spirit as well as his body. Taylor, who had come so unexpectedly into his life and changed everything, forever.

Oh, God, he thought, clenching his fists. *Please let her be safe*. With any luck he would be reunited with her in a matter of hours, and nothing, he vowed, nothing except her own wishes to the contrary would separate them again.

The ensuing hours were a torment as they waited for nightfall. As they drew nearer, however, their arrival was heralded by those on the castle keep, and when they dropped anchor, they were confronted by the entire garrison on the steep hillside. The scene was like something out of a movie, with torches lighting the night, and primitive soldiers with bows at the ready. At first, he thought they were going to be attacked in a shower of arrows, but the soldiers held their fire. A small boat moved from the protection of the cave at the foot of the cliff, and he instantly recognized the stocky figure of Governor Ogilvy.

"Ahoy, Captain Fraser, and welcome!" said the Governor as the oarsman drew the skiff alongside the bigger ship. "We recognized not thy vessel until we sighted th' one behind. Pray tell, what hath ye brought us?"

"Good evening, sir," Duncan replied, relief washing through him. He smiled broadly. "I chanced upon this good ship laden with victuals just off Scurdie Ness, and I thought it imaginable that thy garrison might enjoy a bit of a feast tonight."

A cheer went up from those on shore who had heard his words from across the short distance. A warm, huge, welcoming smile saturated the governor's face. "Aye, Captain. Aye."

Duncan climbed aboard the tender and took a seat in the bow, leaving the off-loading of the ship to someone else. He'd fulfilled his duty. "Your Excellency," he said urgently to the governor. "My wife? Is she well? And the boy, did he recover?"

The cheer faded from Ogilvy's face. He did not answer immediately, and Duncan's heart turned cold in his breast. "Aye, sir," said the Governor at last. "They are both well, and safe . . . but . . . they are no longer at Dunnottar Castle."

Although the winds of March were brisk, they'd lost their wintry bite. The sun overhead was almost warm against Taylor's face as she walked along the shore toward her appointed dulse-gathering duties on the rocks far below Dunnottar Castle. She had been making this trek for almost two weeks now, and although her muscles had become accustomed to the long walk, she was tiring of the daily chore, finding the seaweed repulsive to harvest and even more so to eat. Mrs. Grainger had told her it was considered a delicacy to the people in the area, but Taylor had no taste for it. She'd never liked sushi either.

It wasn't the seaweed that kept her going, however. It was her pledge to her good friend Mrs. Ogilvy to complete the task she had agreed to, and the daily appearance on the shoreline was part of the plan. She had been stopped only once by a stray sentry from the Cromwellian army, but she had pretended to be deaf to his speech and frightened of his manner, until he gave her up for a harmless peasant woman trying to feed her family in these desperate times.

She always wore a disguise, a dreadful rag of a dress and a kerchief that completely covered her blonde hair. She wiped dirt on her face before she set out, and hunched over, haglike when she got within viewing distance of the troops. Thank God Duncan wasn't here to see her like this, she'd thought on more than one occasion. In her arms, she carried a heavy creel, a long, slender basketlike container into which she lay the slimy green seaweed with an odor that clung to her long after she'd handed her daily harvest over to the minister's wife.

As she approached the castle, Taylor stopped as she always did, behind the protection of a large boulder, and searched the horizon, still holding out hope that somehow, one day Duncan would return. But that hope faded as each day passed and there was no sign of an approaching ship. Her vigil grew shorter as winter turned to spring, as her heart slowly accepted the painful idea that Duncan had been killed, that she and Pauley were now alone, and that unless she somehow found a way back through the Ladysgate, she would spend the rest of her days in this harsh and primitive time.

She slopped in the water, bending to retrieve the dulse and tangles that floated in the shallows, starting her chore farther from the castle than usual. She was tempted to fill her creel and turn for home quickly, but then she remembered Governor Ogilvy's instructions: ''Repeat th' same actions every day. Make no changes. They will be watching. Fill thy creel almost t' th' top as ye arrive at th' castle, linger behind th' castle rock out of their view for a short time, then move back along th' shore more quickly, but not too hastily lest ye appear as if ye are fleeing.''

Heartsick, exhausted, grieving for a love she'd lost before she'd ever really known it, Taylor wanted nothing more than to flee altogether from this unbearable existence. She wanted to get back to her time, her apartment, her life, although she knew nothing would ever be the same again. It wasn't just that Pauley would change things, although his presence would definitely alter her lifestyle. But her life had been changed forever by another, a man who had given her the greatest gift of all . . . the ability to love.

If she could just hold him once again, and thank him for that unutterably precious gift. . . .

Governor Ogilvy had promised "Janet" that the time was approaching when they would make the daring attempt to rescue the Honours. His anxiety was rather anticlimactic for her, since she knew already that they would succeed, and that Mr. and Mrs. Grainger would successfully hide the crown, sword, and scepter in the church until the Restoration. However, she'd learned that although history proved the outcome, achieving it might be difficult, even dangerous. For that reason, and because she had come to the firm decision to try to return to her own time soon afterward, she was ready to get it over with.

Only one regret hung around her heart like a black cloud when she thought of returning to the twentieth century. Once she left this time, she believed there would be little hope of ever seeing Duncan again. The thought carved a thin line of pain around her heart. She let out a heavy breath and wiped her face with smudgy green, dulse-stained fingers, leaving grubby marks on her sun-burnished cheeks.

Taylor turned and peered up the steep, black cliffs to the castle ramparts, always heartened to see the royal banner flying in the stiff ocean breeze. How much longer would the Governor be able to hold out? History said spring, but that was not very specific.

She looked for her signal, a small red kerchief that would be lowered on a rope over this side of the castle wall, invisible to the army that surrounded the other three sides, that would indicate this was the day. But there was no kerchief.

Rounding a curve in the wall of the cliff that hid her completely from the view of the armed forces, Taylor's heart almost stopped. There, floating on the tide in the safe harbor of the small cove, were two sailing vessels.

And on the shore in front of her, standing tall and handsome, skin bronzed by the sun, was Duncan Fraser.

Governor Ogilvy had warned him about Taylor's appearance. "Thy Janet's not th' pretty lass ye left," he said, laughing incongruously at Duncan's dismayed expression. But he quickly explained. "We've disguised her t' make her as ugly and unappealing as possible. She looks, and smells, like a fishwife. So prepare yourself, Captain."

Even forewarned, Duncan would never have recognized her. She indeed looked like the hag the Governor had described. But dirty face and ragged clothes and all, she was the most beautiful sight he'd ever seen. And she was safe, and well, and almost in his arms. When she saw him, her eyes widened, and she dropped her creel and covered her hands over her mouth, muffling a squeal of surprise. His heart pounded as she ran into his arms.

"Oh, Duncan, you've come home! You're safe! Oh, my God. . . ." She kissed his lips a hundred times in between the hundred he returned to her.

"Dare I assume you've missed me?" His voice was ragged, catching on the tightness in his throat.

"Miss you? Oh, my God, yes, I missed you! I thought you were dead! Oh, Duncan, this has been so horrible. . . ."

"Shhh," he said, holding her against him, feeling her slight body quivering against his massive one. "Mrs. Ogilvy told me what happened." He raised her head and traced the outline of her face with his fingers. "Tell me you are unharmed. They didn't physically. . . ."

"They threw some rocks, that's all."

Fury at his "kinsman" and the rest of the villagers burned in his guts. "Rocks! How did you get away from them?"

He was astounded when she began to laugh. "I gave them

what they wanted. I pretended to be a witch.'' When she told him how she had worked her ''magic,'' he was both impressed at her quick-witted ingenuity and horrified that she'd had so little with which to defend herself.

''Taylor, I am so sorry I wasn't there for you.''

She put her finger against his lips, as she had once before, when they had first kissed in front of the fire at the crofter's lodge. ''A man's gotta do what a man's gotta do,'' she whispered with a smile, and this time, her words held no trace of anger and bitterness. ''I mean it, Duncan. I understand that you had to make that trip, and I respect you for going. It's because you're that kind of man that I. . . .''

Duncan's heart leapt, and he held his breath in hopeful anticipation. ''You what?''

Her eyes searched his for a moment, and he saw her swallow. ''I . . . love you.'' Duncan closed his eyes and kissed her forehead.

''You don't know how I have longed to hear that from you,'' he whispered. ''Because I have loved you since the beginning of this crazy ordeal.''

Their lips met again in the tentative, gentle kiss of friends turned lovers, but it quickly became a hungry, passionate declaration of the love that had gone for so long unspoken. At last she drew away, breathless.

''Duncan, what's to become of us? Can we ever get out of here? I mean really *out*, back to our own time?''

Tossing away the rag of a cap she wore, Duncan entwined his fingers in the golden richness of her hair, wishing he had a more positive answer for her. ''I'm not certain about getting back to our own time. We can try. But I promise you, if you want to leave the Graingers' house, I'll confiscate Mr. Young's boat for good. It is sound and will take us to someplace that is safer than the here and now.''

''What about Pauley? At one time, you said you didn't think it was a good idea to take him back into the twentieth century, but Duncan, if we try to go home, I can't leave him here.''

''Neither can I.'' He saw the relief on her face and knew how much the boy had come to mean to her.

Then she gave him a doleful look. "And I can't go any-where until I've helped rescue the Honours of Scotland."

In his fervor to be with Taylor again, Duncan had almost forgotten about the plan Governor Ogilvy had asked him to help with today. The plan in which Taylor played a crucial role. Was this the reason *she'd* been forced back in time? he thought suddenly. Was she assigned the duty of smuggling the crown, sword, and scepter out from beneath Cromwell's very nose? Was she the peasant woman collecting dulse he'd read about in history who hid the regalia beneath the seaweed and walked the ten miles to Kinneff Kirk with her heavy load?

The concept boggled his mind. But if not Taylor, then who? If not now, then when?

As if on cue, tiny pebbles rained down from above. "What the heck?" Taylor craned her neck and saw far above her the tiny speck of a figure attempting to get their attention. "There's the kerchief," she said, pointing to a red dot waving on a rope high above them. "It's time."

Dunbar Castle
27 April 1567

There are times when we wish we had never left France. Being the queen dowager and under the control of Catherine de Medici, a fate we once abhorred, surely would have been more desirable than that which we have suffered of late. Our despair envelopes us like a fog, and we are unable to think clearly. We no longer have the will to fight back, or to make sensible decisions, and we despise our weakness.

We have succumbed to Bothwell's scheme to take control of Scotland. We had privately negotiated for an agreement between us, that we would marry him in re-turn for his absolute loyalty and protection in these times of terror and uncertainty. We had agreed that upon leav-ing Stirling and our visit to our son James, he would meet us at the Bridges, appearing to protect us from some harm that lay in store in Edinburgh. We believed in his loyalty and entrusted our person to him, allowing him to take the bridle of our horse and lead us away to Dunbar. Once the castle doors were shut behind us here, however, we have suffered the most degrading and reprehensible treatment, a betrayal by this once trusted ally so cruel, it has near taken away our mind. We accompanied Bothwell with no protest, as we agreed, and we had also agreed to marry him. But this was not enough. That first night, he came into our chambers and ravished our person and lay with us against our will. Although he spoke with words and answers gentle, still his doings were rude and uncalled for. He has forced us into a hasty marriage, in which there is no joy, indeed much fear and despair instead. We spend our days a prisoner of Bothwell, awaiting our return to Edinburgh with a melancholy we cannot shake. We wish that we were dead.

Robert Gordon laid the small book gently back onto the table and wiped his face with a large handkerchief. This was a story not found in most history books. Bothwell had raped the Queen. Gordon found himself surprisingly shocked and outraged, touched by her account that revealed her depression, humiliation, and fury. He'd never thought of Queen Mary, indeed of any royal person in history, as being like everyone else, human and vulnerable. But after his intense hours of translating Mary's diary entries, he felt as if he knew this woman intimately.

The Casket Letters had been shown to have been altered, their revised content used to condemn Mary to death for being a conspirator in her husband's murder. When the diary was made public, it would clearly prove otherwise.

As would the charge that she had wantonly run away with Lord Bothwell, a known accomplice in the king's death.

Gordon suspected the authenticity of the diary to be immediately challenged. After all, this was a major change in the modern view of history. Would he, as Taylor Kincaid's lawyer, be called upon to defend it in court?

Initially, the idea intrigued him. At last, his day in the sun. He would be in all the newspapers. On television. But what if he lost? What if he couldn't count on John Doggett's appraisal? Hell, he thought, I'm defeating myself before I've even begun. As always.

Robert Gordon sat down heavily in the chair and picked up the diary again, thinking that he never should have become a lawyer.

TWENTY-THREE

⤳

Electric excitement coursed through Taylor as she leaned back into Duncan's arms and together they watched the drama begin. From on high, a bundle began its slow descent, bumping against the rock walls, snagging every so often until the dispatchers managed to free it and move it along its way.

"Can you believe this is happening?" she breathed, wishing for all her life that Barry and Rob and her camera equipment were here. Camera. Oh, dear, she thought. She'd brought the camera, as she had every day since she'd begun her hikes to Dunnottar, but with Duncan here, she was hesitant to use it, knowing he did not want to risk exposure of such high-tech sorcery. But that sorcery had saved her life. Besides, no one was there to witness her photography except the two of them, and she'd never have another chance to record this remarkable episode in history in which they somehow were playing a vital part. She wriggled away from him and reached beneath her skirts.

"Something I can help with?" Duncan remarked with a wicked grin.

"Later," she promised with an equally provocative smile. Achieving her goal, she brought the small black box into the daylight. "Right now, I have a job to do."

"You've got to be kidding me," he muttered, seeing what she was about to do. "Don't you ever give up? Have you had that thing with you all along? Don't you realize what danger that could have put you in? Still could?"

"Don't you realize you ask too many questions?" she shot

back, aiming the camera at the descending bundle. "Here it comes!" She snapped off one shot. She had eighteen left on the roll. Enough to document this entire procedure and have some left over. She felt a surge of the gratification she used to enjoy from her job, capturing an exciting story on film, except this was a real life story unlike anything anyone else would ever photograph. "This is going to be great!" she exclaimed.

But when she turned to Duncan, his expression was both angry and exasperated.

"What's the matter?" she demanded. "We're safe enough down here. There's no one around to see this. . . ."

"What are you planning to do with that film?" he asked.

Taylor looked at him as if he were nuts. "What do you think? I'm a television producer. This is the story of a lifetime. Several lifetimes maybe. If I can just bring back proof. . . ."

But she broke off as Duncan placed his hands on her shoulders. "You can't do that."

"Why not?" Her cheeks grew warm. She'd forgotten the God-complex side of this man. "Who are you to say what I can and cannot do? It's my camera. My career."

"This is not some damned travelogue, Taylor," he growled. "What if you produce a show, and some of your 'lunatic' fans decide to follow in your footsteps? What do you think might happen?"

Taylor sniffed. She started to lash out at his high and mighty attitude, but his questions unsettled her. What indeed would happen if some viewer, or lots of them even, descended upon Stonehaven, hired the likes of Fergus McGehee to take them to the Ladysgate and took this little vacation back into time? How many would perish on the rocks before they got here? How many would burn as witches after they arrived?

Her shoulders slumped, and she was decidedly put out with Duncan for bursting her balloon. "I suppose you're right," she admitted, "but I'd still like to photograph this rescue, if for no other purpose than to put the pictures into my personal scrapbook. Maybe under 'Adventures I Have Survived.' "

Duncan gave her an understanding squeeze. "I know it's hard."

The bundle reached them, falling with a metallic clunk onto the rocks. Together, they carefully untied the rough cloth that had been formed into something resembling a gunnysack, exposing to the light of the hazy spring day the crown and the scepter, ancient relics of the kingdom of Scotland.

"Holy man," Taylor murmured, awestruck at the sight. "I'm supposed to put that crown under the seaweed?" The purple velvet of the bonnet had faded, but still, it was royal fabric, not something one slings lightly into a creel full of slimy dulse.

"Well, I don't think they mean for you to wear it out of here," Duncan replied wryly. But it was with equal awe that he removed the crown and the scepter from the bag. He pulled on the rope to signal the Governor to raise it again to the castle, where he would attach its next delivery, the sword of state. Then he looked at Taylor, relenting of his objections. "Go ahead," he conceded, holding up the two pieces of the regalia. "I'll say cheese."

Duncan had made his point, and even though she didn't like it, he doubted if she would follow through with her plans for producing a television show featuring their little adventure back in time. *If* she made it back to a time that had television. So he posed for her camera.

But even as he did, he was struck by the differences in their lives. She was an American woman committed to a glamorous career. He was just a lonely Scotsman living in a house filled with tormented memories. And Pauley . . . a deaf, mute orphan from the seventeenth century. Could they make some kind of sense of it all, when, and if, they returned to their own time?

For the first time since he'd vowed to himself they would always be together, Duncan suffered doubts.

"Get the creel," he said when she had taken the photos she wanted. He nodded to the basket, which in all was over three feet in length and a foot wide. Taylor brought it to him, and together they knelt on the rocks and arranged the regalia as best they could beneath the smelly seaweed.

"Where's a Ziploc when you need one?" Taylor remarked, making a face when Duncan loaded a handful of the dulse over the crown.

"In the big picture, it won't make a bit of difference that this velvet gets ruined," he replied with a grin. "I saw this crown once when I took the boys to Edinburgh Castle. It got a bright new red bonnet only a few years back, and. . . ." He caught himself in mid-sentence, startled at what had just happened. He had spoken about his sons, easily and without a shred of the grief that formerly had accompanied his memories of them. He had felt happy when he'd recalled their trip together, rather than filled with the ashen gray despair that before had always tightened his gut.

"What's wrong?" Taylor glanced up at his sudden silence.

He looked at her for a long moment, then drew her into his arms, and an indescribable sense of peace settled over him. They would make it work. They had to. Because their love had made it possible for him to live again. Taking a strand of her now very long hair between his fingers, he tucked it behind her ear. "Nothing," he said, bending to kiss her tenderly. "Nothing at all. . . ."

Their embrace was interrupted suddenly by a clanking sound, and they looked up to see the bag coming down again like a lumpy dumbwaiter. "Let's get this over with." Duncan stole one more kiss before the parcel reached them. "I'm ready to get on with life."

Taylor took his hands in hers, her touch sending an electric jolt up his spine. "Me, too," she replied emphatically. "The way I figure, we have a lot of good years ahead of us. Over three hundred and fifty by my reckoning."

The sword presented more difficulty in hiding than had the other two pieces of the regalia, for it was over a yard in length and enclosed in a stiff scabbard that was even longer. "This will barely fit in the basket," he said, turning it in various positions to try to make it fit. "No one would probably notice from a distance, but if you should be stopped, it wouldn't take

much to discover that you are carrying more than seaweed."
Then he remembered something from his schoolboy history
lessons. "I have to bend it."

"What?" He could see that Taylor was mortified at the
thought. "You can't bend the Scottish sword of state."

"Watch me."

"Duncan! No!"

He turned and kissed her lightly. "Dinna worry, my good
lass," he said, reverting to the Scots dialect. " 'Tis part of
history. Ye shall see when we visit th' sword again, long in
th' future." He saw Taylor shake her head in resignation but
wasn't surprised when she took his picture as he bent the
sword and scabbard in two places, allowing it to nestle perfectly along the bottom of the creel.

The time had come both had dreaded, when Taylor must
leave him and make her final trek southward to Kinneff Kirk,
where these treasures would lie, safe from the desecration of
the pillaging English until the monarchy of Britain was restored. "Why don't you let me do this for you?" he said,
despising the danger Taylor would be in until she reached
Kinneff. But he realized immediately the impossibility of taking her place. The soldiers were used to a peasant *woman*, and
even if he were to don her dress, he would never pass for a
female.

"I'll be fine," Taylor assured him, replacing the camera in
its bag beneath her skirts.

"I wish you'd stop that," Duncan tried to keep his voice
light.

"What?"

"Raising your skirts like that. You can't imagine what it
does to me."

Taylor didn't lower her skirt after she had zipped the bag,
but rather leaned back against the rock wall of the cliff and
with a saucy grin, struck a chorus girl pose. "Why don't you
show me?"

"Cut that out!" Duncan looked at her, wanting with all his
heart to take her up on her invitation, but time was critical to
her safety. "You must leave. Now! You've already lingered

longer than the soldiers are accustomed to you being here.''

The humor left her expression and her shoulders sagged. ''I suppose you're right.'' Then she brightened again. ''Raincheck?''

The final entry in the diary was scrawled across the pages in a shaky, unstable hand, as if it had been written in great haste. Robert Gordon knew enough of history to guess what the translation might reveal, and his heart was heavy as he began:

Holyrood Palace
16 June 1567

We take great risk in writing this, for we expect at any moment our gaolers will appear. We hold out hope that the Hamiltons will rally to us, but our future looks bleak, as Lord Bothwell has fled to Dunbar, and we have become the prisoner of our lords, to whom we surrendered in good faith and who have now treated us so grievously. What have we done to deserve this end? We sought nothing more than to rule Scotland in peace and decency. Yet through our misplaced trust in Moray, loathesome brother, and Maitland, who will not raise his eyes to us, and the rest, we have fallen prey to the avarice and greed we saw in their eyes the day they knelt and declared their fealty to us. They were liars then, and they remain liars to this day.

Mark this, that when we are free again, and we will not believe it could be otherwise, we will hang and quarter every one of these treasonous savages. Our Holy Father, forgive us.

We turn this book into the safekeeping of Mary Seton, our beloved, loyal Marie, for it is the only record that we have with which to defend our thoughts and actions when so many lies have been spread about us, our letters having been stolen, along with their silver casket. Mary S. also has the Scottish Rose and our letter expressing our wishes for it to be joined to the Honours. It must survive, even if we do not. The Scottish Rose is our hope, our prayer for Scotland. It must not perish, but must fulfill the destiny for which we have suffered so much—Peace in Scotland, and unity. An end to the hatred and deceit, even if it means the death of those who continue to perpetrate these abominations amongst us. We shall rise again. We shall be strong again. We shall reign v——

The ink smeared at this point, almost wiping to the edge of the page, and in his mind's eye, Gordon saw a terrified young queen hastily drop her pen and hand off the book to her trusted Mary Seton before her "gaolers" took her away to be imprisoned in the gloomy castle on an island in the middle of Lochleven. The Mary who had just written these words obviously believed she would be freed and would reign again as Queen of Scots. But Gordon knew it was not to be. She would never see Mary Seton again. Or wear the crown. Or hold the sword or scepter. She would be free again, but only for a short time, after her escape from Lochleven, when she made her final fatal error in judgment and trusted her future, indeed her life, to her jealous cousin, Elizabeth.

Robert Gordon was duly overwhelmed with the remarkable history lesson he had just translated. In little over twenty-four hours, he had come to know, and respect, the queen whom historians had often treated poorly. Perhaps he would be the agent responsible for restoring Mary to her deserved respect in history.

He looked at his watch. It was almost time to meet the antiquarian. It was Doggett's turn to decide if the diary was authentic.

But in Robert Gordon's mind, there was no doubt.

TWENTY-FOUR

⤳

Duncan's eyes followed Taylor until she became only a tiny speck at the base of the black cliffs on the far side of the cove. She did not turn, nor wave, as they had agreed, for if the enemy noted her progress, her farewell would give away that she had had a rendezvous with someone from the castle. He felt as if his heart was being torn physically from him when she disappeared behind the rock formation. He closed his eyes and sent up a silent prayer that she would make her way safely back to Kinneff Kirk with her heavy load.

He believed she would, because he'd learned to believe that, at least in this matter of the Honours of Scotland, history had been recorded correctly.

There was nothing he could do now but wait. Seated on a flat rock, he leaned back against the cliff wall and allowed his thoughts to consider Taylor Kincaid and what, if any, future they might share. He wanted to marry her, but was she interested in getting married? She was such a beautiful woman with an obviously healthy sexuality. How had she remained unattached for all of her thirty-three years? Surely, she must have had men lined up and could have taken her pick. She must have *chosen* to stay single. But why? Was her career really all that great? And if it was, could he compete? He had nothing special to offer her, except a love that would be true and a husband she could always count on. Would it be enough?

It seemed to Duncan as if they were living in some kind of a storybook world at the moment, complete with kings and castles and crowns, and he wondered, when she returned to her real life, would this princess leave him for good? Was their love only make-believe, or would it last for all those years Taylor said she believed awaited them . . . ?

Not wishing to return to the castle and the miserable plight of those therein, Duncan spent the afternoon with thoughts of his hopes for a future with Taylor comingling with plans of how to make their escape. At last the sun dropped behind the western horizon, throwing its rays eastward to deflect in rosy, golden splendor against whipped cream clouds piled high into the sky. This celestial delicacy was itself then reflected in the quiet waters of the cove, where peacefully at anchor lay their best hope for escape. Could he pull it off?

At deep twilight, Duncan ascended the narrow path to the castle and made his way as quickly as possible to the dining room. He was anxious to conclude his negotiations with Governor Ogilvy, but he joined the small group gathered at one end of the long table, enjoying their first good meal in months and celebrating the successful scheme they had pulled off in smuggling the Honours out of the castle. Ogilvy stood when Duncan entered.

"Come in, come in! We were hoping you would arrive in time for this wonderful repast for which we have you to thank!"

Duncan bowed. "I am honored, sir," he replied, and took a seat opposite Elizabeth Ogilvy, who looked at him expectantly.

"Well," she said with unconcealed delight. "Was Janet surprised to see you? Did things . . . go as planned?"

With a hint of amusement, Duncan winked at the woman. "Aye, Madam, and better."

She tittered into her napkin. "Captain, I am filled with hope. Now that th' Honours are rescued, and ye are safely returned, surely th' next good news will be that our lookout will sight th' King's ships coming t' save us!"

The amusement fled from Duncan's face. How he wished he could reassure this steadfast woman that her hopes would be fulfilled, but indeed, he knew just the opposite, that the King's ships would not sail for Dunnottar Castle, that her husband would eventually be forced to surrender, and that when General Overton discovered that Cromwell had been cheated once again of the Honours of Scotland, Dunnottar would be ravaged of all its rich treasures.

He would not allow himself to think about the fate that lay in store for this valiant governor, nor especially for this good woman, Elizabeth, who had so befriended "Janet" and Pauley. He could barely stand to meet her eyes. He turned instead to her husband. "May I have a word with ye, Governor, after dinner?"

"Ye can have anything ye want, Captain. Ye are th' hero of th' day."

Duncan did get everything he wanted. And the Governor's blessing as well. "Godspeed, Captain Fraser," he said, overcome with emotion. "We thank ye for all that ye hath done for us. Thy work here is completed. Go, with my blessings, and sail away with thy wife and th' bairn t' a safer harbor than ye hath known at Dunnottar."

Duncan was seized by the urge to encourage the Governor and Mrs. Ogilvy to come with him, to escape the grim destiny that awaited them. But he reminded himself of the dangers he perceived in meddling with history. Their fate was written already. History had assigned them their roles, just as it apparently had to he and Taylor, but unlike the two visitors from the future, the Ogilvies had not yet completed their performance.

At midnight, by the light of an almost full moon, Captain Duncan Fraser, along with the skipper and crew of the ship he had commandeered, hoisted its anchor and slipped out of the cove and into the moon-washed waves of the North Sea. Once out of range of Cromwell's heavy artillery, Captain Fraser ordered the skipper to head south.

"Ye'll soon have thy vessel returned to thy command," he assured Mr. Young, who upon learning that Duncan was sailing to rescue his "wife" and child, eagerly joined the cause.

Duncan, however, did not fill him in on the details of the final plans for their voyage.

*　*　*

The muscles in Taylor's arms shook from the strain of carrying her heavy burden, but she reached the kirk at Kinneff just at sundown.

"Aye, Mr. Grainger, she has come!" A cry of delight and relief fell through the open windows of the manse as Mrs. Grainger rushed out to greet her. "Ye were so late today, we began to worry. . . ."

Taylor handed her the basket, watching in weary merriment the look on her face when the weight of it almost toppled her to the ground. The minister hurried toward the women.

"Are ye safely returned, madam?"

"Look, husband, at what she hath returned with." Mrs. Grainger handed him the basket in turn. His eyes grew large when he realized what he held in his hand and remained like saucers when he raised them to Taylor. "Doth ye mean. . . ."

"Aye, sir," Taylor said in exhausted triumph. "'Tis done."

"Thy toil is done, daughter," he replied gravely, "but ours hath only begun.

"Where is Pauley?" Taylor was eager to attempt to explain to the boy that Duncan had come back. The child had been ill when he left, and when Pauley recovered, he had not understood totally about the disappearance of the man to whom he had become so attached. Taylor had used the toy boat as an illustration, trying to convey that Duncan had gone to sea, but she realized that Pauley had no concept of there being a shore on the other side of the water, a place called France. When the child looked out to sea, all he saw was an infinite ocean. Taylor was unsure if she hadn't just made matters worse, for she had caught the boy on a number of occasions staring out toward the sea, a look of deep melancholy on his face.

She found him now milking the cow. Somehow, a bond had formed between the human child and the animal, although neither could speak. Pauley knew the milk he thirsted for came from the cow, and Mrs. Grainger had shown him how to squirt it into the pail. Taylor suspected Pauley got as much satisfaction from petting the warm, generous beast as he did from drinking her milk. The child was starved for love and sought affection wherever he could. Her heart skipped for joy, convinced that somehow, someway, she and Duncan would provide him with a better life in the future.

"Pauley," she said, touching his shoulder. The boy's face lit up when he saw her, and he jumped into her arms. "Hey, kid, have I got some news for you," she whispered. Taylor carried Pauley into the room they shared and picked up the toy boat. She made the same motions she had when trying to explain Duncan's departure, only this time, she turned the boat and headed it toward Pauley. But the boy just looked at her blankly.

She set him down and replaced the toy on the windowsill. Maybe it was just as well. How could she explain that Duncan had come back, but not to them? At least not yet.

And how could she tell him that she didn't know when they'd see him again? Or what they would do when they were reunited? Duncan had said he would take them away from here. But where would they go? Would he attempt to take them back through the Ladysgate? Or would they have to settle for a new life in this time, somewhere out of harm's way?

Either way, she hoped they would leave soon. She was tired and lonely, and she wanted to be with Duncan once again.

Returning Pauley to his milking, Taylor helped Mrs. Grainger clean the seaweed from the regalia. The bonnet, she thought after scrubbing it with her best efforts, would never be the same again. They placed the three pieces beneath the mattress at the bottom of the Graingers' bed for the moment, wanting them out of sight in case Taylor had been followed.

But later that night, working by the glow of a single rushlight, the minister, his wife, and Taylor dug up a pavement stone squarely in front of the pulpit.

"They'd be less likely t' look in th' most obvious place," Mr. Grainger declared. They placed the crown and the scepter into the hole and covered them with a cloth, then replaced the stone, dusting it and arranging it so when they were finished, it looked undisturbed.

The sword was situated in a similar grave at the west end of the kirk beneath some "common saits" as the reverend called them. To Taylor, they were very reminiscent of modern-day church pews. This work was accomplished in almost complete silence, the three intent on finishing the task as rapidly as possible lest anyone discover their royal secret.

By the time Taylor crept into the bed beside Pauley, the large silver disc of the moon shone brilliantly through her window, and she wondered just before she drifted off into much-needed sleep if Duncan was looking at the same moon and longing for her as fiercely as she was for him.

She awoke the next morning to the sound of the wind lashing the budding tree branches outside her window. Gray clouds portended an early spring storm. Over a breakfast of oats and milk, Taylor told the Graingers about Duncan's return to Dunnottar in a ship he had "commandeered"—he seemed to like that word better than "stolen"—and that he had brought much needed food to the castle. They wanted to know if she was going to return to the castle now that he was back, but she shook her head. "I'll not place Pauley in that danger again," she replied. "As for my . . . husband, I shall hear from him in time," she said, ignoring the looks on their faces that questioned a wife's decision to remain apart from her husband. "This he promised me, and I await his will.".

Early in the afternoon, Taylor was alone, the Graingers having gone out, braving the rainstorm to go about their missionary work. She was wiping the plates and cups from the noon meal when she heard the sound of horses' hooves beating rapidly toward their door. "Oh, Christ," she uttered a low curse. "How did they find out so fast?" Quickly, she gathered Pauley and ducked into the dark, stablelike room that was cordoned off from the back part of the house with a curtain. "Move over," she nudged the cow, crawling beneath it, hoping it wouldn't kick them.

And there they crouched, Taylor's heart slamming against her chest, her arms clasping Pauley in a death-grip. At any moment, she expected to hear the rough voices of Cromwell's men, searching for her and the treasure she had stolen from them right beneath their noses. She heard a knock on the door.

Polite raiders, she thought, not expecting such courtesy from what she'd heard of the troops. The door opened with a small squeak, and over the sound of the wind, she heard the thud of boots on the planked floor.

And she couldn't believe what she heard next!

"Janet! Janet Fraser, are you in here?" Duncan's deep voice boomed through the tiny manse.

"Duncan!" she whispered, her heart flooding with joy. She grabbed Pauley's hand. "C'mon," she said, dragging the thoroughly confused child out from under the cow. Still cautious, she peered around the edge of the curtain. Filling the room with his presence, Duncan Fraser looked around him in curiosity and dismay, obviously thinking the place deserted. But before he could call out again, Pauley saw him and dashed from his hiding place and into the large, strong arms that he knew would protect him.

Taylor wasn't far behind.

"How did you get here? Where did you get horses? How did you get out of the castle?" Breathless with relief and excitement, she shot questions as fast as bullets. Duncan laughed and embraced her with his free arm, kissing her soundly. "Now you're the one asking too many questions." Then he grew serious. "Come quickly. We have only a short time before the tide leaves us stranded in Catterline."

"You came by boat? What boat?"

Duncan nodded through the window at the other rider who was holding the two horses beneath the shelter of a large tree in the yard. "Yon skipper, Mr. Young, continues to cooperate with me. It was his ship that brought me to Dunnottar. It will be his ship that will hopefully get us out of here." He brought something out of his coat pocket, a scrap of material that looked vaguely familiar to Taylor. "Governor Ogilvy said you had taken all our belongings with you in the chest. Are they here?"

Taylor knew what he meant. He was talking about all their twentieth-century belongings, such as the medicine box. "Yes, they are still in the chest, in our room." She followed Duncan, who had to bend low to enter through the cramped doorway.

He opened the chest and placed the orange plastic container into the sack, which Taylor recognized now to be the same as was used the day before to lower the regalia to the beach. She laughed at the irony.

"What else?" Duncan asked.

Taylor reached over him to the bottom of the chest and she brought out her jeans, sneakers, sweaters, and the waistline pouch. "Can't forget this," she said with a grin, dropping it into the gunnysack. The rest of her things were of this century, and she would not miss them.

"Let's go," Duncan said, taking Pauley beneath the oversized cloak he wore. Taylor donned her own mantle, and the three of them headed for the door. Taylor paused a moment and looked back into the room.

"I wish I could have said good-bye."

TWENTY-FIVE

Duncan noted that instead of subsiding, the tide had risen almost two feet from the time they'd borrowed the horses and left Catterline to fetch Taylor and Pauley. The strong offshore wind fought their efforts to row to Skipper Young's vessel that rocked violently on the waves, testing the endurance of the line and anchor. It took every ounce of his strength to hold the small tender alongside the larger boat so that the woman and child could board safely, but Taylor's courage and determination added to his physical efforts, and together, they all managed to climb the raggedy rope ladder onto the rain-soaked wooden decks.

"Weigh anchor, skipper, and take her north again," Duncan commanded.

Mr. Young looked at him askance. "In this storm, sir, it will be dangerous to attempt to return to Dunnottar."

"We're not going to Dunnottar," Duncan replied. "Set sail, and I'll return to take the helm shortly."

He guided Taylor and Pauley down the companionway to the relative warmth and safety belowdecks. "You two stay here," he said. "It's dangerous for you to come on deck."

Taylor shoved the hood of her cloak from around her head and shook her wet hair. "Don't you think it's too dangerous to set out in this storm? I mean, we've waited this long, can't we wait for better weather?"

Duncan considered this, but only for a moment. "You want to get back through the Ladysgate, don't you?"

"The Ladysgate! Is that where . . . ?"

"We're going to try." His face was grim. "Stay below and take care of Pauley. I'll come for you when it's safe."

Duncan returned to the storm-ravaged deck and took the helm from a white-faced Mr. Young. "Don't worry," he reassured the boat's rightful skipper, "Ye'll have your ship back soon enough."

He prayed he was right. As a ship's captain, Duncan Fraser was not a risk-taker. Safety was his watchword at sea, but what he was about to attempt was anything but safe. But it was, he thought, their only chance. The tide, already high because of the full moon, was running even deeper with the storm and the wind. Maybe, just maybe. . . .

Several hours later, he heard a cry from above. "Ahoy, captain," shouted the lookout from the crow's nest. "Yon lies th' Ladysgate." Duncan closed his eyes.

God curse the Ladysgate.

But then he took up the spyglass and searched the shoreline for some sight of the *Intrepid*. Was it still there? Still stranded? Or had Cromwell's army come upon the "monster," as he felt such a vessel would be considered by people of this day. Had they, in their ignorance and fear, dismantled it? Set fire to it?

Through the slanting rain, the arch of the Ladysgate grew larger as the ship approached. And as it grew nearer, Duncan's pulse pounded and a smile etched itself firmly into his face. Ahead of them, he could see the *Intrepid*, apparently intact. But instead of standing on dry land, waves now lapped around its base. But was the water high enough to float the heavy vessel? They would soon find out. . . .

He turned the helm over to the skipper with directions for his point of sail, then went below.

"We're almost there," he said, sitting on a bunk beside Taylor, whose face was just this side of green.

"Thank God," she uttered. "I'm having a hard time holding it down. . . ."

Duncan took her face in his hands. "You look beautiful," he said, gazing into her eyes. "I love you, Taylor, and we're going to make it through this, if it's the last thing we do."

"It feels like it might *be* the last thing we do," she replied. "Where are we, and what's happening?"

"We're nearing the Ladysgate. We're going to try to go through it."

Her face went totally white. "In this storm? In this boat? Duncan, what are you talking about? The thing is on land, at least in this lifetime."

"Mother Nature seems to be lending us a hand," he replied with a mysterious smile, then explained that the storm tide was many feet above normal. For the first time, he saw hope light up her face.

Then he laid out his plan.

When the ship reached the point where Duncan felt it was endangered by the underwater rocks, he commanded the skipper to head into the wind and douse the sail, then drop anchor until they could safely get off the boat. "Your ship's your own, again, Captain, but I must take th' tender. I'll leave it secured ashore," Duncan said. "Unless," he added jokingly, "ye wish t' row us there."

Mr. Young straightened his shoulders. "I admire thy courage, Captain, although I do not understand thy actions. Take th' tender. I wish you Godspeed."

It took two sailors to bring the small boat that had been trailing behind the larger vessel alongside, and Duncan made the treacherous descent into the bobbing skiff. The gunnysack was lowered into the boat, then Mr. Young literally handed Pauley over the side and down into Duncan's arms. It was obvious from his wide eyes and stiffened muscles the boy was terrified, but he made no effort to resist. Taylor, who had changed into her jeans and sneakers, climbed down the ladder with clenched jaw and white knuckles, but at last, all were safely aboard, and Duncan took the oars in his powerful arms. It would be a rough row in to shore, but adrenalin pumped in his veins, and he gave himself no option to fail.

"Well, I'll be damned," he heard Taylor exclaim when they were several yards away from the vessel.

"What's wrong?"

"Nothing's wrong," she replied, a strange look on her face. "I just saw the name of the ship."

Duncan read the words painted on the ship's stern in tall, ornate letters: *Scottish Rose*.

Taylor's earlier seasickness rolled into a tight ball of fear in her stomach when she stepped into the pitching dinghy. She pulled Pauley tightly against her, feeling reassurance in the human contact, even the thin body of this child, and wondering who was calming whom. This was insane! They would all surely die out here in the freezing waters of the North Sea. Duncan Fraser was as irresponsible, she believed at the moment, as Fergus McGehee.

Turning to look back at the ship they had left behind, as if the sight of it would somehow quell her trepidation, she gasped in astonishment at the name on the stern. She'd never given any credence to coincidence, but this had her full attention.

She had rescued the Scottish Rose for Mrs. Ogilvy, and now, another Scottish Rose, it seemed, might have rescued her.

Taylor realized even as she pointed the name out to Duncan that she had never told him about the other Scottish Rose, or her midnight mission to secure it in the belly of the castle rock. Neither had she shared with him the photocopied letter which, although bedraggled from its experience, remained safely tucked away in the pouch. If they somehow miraculously survived this voyage, she would ask him about the rose chalice. Maybe he would know if it had ever been found. After all, she'd learned that it was a very real part of Scottish history.

But for now, she had enough to think about just to stay alive and keep Pauley safe through the upcoming danger.

"Look!" Duncan cried jubilantly. Over his shoulder, she could see the reason for his excitement, for where once it had been stranded on the sand, the *Intrepid* now floated on the tide.

When they reached the shore, Duncan quickly pulled the tender up onto the beach and handed Taylor and Pauley out onto solid ground. Although her knees shook, her relief was enormous. But she knew they were far from being out of peril. She scanned the shoreline, looking for any sign of a sentry, in case Cromwell's men had discovered the vessel and placed a guard around it. But there was no one in sight.

"Stay here," Duncan said, "I'll be right back."

She watched as he tugged the small boat up onto the shore and secured the line around the same boulder from which he detached the bowline of the *Intrepid*.

"Come on," he shouted urgently, dashing to pick up Pauley and guiding Taylor to the iron ladder that led to the deck of the boat. They scrambled up the steps, and Taylor felt the boat floating free from shore. "Put these on," he said, giving her two life jackets. "Sit here and hang onto Pauley." He almost shoved Taylor onto a seat in the shelter of the pilot house of the boat. She wouldn't have moved even if her terrified body had allowed her to do so.

She saw him turn the key, then press a button for a few minutes, and was alarmed when nothing happened. But a buzzer sounded from somewhere, and Duncan's face washed with relief. He pressed another button, and the engines roared to life. Pauley felt the vibrations, and he buried himself into Taylor. "Poor little guy," she called to Duncan. "He's scared out of his mind."

But she could tell Duncan's mind was on other matters. The engines had not been used in months, and at first they sputtered and faltered. But after several attempts, they began to hum with a steadier sound, and he shifted into reverse. "I just hope the water's deep enough to get us out of here," he muttered, almost to himself.

"But what about . . . aren't you going to try to go through the Ladysgate?"

Duncan looked up at her, his face more serious than she'd ever seen it. "That's what I mean. Out of *here*."

Taylor closed her eyes each time the boat scraped on a rock as Duncan steered as closely as he could to the land side of the granite arch. She tried not to think about Greta's prediction that they would not be able to go back into their own time. Instead, she thought of her film crew being safe and sound in the warmth of the Hook and Eye Lounge Bar, of the bed she would sleep in at the inn. She thought of airplanes, and Manhattan, and taxicabs, dinner at Sardi's. She remembered a playground near her apartment, and pictured Pauley in a swing there.

"Here we go," Duncan called out, just before Taylor felt a strong surge take hold of the *Intrepid*. To her horror, the engines died again, but the boat continued to make way nonetheless. "Hold on," he warned, grasping the wheel with all of his strength even though at the moment, he was not the one in control of the boat.

The Ladysgate seemed to have an energy all its own. Taylor felt the strength of its power like a rush of electricity shimmering through her body, and she feared for a moment that she was losing consciousness as darkness closed in around her. The smell and dampness of fog assailed her senses, and for an instant, she recalled that same sensation just before being thrown into the water from Fergus McGehee's boat.

Duncan continued to try to start the engines, but to no avail. The vessel pitched and rolled violently, sending the big man flying across the pilot house.

"Damn!" he swore, but he righted himself immediately and returned to the helm.

Pauley begin to cry. "Shhh," Taylor whispered to his ears that could not hear, wishing she had some better way to comfort this terrified child. She pulled him onto her lap and kissed the top of his head, soothing his cheeks with her fingers. "It's going to be all right. Everything's going to be okay." She signed "okay," and he looked up at her with eyes swimming in tears, his expression clearly revealing that he did not think anything was "okay."

Suddenly, the waves calmed and the boat drifted in deathly silence. Duncan glanced uneasily at Taylor. "What happened to the storm?"

She shrugged and said hopefully, "Went away?"

He tried again to start the engines. They both fired on the first try. "Yes," he uttered, "yes, baby."

She watched, her own terror subsiding, as Duncan Fraser

checked the compass and punched buttons that lit friendly dig-
ital numbers on a small white box above the nav station. He
shifted into gear. Slowly, he inched the throttle forward, and
she felt the boat gain inertia, traveling easily across the waters.
She held her breath, knowing that at any moment, they might
strike a submerged boulder. But she allowed herself a small
ray of hope, because their course was taking them directly out
to sea, and behind them lay the Ladysgate.

After more than ten minutes, Duncan slowed the boat and
put it in idle. He stepped out of the protection of the pilot
house to check the weather. "Taylor. Come here, and bring
Pauley."

They followed him onto the aft deck, and Taylor looked at
the sky in wonder. The heavens were crystal clear, with silvery
stars sparkling against a pitch black firmament. Above them
hung the brightest full moon she had ever seen.

"We've gone somewhere other than where we were," Duncan
said at last. "A storm like that one doesn't just dissipate in a
matter of minutes."

"Do you . . . think we've come . . . home?" Taylor's quiet
question reflected his own mix of hope and fear.

"I don't know." Duncan stepped back inside and picked up
the radio transmitter. "This is the crew boat *Intrepid*, calling for
a radio check. The vessel *Intrepid*, calling for a radio check."
His heart beat so hard in hopeful anticipation he thought it
might explode through his chest. The airways were silent, except for the familiar scratchy sound of the open receiver—the
sound that had completely disappeared when he had gone
through the Ladysgate the other way. Did that mean . . . ? But
he didn't have time to ponder further.

"Crew boat *Intrepid*, this is RNLI Stonehaven. Do you
read?"

Hearing the message, Taylor dashed back inside with Pauley
and threw her arms around Duncan. "We did it! We're back!"

Relief washed over him as solidly as the rain had doused
him earlier, and he encircled Taylor and Pauley, kissing them

and hugging them with all his might. "Yes, I think we're back."

"RNLI Stonehaven, this is *Intrepid*. Switch to channel nineteen." Quickly he moved the dial to a channel open for communication. "RNLI Stonehaven, this is the crew boat *Intrepid*. Do you read?"

"Loud and clear, Duncan. Where the hell are you, man?" Andy McDowell's brusque voice was brimming with undisguised anxiety. "Fergus McGehee's met with some serious trouble, and one of his passengers, that American lady television producer, was washed overboard near the Ladysgate. Her crew is here about to fall apart with worry. According to McGehee, he almost lost his boat in the search for her. Have you heard about any of this on the radio? Where have you been for the last two days?"

Duncan smiled down into Taylor's tear-streaked face. "Tell everybody to relax," he said. "She's with me, and she's safe. We'll be in port in less than half an hour."

TWENTY-SIX

꒰ᔆ

Robert Gordon put the last of the heavy legal books in the cardboard box and placed it outside the door to his office, marked for contribution to the law school from which he had graduated what seemed like eons ago. Once this business with Taylor Kincaid and the diary and old letter was cleared up, he was going to retire, at last.

At one minute past ten, his phone rang, sending his heart rate soaring. Could John Doggett have finished his appraisal so quickly?

"Gordon here. Yes. Yes, John. I see. Well, actually, yes I would. I can be there in half an hour." He hung up the phone, his mind reeling. They were the genuine articles, according to Doggett. Gordon trusted the antiquarian's judgment, even though he disapproved of the man's reputation for some rather unscrupulous "placements" of some of Scotland's most rare antiquities. But then, he thought, taking his umbrella and raincoat from the hall tree, glancing into his office one last time, turning out the light and closing the door behind him, who am I to disapprove of the way a man earns a living?

Taylor wanted to kiss the dock when Duncan eased the bow of the *Intrepid* against the pilings. She was overjoyed to see Barry and Rob, who greeted her with unabashed enthusiasm, their voices scared and excited and relieved all at once. Fergus McGehee was nowhere in sight.

"What happened?" Rob asked as they helped Taylor from the boat to the solid structure of the dock. "We looked all over for you.'' He paused and frowned. "You look . . . different. Like you've lost weight. And your hair. Was it that long when we left the other day?''

She hugged them both tearfully. "You ask too many questions,'' she laughed, realizing how different she must look. "I'm just so happy you two are okay. I've been worried sick. . . .''

"You've been worried!'' Barry replied. "You were the one who went overboard. We searched for you all along the coast, clear until dark yesterday. We went with the helicopter search team today, but we couldn't find any sign of you. I've never been so scared. Who picked you up?''

Taylor turned and saw Duncan step out of the pilot house with Pauley in his arms. Her heart surged with love and gratitude for this man who had touched her life in so many ways. How could she ever explain any of it? Duncan came to stand beside her, the look in his eyes reflecting feelings as deep as her own, and she felt an unspoken bond tighten between them. "Welcome home,'' he said wearily.

"Glad you're back, Duncan.'' Andy McDowell finished securing the lines and ran to his friend and fellow RNLI rescuer, shaking his free hand. "When'd you grow the beard?'' Then he saw Pauley. "Who's the lad?''

Taylor slipped her hand into Duncan's. How would they ever explain Pauley?

"It's a long story,'' Duncan replied, giving her hand a reassuring squeeze. "We're calling him Pauley,'' he replied, "and I'd bet right about now, he's a hungry lad.''

"When we got your message, we had Dave over at the Hook and Eye make up some hot coffee and sandwiches for you,'' Andy said. "They're inside.'' He gestured for them to follow him back to the small shack. "I didn't know about the lad, or I would've had him bring a soft drink or something.''

A soft drink.

Taylor thought about the implications of a can of soda. It was twentieth-century. Familiar. A common commodity, something everyone took for granted. And yet, this child had never seen nor heard of a Coke or a Pepsi or a Dr Pepper.

He'd never had anything to drink other than milk and water, as far as she knew. Pauley's first soft drink would be a Very Big Deal.

For the first time, anxious doubts that they had done the right thing for him gnawed at Taylor. Pauley would be as out of place in this time as she and Duncan had been in his. Was it fair to thrust this frail, young child from a time long ago into a time so foreign to him it might scare him to death? A child who could not even ask questions about what was going on around him, or hear the answers?

Her heart ached for all he faced, but there was no going back now.

They entered the brightly lit RNLI station, and Taylor saw the fear and confusion on his little face, and how he clung desperately to Duncan's neck. She also saw that Duncan did not try to disengage from his vise-grip, but instead patted him reassuringly on the back.

Somehow, they would do right by Pauley. Duncan took a seat at the small table and set the child on his knee. "The lad can't hear," he said, taking a half sandwich and offering it to him, signing for him to eat. Pauley scrunched up his face and gave Duncan a what-the-hell-is-this sort of look, and Taylor had to cover her mouth to keep from laughing. But she watched the child's reaction when Duncan demonstrated how to eat a sandwich, and saw the look of surprised delight when he sunk his teeth into the crunchy white bread layered with ham and cheese.

"Where'd he come from?" Andy wanted to know.

"We . . . uh . . . just happened upon him," Duncan began, flashing a look at Taylor that warned her not to go into the details of the trip through the Ladysgate. She smiled and gave him a slight nod, knowing that as fascinating a documentary as their adventure would make, she would never put it on film, for all the reasons Duncan had given her before, and for one very important reason that surmounted the rest . . . Pauley. She knew what would happen if tabloid TV got hold of a story about a boy from another century.

"Does he come from around here?" Andy pressed.

"He appeared very hungry and cold when we found him," Duncan evaded the question between bites of his own sandwich. "My guess is he's an orphan, or he's strayed from one of the remote farms and couldn't find his way back."

Taylor bit into her own sandwich which, after months of gruel and oats and other strange meals in their siege-starved existence, tasted divine. "We thought it would be better to bring him along than leave him to fend for himself."

"Shall I call for the authorities? They could take him to the children's home until they find his parents."

Taylor knew Andy McDowell was only trying to help, but the thought of Pauley being turned over to people, no matter how well-meaning, who had no idea of his true background, turned her to stone. "No!" Her word was an overreaction, and it brought startled stares from Barry and Rob, who had sat quietly by until now, content to let the refugees eat and rest.

"What are you going to do," Rob said with a cynical grin, knowing of Taylor's adamantly single lifestyle. "Adopt him?"

Duncan came to her rescue, which seemed as if it was becoming a habit. "I'll call the authorities in the morning, Andy," he said quietly, tousling the boy's hair. "But I think he's had quite enough adventure for one day. We'll . . . I'll keep him at my house tonight."

The young men didn't miss his slip-up. They exchanged quick glances, then Rob stood up, faking a yawn. "Well, now that we're all safe and sound, what's say we go back to the hotel and catch some MTV?"

Barry snickered. "Yeah. Right. Think I'll do some darts at the Hook and Eye. Wanna come, Taylor?"

To her dismay, Taylor flushed. She hadn't made plans for what she would do once the *Intrepid* brought them back to Stonehaven, much less what she would do with the rest of her twentieth-century life. But throwing darts with these two "lads" held no appeal whatsoever.

"Thanks, but I'll pass," she said, turning to Duncan. "I need to help Duncan . . . uh, Captain Fraser, with the boy. I'll catch up with you tomorrow."

"We still going to the Maidenstone?" Barry asked his boss. "Our equipment is all okay."

Taylor had to think a moment to remember what the Maidenstone was. A carved rock. A storyline. An object that at the moment seemed utterly meaningless. "No. No, we're not going anywhere for a while. Take the day off."

Duncan's house was dark when he and Taylor drove into the driveway. She held Pauley closely, wondering what the child thought about his boat ride aboard the powerful *Intrepid*, the electric lights that lit his native Stonehaven, the automobile that he rode in. His life had taken a quantum leap in the last twelve hours. She remembered how frightened and confused she had been when she arrived in seventeenth-century Stonehaven and knew he must feel the same. At least in his case, though, there were no horsemen carrying messages that the "bloody English" were about to pounce upon them. Nor was he in any way threatened by others, and was, in fact, loved and nurtured and comforted.

Surely, that would make a difference.

"Let me take him," Duncan said, coming to her side of the car and opening the door. He lifted Pauley into his arms and gave him a little kiss on the cheek. He nodded to Taylor. "Follow me."

He led her through a gate and up a flagstone path to the front door. "Reach under the mat, will you? I keep an extra key there."

She unlocked the door and flipped the light switch on the wall, flooding the entryway in a soft incandescent glow. Pauley jumped.

"It'll take him some time to get used to our conveniences," Duncan said, starting up the stairs with his bundle. "But I bet his transition is easier than ours. Wait till he learns about Nintendo."

Taylor followed him upstairs. He reached a closed door, and his long pause before he opened it told her how difficult this was for him. When he opened the door, she understood why. It was his own boys' room. Twin beds were covered with navy spreads trimmed in bright red with ships of all kinds printed on them in white. A yellow kite hung in one corner. A teddy bear sat on one pillow, a stuffed lion on the other. Her throat constricted painfully, and she wondered how Duncan was dealing with this.

"Turn down one of the beds for me, will you?" His voice was intense and husky.

"Don't you think he needs a bath first? And some pajamas?" she asked, nodding toward the boy's muddy feet and rain-soaked clothing.

Duncan laughed. "You and your bloody baths. Okay, okay. The tub's across the hall. Run him some water, and I'll try to make him understand that his new mum wants him to go to bed all scrubbed up."

Taylor slipped out of the room, her heart racing at what Duncan had just said. *His new mum. . . .*

But could she, should she, consider being Pauley's mother? When they were at Dunnottar Castle and later at the Graingers' house, she had fulfilled that role, not just because she loved the boy, but also because there was no one else there for him. But suddenly that seemed very long ago. Being reunited with Barry and Rob had brought her quickly back into the reality of the present day.

She had a life, a career, commitments which would be difficult to break. She was filled with questions. Taylor knew that she loved Duncan. She believed that he loved her. At least, they had shared a love three hundred and fifty years ago. But that was then and this was now. On this side of the Ladysgate, the differences in their lives were vast. Could their love ever be the same again? Could they find some mutual ground upon which to build a solid relationship? The thought of a committed relationship filled her with familiar anxiety, made worse by her suspicion that Duncan, who had tragically lost his sons, would want more children. When he learned of her barrenness, would he still want her?

The whole idea of motherhood scared her to death. It was fine to pretend to be a mother, in a crazy and inexplicable warp of time. But on this side of time, wouldn't it be better for Pauley to be adopted by someone more qualified than herself to be his mother?

Troubled thoughts and mixed emotions spilled through her as fast as the water ran into the tub, and her heart ached. Could they overcome all the obstacles that confronted them in this century?

She simply didn't know.

When the bath was drawn, she turned to go tell Duncan it was ready and jumped a foot when she saw him standing in the doorway, watching her. "You scared me." She put her hand to her chest and laughed nervously, as if he'd been listening to the unquiet conversation in her head. To her astonishment, she saw Pauley start to laugh, too. She'd never seen him laugh before, *really* laugh. Granted, it was a silent, squeaky sort of laugh, but it was filled with what she could best describe as . . . glee.

"What have you two been talking about? Did you scare me on purpose?" she teased.

"I told him, and I think he understands, that this is his home now. That we love him and will take care of him. That he will never be hungry again, and that he can have. . . ." Duncan's eyes misted over at this point . . . "the teddy bear and the lion."

TWENTY-SEVEN

❧

Duncan left Pauley to Taylor's scrubbing. He went back across the hall and entered the room that had belonged to Jonathan and Peter. It had taken every ounce of his courage to carry Pauley into that room, because that door had been closed, both literally and figuratively, for over four years. Duncan sat on the turned-down bed and ran his hands across the sheets. He supposed they were clean enough. He had had a friend in to make up the room sometime during those horrible days following the accident, and then he'd shut the door, trying not to think about the emptiness it held.

But bringing Pauley up the stairs, he knew it was time to open it again, and to open his heart to this other lad, not a child of his blood, but one who desperately needed him. Picking up the teddy bear, Duncan stroked it absently, turning over in his mind the incredible events that had occurred in the last few days, twentieth-century time, that he was certain had changed his life forever.

Could it have been only three nights ago, a little earlier than this, that he'd first seen Taylor Kincaid? The woman that tonight he hoped would agree to marry him? Could he seriously be considering adopting a child, a waif from a place so far away it boggled his mind?

The whole thing boggled his mind.

And, yet, the whole thing felt so right.

If Taylor felt the same way.

She had told him she loved him. But that had been three hundred and fifty years ago, in a time of tremendous stress and danger. Did she feel the same now? Would she tomorrow? Or would her career beckon to her once again, and would the call be strong enough that she would leave him and the boy?

Another doubt struck him. Suppose she chose to marry him and live in Scotland. What would she find attractive about a small town like Stonehaven after the excitement of living in New York City? Would she become bored and eventually leave him? He'd rather she'd not stay in the first place.

Exhaustion and gnawing uncertainties began to draw him into a downward spiral of apprehension, sapping his earlier exhilaration at having arrived safely back in their own time. With a weary sigh, he replaced the teddy bear on the pillow. It had all seemed so much simpler seen from the past.

From across the hall, he heard Taylor talking to Pauley as if the child were able to hear every word, and he knew she was signing to him in the private language they'd developed between them. They had grown close during their time together, but what did Taylor really think about becoming his adoptive mother?

Taylor had never had children and had told him that by choice she had not been around kids much. And yet motherhood seemed to come so naturally to her. But, again, that was centuries ago. Would she be so maternal in this time?

Duncan's heart went out to the boy from long ago who needed so much—medical care, education, nurturing, love. Duncan and Taylor as adoptive parents could give him all that, and more. But if she didn't want to get married, or adopt Pauley, what then? He thought it would be damned difficult for a single father to adopt him, although he would try his best to get the courts to see it his way.

Duncan ran his hands through his hair and rubbed his eyes, feeling the intensity of his fatigue. Not just fatigue from all that had happened, but fatigue for all that remained to be sorted out.

"Duncan," he heard Taylor call him. "I need you."

Quickly, he returned to the bathroom to find Taylor looking oddly embarrassed. "He needs to use the toilet," she explained, laughing self-consciously, "only he doesn't know what it is, or how to use it. Can you . . . help?''

She left, closing the door behind her, and Duncan took charge of starting Pauley's education. There is so much that we take for granted, he thought, finishing the toweling Taylor had started, so much this little lad has to learn. He dressed him in a pair of Peter's pajamas, taking pains not to laugh at the boy's reactions to being fussed over in such a manner.

With a squeaky clean kid in his arms, Duncan returned to the child's room to find Taylor waiting for them. In her hands, she held a mug. "I found your milk, and your microwave," she said, holding the warm milk out to Pauley, who for once found himself with something familiar. He drank it eagerly. "Do you think he'll be content to sleep here by himself? He's used to sleeping with me.''

Duncan scowled. "I had . . . other sleeping arrangements in mind," he grumbled, but then gave her a smile. "Let's give it a try. I'll sit here with him until he falls asleep, if you'd like to indulge in that unfamiliar luxury called a bath.''

"I would kill for a bath. Is there shampoo?''

"On the window ledge.''

In the bathroom mirror, Taylor saw that her hair was matted and tangled from the wind and the rain, and it took ten minutes with her hairbrush to unravel the long strands that had grown at least four inches since she'd been gone. Her body was thin, as Rob had noticed. She laughed. She'd wanted to lose weight, but that was one hell of a way to go on a diet. Her face appeared tired, almost gaunt, a look that evidenced her acute need for rest. She took a long shower and followed it with a hot bath for dessert. After all, it *had* been more than three hundred years. . . .

She remained in the tub until the water cooled, then with pruney fingers and toes, reluctantly emerged from the soak, feeling refreshed but rubbery. Only then did she realize she had nothing to wear. There was no way she was going to step back into the grubby jeans or the filthy dress that lay in the gunnysack. She shivered in her nakedness, noting that, like the innkeeper, Duncan also kept the thermostat set very low.

That was just one of the things they'd have to work out between them if. . . . But she shut out that thought. The possibility of a future with him was just too monumental for her to deal with at the moment.

Wrapping her body in a thick towel, she picked up another and blotted her hair until it was almost dry. Then she brushed it until it hung long and straight, if uneven. Her bare feet were cold against the linoleum floor as she tiptoed to the door. ''Duncan!'' she called out in a loud whisper. But there was no answer. The door to Pauley's room across the hall was open a crack. Quietly, she crept toward it and peered into the room. A small night light offered a dim glow, enough for Taylor to see that the boy was sound asleep and the man was no longer in the room.

A soft, warm fabric dropped around her shoulders, and Taylor turned abruptly, then caught her breath. Duncan stood before her, clean-shaven, clad in fresh jeans, naked from the waist up, his own hair wet, his body glistening. ''I took a shower downstairs,'' he replied to her look of curiosity as to how he'd been able to bathe while she loitered in the tub. ''I thought you might need this,'' he added, tucking the lapels of an oversized terry robe around her chest. ''I realize it's a little big, but. . . .

Taylor almost stopped breathing. Never had she seen Duncan look so sexy. She usually avoided superlatives, but the man standing in front of her now could only be described as the most magnificent male she'd ever laid eyes on.

''Thanks,'' she managed, her cheeks burning, her skin suddenly feverish.

He lifted her chin and kissed her lips. ''Do you feel like talking?'' He brushed a strand of hair away from her face. His manner was composed, but she saw a quiet urgency in his eyes.

''What about?''

''The future. Our future.''

''Oh.'' Taylor dropped her eyes. No, she didn't want to talk, especially about their future. She doubted that they had one. She didn't want to talk about anything. Not tonight. Tonight she just wanted to be together with Duncan, to make love like they had when they were "pretend" husband and wife, before tomorrow came and reality set in once more. Before things like long-term commitments, careers, and issues about family destroyed the magic.

But it appeared they'd already come back to reality, and Duncan seemed determined to talk about it. She bit her lip and forced back the moist emotion that sprang to her eyes as she felt that magic already slipping away. The reality was that their relationship had already changed. At Dunnottar Castle, they'd lived as man and wife, even if it was only make-believe. But here, she was nothing more than a guest in his house, a house she knew was still haunted, at least for him, by the memories of his wife and sons. She didn't belong here. She couldn't take the place of his wife, and she no more wanted to sleep in Meghan's bed than she had wanted to wear Kenneth's dead sister's dress. And as for his children, well . . . if he married her, there would be no more for him.

No, she didn't want to talk, for in talk lay the end.

But she could tell that the stunning but stubborn Scot wouldn't take no. Well, she thought, her desire subdued by the sobering reality, we might as well get it over with. "Let me put this back in the bathroom," she said, indicating the towel that still encircled her body. She felt wretched. "I'll meet you downstairs."

"Would you like a Scotch?"

Taylor laughed bitterly to herself. She'd rather have a *Scot* instead. That certain Scot who stood like a mountain of masculine sexuality right before her eyes. But when they got through with their pending talk, she was certain that wouldn't happen. A little alcoholic courage to face the inevitable wouldn't hurt. "Sure. Just a tot."

Duncan waited for her on the sofa, where he lounged, feet on the ottoman of the chair next to it, comfortable in his familiar surroundings. Taylor wished she were as comfortable. She noted he had not put on a shirt and was disturbed to feel the rush of desire renew itself involuntarily. He handed her a short glass with a shot of single-malt whiskey. "Need ice?"

"I'm fine," she replied, taking the glass with an unsteady hand. The only ice she needed was of the emotional type, to cool her seemingly uncontrollable desire. She took a seat at the opposite end of the couch and drew the robe securely about her nakedness, determined to keep her distance.

"I can't talk with you that far away," Duncan said.

Taylor shot him a nervous glance. "And I'm not sure I can talk if we get any closer."

But he leaned toward her and touched her face, his shower-clean scent inviting intimacy. "Don't be afraid," he murmured. "We'll work it out." He'd read her mind, she was sure of it.

She *was* afraid.

And not at all sure they could work anything out.

But the moment his fingers touched her skin, the hunger for him she'd been fighting overwhelmed her. At his insistence, she moved to his end of the couch and nestled against him, the palm of one hand resting against the dark hair on his chest. He held very still, but she could feel the heavy beat of his heart just inches beneath her fingers. She moved her hand, entwining her fingers in the wispy hair, willing herself to stop but unable to control the force of her yearning any longer.

"Remember that raincheck?" she murmured.

"Taylor, wait. . . ." She heard his voice, but it sounded like it came from a great distance. Her hand lowered to the smoothness of his belly, where she let her little finger dip below the waistline of his jeans. She felt his muscles contract as he drew in a sharp breath.

One more night, Duncan. Please. Just one more night before the whole fairy tale comes to an end.

But he grasped her wrist and moved her hand away from his body. "You know what you're doing to me," he said, his voice low and tense. "Please stop, or I won't be able to."

But her reply was to place her lips against his chest. "I don't want to stop, Duncan." She kissed the words into his skin. "I want one night with you, here, now, where it's safe and warm."

He let go of her wrist, but took her head between his hands, forcing her to look at him. "Is that all you want, Taylor? One night?"

Her gaze shifted rapidly from one of his china-blue eyes to the other, their faces were so close. Blood coursed through her veins in a pulsing torrent. Her skin felt as if it were on fire, and her breath grew ragged. No, it wasn't all she wanted. But she knew it was likely all she would have, and she was willing to take what she could get.

"I want you, Duncan. Now. Tonight."

He closed his eyes and leaned his forehead against hers for a long moment, as if trying to decide something, then let his hands slide down her back, inside the bathrobe. "Yes," was all he said as he dropped his arms around her shoulders, leaving them bare of the garment. His mouth melted against hers, and Taylor slid her arms the rest of the way out of the loose sleeves. Aching for him with a desperation she had never experienced before, she pressed her bare breasts against the wall of his chest, where the texture of his hair teased her nipples. Her nails grazed into the skin of his back, and she heard him moan and felt his kiss deepen in response.

He removed the robe altogether, his hands caressing the curve of her back and coming to rest on her hips. She felt his strength as he pulled her against him, felt the tension in his body that heated her own desire to just short of volcanic.

Taylor could not get enough of him. She twisted in his arms and threw one leg across his lap, a motion that upset their balance and sent them both sliding to the floor, along with the sofa cushion. She scarcely noticed. Her hands were working on the buttons of his jeans.

"My God, how I love you," he whispered hoarsely. "I want you, Taylor. I want you for all time."

Already trembling with need, his words only increased her torment. But she was aroused even further when upon achieving her goal, she found he wore the jeans, and nothing else.

Taylor lost all control as they rediscovered one another on the carpeted floor of Duncan's living room. She did not care that there were no sheets, no soft mattress. Her only thought was of him, of her need for him, of the fulfillment he brought to her. Her mind began to spin as Duncan's body fused with her own. She felt as if she were caught in a vortex of energy and wondered briefly if she were being swept through the Ladysgate again, back into the time when the constraints of modern life didn't count. It was her last conscious thought before completion obliterated reality and she swirled into the exquisite realm which only lovers know.

Duncan propped himself against the ottoman and drew Taylor into the warmth of his embrace. Sleepily, she nuzzled against him, and he knew there was going to be no talk tonight. Maybe it was just as well. He sensed her reluctance to approach the subject of their future together, and with a heavy heart, he acknowledged that likely she wasn't interested in giving up her career to settle down to a quieter life and the restrictions that marriage and family would impose upon her freedom. Gazing down on her sleeping face, however, Duncan wanted her worse than anything he had ever desired in his life. She had made him whole again, and for that, he could never express the measure of his gratitude. The thought of losing her filled him with pain, but he knew it would have to be her decision to stay with him, just as it had been Pauley's to come with them to the castle. There wasn't a damned thing he could do to make her stay, except let her know how much he wanted her. She'd have to take it from there.

The cool air in the room began to chill his sex-sweatened skin, and he wondered suddenly about those sleeping arrangements he had had in mind earlier, the ones that involved the large bed in the room upstairs. He didn't want to take this woman there. He didn't even want to sleep in that bed again himself, ever again. That room represented things past, things that needed to remain in the past. He glanced at the sofa. It was long and comfortable. He'd taken many a nap there. Quietly, he shifted Taylor out of his arms and braced her sleeping form against the ottoman, then went to the linen closet, where he found clean sheets. He made up a bed for her and lifted her onto it, unable to tear his gaze from the naked beauty of her slender body. She was deeply asleep.

"Sleep well, my love," he whispered, brushing a kiss across her forehead. "But tomorrow, we have to talk."

Picking up his jeans, Duncan felt his own exhaustion now weaving itself around him like a web. He considered his options. He'd rather stretch out on the floor beside Taylor, but he knew the small boy asleep alone upstairs might need him should he awaken in the night. So he climbed the stairs and gave that small boy another kiss, tucking the covers around him before dropping wearily into the twin bed next to him. It was shorter than his own, and narrower, but Duncan was asleep almost before his head hit the pillow.

Something crashed nearby, and Duncan bolted out of bed, expecting to find himself in a crisis on board the ship that he had dreamed he was sailing back from the Continent. Instead, he saw a yellow kite, a window through which golden sunlight streamed, and a frail child eyeing the chaos of Legos he'd just dumped on the floor. Pauley looked up at him, and a grin crossed the impish face.

Duncan signed to him that it was okay and got out of bed. He slipped into his jeans and joined the boy on the floor to show him how to fasten the blocks together. Only then did he become aware of the aroma of coffee seeping through the partially open door. Coffee. And bacon. "Come with me," he motioned, helping the boy gather the plastic pieces back into the bag and letting him bring them downstairs. "I think I smell breakfast."

Taylor stood in front of the small stove in the kitchen, turning a strip of thick bacon in a skillet. The coffeepot percolated on the back burner. She still wore his robe, but he heard the rumble of the electric clothes dryer in the small utility closet and guessed she had already attacked the laundry.

"I . . . made myself at home," she said, turning to him with an uncertain smile. "I hope you don't mind. I have breakfast almost ready."

Duncan set Pauley on the living floor and went to Taylor, but he stopped at arm's length. Something in her demeanor warned him against getting too close. Where was the warm, eager woman of the night before? He hesitated, then leaned over and kissed her cheek. "You know I want this to be your home."

"I've been thinking about that," she replied tensely, removing the bacon to drain on a paper towel. She didn't continue, and Duncan knew what was wrong. His heart wrenched. She was going to leave him.

He knew he shouldn't press matters, but he felt if he didn't say what he wanted to say right now, she might not give him another chance. He took the long fork out of her hands and laid it on the porcelain of the stovetop. Then he placed his hands on her shoulders. "You didn't want to talk last night, but we have to, Taylor. Because the fact is, I love you, and I don't ever want us to be separated again." He held his breath and scanned her face for some sign of hope, but he found none.

"I know," was all she said.

"Marry me."

She looked away. "Can we eat breakfast?"

He let his hands fall away from her. He wasn't going to beg, damn it.

He found some placemats and utensils and set the table while Taylor cooked the eggs.

Neither spoke.

He retrieved a jar of apple juice from the refrigerator and poured the golden liquid into three jelly glasses. He took three mismatched and chipped plates from the cupboard and handed her a platter for the bacon and eggs.

Neither spoke.

When breakfast was on the table, he went to get Pauley, who had by now built an impressive tower of red and blue blocks. "He's a sharp lad," Duncan broke the silence at last.

"Yes," Taylor said, "he is." She served their plates, and Duncan read an anguish in her face that confirmed his doubts. She was going to leave Pauley, too.

So she was going back to her life. Her career. And he and Pauley would be just memories of a larger-than-life history lesson. Just another legend for her to dismantle. He wondered if later she would deny it even happened. Anger and despair tightened his stomach, taking away his appetite.

She noticed. "Not such a good cook, huh?" But he saw that she was only picking at her own breakfast.

He laid his fork on his plate. Better to get it over with. They'd all had more stress than they needed lately. And after four years of self-imposed emotional exile, Duncan suddenly felt an urgency to get on with his life. He reached for her hand. "Talk to me, Taylor. What are you so troubled about?"

It took her a long moment to reply, and when she did, her voice was hoarse. "Family."

Duncan raised his brows in surprise. It wasn't the reply he'd expected. A glimmer of hope lit in his heart. What did she mean? Her family? Or theirs . . . together? She'd never spoken much of her family in the States. He knew her parents were dead. She had a married sister, some nieces and nephews. "What family?"

Taylor withdrew her hand and clutched her coffee mug. "That's just it," she said, looking down into the black liquid. "You've had a family, kids of your own. I haven't. . . ."

"We can have children, Taylor," Duncan broke in. "I'd love to have children with you, if that's what you want."

She looked at him, her face terrifyingly bleak. "No, we can't." She hesitated. "Is that what you want, Duncan? More children? A family to replace the one you lost?"

Her words cut like a knife. Her voice sounded almost angry, as if she were accusing him of something terrible. "I can never replace the family I lost." His heart felt as if it were a lump of stone. "I never sought to. But what do *you* want, Taylor? What are you looking for? Do you want children of your own?"

He saw her jaw clench. She chewed on her bottom lip. She glanced at Pauley, then at Duncan. "Yes," she whispered, "that's what I want. A child. With you."

"I just told you, I want children. And I want you to be their mother."

"And I just told you," she said, and cleared her throat, "that it can't be."

Duncan heard her this time. "Why not?"

Taylor leaned back in her chair and twisted her napkin. "Because . . . I . . . can't have children. Physically, I mean. It's an impossibility."

TWENTY-EIGHT

❧

There. It was out. And Taylor felt as if her heart was being torn from her breast, because she believed that once he knew the truth, Duncan would no longer want to marry her. Surely he must want more children. He would want, and deserve, a wife who could give them to him. She fought for emotional distance, but lost, and looked away to hide the tears that threatened. Damn! How had she let herself become so vulnerable?

When she regained control, she glanced at Duncan. He regarded her with a thoughtful expression, but for a long time he didn't respond, and Taylor suspected he was groping for words to cover the chasm that now stretched between them. Then he drew in and exhaled a deep breath. "I guess we've both had our tragedies in life, haven't we?" he said at last. "I don't know which is worse, to have had children and lost them, or never to have known them at all." He looked at her, a slight frown creasing his brow. "Is that your hesitation about marrying me? You think I want a replacement family? Because if so, you're wrong."

Taylor's heart leapt momentarily, but her rational mind quickly squelched her hope. She dropped her gaze to the tabletop and fiddled with a fork. "You just said you wanted children."

"Only if you do."

"*Want* is not the issue. *Can't* is the issue."

Duncan pointed toward Pauley. "You don't have to bear children to love them, Taylor, or to call them family. But children are not what a marriage is all about anyway. Marriage is between us—the man and the woman.''

She gave him a bitter laugh. ''I know that intellectually, Duncan. But in my heart, marriage and children go hand in hand. Not being able to have kids has kept me from even thinking about getting married. I find it . . . difficult. . . .''

Pauley took that moment to topple over his juice glass, interrupting them momentarily. She watched how easily Duncan dabbed up the spill, unperturbed by the disruption.

''I guess we've just got to go with what life hands us,'' he said, removing the child's empty plate to the sink. ''Like this little guy,'' he added, tousling the boy's hair and giving him permission to go back to play in the living room. Returning to his place at the small table, Duncan leaned his arms against the edge and clasped his hands together tightly. ''I thought when my sons were killed I would never want another wife or family. I closed myself off, until you came along.'' He took a deep breath. ''To think of what I would have missed if I hadn't known you. Or Pauley.''

Taylor swallowed hard. She appreciated his thoughts about her and Pauley, but despite that, and what he had said about taking what life hands you, she'd also heard that now he was ready for another wife, another family. What if Pauley wasn't enough to fill his need? What if she married Duncan, and later he changed his mind and wanted more kids?

She didn't think she could stand the pain. Better to deal with it now, get it behind her, and get on with life.

Taylor was so lost in her turbulent emotions, she scarcely heard Duncan speaking to her, and she jumped when he took her hand again. ''What?''

He gave her an encouraging smile. ''I said, marry me. I know you love me. Share my life. And Pauley's.''

She wiped a light sheen of sweat from her forehead with her napkin. ''I . . . don't know if I can,'' she stammered. ''I'm . . . not sure I'm good marriage material. Or have what it takes to be a mom.''

Excuses. Bricks with which to rebuild the emotional wall

around her she had so carelessly let crumble. She was paying for that foolishness now.

Duncan's face clouded, and she saw the exasperation in his eyes. "That's ridiculous," he burst out. "You've already been a wonderful mother to Pauley. As for being a wife, how will you know what it's like until you try?"

He was all but begging her, but with each of his attempts to convince her to marry him, Taylor's fears mounted. Doubts overwhelmed her. *Could* she be a wife? Even if children weren't an issue?

She'd lived as a single career woman for so long, avoiding the very idea of marriage, it was hard for her to picture herself in the role of wife. She looked around at the house, the picket fence she could see through the front window, the car parked in the driveway. It was appealing, and yet terrifying in its very foreignness. In New York, she didn't even own a car.

But that was a cop-out and she knew it. Marriage wasn't about where you lived or your mode of transportation any more than it was about children.

There was something else holding her back, something imperceptible forbidding her heart to take a chance with Duncan. She did not understand it, in fact at the moment, she felt hopelessly distraught and confused. Needing distance from Duncan, she pushed her chair back and went to the window. Outwardly she appeared calm as she stared absently at the breakers rolling into shore, but within, an emotional war waged.

Her heart was screaming at her—*you love him. Marry him!* But her mind was shouting even louder—

Run!

Always, she'd listened to her mind. It had been safer that way. And now it was telling her to go back to the life she'd come from. The existence that was safe, where she was in control, not her heart. The place where she wouldn't get hurt.

But her heart took over again, reminding her how she had loved Duncan, secretly, their last night together in the castle. *As a wife does a cherished husband.* She'd felt it again last night, and she knew she loved Duncan in just that way. As a husband. She blinked back those irritating tears again. What *would* she be missing if she listened to her mental arguments, got on a plane, and never knew what it was like to be a wife?

Duncan's wife.

She turned and gazed into his troubled face, wanting with all her heart to say yes. To make him smile again. But a lifetime of listening to her mind rendered her unable to do it. Taylor knew that no matter how much she loved Duncan, she couldn't make the commitment he was asking for. Not yet. Not until she could look him straight in the eye and accept his proposal without a flicker of doubt in her mind or fear in her heart.

"This is . . . the most important decision I've ever made in my life," she faltered instead. She clasped her hands together, feeling their cold, clammy sweat. "Duncan, I need some time . . . in this century . . . to think about all this. I can't just. . . ."

Duncan threw his head back and bored his gaze into the ceiling. "It's your career, isn't it?" he interrupted her tersely.

Something about the way he said it punched her buttons, and she started to snap back at him, but she stopped short, realizing suddenly that at the word "career," the nauseating, anxious knot in the pit of her stomach relaxed.

Career was familiar. Friendly. Nonthreatening.

Career meant that *she* was in control.

Career meant never having to risk that Duncan would eventually want kids. Or that she would be hurt.

She looked back out over the ocean. "Yes," she said at last, in a voice barely audible over the tightness in her throat. "Yes, Duncan, I guess it is."

He'd accepted the possibility that she might leave him, but that didn't make it hurt any less when she did. After she'd admitted that her career stood in their way, he'd tried to assure her that she could continue her work as before, but he could tell she didn't believe him. He hadn't really meant it anyway. As badly as he wanted her to be his wife, he also wanted a wife who would be at home, with him, with their son. Meghan hadn't thought this kind of togetherness was important, and it had caused him untold grief and anguish during their marriage.

He sighed and ran his hands through his hair. Maybe it was just as well. Maybe it wasn't meant for him to be with Taylor, no matter how much he loved her. Their lives were just too diverse.

But Duncan didn't believe that for a minute. If Taylor would just give it a try, he was certain they could sort through their differences and work things out.

But Taylor was gone.

He looked around the kitchen where only moments before, without further conversation or argument, she had taken her clothing from the dryer and gone upstairs to change and collect her hairbrush.

When she came down again, Duncan had offered to take her back to her hotel. "I can walk," she'd said.

"What about Pauley?" he couldn't help but ask, knowing that she was about to break the child's heart as well as his own.

She'd paused a fraction of a second too long, and he knew she felt guilty, at the very least, about leaving the boy. She ought to feel guilty, he thought, angry at her even as he tried to understand her. Duncan couldn't comprehend how she could just walk out on the lad.

But hadn't she made it clear?—Her career came first.

"You're a wonderful father, Duncan," she'd said at last. "You will be good for him, and he for you."

"If they let me keep him. Single fathers aren't exactly a social worker's ideal for an adoptive parent."

He'd seen her shoulders sag. "Duncan, I can't marry you just because of Pauley."

"No. I'm not asking that. I'm just giving you the reality of what is likely to happen to him. Because I'm not married, unless I can convince the courts otherwise, Pauley will likely be placed in a foster home. Hopefully, I can help find a loving couple who might adopt him, although his age and disability will make it more difficult."

"I'm a selfish bitch, aren't I?"

Duncan would never have accused her of that, but at the moment, he couldn't agree more. "A woman's gotta do what a woman's gotta do." He didn't mean to be bitter, but the words were out before he could stop them.

"Touché." She knelt and gave Pauley a hug, signing to him that she had to leave. The boy returned her embrace and gave her a kiss.

He didn't understand that she meant forever.

I will not cry, Taylor told herself as she went out of Duncan's front gate. I will not. Better to do this now than to allow her emotions to become even more entangled in a hopeless situation.

Because that's exactly what it was.

Before they'd come back through the Ladysgate, and even when the boat had first docked, she had hoped they could work it out. For Pauley's sake as well as their own. But as each minute ticked away in 1996, she was ever more convinced it just couldn't be. The feelings that had grown up between her and Duncan during their sojourn through history had no basis in reality. Indeed, that time seemed almost dreamlike now.

But the present day *was* reality. And Taylor's reality was that she was afraid to trust in any future with a man who wanted children. The only relationship she could allow herself to depend upon was that between herself and her work, where the only person who could let her down was Taylor Kincaid. The arrangement had sufficed for over ten years. It would have to continue to do so.

But back at her hotel, she shut the door behind her and leaned against it, closing her eyes. Hurting. She'd just walked away from the only man she'd ever loved. The only child she might ever have. Why? Because she was afraid of taking a chance?

"Grow up," she uttered, throwing the bum-bag across the room with an audible curse.

Surely it wasn't fear. Taylor had never been afraid of anything.

Except relationships. And more, loss of control over her life. Maybe that was it. When nature had taken control over her ability to bear children, had she retaliated by demanding control over everything else about her life? The idea was uncomfortable, and yet it settled in her gut with alarming alacrity.

Whatever amateur psychological explanation she chose, it didn't matter. She'd made her decision, taken her leave, and would have to depend on time to heal the pain.

Trying to refocus her thoughts on the career she deemed so all important, she rummaged through her briefcase, looking for her notes on the story ideas that had brought her to Scotland in the first place. But none of them worked anymore.

She couldn't go back to the *Legends, Lore, and Lunatics* series, not after what had taken place in her own life. Never again would she take a legend lightly.

Nor could she produce a show about her incredible voyage through time. For all the reasons Duncan had given her, she'd decided against exposing the secret of the Ladysgate to the exploration of her viewers. So what did that leave her?

The diary of a Queen.

The letter from Lady Ogilvy.

And a lost treasure that only she, and Pauley, knew where to find.

"The Lost Treasure of Scotland."

Perfect.

She would produce a show using the actual artifacts that she'd inherited to set the stage for the drama, and she'd film the live excavation of the cliff, as she took her viewers into the "belly of the castle rock," as Mrs. Ogilvy had called it, seeking the Scottish Rose.

The idea stirred some small excitement in her, but it was pale in comparison to the eager enthusiam she'd once felt at the start of a new project.

This is what you wanted, she reminded herself again. No risk. No entanglements.

No joy . . . ?

It was her heart talking again. She ignored it.

Going to the phone in the hall, Taylor used a phone card she'd purchased at the airport to reach Robert Gordon. Had he had enough time to translate the diary? Authenticate it? It had only been a few days. She knew from experience the letter and the diary were both the real thing, but she couldn't very well state on camera just how she knew that. An expert's opinion was critical.

The phone rang twice, then the ring was replaced by a message saying the number had been disconnected. Must have dialed the wrong number, Taylor thought, and redialed. When she received the same message, she replaced the receiver with the shadow of a nasty suspicion building in the back of her her mind.

She knocked loudly on the door to the room where her crew members were likely still sleeping off their night at the Hook and Eye. "Need the car keys, fellows," she said to a bleary-eyed Barry, who returned in a moment and dropped them into her hand.

"You want us to go with you?" he said, his voice clearly revealing he'd rather she didn't.

"Nope. Sleep till supper if you want."

It was early afternoon when Taylor made her way through the bustle of the city of Aberdeen to the lawyer's office. Although the outside door to the building was open, she found the offices of Robert Gordon, Esquire, were shut down.

Permanently.

A note on the door referred her to another attorney whose office was upstairs.

"What do you mean, he retired?" Taylor was beside herself when the man told her the news.

"I didn't know Mr. Gordon well," he told her. "He came in late yesterday and explained to me that he was old and tired and wanted to spend the rest of his days on a beach somewhere in the Caribbean."

"And I'll bet I know what he's going to live on, too," she growled, furious with herself for entrusting the inherited artifacts to the old lawyer. That's what happened when you lost control of a situation. You got taken.

"He left an envelope for you," said the attorney's attorney. "Just a moment, please."

Taylor signed for the letter and opened it with fingers that trembled with rage. As she read its contents, however, she saw that Robert Gordon had had some shred of honor in him, even though the temptation of the ancient relics had been too great:

Dear Miss Kincaid,

I must apologize for my unseemly behavior as regards the matter of the two items given by Lady Agatha Keith into my keeping. As agreed between us at our meeting, I translated enough of the diary to discern that it was historically correct, after which I contacted a known antiquarian. Unbeknownst to me, he was in possession of another letter, already authenticated, authored by Mary Queen of Scots, the one referred to in the Ogilvy letter, and he offered me such a sum on the spot for the articles belonging to Lady Agatha, I was unable to overcome the temptation. I have been a lawyer for forty years, and I have seen others whose scruples did not match my own honest ones take advantage of opportunities presented them, whether or not it was the moral high ground to do so. I have worked hard for these many years, and have little to show for it. Therefore, I beg your understanding and forgiveness.

I am not the complete thief you might think me, however, for I took the liberty, upon receipt of the money for the letters, of paying off the mortgage on Lady Agatha's house. Her will states explicitly that it is yours, as well as the belongings within it. I have concluded my duties as executor of her estate, and I find this to be the sum total of her worldly possessions. With this letter is the deed to the property, a copy of Lady Agatha's will, and the key to the front door. I trust you will have no difficulties in the matter, as you now own the property free and clear.

Do not pursue me, I beg you, but allow me to enjoy the compensation I believe was my due for my long, sometimes trying, service to your relative. What was paid for the mortgage is more than four times what I have reserved for my quiet retirement. It is a fair arrangement, I believe.

Yours very truly,
Robert Gordon, Esquire

TWENTY-NINE

Taylor drove back to Stonehaven, stunned, angry, and emotionally drained. She didn't give a damn that Robert Gordon felt vindicated in his theft because he'd paid off the mansion. What good was a mansion in Scotland to a woman who lived in New York? What she wanted were those artifacts. Without the documentation, she had no story. Unless, of course, she could unearth the Scottish Rose. But without the diary, which she felt must contain mention of Mary's rose chalice, and the letter to provide evidence of where it had been hidden, Taylor doubted if she would be allowed to attempt to search for it on the grounds of the castle ruins.

She had to find the unscrupulous lawyer and his antiquarian buddy immediately and get those papers back. She considered going to the police but decided against it, not wanting the investigation to get bogged down in bureaucratic procedure. She had to move fast to retrieve what belonged to her, before the antiquarian sold the goods to a private collector.

But Taylor felt uncharacteristically helpless, not knowing anyone to turn to in this entire country. Well, there was one person she knew who might possibly help her, but she was not at all sure he would want to. She knew she had hurt him badly.

But she also knew she could trust Duncan Fraser. He was a man of honor, a man who couldn't *not* help.

A man who loved her.

She tried to keep her mind on the road, since driving on the left was a new experience for her. But the face of the handsome Scotsman kept looming in her mind's eye.

Marry me.

It would be so easy to say yes, she thought, but warned herself that it was only because she was feeling vulnerable at the moment, in need of help.

Her heart spoke up. So what's wrong with having a help-mate? it wanted to know.

When she reached the house at the top of the hill, Taylor noted there was a second car in Duncan's driveway and another parked out front. She pulled to the curb and set the brake, a sixth sense alerting her suddenly that something was wrong.

She knocked on the door, nervous but undeniably anxious to see Duncan again. When he opened it, she was shaken by the bleak look on his face.

"Thank God you're here," he said in a low voice. "McDowell's called the social services bureau about Pauley. They're talking about taking him away. Right now."

"Oh, no!" Taylor's blood ran cold. "Where is he?"

"Upstairs playing."

Taylor hurried into the living room, forgetting her own dilemma in the face of this new, more critical one. Andy McDowell sat on the edge of the ottoman, and a large woman dressed in a dark suit took up most of the corner of the couch where she and Duncan had made love the night before. Taylor didn't wait for Duncan's introduction.

"I'm Taylor Kincaid," she said, extending a hand to the woman, forcing what she hoped was a warm smile to her lips. "Duncan's fiancé. It was so good of you to come."

"Marguerite Claiborne," the woman replied, appraising Taylor with open curiosity.

Taylor saw Andy McDowell's mouth drop open at her announcement, and she gave him a discreet wink. She wasn't really Duncan's fiancé, of course, but he *had* proposed to her, and Taylor's instincts told her the social worker would be more cooperative with an almost-married couple in allowing Pauley to stay where he was.

She turned to Duncan, who was busy hiding his astonishment and confusion behind the face of a concerned potential parent. Taylor grinned and moved quickly to stand beside him. She slipped her hand into his and gave it a squeeze, hoping he'd play along with the ruse, the way she had when he'd introduced her to Kenneth and Greta as his wife, Janet Fraser. Their lives had depended on it then, and Pauley's future might very well depend on it now. His hand felt warm and secure around hers and gave her courage. "So, Mrs. Claiborne, I assume you are here because you've found Pauley's parents?"

"I am here because Mr. McDowell has made us aware of the child's circumstances," she replied stiffly. "Perhaps you can enlighten me more about the exact location where you found him. Mr. Fraser has been a little vague on the point." Marguerite Claiborne gave Duncan a disparaging look that made Taylor want to throttle her. She wanted to throttle Andy, too, for interfering, although she knew he had meant well. But most of all, she wished she knew what Duncan had already told the social worker.

"I . . . I'm not from around here," Taylor replied, "and Duncan had just rescued me. I'd been thrown overboard in a boating accident, you see. So you will have to forgive me if I must be vague as well. All I know is that when we found him, he was filthy and hungry and appeared severely neglected. Have you met Pauley, Mrs. Claiborne?"

"Uh, no, I haven't."

"We'll bring him down in a moment so you can be introduced. He is deaf, by the way. We haven't had time to take him for an examination yet, but I suspect his condition may be a birth defect." Taylor reluctantly left Duncan's side and took a seat next to the woman. She lowered her voice, continuing confidentially, "I also suspect that he is a victim of severe child abuse. When we found him, he was so hungry, he was almost sick. His clothes were so dirty we had to burn them and give him new ones."

Marguerite Claiborne put her hand to her mouth. "Oh, dear. He is in ill health then?" she said, making a note on the clipboard that rested upon her wide lap.

Taylor knew she'd made an error in wanting to impress this woman when she saw Pauley's excellent state of health at the

present, for she'd forgotten that the sickly Pauley they'd rescued had had months to recover and gain weight. "I . . . I only
meant sick as in . . . weak," she added hurriedly. "As soon as
we gave him a sandwich when we got back to the RNLI station, he seemed to perk right up."

"Could I see the lad now?" she asked.

Duncan turned to go upstairs, but Taylor shook her head.
"I'll get him." She hurried up the stairs, anxious to see the
child again, worried that this do-gooder would make a decision
about his future that would inadvertently harm him instead.
They had to make her see he belonged here, with them.

Them.

Mr. and Mrs. Duncan Fraser.

Taylor paused just outside Pauley's door. *Mr. and Mrs.* It
suddenly felt good to her. The knot did not tie itself in her
stomach again. Her fears vanished as determination took their
place, determination to keep her "family," as strangely composed as it was at the moment, together.

Because clearly she wanted that family. Fiercely. She told
her head to stay out of it. She was listening to her heart now.
Pauley needed her. Duncan needed her. And she needed them.
"We're all we've got," she'd once told Duncan, and it was
as true in this century as it had been in that one.

She stepped inside the child's room. Yes. She wanted them
to be again the family they had been in 1651. Only this time
for real.

"Hey, Pauley," she said, touching the boy's shoulder.
"You're really getting those Legos down, aren't you?" She
studied the plastic structure that was rising out of the floor,
and she could swear she discerned the rudiments of a castle.
She knelt and signed to him that someone was here to meet
him. But instead of eagerly following her instructions as he
usually did, Pauley gave her a look that reflected his doubt. It
was as if he sensed the danger this visitor presented.

"It's okay," she signed and gave him a reassuring smile.
She must remember not to sign to him in the presence of the
social worker, however, lest she wonder where an abused boy
had learned sign language.

She combed his hair, noting that Duncan must have cut it after she'd left. She also saw with satisfaction that Pauley wore a pair of clean jeans, a nice striped knit shirt and sneakers. It must have taken all of Duncan's strength of will to dig through his sons' clothing to find things for Pauley, she thought, a wave of pure love surging through her. She was glad he had taken pains to groom the boy, for she knew Mrs. Claiborne's visit had come as a surprise, and it was important that Pauley be dressed like a child who was lovingly cared for.

She took him by the hand and led him down the stairs. His grip tightened around hers. In his other hand, he clutched both the teddy bear and the stuffed lion, and Taylor sensed the little boy clung to both her and the stuffed animals for protection. At the foot of the stairs, Taylor knelt and gave Pauley a re-assuring kiss. There was no way, *no way,* this woman was going to take her new son from her.

"Mrs. Claiborne, this is the boy we rescued from the cliffs yesterday," she said with great composure. "We don't know his name, but we call him Pauley."

She could feel Duncan's body heat as she returned to his side, and she saw him put a hand protectively on Pauley's shoulder. In the next moment, his other hand came to rest equally protectively across hers, and Taylor allowed herself to take heart from its strength.

The social worker leaned forward, and Taylor held her breath, trying to ascertain the woman's first impression, but her face remained impassive. "Come here, Pauley." Mrs. Claiborne motioned to him with her hands to come to her. But Pauley wouldn't let go of Taylor's leg.

"He's . . . we've . . . sort of bonded in the past twenty-four hours," Taylor said in apology for the child's reticence.

"Well, it's not important that he come to me," Mrs. Claiborne replied. "I can tell from here he has been well-treated. You are to be commended in the temporary care you have given him. If we don't find his family, I'm sure we'll be able to find a good home for him."

Duncan finally stepped forward. "He has a good home. Here. With us."

"I'm afraid that won't be possible, Mr. Fraser. You see, it is the policy of the agency to. . . ."

"To take him away from the safety and security of familiar surroundings? What kind of policy is that?"

Taylor was alarmed at Duncan's adversarial stance toward this woman. "Don't you think it's kinder to let him stay here?" she pleaded. "At least he knows us. He trusts us. And in all honesty, Mrs. Claiborne, once we are married, it is our intention to petition the courts to adopt him. Provided, of course, you are unable to find his real parents." She felt Duncan's hand tighten encouragingly around her shoulder, and she was glad. This was really scary territory for her. Marriage. Adoption. But it was also wonderful new territory.

"But, it would be highly irregular for me to leave him in a household where the potential parents aren't married yet," came back the official reply.

"Our vows are set for the very near future," Taylor blurted out. "It seems to me that it would just make things extra difficult for him to have to adjust to more strangers right now, and as you can see, he's obviously happy right where he is." Her heart pounded. Oh, please, lady, do what's right by this kid, not by your damned books.

Mrs. Claiborne looked at her watch. She looked at Duncan, then at Taylor, then at Pauley. "I'm in something of a hurry," she said, standing to go. "I will leave him with you for the time being, but I can't guarantee that I will be able let him stay more than a few days. It will be up to the board to decide when we review his case. In the meantime, don't take him out of the area."

A sudden thought struck Taylor.

"But, Mrs. Claiborne, I had planned take him tomorrow to Aberdeen. I . . . am hoping to get an appointment with an ear specialist."

The woman's face softened. "Be careful, Miss Kincaid. I know it's easy to lose your heart to this kind of lad. But believe me, it's better not to get too emotionally involved. If his parents are found, he'll be returned to them, unless they are found to have been abusive, of course. But even if he is an orphan, you will have to prove your fitness as adoptive parents, and the process takes some time. Go ahead. Make your appointment in Aberdeen. But just don't set yourself up for disappointment."

Andy McDowell rose to leave as well. He looked at Duncan as if he couldn't believe the scene that had just transpired before his eyes. Then he extended his hand smiled. "I'm happy for you, mate. And for this pretty lass. Y've been needin' t' find a good woman for some years now."

He'd found a good woman all right, Duncan thought as he closed the door behind the pair. But had she meant it when she'd called herself his fiancé, or had it been just an act for the benefit of the social worker? He turned to Taylor. "You can't marry me just for the sake of Pauley," he said heavily, throwing her earlier words back at her.

Taylor did not reply. Instead, she picked the child up in her arms, gave him a big kiss, then put him down again. "Getting too big for me, little buddy," she said, and signed that he could go back to his Lego construction work if he wanted to. He grinned and was up the stairs in a flash.

She gave Duncan an enigmatic smile. "You got any of that Scotch we never got around to last night?"

Duncan saw that something had changed since this morning. Did he dare hope it was her mind? Quickly, he poured them each a shot into the same glasses that he'd emptied and washed when he did the breakfast dishes. Taylor took her same seat at the round table in the kitchen where only hours before she had made a decision to leave him.

"I guess we're not through talking," she said, taking the glass and sipping at the scotch.

Duncan turned his own chair around and sat astride it, his arms leaning against the wooden backrest. "I'm listening," he said. "I think I've said all I can say."

"Fair enough. Let me start by telling you that little bit about a doctor's appointment in Aberdeen was not exactly true. But I wanted to get her permission to take Pauley on a little trip tomorrow."

"What kind of little trip?"

"To see a house."

Duncan frowned. The woman continued to confound him. "What house?"

She gave a small laugh. "Before I answer that, let me ask you a question . . . is that marriage proposal still open?"

Duncan felt a smile permeate his entire face, and a warm glow settled around his heart. "You know it is." He set the glass down on the table top and took her hands in his. "Have you changed your mind, Taylor? Will you marry me?"

He saw a twinkle in her eyes. "Well, I might, provided we can agree on some details."

He kissed her fingertips and longed to take her in his arms and kiss all the rest of her. But he'd almost lost her earlier by pushing too hard. He'd listen to what she had to say. Then he'd kiss all the rest of her. "You make this sound like a contract negotiation," he commented on her business-like request.

"Well," she answered softly, "isn't marriage the biggest contract two people ever make between each other?"

"I suppose it is." He could tell she had something important on her mind, even though her banter was light. Something that needed to be settled between them before she'd give him her total commitment. He suspected it had to do with her career. "What details need sorting out?"

He expected her to tell him she'd marry him if he would come to live in New York. Or at the least, that she wanted continue her glamorous lifestyle, even from a base in Scotland. As deeply as he loved her, neither was an option he wanted to live with.

Instead, she started talking about an inheritance—some papers and an old mansion, and at first, Duncan had a hard time following her. She'd never mentioned any of this during their time together at Dunnottar Castle. "Wait. Start over, please," he asked. "I don't understand."

"You didn't know you were marrying nobility, did you?" she said with a casual laugh, then repeated her story of how she came to Scotland in the first place to claim her inheritance from Lady Agatha Keith.

"But I thought you came to shoot a television show," he said, trying to make some sense of it all.

"I decided to accomplish two things during the trip," she replied, then added with a grin. "I always was an over-achiever."

"Yeah, uh, maybe we should talk about that."

"In a bit. But listen to this first." She told him about Robert Gordon and the letter and the diary, and what the lawyer had done. "He seems to think it was okay for him to steal those artifacts and sell them because he paid off the mortgage on the house with part of the money."

"What house?" he asked for the second time.

"My ancestral mansion." She hesitated for a long moment, biting her bottom lip, then added, "Our new home. Maybe."

This woman had brought a lot of surprises into his life since they'd met, three nights and three and a half centuries ago. And it appeared she wasn't finished. "Ancestral mansion. Where?"

"In Aberdeen. I haven't seen it, and I understand it is rather rundown." She unzipped the pouch at her waist and took out an envelope. She opened it and handed him a piece of paper. It was the deed to a property in an old district of Aberdeen. "But I own it free and clear."

She set her glass on the table and entwined her fingers with his. "Duncan," she said tentatively, "if the place is not too awful, would you consider . . . moving?"

Taylor could tell this was about the last thing Duncan was expecting from her, and she grinned to herself, sympathizing with his confusion. The idea had only just come to her, but it hit her like a lightning bolt that perhaps that old ancestral mansion might just be the thing to bridge the final obstacle that lay between them.

Taylor's decision to take the risk of loving Duncan, to trust him when he said he didn't have to have more children to make his world complete, hadn't come easily, but when she'd made it, she knew in her heart it was right.

And just moments ago, she'd put her finger on what it was that had been gnawing at the back of her mind, telling her she couldn't be happy if she married Duncan. It had nothing to do with the man or her feelings toward him. It didn't even have anything to do with not being able to bear children.

It had everything to do with her need to keep her hands firmly on the wheel of her own life.

To remain in control.

She realized that in her usual obsessive, hard-headed way, she'd believed that if she married Duncan, it meant that she must give up her world, her career, and subjugate her needs to those of her new family.

Now, she recognized the folly of that thinking. Duncan had never asked her to give up anything. She had just assumed he would. If she gave up her career, or changed it, it would be because she wanted to, not because anyone was forcing her to. The relief that washed over her was almost tangible.

"Moving? To your inherited mansion?" Duncan asked, bringing her out of her reverie.

"Let's take a look at it. Consider it. That's all I'm asking. Unless there's some reason you can't, or won't, leave Stonehaven."

Duncan looked thoughtful. "No. I've been thinking about moving out of this place for some time, but I hadn't thought about leaving Stonehaven."

"Is . . . that a problem?"

He shook his head. "There's nothing to keep me here but tradition, I suppose. My people have lived here for generations." He gave a dry laugh. "Maybe as far back as Kenneth and Greta."

Taylor groaned, then asked, "What about your work?"

"Aberdeen is the heartbeat of the offshore business," he said. "It would actually be more convenient for me."

Taylor allowed a ray of hope to shine on her idea. It just might work. . . .

Duncan stood up and drew Taylor from her chair. He encircled her in his arms and kissed her gently. "Does this mean you wouldn't be going back to New York?"

"I'm not going back to New York in any case," she said, tilting her head back, her lips eager for more of his kisses. "Except to pack up and move to Scotland."

She saw the delight on his face. "But what about your career? This morning, I thought...."

"I know. I 'thought' too. But I thought wrong. It wasn't my career, Duncan. It was some other old baggage I had to get rid of." She touched his cheek with the palm of her hand. "Some other old 'divils' I had to put to rest."

THIRTY

༝

The traffic in Aberdeen was heavy, and Duncan steered his small car carefully through the flow of automobiles, wondering how he would like living in this busy place. But moving here was a small compromise to make, one he'd happily undertake for Taylor. She had assured him that she did not wish to return to New York or the production of her show. "It had a good run, great ratings. I think I'll stop while I'm ahead," she'd said. But she'd also told him she wanted to continue to work in television, maybe develop a children's series, and Aberdeen offered more of the facilities she would need. "I've always been an independent producer. What's to say I can't do it from here, instead of New York?" Duncan wanted Taylor to pursue the work she loved, especially if it no longer meant that she'd be traipsing around the world like she once did.

They had resolved a lot between them over their scotch the afternoon before, and when they were finished, Duncan knew he must be the happiest man alive. To be sure, there were obstacles they would have to overcome and compromises to be made along the way. But both he and Taylor agreed in the end that their love was strong enough to overcome anything.

Duncan had taken Taylor back to the inn, where she'd checked out, handed the keys to the rental car to her two totally dumbfounded crew members, given them her corporate credit card, and told them to return to the United States and find another job.

They'd stopped at the market for groceries, then returned to Duncan's house, where together in the tiny kitchen they'd prepared a lovely meal comprised of a roast of lamb, mashed potatoes, and fresh vegetables. Pauley's eyes had almost popped out of his head at the abundance and flavor of the food, especially when he had his first taste of ice cream.

Duncan's dessert came later, when Pauley was sound asleep, and he and Taylor were at last alone, when his wish to kiss all of her finally came true.

"Watch out!" Taylor cried out a warning just in time for Duncan to avoid a collision when a large truck cut in front them. Silently, he reminded himself to keep his mind on his driving instead of what he and Taylor had done in bed last night. To think he would be able to hold her and make love to her like that every night of his life from now on. . . . He felt the beginning of an erection and realized if he was going to stop thinking erotic thoughts about her, he'd have to do it out loud. He switched to another intriguing but not so dangerous subject.

"When we were in the castle, did you ever see the letter and the diary that Gordon stole?" he asked.

"Oh, sure," Taylor replied, turning in her seat to check on Pauley, who was securely strapped into the back seat. "I actually saw Mrs. Ogilvy write the letter. She had the diary there, too. Right in her little privy closet. She smuggled them both out to Lady Keith, who, from the name, I think must have been my ancestor."

"And what about the Scottish Rose? Did you ever see it?"

"Well, actually, I helped Elizabeth bury it in a cave deep within the castle rock," she said. "That's what Pauley and I were up to the night Greta and Kenneth and all those good folks bagged us and almost burned me as a witch."

Duncan swerved, veering into the next lane. "You did what? Good God! You could have been killed, you could have fallen from that cliff, you could have. . . ."

"Was the Scottish Rose ever recovered? Have you ever seen it mentioned in your history books?"

Her question stopped his stream of remonstrations, which he realized were about three hundred and fifty years too late. Duncan thought about his history lessons. "I don't recall mention of any such item, especially in connection with the Scottish regalia. You said there was a letter, Mary's request that it be joined with the crown, the scepter, and the sword when peace came to the land, but I don't think it ever happened. I guess we could go to Edinburgh Castle and see. That's where the Honours are today.''

''When we get things sorted out, why don't we go to Dunnottar Castle instead? The Scottish Rose might still be right where we left it.''

They reached an older part of town, and Duncan drove slowly through the streets, looking for the address of the house deeded to Taylor.

''Don't you think we should try to find him?'' Taylor asked, speaking of the crooked attorney one more time. ''It really irks me that I trusted him. And I don't care what he did with the money, it isn't right. He ought to be caught and brought before the law.''

''If he really wanted to disappear, I doubt if we'd be able to find him easily,'' Duncan replied. ''He probably left the country on a fake passport and has the money in a Bahamian bank by now.''

Taylor heaved a sigh. ''I guess I shouldn't begrudge him his retirement.'' She slipped her hand into his. ''Only a few days ago, it was just me and my TV show. Now, because of him, I have a fiancé, a child—we hope, and a paid-for mansion.'' She laughed. ''Maybe it was a fair arrangement after all.''

They reached the ivy-covered gate described in the lawyer's note that was with the deed, giving them directions to the mansion. Robert Gordon was nothing if not meticulous. Duncan steered the car through the gate and up the cobbled drive that led to a large house, the rear of which overlooked the sea.

''This is amazing,'' Taylor uttered.

Duncan crooked his head to peer up at the impressive gray stone mansion that stood like a silent sentinel, its drapes drawn, closing out the world after the death of the old lady who had been its last inhabitant. Its walls reached three stories into the gray sky above, with several large, nine-paned windows overlooking a formal garden that was now overgrown by weeds. On either side, wings had been added, their design more modern than the original structure.

"When did the papers say the place was built?" he asked, parking the car in the drive.

"Around 1700, but it has been added onto. I guess that's why the architecture is sort of . . . eclectic."

Inside, "eclectic" was the kindest word Duncan could come up with to describe the mishmash of nineteenth-and twentieth-century décor and furnishings that greeted them. Pauley was fascinated with the bric-à-brac of all descriptions that cluttered every shelf and table. Chairs and sofas were covered with faded chintz in busy prints. Paintings vied for wall space with old calendars, notes, and newspaper clippings taped to the wallpaper, and an occasional ornament of some kind.

The main parlor, just to the left of the entry hall, had been dealt the worst blow, Duncan decided, drawing back the draperies to let the daylight in. He could picture the original walls being much like those at Dunnottar Castle, made of stone and draped with tapestries. But sometime within the last twenty years, these walls had been covered over with tacky, dark wood-grained vinyl paneling. Olive green shag carpeting lay like an old dust mop on the floor and the cheap drapes sagged from the front windows.

"Looks like a seventies decorator got hold of Auntie Agatha," Taylor commented wryly. "But I think I can see potential here."

Duncan could see the potential too, and found that he was excited over the prospect of relocating here. Perhaps this structure of ancient rock would be their modern-day castle by the sea.

Taylor went into the adjoining dining area and looked out over the back of the property, which spread in a flat lawn before disappearing over a cliff into the sea. Duncan came to her side and put an arm around her. "I like the view."

"We'll have to make sure Pauley is safe out there."

"The lad is almost twelve, Taylor," Duncan reminded her. "He's plenty old enough to be allowed to explore out there."

"But his hearing problems. . . ."

Duncan kissed the top of her head. "I talked to a doctor friend of mine while you were in the shower this morning, and he told me there's a chance Pauley's hearing might be largely restored by surgery. But other than his deafness, he's a perfectly normal lad. Would you quit worrying?"

Taylor gave him a good-natured punch in the ribs. "You got any other little tidbits of good news like that to drop on me, mister?"

"Actually, yes. I have a friend in the juvenile division of the police department. They've combed high and low around the area where we found Pauley, but there's been no word that someone is missing a child."

"Surprise, surprise."

"But, even better, I told him about us, and that we want to adopt him, and, well, you know how it goes, it pays to have contacts in the right places. He said he'd talk to his friend who happens to be the head of the social services bureau."

"Oh, Duncan, does that mean . . . ?"

"It means maybe. But a definite maybe," he added, giving her a quick kiss on the cheek.

As the three of them went up the stairs, Taylor trailed her hand on the bannister, letting the silkiness of the dark wood slip away beneath her fingers. "It's kind of neat to think about all the ancestors who must have climbed these same stairs over the past three centuries. This place was likely under construction only a few decades after the time of Cromwell's siege."

"True."

"And you know what else? I'm almost glad Robert Gordon did what he did. I doubt if I would have taken the money and sunk it into this place. But now that I own it, I know I'm already a part of it. It's . . . like family."

Duncan didn't reply, knowing that Taylor was still getting used to the idea that she could have, indeed, did have a family.

At the top of the stairs, a large sitting room overlooked the front of the house, but it had been converted into a bedroom for Agatha Keith's last few years. The walls were covered with an old-fashioned floral printed paper, the bed with a spread of a clashing design. Three tall bookcases stood uniformly against the far right-hand wall, the shelves brimming with volumes. Those that couldn't be crammed onto the shelves were stacked on chairs as well, along with magazines dating from the 1950s.

"Looks like Auntie was also a packrat." Duncan grinned, picking up an old periodical. "I was only two when this one was printed." He went to the shelves and took down an ancient-looking volume and opened it. "*Childe Harolde*," he read from the title page. "By Lord Byron. Published in 1812 by John Murray Publishers, London." He closed the cover and blew dust off it. "It's quite old. I wonder if it's valuable?"

"Could be." A single book on the bedside table caught Taylor's eye. She picked it up and read its title on the spine. "*The Abbott*. By Walter Scott." She opened the aged cover. "Duncan, look at this." There before them was a photogravure of a young woman in a most unusual but elegant costume, with a wide ruff at the neck and a cumbersome headdress topped by what looked like a man's bowler hat incrusted with jewels in the shape of a cross. Across from the picture, printed in red ink on a thin onionskin paper, were the words: *Mary Stuart, from a drawing by Fr. Flameng.*

"I wonder if Aunt Agatha was reading up on Mary Queen of Scots before she died," Taylor remarked. "What an outfit," she added, running her finger over the yellowing page. "And what a remarkable woman she must have been. Ahead of her time, at least where peace and the unity of Scotland were concerned." She scowled. "Damn, what I wouldn't give to read that diary!"

"At least you got to see the Scottish Rose."

She closed the book again. "I wonder what ever happened to it. Maybe Scott mentions it in this book," she mused, tucking the volume under her arm. She went to the window and peered down into the weed-infested garden, appearing to be lost in thought. A few moments later, she spoke. "Duncan," she said in a faraway voice. "I want to go back to Dunnottar Castle."

* * *

Dunnottar Castle in 1996 sported a large gravel parking lot at the top of the hill opposite the ruins of the fortress where once—was it only a matter of a few days ago?—Cromwell's army had set up camp. "Looks a little different, doesn't it," she remarked as Duncan swung his small car into a parking space next to several tour buses.

Almost two weeks had passed since Taylor, Duncan, and Pauley had returned through the Ladysgate. They had postponed this visit to "their castle" because they'd been caught up in making plans for their future and getting Pauley's legal life in order. Fergus McGehee had finally shown up, guilt-ridden and apologetic, and offered to turn in his captain's license. Duncan had given him a stern, Godlike lecture, but he hadn't taken away the man's means of making a living. Taylor's only disappointment had been that her photographs hadn't turned out. "Looks like it went through an X-ray machine," the lab tech told her when she learned there was nothing on the film. "Got to be careful about that in airports."

Their wedding plans were set. They were to be married the following week at Kinneff Kirk, in the chapel where Taylor had helped Reverend and Mrs. Grainger hide the Honours of Scotland. But before they took that next step in their new life together, Taylor wanted to put closure on the one they'd shared here in this ancient castle. She wanted to return to Dunnottar and see what had become of the buildings and grounds. But most of all, she was anxious to learn the fate of the Scottish Rose. A call to the Stonehaven Library had confirmed Duncan's belief that the golden chalice had never been joined to the regalia. It was a stretch to believe it might still be sitting on that rock outcropping in the cave, but if there was anything Taylor had learned recently, it was that she could stretch her beliefs.

She helped Pauley out of his seat belt and watched the child's eyes grow enormous when he recognized the structure that still perched atop the high black cliff. "Get used to it, sweetie," she murmured under her breath, remembering her own shock when she'd first been forced to deal with things out of their familiar time.

Duncan took Pauley by the hand and Taylor followed them, their steps accelerated by gravity as they wound down the path. Duncan paid the entrance fee at the small house at the foot of the ramparts, and they began the upward climb.

"I have the strangest feeling I've been here before," Taylor joked, trying to control the emotions that threatened to overwhelm her. Like any other tourist, she was just another visitor to this famous castle, but unlike for any other except the three of them, she had called it home for those terrible stormy months in Scotland's history. And she and Duncan, for whatever reason, had played their part in that history. She could never explain it logically, as once she would have tried, but she could never deny that it had happened. Pauley was physical proof.

Maybe today they would find more physical evidence of that participation. After lengthy discussions about the ramifications of searching for—and finding—the Scottish Rose, they had decided that if they somehow miraculously recovered it, Taylor could fulfill her role as Keeper of the Rose and make Queen Mary's dream of joining the chalice with the rest of the Honours come true.

The condition of the gray, rubble-strewn ruins saddened her, for Taylor clearly recalled the earlier splendor of the now crumbling walls and roofless chambers. They climbed the tower where the Honours had been hidden, peering along with the rest of the tourists into the small vault where Governor Ogilvy had once proudly displayed his custodial charges to his small audience.

The quarters that they had shared were starkly barren and roofless. Small yellow flowers grew from roots hidden away between the rock walls. Taylor slipped her hand into Duncan's, a tight knot in her throat. "Could we really have lived here?" she whispered.

"I think we did." He enveloped her in his arms. "At least I recall a couple of rather spectacular nights, lying in a bed with you, right about here." They were alone in the space at the moment, and Taylor allowed herself to relish his long and tender kiss delivered in the present day upon that same spot.

But Pauley sought them out, pulling at Taylor's jacket, eager to cavort further about the ruins that looked vaguely like the castle he remembered. They continued their tour, at last reaching the drawing room, one of the areas that had been restored. "Look at that," Duncan said, pointing to the relatively new wooden ceiling. "I've seen those initials before when I've visited Dunnottar, but they never meant much to me."

Taylor read the initials that were carved into the wood. "What do they stand for?"

"The first is for King George V and his Queen Mary. Then Lord and Lady Cowdray, who bought the estate and the castle in the early part of this century and who were responsible for most of the excavation and restoration of it. And look there . . . George Ogilvy and Elizabeth Douglas. Don't we know them?"

"In Defens, Regi et Regno. A.D. MCMXXVII."

A new lintel had been placed over the large fireplace. Taylor approached it and ran her fingers over the large lettering: *In commemoration of the defence of the Honours of Scotland, From September 1651 to May 1652, by George Ogilvy of Barras, Governor of Dunnottar, and of the help given by his wife, Elizabeth Douglas, and by her kinswoman Anne Lindsay.*

"Anne Lindsay left just as we arrived," Taylor murmured. "She took with her all of King Charles' valuable papers, tucked up in her girdle." She laughed. "All those clothes had to be good for something." Then she sighed. "I wonder what happened to the Ogilvies."

Duncan put his hand on her shoulder. "I'm afraid our good friends suffered a great deal after we left," he said. "When Ogilvy finally surrendered, Cromwell's commanding officer was furious that the Honours had eluded them. They held the Ogilvies in prison in the castle, I imagine in that dungeon next to the kitchen, trying to get them to divulge the whereabouts of the regalia, but they never did. The Governor lived to tell of what happened, but Mrs. Ogilvy died from her ill-treatment."

I would die before I would give it away t' the English.

Taylor put her hand to her mouth, feeling as if she might cry. It was odd, grieving for the death of a woman who had been gone for centuries. But it had only been a few weeks since she and Elizabeth Ogilvy had plotted with Mrs. Grainger for the rescue of the Honours right here in this castle. "She was a brave woman," Taylor whispered, but a shiver involuntarily shook her body. "This gives me the creeps. Let's get out of here."

They went to the far eastern wall of the castle and found the niche where she and Pauley had slipped and slid down to the entrance to the cave. It was wider than she remembered, the rocks knocked down over the eons by wind and weather. They climbed through, ignoring a "Danger Keep Out" sign. The path no longer existed, so they had to pick their way through gorse bushes and over fallen rocks, but in a few minutes, Taylor spotted the boulder that marked the entrance. She stopped to catch her breath.

"It's still there, just like I remember it." Excitement tingled through her. The boulder had not moved in three hundred and fifty years. Had the cup?

Pauley tugged at her hand and pointed, nodding his head. He remembered, too. She touched the soft skin of his cheek. "Let's go get it, little buddy."

Duncan, like Mrs. Ogilvy, was too large to fit through the opening, and he was not happy that Taylor and Pauley wanted to go inside the cave alone. "We'll be fine," Taylor assured him. "Give me the flashlight and wait for us here. It'll just take a little while." She appreciated his concern, however. "Don't worry. Either it's there or it's not. We'll be right back."

Pauley reached for the flashlight, totally unafraid of it now. He was adapting to his new century like lightning. Taylor gave it to him, and together they ducked into the darkness behind the boulder. There lay the passageway, just as before, although the corridor seemed narrower than she recalled. The further they went, the closer the walls seemed to encroach upon them. Finally, they reached a place where rubble began to form a solid barrier in front of them.

"I don't think we're going to make it, Pauley," she said aloud, disappointed. "I think maybe the mountain has shifted since our last visit here. We're not going to get to the Rose unless we have some professional excavators to do it."

Her voice echoed in the chamber, and the sound pried loose a few pebbles from the ceiling, sending them down on the explorers. "Uh-oh," Taylor said, suddenly alert and aware that she might have placed them both in great danger. "Let's get out of here."

Pauley sensed the danger, too, and he took Taylor's hand, motioning with his flashlight for her to return to the entrance. She tightened her grip around his and together they quickly ran back along the path, the boy trying to illuminate their way in their hurry. Behind her, she heard the sound of still more falling rock.

They reached the crevice and stepped out into the fresh air, brushing debris from their sleeves and coughing from the dust they had breathed in.

"Good God, what happened?" Duncan said, drawing them instinctively away from the cave. They stood, watching, waiting, as if expecting to see the mountain collapse. But from the outside, all was quiet, even though Taylor guessed that inside, the rock continued to shift and settle from the inescapable demands of gravity, sealing away the cave forever.

"Well," Taylor said at last, "I guess that settles that. No story about the Lost Treasure of Scotland. No Scottish Rose to join with the Honours. If Mary's chalice is still in that cave, I guess it's going to remain a lost treasure for all time."

"Dinna grieve, my good wife Janet," Duncan said, lifting Pauley to his shoulder and taking her in his arms. "Peace and unity have long since come to Scotland. And as for the chalice, hath we not found a treasure far greater?"

"Aye, husband," Taylor agreed, reaching to give him a kiss on the cheek. For here in this gloomy sentinel of stone, they had found their own peace and unity, and the greatest treasure of all, love.

EPILOGUE

❧

Sunlight streamed through the windows of the dining room, crossed Duncan's wide shoulders and fell in a shimmer onto the newspaper he was reading. Taylor studied him from the adjacent kitchen, filled with love, marveling still at the way their lives had turned out. It was nothing short of a fairy tale.

"Want more coffee?" she called to him.

Duncan looked up from his paper, then shook his head. He glanced at his watch. "Shouldn't we be going?" he said. "It's almost high tide."

"I've got our lunch basket all ready. Will you get Pauley?"

Duncan stood up and went to the foot of the stairs. "Pauley, lad, come, let's go."

Taylor heard a youthful reply from somewhere upstairs. "I'm coming, Daddy." The voice had a tinny, somewhat robotic quality to it, but the speech therapist had worked wonders with Pauley since his operations. If ever Taylor had doubted the wisdom of bringing him into the twentieth century, those doubts had vanished the day when first he heard the world around him. Modern medicine and technology had joined forces, and a cochlear implant in each ear had replaced the nerve-damaged organs, enabling the boy to hear normally. She would never forget the look of wonder on his face when she'd spoken to his hearing ears for the first time.

That had been over a year ago. Since then, Pauley had progressed at an amazing pace. He was brighter than average, brilliant when it came to things electronic, like his Nintendo games and the computer he was learning to operate. Most of all, he was a loving child, a joy for her and Duncan.

Today, he was to have his first lesson in navigating the *Intrepid*, using the Satnav system on board. Taylor herself had overcome her anxiety concerning boats, since Duncan had patiently introduced her properly to seamanship.

The weather was crystal clear and warm this summer Sunday, and the three of them drove beneath leaf-laden trees to the marina where the boat was docked. These ocean outings had become a family tradition on Sundays when the weather permitted, and as soon as the car was parked, they hurried aboard the vessel, eager to get under way.

"Want to take the helm?" Duncan asked Taylor.

"If you'll stand right behind me while I navigate out of the boat traffic."

"Now that's an offer," Duncan laughed. He started the engines, and Pauley and Taylor cast off the dock lines, as they'd been shown how to do. Together, they made an efficient crew.

Carefully, Taylor backed the boat out of the slip, shifted into forward, and slowly made her way out of the busy marina. As promised, Duncan stood right behind her, his hands on her shoulders, his rock a body pressed against her back. She found his presence at once comforting and distracting, for she could feel his arousal against her hips. "You'd better back off, Captain." She laughed.

"Raincheck?"

Taylor turned the wheel over to her husband, giving him a kiss on the cheek. "Raincheck."

"Where to, then, my lovely first mate?"

Taylor squinted out over the expanse of ocean that lay in front of them. Mostly they headed north on these outings, but today, she had a strange notion.

"Duncan, if we didn't get too close, since it's such a lovely day, could we go the the Ladysgate?"

He looked at her askance. "You can't mean it."

She shrugged. "I didn't say go through it." She saw Duncan glance at Pauley, who had by now tied the lines in a neat coil and hung them where they belonged, ready for when they returned to the dock, and she guessed his thoughts. "Do you think it would upset him to see the arch? Or do you think he'd even remember it? He's come so far since that day. . . ."

Duncan turned south. "I guess we'll find out. Maybe it's time for him to deal with that truth about his life, if he remembers where he came from." Pauley's past was a subject they had avoided with the boy, focusing instead on what lay ahead for him.

It was a fair distance between Aberdeen and the Ladysgate, but Taylor stretched out on a cockpit cushion and enjoyed the warmth of the sun on her face and the brush of salt air against her cheeks. She watched with love and admiration as Duncan carefully showed Pauley how to use the sophisticated navigation equipment. Never had she felt so content.

She'd learned one lesson for certain from everything that had taken place in her life since the last time she'd been to, and through, the Ladysgate . . . that letting go of fear, releasing the need to always be in control, made room for wonderful things to happen.

She'd let go of her flashy American television stardom only to find herself head of a British national children's television development team. It was a project that engrossed her mind, demanded hugely of her creativity, and yet allowed her time to integrate her new role as a mother as well.

She'd let go of her fear that Duncan would want more children and watched him become Pauley's father in every way. It was no small task, nurturing this boy, changing him from the ragged waif he was when they found him three centuries ago into the bright, capable twentieth-century lad he was today. Taylor attributed much of his progress to the fact he knew he could trust Duncan to be there for him. A teenage boy needed the strength and wisdom of just such a father.

Taylor had also discovered that as she let go of the obsessive drive that once fueled her ambitious career, she found time to see the beauty in life. She'd cleared the garden, and it flourished now with bright summer blossoms. She'd undertaken the renovation of their "castle," as Duncan called the big old house, and it fairly oozed with authenticity. She had consulted with an expert in historical restorations who had made suggestions as to how they could return the mansion to its original splendor, keeping of course, their modern conveniences. Her favorite touch was the antique tapestries that now hung on the exposed rock walls of the front rooms of the house. They reminded her of the ones Mrs. Ogilvy had used to warm the walls at Dunnottar Castle.

No sign had been found, however, of the Scottish Rose. They had visited the Honours of Scotland in their royal display in Edinburgh Castle, and Taylor had laughed quietly when Duncan pointed out the two places where he'd bent the sword. The guidebook told the story of how these emblems had been rescued by brave, patriotic Scots from certain destruction at the hands of Cromwell's army.

"Mum! Look!" Pauley's excited cry startled her and she sat up abruptly.

"What is it, son?"

He pointed toward the shore. There, looming darkly against the cliffs was the Ladysgate. Duncan slowed the boat, slipping it into idle. "I guess that answers our question about him remembering," he said, coming to sit next to Taylor.

She shivered. "It's an ominous thing, isn't it?"

Duncan had brought her sweater, and he draped it protectively across her shoulders. "Let's just say, I won't venture any closer than this."

Pauley picked up a pair of binoculars and climbed to the roof of the pilot house. "What is it, Daddy? What is that rock?"

"It's called the Ladysgate, son. Do you remember it?"

"I don't know. I think so. Did we once go there?"

Did we once go there? What a haunting question, Taylor thought. She strained her eyes, trying to see through the giant portal. Today, there was no fog, no swirling mist, no treacherous ocean conditions, and all she saw was the calm blue water lapping through the gate. But in her mind's eye, she caught a glimpse of smoke rising from a crofter's lodge, of riders racing to spread the warning of impending invasion. She saw a castle, resplendent with the treasures of a bygone day, and the king's standard, snapping in the brisk air, defying the enemy to trespass. Taylor could almost smell the smoke from the villagers' cooking fires, hear the voices of the soldiers in the barracks. And she felt the warmth of her husband lying next to her in a primitive bed, and his love that changed everything.

"Yes, son," she whispered, her throat tight. "We did go there once."

Turn the page for an exciting sneak preview of a wonderful new historical romance from St. Martin's Paperbacks—

DEEP AS THE RIVERS
by Shirl Henke

A Maryland post road, 1811

The air was redolent with a hint of spring. Samuel looked around the low marshy countryside, still sere and brown from winter's cold. Tall patches of marsh grass grew in thick clumps off to the east side of the wide rutted road. Two gulls circled in the distance and the bare branches of a willow tree rustled softly in the brisk breeze.

By the time he reached St. Louis the weather should be breaking. The thought heartened him, as did the fact that he would be leaving Tish and her whole family behind. He threw back his head and took a deep breath of air. The slight movement saved his life as a bullet whistled a fraction of an inch from his temple.

Years of conditioning took over as he responded with pure reflexive action. He swung low to the right side of his mount, but before he could turn the horse and kick it into a gallop, another shot rang out. His horse stumbled to its knees. Samuel kicked free of the stirrups and threw himself away from the dying animal. He landed hard, thrown onto his right shoulder, striking his head a glancing blow against the hard rocky earth. The gelding nearly fell on top of him as it convulsed in its death throes, then lay still. A third shot grazed his cheek before he could flatten himself behind the fallen horse. Quickly he studied the terrain, trying to locate better cover. There was a dense copse of pampas grass in a slight swale to the east of the road. His eyes swept the rest of his surroundings, searching for a way to cover his retreat even as his hands pried desperately at the stock of his Bartlett Flint Lock, which was wedged firmly in its scabbard beneath the dead horse.

No help there, and his Martia l pistols were not accurate enough at the range from which the assassin fired. Mercifully there seemed only to be one man, but he was damnably proficient at reloading and firing. Cocking a pistol, Samuel futilely returned a shot where he saw faint movement in the brush. Cursing, he pulled out the second pistol.

Quiet. For several moments Shelby heard nothing. Then another shot rang out, this time burning through his jacket sleeve and slicing a furrow across his left bicep. The killer had circled around to his left. Soon Shelby would be without cover. He surveyed the clearing in which he lay and decided his only chance was to make a run for the tall grass at the opposite end from which the last shot had come. If only his foe had not again circled back, waiting for him to do precisely that.

Shelby shook his throbbing head to clear it, ignoring the raw burn of his arm. Just as he tensed his muscles, preparing to make the deadly dash, the drumming of hoofbeats broke the deceptively bucolic quiet. A faint rattling of harness grew louder as the tempo of the hoofbeats accelerated. A vehicle was coming around the bend in the road, the galloping horses headed straight for him.

The driver, hidden in the shadowy interior of the small phaeton, slowed the team as they neared Samuel's position. A high clear voice yelled out "Jump aboard!" as the wheels narrowly missed the fallen horse.

Samuel tumbled onto the seat, sprawling half on the floor of the small carriage as another shot rang out, whizzing past his head. The driver whipped the well-matched team of bays into a gallop with a sudden lurch. Dazed, he hung onto the side of the phaeton and struggled into the seat. Another shot whistled harmlessly over the top of the carriage as they hurtled toward the capital.

"You're bleeding all over Uncle Emory's new velvet upholstery," a soft feminine voice said in lightly accented English.

"So, we meet again," Samuel replied, arching one black eyebrow at his rescuer.

"We never *met* in the first place," Olivia said sharply, recalling the cool way he had cut her, turning his back and stalking across the ballroom floor.

"We've not been introduced, no." He could see that she was piqued at his dismissal last night. The spoiled little cat wasn't used to having men ignore her. "Given that a beautiful young lady has just saved my life, the very least I must do is offer my name. Colonel Samuel Sheridan Shelby, at your service, my dear." He grinned as her cheeks pinkened at the suggestive tone of his voice.

"I am not your 'dear'," she snapped, giving the reins a sharp slap, although the horses were already galloping. "Use my scarf to bind up your arm. I can't have you passing out and falling beneath the carriage wheels before we make good our escape."

He pulled a heavy woolen scarf from her neck and wrapped the cloth securely around his throbbing arm. The roadside moved by them in a blur. When the phaeton took a curve on two wheels, then righted itself with a swaying bounce, he cautioned, "Careful or you'll overturn us."

"I've driven some of the finest and the worst carriages ever made as fast as they can go, and I've never overturned one yet, 'my dear'," Olivia replied smugly.

"Beautiful and modest, too," Shelby said dryly, his eyes assessing her delicate profile with amusement. Damn, but she was a stubborn beauty with her chin jutting pugnaciously and her pink lips pursed in concentration. He was forced to admit that she handled the reins with considerable expertise. "Am I not to receive the favor of your name, at least? After all, according to custom, when one person saves another's life, it belongs to the rescuer from that day forward."

"I've never heard of such a custom," she said, curious in

spite of herself. She pulled on the reins and slowed the lathered team to a trot.

" 'Tis a common belief among certain of the Indians of the Far West.''

"You've been West?" she asked, turning to look him full in the face for the first time. A slight bruise had begun to discolor his left temple and his face was smeared with dust and sweat in spite of the chilly air. For all that, he was still so devastatingly beautiful and disturbingly male, that her breath caught in her throat. Then he smiled, and Olivia was lost. The brilliance of that smile outshone all the candles on the biggest chandelier in the White House.

"Yes, I've been West. I've spent some time among the various tribes on the Great Plains, even those living in the vast mountain ranges that crossect the continent.''

"You sound as if you've traveled with Lewis and Clark,'' she said, her eyes alight with curiosity.

Samuel realized he had already revealed more of his background than he normally ever did to a strange female, no matter how beautiful or plucky she might be. "No, I was not privileged to make that journey. I've had other assignments across the Mississippi. You still have not told me your name. I know you're French." He cocked his head, studying her with blue eyes so piercing that she looked away.

Olivia could feel his gaze on her and knew her body was responding most unsuitably, making her face an unbecoming shade of pink that clashed with her hair. *Merde!* Why did he have to fluster her so? "I'm Olivia Patrice St. Etienne. Also, it would seem, at *your* service for this afternoon's work." There, dare him head-on! If only she could muster the nerve to return his stare. Olivia forced herself to meet those penetrating dark blue eyes, which at the mention of her surname seemed to grow an infinitesimally bit wintry. Then he smiled again and she was not certain if she had imagined it.

"Charmed, Mademoiselle St. Etienne.''

"How did you know I was French?" she blurted out, curious about his reaction—or her imagining of his reaction—to her name.

"Although your English is fluent, there is a faint trace of an accent," he hedged. He had no desire whatsoever to discuss his mother with the beauteous Mademoiselle St. Etienne.

"Have you some aversion to my countrymen, Monsieur Colonel?"

"Certainly not to the lovely young lady who has just saved my life," he replied gallantly.

Olivia recognized evasion when she heard it, having been raised by Julian St. Etienne, a luckless gambler who had been more expert in his choice of words than his choice of cards. She chose a frontal assault to test how much Samuel would reveal—or conceal. "Why was someone trying to kill you back there? Do you know who it was?"

Samuel shrugged. "I have no idea. Probably a simple robbery. My horse was quite valuable."

"But of course! Precisely why the assassin shot it out from under you, so he could lug it off to the meat market," she responded scornfully, meeting his eyes with a dare.

"Maybe it was an unlucky shot," he said smoothly. "His first shot nearly took off my head. I was turning the horse suddenly, trying to reach cover when it went down. Lucky for me the brigand was something amiss as a marksman."

"He was not all that bad a marksman, or you would not be dripping blood like that," she replied with asperity. The woolen scarf was soaked dark red now, in vivid contrast to the colonel's face, which was growing decidedly pale beneath his sun-bronzed tan.

"Don't worry. I won't pitch over the side and spook your horses," he said in grim amusement. "I've suffered far worse. It's just a scratch."

"That *scratch* is bleeding profusely," she countered. "How can you remain so calm while your lifeblood just seeps away?"

"Practice." He swore beneath his breath. Between the burning nuisance of his arm and the throbbing misery of his skull all he wanted was to lie down, preferably on some surface not bouncing wildly up and down.

Olivia reined in the team as they neared a farmhouse situated on the outskirts of the capital. There was a well by the roadside with a bucket beside it. "Maybe you'd better clean up your wounds. We must stop the bleeding before you ruin the upholstery. We could see if the people here have some fresh bandages. If not," she fluffed her voluminous skirts and added boldly, "I can always use one of my petticoats."

He grinned at her cheerful voice, noting that she turned a bit green around the gills when she looked at his blood-soaked arm. "Now you must promise not to faint and fall beneath the horses' hooves," he teased.

Olivia gave an indelicate snort as she jumped from the phaeton, scanning the farmhouse door for signs of occupancy. A mangy old yellow dog eyed them suspiciously from the rickety porch and bared his gums in a toothless growl. "No one seems to be about," she said with a sigh, turning back to Samuel, who by now had climbed out of the carriage.

He walked determinedly to the well and lowered the bucket, then cranked it back up with his uninjured arm. Lifting the moldy oak container, he leaned forward and poured it over his head, then let it drop by its rope once more into the depths below with a splash.

Olivia watched as he shook his head to clear it and combed his finger through his glossy black hair. Brilliant droplets of water sprayed around him in a rainbow arc of color. She felt her heartbeat accelerate when she observed a fine sheen of droplets forming on his face and rolling slowly over his boldly masculine jaw and down his throat to vanish beneath the collar of his uniform. This was not wise, not wise at all. Other than the fact he was devastatingly handsome and charming, what did she really know about Colonel Shelby? He seemed to be involved in some mysterious intrigue, and people most certainly were trying to kill him. She was altogether too attracted to this stranger.

"Damn. I lost my hat when I fell. It was brand new. This whole uniform is ruined," he grumbled, inspecting his bloody, torn and dirt-smeared clothing.

"You . . . you had better see about that wound, else more

than your uniform will be ruined," she said, moistening her suddenly dry lips with the tip of her tongue.

"Not out here," he replied distractedly as he pulled up the bucket and unfastened it from its rope. "It's a bit cool now that the sun's setting . . . and it's too exposed."

After a quick glance back down the road, she watched him stride toward the front door of the log cabin. "What if no one is at home?"

He turned at the uncertainty in her voice and raised one eyebrow. "Then we just go in. I don't plan to rob them, just use the shelter long enough to change this dressing . . . that is, if the offer of your petticoat still stands good?" He waited, watching her to see what she would do.

She walked up to him as if taking the dare, but then as he turned to open the door she said, "It really isn't proper for us to be alone . . . indoors, that is."

Samuel threw back his head and laughed heartily. "You are a caution, *ma petite*. It is a bit late for the proprieties now. First you come thundering wildly to my rescue out of nowhere, alone and unchaperoned. Then you drive like a London hackney and nearly kill us both on the road. Now you suddenly turn vaporing belle."

Olivia felt like stomping her foot at his mocking laughter. "For a man who owes me his life, you are very rude, Monsieur Colonel." Anger thickened her accent.

Samuel noticed the shift in cadence as well as the blaze of emerald fire in her eyes. "My apologies, Mademoiselle. But you still have not explained why you were driving alone in the middle of nowhere," he could not resist saying as he turned and entered the obviously deserted house. The hound on the porch raised its head once, then thought better of the exertion of further protest and instead slunk inside the shelter of the cabin behind Shelby.

Olivia stood alone in the yard for a moment. The impulse to dash to the phaeton and take off leaving the arrogant colonel stranded was tempting. But he was injured, and she was more attracted to him than she had ever been to a man before in her life. *Fool*, she berated herself.

Olivia reluctantly followed him into the dark interior of the cabin and watched as he unwrapped the soaked scarf from his upper arm. In spite of a slight wince of pain, his hands remained steady. Then he began to unbutton the heavy uniform jacket. As he slipped it easily off his good arm and began to work it carefully free of the injured one, Olivia stood rooted to the floor of the deserted cabin. The sheer white lawn shirt beneath his jacket stretched across his broad shoulders and clung lovingly to every inch of his lean muscular torso. Then he started to remove the shirt, too!

"What are you doing?" Her voice cracked on the last word.

"If I'm going to wrap this wound to stop the bleeding, I first have to bare the skin," he replied reasonably, continuing to pull the ruined shirt off.

She had thought his chest and shoulders were revealed through the sheer lawn covering. Now she could see how mistaken that assumption had been! Darkly bronzed skin rippled with sleek muscles as he tossed his shirt onto the crude wooden bench beside the table. A heavy pelt of black hair covered his chest, then tapered into an enticing vee that arrowed down to disappear beneath the belt buckle at his narrow waist. Her eyes would have strayed scandalously lower, but a bitten-back groan distracted her.

Samuel cursed as he tried to flex his injured arm. "The bleeding's grown worse. If I don't get it stopped, I might pass out and bleed to death before you can summon help. I'm afraid I'm going to need those petticoats."

"M-my p-petticoats," she stammered, then instantly felt like a fool.

"You're not going to faint now that the shooting's done, are you?" His voice was light, but a sheen of perspiration glistened on his forehead in spite of the chilly evening air. "I'd search around here for some cloth for bandages, but somehow I suspect that any to be found in here would blood-poison a possum," he added wryly as Olivia came out of her trance.

His whole arm was soaked with blood, and here she had been gawking at his naked chest as if she had never seen one before! Well, come to think of it, she *had* never seen a grown man's bare chest before. With clumsy fingers she began to tear at the top layer of her petticoats, but the heavy linen would not give.

"Here, allow me," he said with mock gallantry as he knelt in front of her and reached for the snowy slip with his uninjured hand. In the other one a wicked-looking knife gleamed. He sliced through the hem of the undergarment, then let her tear it until she had a little over a yard of cloth with which to wrap his arm.

"Tear another piece about the same length," he commanded as he lowered his injured arm into the bucket of cool water he had placed on the table. A small hiss of pain escaped his clenched jaw, but he made no further sound as he bathed the injury until the water ran red between his fingers.

Olivia stood holding the makeshift bandages, feeling utterly useless and somewhat queasy as she watched. An ugly furrow marred the perfection of his upper arm, slicing in a nasty angle across his bicep. She swallowed and moved closer as he raised his arm out of the water. "I'll wrap it," she said.

He held out his arm and let her cover it with the linen. He could feel the tremors that wracked her body vibrating through her hands as she worked. "Pull it tight so the bleeding stops. Aargh! Yes," he rasped as he pressed the end of the linen against the wound to hold it in place.

"I'm hurting you!" she gasped, dropping the bandage.

"No! I mean yes, but it can't be helped. Just get the damn thing wrapped around my arm and tie it off good and tight." He began to wrap the bandage himself. Suddenly Olivia's fingers, soft and cool, brushed his hand as she once more took over the task, pulling on the wrapping the way he had instructed her.

As they worked, their hands continued to touch each other. Her skin felt silken and she smelled of jasmine. He watched her bite her lower lip in concentration as she tied off the bandage. Her mouth was soft, pale pink, utterly kissable. And he was utterly insane. He was still a married man and he knew nothing about her except that she was young, French and spoiled. That should have been enough to deter him, but some-how it was not. Her hair had come loose from its pins during the wild carriage ride, and a fat bouncy curl of pure flame brushed against the sensitive inside of his wrist.

Without thinking, Samuel cupped his hand around the back of her slender neck and lowered his face to hers as he drew her against him. "Such good work deserves a reward," he murmured as his mouth tasted the soft pink lips that had beck-oned him.

Olivia felt herself melting toward the hardness and heat of his chest. Her palms pressed against the crisp hair and her fingers kneaded in it as her lips tilted upward to meet his descending mouth. The kiss was fierce and hungry, yet oddly delicate and exploratory at the same time. His lips brushed, then pressed hers and his tongue lightly rimmed the edges of her mouth until she emitted a tiny gasp of delight, allowing him entry to taste the virgin territory within.

She'd had the adulation of legions of lovesick young swains, but she had never been kissed like this. Olivia could feel the pounding of his heartbeat against her palms and the answering acceleration of her own wayward heart. The exotic texture of crisp chest hair delighted her questing fingers, but it was her mouth that felt the full drugging persuasion of Sa-muel's sensual coaxing. The tip of his tongue dipped and glided inside her lips, then danced a duel with her tongue and retreated only to plunge in for another jolting foray. She heard a low mewling sound like a lost kitten crying, without real-izing that it was her own voice.

She was pliant and willing, yet there was an inexplicable sense of surprise and wonder in her responses that did not befit a belle of her apparent experience. Yet the hunger that he felt left no time for further consideration or caution. It had been far, far too long since he had lain with a woman. As the enmity between him and Tish had grown, their physical hun-ger for each other had waned. Two years ago he had quit her bed when he learned that she had visited a notorious abortist in Maryland. Sickened and desolate, he had never touched her since. When his physical needs became unbearable he betrayed his marriage vows with carefully chosen professionals. The encounters always left him with such bitter, sordid regrets that he seldom succumbed. Instead he buried himself in his dangerous work.

His compelling attraction to Olivia St. Etienne was utter madness. She was obviously from a good family, gently reared with the expectation of a proper marriage, even if she did behave irresponsibly. There was no place for such a female in his life. Then why was he drawn to her with such an inexplicable longing? His hand, deft and sure, had found the small sweet enticement of her breast, cupping it through the soft linen of her jacket. When he rubbed his thumb against the hard bud of her nipple she cried out against his mouth and pressed closer to him in the mindless desire they shared. His fingers tangled in her thick, lustrous hair and he twined the curls around his fists like scarlet ribbons.

If he did not stop at once he would take her here in this filthy deserted cabin on the crude plank floor, rutting like the cur dog that lay quietly in the corner of the crude bare room watching them. This was insanity born of simple deprivation. Surely it couldn't be anything more. With an oath he pulled away, supporting the breathless, dazed girl by holding her shoulders. He could feel a shudder of surprise rippling through her. She raised her head and their eyes met. Hers were wide and dazed, turned the deep green of a tree-shrouded forest pool.

The pull of her mute entreaty frightened him with its intensity. Without words she asked him why he had ended the passionate interlude. Without thinking he replied, ''I've wanted to do that since the first moment I laid eyes on you. Don't deny that you wanted it, too,'' he added, stung by her wounded expression and his own guilt.

Shame washed over her in waves. Feeling her face flame, she raised her hands and pressed them to her cheeks, backing away from him. Dear merciful Lord, what had she almost done—allowed him to do? ''No, I am scarcely in a position to deny anything.'' Her voice was hoarse, soft as if coming from a great distance. She could still feel his heat, the magnetic presence that held her in thrall. His eyes pierced to her very soul. She felt naked as he was, defenseless.

Samuel could feel her vulnerability, and the pain of it hit him like a slap. He turned to pick up his discarded clothing. The shirt was a blood-soaked mess which he quickly abandoned, attempting instead to slip his injured arm through the sleeve of the heavy uniform jacket.

Olivia watched him struggle with the stiff coat, then stepped closer and pulled the blood-caked sleeve straight, helping him ease it over his bandaged arm. He shrugged the other arm into the uniform, then began to button it. She stepped back, yet their gazes locked and held. When Samuel had completed the task, his arms dropped to his sides.

He continued to study her with those unnerving blue eyes. "I'm truly sorry," he said stiffly. "You saved my life and I behaved abominably."

"You dared nothing I did not allow," she replied with candor, meeting his gaze unflinchingly.

"There is something between us, Mademoiselle St. Etienne, something quite remarkable . . . disturbing . . . and dangerous," he said, groping for a way to express his tumultuous emotions without revealing too much.

She smiled wistfully. "Yes, I believe you are right." Then, appearing thoughtful, she added, "Since I've already been as bold as any hussy, I may as well be even bolder. Don't you think after all that has happened, you might call me Olivia?" Her bones melted when his face, so harsh and austere a moment earlier, split into a heart-stopping smile.

Olivia. How classically lovely. It fit her perfectly. "Hussy you are not. Bold you definitely are. My name is Samuel, Olivia." The sound of her name rolled off his tongue like song. Damn, he was bewitched! "We had better return to the city before you are missed by your family."

She returned his earlier smile. He was clever at extracting _____tion without revealing himself. "I have only my guard- _____uel. Emory Wescott, a St. Louis merchant who is _____ in the capital to attend to business matters."

_____uis?" he questioned, caught off-guard.

Olivia picked up on the surprised note in his voice and turned to him as they approached the phaeton. "Yes, that is where we reside, unless Uncle Emory takes me traveling with him."

"Even a guardian so remiss as to allow his charge to go careening about the countryside unescorted will be upset if she's not at home by dark," he ventured as he helped her into the carriage.

"Not tonight he won't. He is yet in Maryland . . . collecting some bills owed him," she said with a mysterious smile. "As long as I present myself all packed and ready to sail for home on Friday, he will not note my absence. Anyway, 'tis I who must see you home since I am the driver and you are the passenger. Now, let's hurry so *I* get *you* home by dark."

A smile hovered about his lips. "Such solicitude for my reputation! How can I refuse so generous an offer?"

Dusk had settled over the city with a glittering cloak of frost when Olivia's phaeton pulled up in front of the elegant three-story Georgian brick house that had been Senator Worthington Soames' wedding gift to his beloved "Tisha-Belle." Samuel hated the looming monstrosity.

Olivia eyed it with amazement. "Your house is as grand as any I've seen, even in London," she murmured, wondering how Samuel could afford it on a colonel's pay.

He could see the questions looming: Mercenary speculation? Or mere curiosity? As the daughter of French émigrés she had grown up living with the grating reality of champagne taste and gin-swill income. Although it had always bothered him to admit the house and its lavish furnishings were a gift, he especially did not want to confess such to Olivia St. Etienne. Nor in their long and earnest conversation on the ride into the capital had he confessed that he was married. *But what if he were free?* Free to do what? Become involved with a wild young French hoyden who drew him like a wet hound to a warm fire?

"It's just a house. I don't even own it," he replied dismissively, raising her hand for a chaste salute. Somehow once he had pressed his lips to the jasmine-scented silk of her skin, he could not release her.

Olivia's fingers curled around his wrist while their eyes communicated in eloquent silence. He surprised himself by saying, "I'll be posted to St. Louis within the month. Perhaps we'll meet again."

Her smile was dazzling. "St. Louis is not so large a city that you could hide from me. I shall delight in tracking you down!"

Letitia Soames Shelby stood behind a Brussels lace curtain at an upstairs window watching Samuel and Olivia say their farewell. Her eyes narrowed to pale golden slits as the sound of their laughter drifted up to her. "Such tendresse. Who is the red-haired tart?"

Her companion peered out in the gloom and swore as Olivia's flame-colored hair danced in the light from the torch held by a servant who had come out to greet Samuel. "That's the rig that rescued him! An expensive lightweight phaeton with those superb matched bays."

Tish turned to face him with a scornful expression hardening her patrician features, robbing them of the doll-like beauty that always turned heads. "Forget the worthless little nobody driving that carriage. Tell me why you failed to kill my husband."

***Deep as the Rivers* by Shirl Henke—
a March 1997 St. Martin's Paperbacks Bestseller!**

Alex Hightower, an American professor, has always been fascinated by Emily Brontë and her brief, tragic life. But what were the secrets she took with her to her grave? The answers begin in the village of Haworth, where Emily lived and died, as Alex delves into the past to unlock a hundred-and-fifty-year-old mystery.

Was Emily a lonely spinster of legend? Or a troubled, passionate woman who loved in secret? And who is Selena, the mysterious gypsy beauty Alex meets on Haworth's storm-tossed moors, who speaks of a family curse, and who knows more than she realizes about Emily's secrets?

EMILY'S SECRET

Jill Jones

"Magnificent!"
—*Affaire de Coeur*

EMILY'S SECRET
Jill Jones
_____ 95576-6 $4.99 U.S./$5.99 CAN.

> *"He played a cruel and cunning game with me. What I took for love, to him was only a conquest."*
> — *The ghost of Lady Caroline Lamb*

Her parents' tragic death has led Boston heiress Alison Cunningham to seek them out at a seance. Instead, she encounters the troubled spirit of Lady Caroline Lamb, whose scandalous 1812 liaison with the charming, erotic Lord Byron ended in bitter betrayal and vengeful madness. Soon Alison finds herself buying Dewhurst Manor, near London, where the winsome apparition begs her to search for Byron's secret memoirs.

Also looking for the memoirs is sexy, arrogant Jeremy Ryder. Together, Alison and Jeremy must reckon with that beautiful capricious phantom, and find out what happened nearly two centuries ago. But will their obsession bind them together or drive them apart?

My Lady Caroline

Jill Jones

> *"A terrific tale...Jill Jones is one of the top new writing talents of the day."*
> —*Affaire de Coeur*

Against the backdrop of an elegant Cornwall mansion before World War II and a vast continent-spanning canvas during the turbulent war years, Rosamunde Pilcher's most eagerly-awaited novel is the story of an extraordinary young woman's coming of age, coming to grips with love and sadness, and in every sense of the term, coming home...

Rosamunde Pilcher

The #1 *New York Times* Bestselling Author of *The Shell Seekers* and *September*

COMING HOME

"Rosamunde Pilcher's most satisfying story since *The Shell Seekers*."

— *Chicago Tribune*

"Captivating...The best sort of book to come home to...Readers will undoubtedly hope Pilcher comes home to the typewriter again soon."

— *New York Daily News*

Once upon a time...

A lovely lady fell asleep in a charmed ring of flowers and dreamed of Comlan, king of the fairy realm. She spent a few magical hours by his side, enjoying the company of the handsome king whose golden hair and green eyes could turn the head of any mortal maid...and whose charming attentions captured her heart.

But the year is 1850, and Amy Danton knows better than to believe in fairy tales. However wonderful Comlan seems, he is nothing but a figment of her imagination.

But then, across a crowded ballroom, she sees him— the man of her dreams...

"An exciting romance...this novel has every- thing a romance reader desires...a beautifully poignant fairy tale."—*Affaire de Coeur*

Once Upon a Time
Marylyle Rogers